MORNINGSIDE FALL

"Gritty action-packed drama so hi-res and real you'll believe you got something in your eye."

Matt Forbeck, author of Amortals *and* Dangerous Games

"Posey has crafted a story that is impossible to put down."

Richard E. Dansky, author of Vaporware

"Jay Posey creates a vivid and mesmerizing world whose characters are so real and so flawed that you'll recognize them immediately. An unforgettable read."

Peter Telep, co-author of the #1 New York Times bestseller Against All Enemies

"The post-apocalyptic world that Jay Posey created in *Three* is brilliantly constructed, it's just chock-full of the cool stuff, futuristic gadgets, augmented people and not forgetting the Weir."

The Book Plank

"A post-apocalyptic adventure tale in the vein of *The Road Warrior*, only with fewer vehicles and a higher tech level and body count… Posey knows how to pour on the tension. 4.5 stars."

Shelf Inflicted

"This powerhouse of an apocalyptic read cannot and will not be denied!"

My Shelf C

ALSO BY JAY POSEY

Three

Jay Posey has asked for a percentage of his fees for this book to be donated to Hope For The Warriors®.

We are honored to bring Hope to the lives of our nation's heroes and their families.

RESTORING: Self • Family • Hope

The mission of Hope For The Warriors® is to enhance the quality of life for post-9/11 service members, their families, and families of the fallewn who have sustained physical and psychological wounds in the line of duty. Hope For The Warriors® is dedicated to restoring a sense of self, restoring the family unit, and restoring hope for our service members and our military families.

www.HopeForTheWarriors.org

JAY POSEY

MORNINGSIDE FALL

LEGENDS OF THE DUSKWALKER

BOOK 2

ANGRY
ROBOT

ANGRY ROBOT
A member of the Osprey Group

Lace Market House
54-56 High Pavement
Nottingham
NG1 1HW
UK

Angry Robot/Osprey Publishing
PO Box 3985
New York
NY 10185-3985
USA

www.angryrobotbooks.com
Blind justice.

An Angry Robot paperback original 2014

Cover design by Steven Meyer-Rassow
Set in Meridien and Bank Gothic by Argh! Oxford

Distributed in the United States by Random House, Inc., New York.

ISBN 978 0 85766 365 8
Ebook ISBN 978 0 85766 367 2

Printed in the United States of America

9 8 7 6 5 4 3 2 1

For Will, Noah, and Jane.

PROLOGUE

In the shadow of the moon, the Thing lay in wait. Its prey was near and drawing slowly nearer. A fresh burst of vital signal pulsed like a heartbeat, a digital vibration that could be neither seen nor heard. Though the Thing could not taste, it processed the sensation into something like that of cold iron on the tongue. Claws extended. Soon.

The Thing no longer knew hunger, or thirst, or addiction. Yet it was compelled. Compelled to hunt. To reclaim. To optimize. Had its companions been near, it might have called to them to chase their quarry and corner it. Alone, however, the Thing was forced to ambush. An abnormal protocol.

Seconds remained. The prey would exit the narrow alley and pass into view. The Thing would strike. Others would come to take the harvest away. The Thing would begin to search anew. That was its process. Its function.

The prey appeared. Stopped, facing away from the Thing. Unaware. The Thing rocked back, muscles tensed to pounce. Then hesitated. Something strange. The Thing scanned, evaluated.

This one was smaller than most. But a sort of pressure emanated, radiated from it. A weight. Its signal was complex, multilayered, multithreaded. More *intricate* than any the

Thing had before encountered. Had the Thing been capable of emotion, it might have felt something like awe. Or fear.

The prey turned to face the Thing. Unsurprised. Unafraid. Waited calmly. Raised its hand. The Thing leapt.

It felt its claws puncture, but the instant it made contact, the Thing experienced a piercing cold that bored into the center of its forehead and streaked through to the back of its skull. It cried out involuntarily, a static burst of white noise. The cold became white-hot behind the Thing's eyes. A cleansing fire, like cobwebs vanishing in a flash of flame. And as the Thing fell to the ground, it remembered.

My name is Painter.

ONE

A man with a knife was standing in the hall. Wren could feel him, and lay still, absolutely still, like Mama had taught him, covers pulled tight to his mouth out of fear that his breath might escape and somehow invite attack.

Mama.

He could call for her. Scream. And then the man with the knife would disappear, and try again another time. Sometime when Wren might not see it coming, when he had no chance to stop it. Better to allow the plan to unfold until the attacker was committed. Maybe.

Whoever was out there wasn't moving. Just standing. Waiting, maybe. Or listening. For an instant, Wren nearly pimmed his mother, quietly reaching out to her through the digital connection. But no. *He* might catch the burst of signal, recognize the warning, and then it'd be the same as a scream.

Wren's eyes scanned the dim room, moonglow blue in the soft light of the night-light near the foot of his bed. Now he felt childish for having kept the light, and foolish for the disadvantage it forced on him. There would've been more places to hide in pure darkness. More opportunity to surprise his would-be attacker, or to slip out and escape. But not now. He'd limited his own options and traded imaginary dangers for real ones.

The person in the hall moved, and moments later Wren could hear a faint scratching at the door. Working the lock from the outside. Help wasn't going to come. Wren would have to figure this one out on his own.

Carefully, carefully, he slipped sideways, stretching his foot out and down, down to the floor that now seemed too far away. When he finally made contact with the floor, he eased himself off the mattress, not daring to breathe, trying desperately to slide silently out from under the covers without shaking the bed. Just as he was about to get his other leg out, the door clicked once and the scratching stopped. Wren froze.

Silence stretched. The person was still there. Did he hear Wren? Or was he afraid that Wren had heard him? The leg that was supporting all of Wren's weight started to burn. As he was trying to decide whether to shift back into the bed or not, the scratching resumed. Good. Still working on the lock then. Wren got his other foot on the floor and quietly shifted the pillows into a lump under the covers.

We often see what we expect, Three had once told him, *and miss what we don't.*

Three, the man who'd given his life to get Wren safely to Morningside. Wren felt a cold knot in his chest, the fear mixing with a sudden sadness of loss. He swallowed and tucked the blankets in around the lumped pillows. Not very convincing, but maybe they'd buy him some time anyway.

The room was simple and small. A desk, a chair. Not many natural hiding places. Did he have time to switch off the night-light? No, the man with the knife might see the light go out under the door and then he'd know Wren was awake and aware. Instead, Wren grabbed the corner of the large comforter on his bed and pulled it towards the night-light. The fold cast a dark shadow across one corner of the room without disturbing the brightness near the door.

Wren's bed was positioned in one corner of the room, the right side pushed against the same wall that held the door and the head against the wall adjacent. Sleeping in the corner had made the room feel smaller, more secure. Now, Wren was grateful to notice that the intruder's likely approach to the bed would put his back to Wren's hiding place.

There was something else, something in the drawer in the desk that might help, if Wren could just open it quietly enough. The door clicked again. Unlocked now. No time for anything else. Wren backed into the darkest corner of the room, diagonal from the door, tight in a ball, the chair the only thing between him and the entry. The first seconds would be the most dangerous; if the attacker scanned the room before entering, he might spot Wren in the corner. But if he was intent on the bed, Wren just might have a chance.

The boy watched the door handle with wide eyes. Tried to keep his breathing steady. His heart thundered so hard against his ribs he feared the man with the knife would be able to hear it.

From across the room, it was nearly impossible to tell if the handle was turning or not. But soon a crack appeared between the door and its frame and Wren knew the man was creeping in. At last the figure appeared, gliding like smoke seeping through the barely-opened door. He was backlit and silhouetted by the night-light, a slender figure with a hood. No, not a hood. Hair, long, past the shoulders. He was short, hunched in on himself; his frame slight, his movement controlled and delicate like a dancer.

The man with the knife crept towards the side of Wren's bed. A momentary gleam in his left hand. The knife, the blade translucent.

Wren's timing would have to be perfect. A few more steps and the man's back would be to Wren, and Wren would have a clear path to the door.

Still. Be still.

The man stopped mid-step, only part way along the bed. Still too close to the door. If Wren moved now, the man might see the motion and have time to react, time to catch him before he made it to the doorway. But maybe the man had realized that Wren wasn't in the bed. Maybe it was already too late. Wren felt cold sweat break over him as he fought the indecision. Try to run for it now? Hold still just a little longer?

The man's head snapped around. Now it *was* too late. The night-light illuminated only the right half of the assailant's face, leaving the left blank in shadow. His right eye fixed on Wren, and for a long, electric moment, the two stared at each other.

It was impossible to make out the man's features distinctly in the dim light, but Wren could tell he was young. His face seemed smooth and soft. Wren couldn't see the knife.

"Please, don't," Wren said.

After a moment, Wren saw the young man's shoulders go slack.

"I have to," the man whispered, his voice thin and light. Not a man at all. A girl. The knife inched upwards, where it caught the light. She rolled the blade over in her hand. Then again, to herself, "I have to."

She shook her head slightly, and in the half-light Wren saw the gleam of her eye disappear. She was looking down, watching the knife blade continue its uneven roll, or maybe she'd closed her eyes. Considering. Wrestling. Her shoulders came up again, tensed. Wren knew what was coming next. He brought his hands up in front of him, palms out, started to rise slowly.

Help, flashed through his mind, help!

"I'm sorry," she said, looking at him again, "but I don't have–"

She didn't finish the sentence. In that instant, Wren launched himself from the corner and drove the hard edge of his right hand into her left wrist, aiming for the nerve there, just as he'd been taught. A split-second later he buried the top of his head into her lower abdomen, just above the pelvis. Together they crashed into the bedframe, and Wren felt a sharp impact on the back of his head that made stars explode in his vision.

They hit the floor, and Wren rolled to his left, found his feet. The room spun. The door wasn't where it was supposed to be. Where did it go?

There. Closed. He leapt just as the girl snatched at his foot and caught it for a split second. Wren went sprawling again at the foot of the bed and heard a metallic scrape against the floor behind him. She still had the knife.

He scrambled, fumbled the door handle with fear-numbed hands, felt her rising close behind. She was clambering over the bed. He clawed the door open and squeezed through just as she reached out and slammed the door on his ankle.

"Help!" Wren called. It was the only word that would come out as he tumbled into the hall. He skittered backwards as the door flew open. "Help!"

He scrambled back, back, back into a wall, hard. Felt strong hands clamp down on his upper arms. Lifting him. Not a wall. Someone else.

The girl stood silhouetted in the doorframe, and Wren felt himself whirling sideways as he was tossed to one side. He landed on his feet, but went down on his knees as the Someone Else stepped between him and the girl. Shielding him. He recognized the shape now. Able.

"Wren!" Cass, his mother, was running down the hall, her eyes glowing their eerie blue in the gloom. In two heartbeats, she was at his side, and then hunched in front of him, eyes on the assassin.

Wren craned around his mother for a view. The attacker was trapped, now, trapped in the doorway of Wren's room, with Able and Mama both ready to pounce. The girl took a step backwards into his room, hands up, submissive. But she still had the knife.

She looked sad in the glow of the night-light. Trapped, defeated. Desperate. Wren recognized the look. Remembered it well. It was how Mama used to look, before Three had come.

"It's OK…" Wren started to say, but the girl was already in motion. Before anyone could react, she plunged the knife into her own stomach, just below the breastbone. A quick twist of the handle, and a dull thump sounded inside her chest. The girl doubled over, hung in an awkward pose for a moment, and then collapsed to the floor.

Lights came on in the hallway as guardsmen rushed in from both directions. Able signaled to them, and they slowed their approach, obviously relieved that they weren't too late. Late, but not too late. Able moved to the girl and crouched near her warily, holding himself ready for any sudden ambush.

Cass turned part way around and pulled Wren in front of her so she could look at him without taking her eyes completely off of Able and the girl. She went down on one knee, cradled his face in her hands, searched his eyes.

"Are you alright, baby?" she asked. "Did she hurt you?"

Wren shook his head. His legs felt hollow and his face hot, and when he shook his head it made him dizzy. "My head hurts a little. We fell. And my ankle."

The guardsmen formed a timid semicircle around the others, waiting quietly for some kind of orders or direction. Cass gently ran her hands over Wren's head and when she reached low on the back of it, he winced and jerked away from a stab of pain where she brushed over a wound. When she brought her hands back, the fingertips of one were stained wet crimson.

"Lane," she said to one of the nearby guards, "would you go get Mouse for us? Ask him to bring his kit?"

"Sure thing, Miss Cass," Lane said, with a quick nod. He turned and hurried off down the hall.

"You might need a stitch or two," she said. Then she motioned with a hand and caught Able's attention. "How's the girl?"

Able shook his head slightly. *Dying,* he signed with his hands. *But not dead yet.*

At least that's how Wren interpreted it. He still had a little trouble following some of Able's faster signs, and everything was starting to feel fuzzy. He pulled away from his mother and approached the girl.

"Careful, Wren," said his mother, but she didn't restrain him.

Able held up a cautionary hand as he drew near. Wren nodded and crouched next to Able, careful to keep the man between him and the girl. From here he could see she was taking quick, jagged breaths, almost like hiccups. Weeping. Or maybe struggling for air. Able rolled her gently onto her side. There was blood in her mouth and fear in her eyes. Able brushed the hair back from her face, an almost tender gesture.

She was a few years older than Wren. Thirteen, maybe fourteen, with hazel eyes and a splash of freckles across her nose and cheekbones. Too thin. Wren wondered when the last time was she'd had a meal. Without understanding why, he felt emotion clawing up his throat.

"It's OK," he said to her. Her wild eyes bounced between Able and him. "It's OK. We're going to get you some help."

Mama was next to him now, kneeling at his side. Able handed her something, and as she was examining it, Wren recognized it as the handle to the girl's knife. The blade was gone. After a moment, Mama turned to him.

"Wren, she doesn't have much time. I'm sorry, but there's nothing we can do for her now."

"What about Mouse?" he asked.

Cass shook her head, and held out the knife hilt for him to see. She pointed to a section of the hilt, showed him how it twisted. "There's a charge in the blade. This makes it explode."

Wren understood then. Rather than be taken, the girl had chosen to detonate the blade inside herself. Why would she do that? Did she think they would torture her or something? For a brief instant, he wondered if it was out of fear of capture or because of some expected consequence of failure. He turned back to her. "I don't understand. I don't know what I did. But I'm sorry. I'm sorry for whatever it was."

Her eyes locked on his as he spoke. Her lips moved, but no sound came except that of her thin, labored breath.

"It's OK. I know you had a reason," he said. "It's OK. I forgive you."

The girl's eyes softened, tears welled. She raised a weak

hand towards him, but Able instinctively caught it at the wrist, held it fast. Still, she never took her eyes off of Wren. Again her lips moved, so pale now he could barely distinguish them from the rest of her ashen face. But the damage was too severe and no matter how much the girl might have willed it, her message to Wren went unheard. As Lane and Mouse came running down the hall, her eyes darkened and her hand went limp in Able's grasp. And there, on the floor of Wren's bedroom, a girl that should've been blossoming into life died instead.

Tears broke from Wren, and he felt sick. He gagged once, then again, but only sobs came. Cass wrapped him in a strong embrace. She tried to turn his face away from the girl's body, but he pulled her hand off, and continued to stare at the girl on the floor of his room.

"Why, Mama? Why did this have to happen?"

Cass replied, "I don't know, sweetheart. But it wasn't something you did. It wasn't your fault, OK? It wasn't your fault."

It came crashing down then, the fear, the relief, the guilt, the horror. Wren let himself cry, let the flood of emotions overtake him while Able rolled the girl gently to her back. Mouse came and knelt by her for a moment, making her seem even smaller and more fragile next to his hulking frame. He spoke in low tones to Able, who signed in response. Wren didn't even try to follow them.

Cass picked him up and carried him across the hall to her own room, and together they sat on her bed, door open, with the light from the hall spilling in. After a few minutes, Mouse and Able came in together. Able stood quietly by the door while Mouse gave Wren a quick examination and cleaned up the wound on the back of his head.

"Well, I don't think there's any serious damage. Nothing missing, nothing broken," Mouse said, flashing a subdued smile. "Just going to put a couple of drops of goo on this gash to seal you up and you should be all set, 'kay, buddy?"

Wren nodded, and Mouse stepped around behind him to do his work.

"Looks like you got a pretty good whack from something sharp and bony. Knee? Elbow? Chin maybe?" he asked.

Wren shrugged. He remembered every terrifying moment with absolute clarity, but he didn't feel much like talking about what had happened. He just kept thinking through it, wondering what he could've done differently. What he should've done differently. Maybe he should've called out sooner. Or hidden under the bed. Surely there was a way for it to have turned out differently, a way that didn't end in death.

"Well, whatever it was, I'm glad it's no worse. You might end up with a little scar, but I think it'll heal up fine."

Wren heard the words, but they didn't really register. He was too busy playing the scenes out in his head.

"Thanks, Mouse," Cass said.

"No sweat, Cass. You need anything else?"

She shook her head. "I think we're OK for now."

"Alright then. I'm going to go see about... uh," Mouse finished his sentence with a little nod towards the hall. Cass nodded. Mouse squeezed Wren's shoulder and left the room. Able bounced a gentle fist off Mouse's upper arm as he passed, a silent gesture of thanks and casual affection. For some reason it made Wren wish he had a brother. And reminded him of the one he had once had.

A thought occurred to Wren, and he sat up straighter in Cass's lap. "Mama. How did you get there so fast?"

"What do you mean?"

"You weren't in your room. You came from down the hall. When I yelled for help, you came so fast. And Able…" he trailed off, realizing that Able must have already been in the hall when he'd called. And Able couldn't have heard Wren calling anyway.

"You called before that, sweetheart. You know. The way you can."

She put special emphasis on the words. *The way you can.* The way he could, without knowing how. The way he'd done it before. And other things. Worse things.

He said, "I wish I knew what she was trying to say. There, at the end."

Cass just nodded.

"Did you hear?" Wren asked.

Cass shook her head. "No, sweetheart, I couldn't." But her eyes flicked up at Able, and there was something to it that Wren picked up on. Able didn't react, but when Wren looked at him, he held his gaze.

"Able," Wren said. "Could you tell what she was saying?"

Able didn't move. Just held Wren's stare. But Wren could see it in his eyes. Able, deaf from birth, was a masterful lip-reader.

"Able."

Able glanced at Cass, a silent request for permission. Cass nodded. He drew a breath, looked back at Wren, and carefully signed. *She said, "They told us you were a demon."*

TWO

The mid-morning sunlight seemed overpowering to Cass's dazzled eyes even through the special veil that covered her face. Though it was never easy for her to see in broad daylight, the veil usually made it bearable for her altered vision. But at the moment the morning glare was creating a pressure behind her eyes and at her temples that threatened to become a full-blown migraine if she didn't head back indoors soon. Of course she hadn't slept in almost thirty hours, and that likely wasn't helping matters.

She and Wren were in a small courtyard not far from the north-eastern gate of the compound. It wasn't as nice or as large as the central courtyard, nor as secure, but it was Wren's preferred place to get outside and Cass knew it'd help boost his spirits before the meeting of the Council. Or rather, she hoped it would. He'd grown distant of late; spending more time alone, less willing to talk, more likely to shut down if she pressed him. He'd hardly spoken at all since the attack. And though she wanted more than anything to gently probe her young son's mind, Cass knew the only chance she had to learn what was going on inside Wren was to wait patiently for him to begin on his own terms. And so they walked in silence with slow careful steps, Cass feeling all the while that her son was becoming more and more a stranger.

The narrow stretch of open space was shaded and rarely traveled. Cass couldn't help but wonder if it was the isolation that attracted Wren so. It wasn't quiet per se. Morningside was never quiet. But the high walls and fortified structure of the compound shielded them somewhat and reduced the noise to a background murmur. She glanced up at the wall separating them from the city at large, and saw a figure moving along the top. They'd put extra men on the wall. Not surprising, given the night's events, but she wondered if it was wise. Citizens were bound to notice the change, and it never took much to start rumors.

"It's nice to be out here with you, Mama," Wren said. His sudden words, quiet as they were, jolted Cass from her thoughts.

"It's nice to be out here with *you*, Wren," she said with a smile.

"I mean, with just you."

"Yeah. Seems like it's hardly ever just us anymore, huh?"

"Yeah."

He went quiet again for a few moments after that, but Cass could tell he was working up to something. Sometimes he just needed time to find the words, and sometimes Wren waited for her to ask the right questions. For a long time it had been easy for her to read her son, but lately it'd been different. Difficult. Maybe it was that they hadn't spent as much time together the past few weeks. Or maybe, more frightening to her, he was just growing up.

"Do you miss it just being the two of us?" she asked.

Wren shrugged and then waggled his head back and forth from shoulder to shoulder slightly, a gesture that Cass had learned to interpret as "kinda".

"I know I've been away a lot lately," she said. "There's just been a lot going on. But I'll try to make more time for us, if you'd like that."

Wren nodded. But there was more to it than that. Not that it looked like he was going to offer.

"Have you been enjoying your time with Able and Swoop and everyone?" Cass asked.

"I guess so."

"Just guess so?"

Wren shrugged. "They're all really nice." His tone didn't carry any enthusiasm.

"But they're not Three."

Wren shook his head.

"I miss him too," she said. "Every day."

"Mama, do you think we could go away?" Wren asked, looking up at her. She must've looked surprised by the question, because he quickly added, "Just for a little while, I mean."

"Hmm, I don't know, baby," Cass answered. "I don't think people would like it too much if their governor disappeared all of a sudden." She'd meant to make the statement light, but from Wren's reaction she realized she'd said exactly the wrong thing. Cass tried to recover, to keep him from shutting down on her completely. "But who knows? I guess if you're in charge you can do what you want. Where would you like to go?"

Wren shrugged again. Cass tried to think of a place to suggest, but found she couldn't come up with one that didn't have some painful memory attached to it. She needed something, though, to keep him talking.

"Greenstone?" she said, and then held her breath. They hadn't been back since their narrow escape from that wild and dangerous city. But for all the threats they had faced, the little time they'd spent there had also offered them a greatly unexpected refuge and, for one precious moment, almost a sense of home.

Wren did his little head wag again.

"Greenstone would be nice," he said, finally. "Or Chapel's, maybe." Chapel's village without walls, just on the edge of the Strand. It sounded like an imaginary place, a fairytale for children in a world of fortified cities and urban wasteland. But Chapel and his people had taken Wren in for a time, and Cass knew as dreamlike as it sounded, it did exist out there, somewhere, on the Strand's fringe.

She said, "I'd really like to see that someday."

"I think you will."

They were just passing the north-eastern gate, and Cass hadn't really thought much about it until Wren stopped walking. She continued on a few steps before turning back. He was just looking off through the gate.

"Wren? You OK?"

"I'm not who they think I am, Mama," he said quietly. And his words held such weight that she knew this, at last, had been what he'd been building up to say.

"Who, baby?"

"Any of them." He looked so small to sound so weary. Cass returned to her son and crouched in front of him. She lifted her veil and took his face in her hands. His cheeks were cool from the morning air.

"Listen to me," she said. "Last night wasn't about anything that you did, or anything you could've done. And you never have to try to be anything that you aren't."

Without taking his eyes from hers, Wren said, "I do, Mama. I do have to try. Every day."

He said it with such quiet authority, Cass couldn't think of anything to say. Her hands slid off his face, down to his shoulders.

Wren looked off towards the gate. "All those people," he said. "It doesn't work like that."

It took a moment before Cass understood. She followed his gaze, and the pieces came together. Though it was technically still an entryway, the north-eastern gate was hardly ever used to actually enter or exit the compound. Soon after Wren had Awakened the first of the Weir, word had spread through the city with surprising speed. And then the memorials had started showing up. Wreaths, ever-burning vigil lights, personal belongings... offerings, really. It wasn't a gate anymore. It was a shrine. To her son.

And then, worst of all, the pictures began appearing. Just one or two, at first. Then each day brought a few more. Now there were dozens and dozens of pictures of people who had disappeared. The taken. And with every one hung a silent, permanent plea for Wren to find them and bring them back.

Cass just pulled him to her then and held him tightly. In that moment she wasn't sure if she was giving comfort or taking it, but Wren didn't try to resist. She knew it was hard on him, of course. To be ruling a city at such a young age. Cass had tried to insulate him as much as possible. But their choices had been so few; after what had happened they could never have stayed within Morningside as normal citizens. And at the time the idea of leaving again, of having nowhere to go and to be always on the run, had been too much for either of them to bear. In the end it had seemed the only real choice, to stay and let her child be revered as governor. Maybe worshiped. Now, feeling his tiny frame in her arms, she wondered that she could have ever been such a fool.

Cass had hoped, and maybe even let herself believe, that with her as his primary advisor and with the help of the Council members, that the burden wouldn't be too much for Wren to bear. Of course it was too much to bear. Of course it was too much to ask. And the pressures of governing were only made worse by the guilt he must have felt, knowing all those people were counting on him, believing he could rescue their missing and deliver them safely back home.

It hardly seemed fair, after all they had been through: the flight from RushRuin, the cold nights of hunger, the utter terror of the Weir, the heavy losses. To have come so far, to have escaped all of that, only to find themselves surrounded by everything they could ever need or want – and discover it was just a different kind of prison. Tears brimmed in her eyes, but she blinked them quickly away.

"Tell you what," Cass said. "What if you didn't come to Council today?"

"I have to. I'm the governor."

Cass rocked back so she could look at her son. "You're the governor. You *don't* have to."

He smiled a little at that. Wren said, "But I should go."

"I'll tell them you needed some time off. After last night, no one would blame you."

"Uncle Aron might."

"Uncle Aron is a grouchy old man. If you came, he'd probably fuss at you for being there." She felt his slight shoulders relax under her hands and knew that skipping the meeting was the right thing. Yet another thing that had been weighing on him. He was just too concerned with what he felt was his duty to have said anything about it. "I'm pulling rank. As your mother, I demand that you not come. So that's that."

"I don't think it's like that anymore, Mama."

Cass was surprised by how much those words cut her. Not because Wren had intended any hurt; he'd just said it as if it were fact. Perhaps she feared it was.

"It is today," she said, standing back up as she did.

"Well," Wren said. "If you think it'll be OK."

"I'll take the heat if there is any. But I'm sure everyone will understand."

"OK, then. Is it alright if I stay here? Just for a little while longer?"

Cass was still weighing the options when someone called through the gate.

"Mister Governor!"

They both looked over to see a couple of teenagers peering through the bars.

"Hey, Painter!" Wren called back. He looked up at Cass, and she nodded, and together they walked over to the gate. The daylight made it hard for her to identify the two from a distance, but as they approached, Cass recognized the other teen as a kid everyone just called Luck. He was the more stylish of the two, always quick with a smile – and had a seriously dry wit. Luck was sporting a pair of dark glasses.

Painter was tall and thin, with arms and legs just a little too long to look like they belonged to him. His hair was a wavy brown nest too loose to call curly but with an obvious mind of its own. He tended to be self-conscious – either because of, or compounded by, the heavy stutter he suffered from. Painter looked in every way like a typical nineteen year-old kid. Except in the eyes; though they were currently hidden beneath dark goggles, Cass knew that where others had iris and pupil, Painter had only softly radiating blue. Both he and Luck had become good friends to Wren. And both had been Awakened.

"Luck, Painter," she said, greeting them both. "What brings you gentlemen around?"

"Actually we were on our way back home, Miss Cass," Luck said. "They wouldn't let us in the front gate."

"The Council's meeting," Cass answered. Normally security wouldn't lock the compound down just for the Council, but what she'd said was true and she hoped it wouldn't invite any further questions.

"Oh, OK. We were just coming to say 'hi'," said Luck. "Guess we'll catch up later?"

Cass looked down at Wren, who in turn looked up at her. His eyes told her everything she needed to know.

"Actually, I have to get to this meeting, but Wren's free. Why don't you fellas walk back around to the north-west gate, and he'll meet you there?"

"Uh, OK, sure," Luck said. "If it's no bother."

"I'd like the company," Wren said.

"Alright, we'll see you there. Thanks, Miss Cass!"

"Sure thing, Luck," she said. Painter dipped his head and waved. Cass smiled back, and the two young men disappeared from the gate. When they were gone, Cass turned Wren towards her. She said, "I know you'll be careful, but watch what you say, OK? It's very important that no one finds out about what happened last night, alright?"

"I know, Mama. I'll be smart."

"I know you will, baby. I'll come find you after the meeting, OK?"

"Kay."

"I love you."

"I love you, too."

Cass bent and kissed Wren on the top of the head, and then sent him off towards the main gate. As she watched him go, she inhaled deeply and exhaled slowly. The attack had raised so many questions in her mind; there were too many moving pieces, too many shifting variables for her to grasp anything solid. But despite the cloud of confused and swirling thoughts, something in her gut insisted that someone from the Council had been involved.

With Wren removed from the meeting, the Council members would be off-balance; some would be less guarded, others more so. Reading them would be critical. Cass needed all the focus she could muster. She drew the veil back down over her face. And with a sharp, short breath she steeled herself, and headed towards the Council Room.

As Wren approached the gate, he crossed behind two guardsmen patrolling through the front courtyard. Neither of them seemed to notice him. He moved behind them and picked up on the middle of their conversation.

"Just a couple of those deadling kids. Said they came by to see the Governor," the shorter one said.

"Ugh. I dunno why we ever let 'em in in the first place. They gimme the creeps."

"Yeah, I don't know," the first guard replied with a shrug, neither agreeing nor disagreeing. "Kid's mom seems alright."

The other guard snorted. "She's alright from behind for sure. I'd like to bend her over a chair, as long as she didn't turn around."

Wren had no idea what that was supposed to mean exactly, but he knew they weren't speaking well of his mama, and something rose up inside him.

"Hey!" he called.

Both guards jumped a little and turned in surprise. Wren guessed the shorter one was in his forties, and the other was quite a bit younger. Twenties, maybe. He recognized them both, but didn't know either of their names. They stood awkwardly next to one another.

"Governor," the older one said, and it sounded like some mix of a greeting, a question, and just a hint of a joke. And in that moment, Wren missed Mama and Able. He had to say something to these men, now that he had their attention, but he didn't know what. They were grown-ups, after all. Tall and muscled and certainly not used to being challenged by little boys. Swoop had been trying to teach Wren how to talk with authority and how to command a room. But Wren realized now it was so much easier to be brave and in charge when you had a couple of warriors at your side.

The young guard made a clicking noise as he sucked something out of his teeth and the corner of his mouth curled up like he was trying not to laugh. It made Wren angry. At least one thing Wren had learned was that anger always sounded scarier when you didn't shout it.

"What're your names?" he asked, not quite knowing where he was going. He just knew that when he got in trouble, the thing Wren hated most was the questions he had to answer without knowing why they were being asked.

"Gaz," the older one said. The younger one just stood there staring back with that look on his face. "This here's Janner."

Wren's legs felt hollow and there was a tremble in his stomach that made him want to throw up. He held his hands behind his back to look more in charge. And to hide the fact that they were shaking. Janner sniffed out a laugh through his nose and looked at the ground. Wren's mind raced for something meaningful to say. A thousand thoughts rushed through his head and jumbled into a huge mass of nothing.

Without raising his head, Janner's eyes shifted sideways

to Gaz. He still had that smirk on his face. And Wren still felt the anger, the need to defend Mama. But everything seemed frozen inside him. Frustration built. He discovered he had no idea how to express what he wanted to say. No way to correct or punish.

"If the governor would be so kind," Gaz said, "we've got a patrol to maintain."

Wren searched one last time for something. Anything. And came up empty. He nodded his head and even though he tried hard not to, he ended up dropping his gaze to the ground.

"Morning, then," Gaz said. Wren watched the two pairs of feet swivel and walk away. And just a few moments later he heard Janner mutter, "Little brat."

It shouldn't have seemed like such a big deal, but in that moment Wren felt like he'd lost something important. He was supposed to be the Governor. Supposed to be in charge. But even his own guard didn't respect him. And why should they? He was just a stupid little boy, playing at being king. Tears rose up, and he hated himself all the more for crying.

Wren dug his palms into his eyes for a few moments, tried to push the tears away. It didn't matter, really. It didn't matter whether people respected him or even liked him. There was still work to do, and it was his job – his duty – to do it. At least until someone else came along.

He wiped his sweaty hands on his pants, and his nose on his sleeve, and made his way to the main gate. Up ahead he could hear raised voices, not quite loud enough to make out the words but enough to get the gist of the tone. Painter and Luck were already there, taking abuse from one of the guardsmen.

"Look, I'm sorry, but I told you already, nobody's coming in or out today," the guard snapped. "And if you don't quit buzzing around here, I'll have to juice you both." He waved his stunrod back and forth for emphasis.

"It's OK," Wren called. "I asked them to come."

The guard turned and saw Wren. It was Lane, one of the guards who'd been on duty when the attack happened, and one of the nicer people in the guard. If he was still posted, that must've meant they'd called everyone in. It also explained why Lane wasn't his usual cheerful self.

"Governor," Lane said. "No one told me anything about these two."

"I know, Lane. But it's alright."

"Does your mother–" Lane caught himself. "Did you clear it?"

"Yeah, it's OK," Wren replied. "You're not going to get in trouble."

"Well, do me a favor and tell that to Connor, huh?"

Wren smiled. "I will."

"Alright," Lane said. He authorized the gate unlock, opened it, and nodded to Luck and Painter as they entered. "Sorry for giving you boys a hard time, but orders are orders. And it's been a long night."

"Hey, it's your job," Luck said with a shrug and his quick smile. "We won't break anything while we're here, promise."

Lane said, "Yeah, see to it you don't. Best to keep a low profile today." Lane closed the gate behind them and relocked it.

"Thanks, Lane," Wren said.

"Yep."

Wren led the two away from the gate. "You guys want to go back over to the side yard?"

"Actually," Luck said. "You mind if we go in? Sun's starting to get to me."

"Um, I guess so. We should probably go around the side though."

"Yeah, what's going on with all that? People seem pretty buttoned up today."

Wren shrugged.

"Old people stuff?" Luck asked.

"Yeah," Wren answered. He adjusted course and took his companions away from the main entrance, around the eastern edge of the building. They passed the two guards on patrol again, who gave them a quick once-over. Wren kept his head down. He asked, "How're you guys doing?"

"Can't complain," Luck said.

"You can al-al-always complain," Painter said.

"Well, yeah, I mean, I've gotta hang out with you, so that's like the worst," Luck replied. He swatted Painter on the arm. "And for some reason I'm having trouble with the ladies lately."

"Not just l-l-l," Painter said, the "L" sticking in his mouth. He shook his head once, quickly. "Lately."

The three walked to a short set of stairs leading down to one of the main building's lesser used entrances, and Wren tried the door. Locked.

"See what I mean?" Luck said. "Buttoned up."

"Just a sec," Wren said. He knew he wasn't supposed to, but he really didn't feel like going back around to the front. And these days, it hardly took him a second. He stretched out through the digital, and in the next moment the lock chirped and he pulled the door open. "Don't tell my mom."

They entered a hallway, one level below the main floor of the building. It was cool, and quiet, and minimally lit. It always seemed to Wren that the place had been built to hold far more people than were allowed in it now.

They found a room off the hall with some plush chairs and made themselves at home. Luck flopped into a chair in the middle of the room and threw his feet onto a low table. Wren sat across from him, perched forward in his chair so his feet could still touch the floor. Painter didn't sit, but instead walked slowly about the room, looking around aimlessly.

"How about you, Painter?" Wren asked. "How's everything with you?"

Painter shrugged. "Alright, I g-guess."

"Just *alright*?" Luck said. "I wish my life was as *alright* as yours. Any time you wanna trade jobs, P, you just let me know."

"Mister Sun is real n-n-n-nice. But you know what it's like."

"I'm sure I don't," Luck said.

Painter frowned a little and went quiet. There was an awkward silence, and Wren wasn't sure why, or how to fix it. Painter and Luck were both good friends, but they were also a good bit older than Wren, and he was never sure exactly how to behave around them.

"So, what's up with you, Wren?" Luck said. "Err, I mean, Mister Governor, sir." He took his feet off the table and bowed forward when he said it, before flopping back again.

"I don't know. Just the usual, I guess."

"Just the usual, Painter," Luck said, looking over at Painter who was now examining some fixture near one corner of the room. He turned back to Wren. "So, that's like what? Running the city, keeping the guard in check, bringing people back from the dead... you know, just the usual." Luck said it with a smile and his kind of teasing affection. "Speaking of which, how come you don't have to be in that meeting, anyway?"

"My mom said I could skip it," Wren answered. "I don't think it's supposed to be important."

"Aren't they all immm-imm... -portant?" Painter said from across the room.

Wren shrugged. "I'm sure the Council thinks so. But most of the time they just talk a lot and hardly ever do anything. I don't know how important something can be if all you ever do is talk about it."

"That's one of the reasons you make a good governor, Wren," Luck said. "You're a man of action."

Wren felt embarrassed at the description, but he could tell Luck actually meant it. "I'd like to be," Wren said. "One day."

"No reason to wait," said Luck.

Painter finally wandered over and took a seat next to Luck. He seemed restless, more on edge than usual. Like he had somewhere else to be, and was running late. One of his legs bounced with nervous energy.

"Have you heard from your sister?" Wren asked Painter.

Painter's attention snapped to Wren, and after a moment he shook his head. "Not since the fuh, fuh, the first time."

Painter had a younger sister named Snow. Wren had never met or even seen her, but from what he could gather, she and Painter had been very close before he had been taken. After his Awakening, he'd sought her out, expecting a happy reunion. It hadn't gone the way he'd hoped.

"I'm sure she'll come around, man," Luck said. "Just needs time to adjust. We all do."

Painter shrugged and shook his head again. "Wouldn't think it'd tuh-take that long."

"Yeah. But every day we've got's a gift as far as I'm concerned. You can't let the regulars get you down."

"Easy to sss – to say."

"Have you guys been having trouble?" Wren asked. "In the city, I mean."

Luck glanced over at Painter. Painter just looked at the floor.

"Just the usual," Luck said, with his quick grin again.

"What happened?" said Wren.

"Nothing really. Just, you know, like I said. Everybody needs time to adjust. Maybe some quarters more than others."

"It isn't fair," Painter said. "We're citizens just as muh-muh-much as anyone."

"Yeah," Luck answered. "But you gotta admit, we're not just people anymore."

"We're better."

"Well, I don't know about that. Different, for sure."

Wren felt overwhelmingly selfish. Yes, he'd had a frightening night, but it hadn't been the first time he'd been exposed to danger. He hadn't been harmed, not really. And here his friends were, facing threats every day for something out of their control. They'd done nothing to deserve being taken by the Weir. And they'd never asked to be brought back by Wren. Twice victims. There might not be anything Wren could really do to make it right for Painter and Luck and others like them, but that didn't mean he shouldn't try.

"Hey, I'm sorry to do this guys," Wren said, getting up out of his chair. "But I've got a meeting to go to."

"How'd somebody get inside the perimeter?" Arom asked. "Then inside the compound? His hall? His room?" He stomped around the room in a rage. "Do you all realize how many separate, total failures had to happen for some stranger to end up even in the same *building* as him?"

The Council had already gathered, having been briefed when they were summoned. It was unusual to bring them all together on such short notice. No one was happy about it. But certainly the circumstances warranted it. Cass stood at the door, silent and thus far unnoticed, watching them through her heavy veil. Aron, the oldest member of the governing body, thundered with a passion more characteristic of a man thirty years younger.

"Aron, please–" said Connor, holding up a calming hand, trying to soothe the older man. A mistake, Cass knew. His tone would inflame, instead.

"Don't *'Aron, please'* me, boy," Aron said, whirling to face Connor. His finger darted out so quickly that Connor actually flinched from across the table. "This is exactly what I've been warning you all about. The disorder, the lack of discipline, the... the... the *chaos* out there has finally spilled over these high walls and infected the very heart of our city."

Already Cass could sense a shift in the Council. Something was different. Off. And in a flash, her instincts confirmed her fear; someone in this room wanted her son dead. But who? And why? Or was she just being paranoid?

She thought of Three and his uncanny knack for reading subtle signs in people's expressions, movements, breathing. What would he have seen? What would he have said? *Trust your instincts.* She would have to intervene soon or else the morning would be lost. But not yet.

"I told you," Aron continued. "I warned you when you opened them gates to those people, I warned you they was gonna bring nothin' but disease and decline. And you did it anyway."

Hondo had his head back on his chair, eyes closed. Aloof, impatient with anything he considered petty or irrelevant. Vye was next to him, staring down at the table in front of her, ignoring the conflict. If the argument got too heated, she would wilt and refuse to take sides, regardless of what she believed.

"The damage was already done," Connor answered. Civilian overseer of the entire guard. Not as skilled a diplomat as he believed, but level-headed. "You know it better than anyone. Those people were submissive only because they knew Governor Underdown would continue to protect them even outside the wall."

"If not for Underdown's tyranny," Rae added, "*those people* would've been our friends. Our neighbors. Our *allies*." She was middle-aged and fiery, ever the champion of the less-fortunate.

North watched with quick eyes and utter stillness. Cass was a little surprised he hadn't noticed her yet.

"Underdown may've been a tyrant," Aron countered, "but at least he brought *order.*"

"Through fear and deception!" Rae retorted.

"Underdown is dead," said a voice, and a chilled silence immediately fell over the group. Cass realized it was she that had spoken.

"Lady Cass..." Aron said with a slight bow, and the hint of a tremble in his voice. From the adrenaline, not from fear. Never from fear when it came to Aron.

Cass was uncertain what point she had intended to make by reminding them of Underdown's death. And she could not afford to seem uncertain. Not in this room. Not now. So, without another word, she strode from the door to a seat near the head of the table, but did not sit. Instead, she placed her hands on the table and leaned over it, addressing them in a low and well-controlled voice, hoping it would command the group's respect, or at very least their attention.

"Last night someone tried to murder my son in his bed. I called you here to discuss solutions, and I see no value in revisiting year-old decisions in light of the difficulties that already lie before us." She looked to Aron first, and then slowly to each member of the council in turn. "If any of you wish to discuss the matter further, you may do so with me later. Privately. Are we agreed?"

"Of course, ma'am," said Connor, half-rising out of his chair. The others nodded their assent, Aron last of all.

Cass lifted her hand to indicate her veil.

"Take it off," Aron said with a dismissive wave. He threw himself heavily into a chair at the table. "I can't stand you hidin' behind that infernal curtain." His gruff words might've seemed like rudeness or disdain, but Cass knew better, and she took it as a good sign. It was more like a father's thin impatience about a cherished daughter's scandalous outfit; and Aron was only polite when he had an angle.

Cass raised the veil and took a seat, but not without noticing how quickly Rae averted her eyes. More than a year had passed since Cass's return, and still some could not bear to look at her directly. Some. Many.

"I apologize for bringing you all here on such short notice," she said. Hondo laid his head back on his chair again, closed his eyes as if to emphasize the point. "But I felt, given the circumstances…"

"Where's Wren?" Rae asked.

"He won't be attending today."

"Is he alright?" North asked, his voice like distant thunder. Built like a mountain, he spoke rarely, listened deeply – and most often heard what went unsaid. A good man.

"A knock on the head, a bruised ankle. We're grateful it was nothing more."

"We're *lucky* it wasn't more," Aron said. "And if he isn't holed up somewhere under lock and key, you're all a heap dumber than I thought."

"I'm not going to imprison my son for someone else's crime, Aron."

"That boy, Cass, you know I love him like my own, I do, but that boy is more than just your son."

"Where would you put him?" said Rae. "If he isn't safe in his own room, where in Morningside could he possibly go?"

Cass defused the beginnings of another squabble by activating the table surface. The marble texturing melted away and was replaced by a number of images of Wren's attacker. "Anyone recognize this girl?"

Hondo raised his head off his chair with an audible sigh, opened his eyes to look.

Vye's hand went to her mouth, but not from recognition. Her compassion was well known. Tears welled in her eyes. "She's so young."

There was a brief silence as everyone scanned the pictures.

"An outsider, no question," Aron said. A quick evaluation; maybe too quick.

"We don't know that," Rae responded. Possibly just to antagonize Aron.

"It's obvious. Look at her. Clothes, dirt, all skin and bones."

"Because Morningside's never had poor inside the wall, Aron?" Rae asked, anger evident in her voice.

"Rae." Connor stepped in. "Let's not make it a class thing, OK? You have to admit, she doesn't look like a citizen." Rae sharply looked back at the images in front of her without response.

"Probably lost her family to an attack or something," Aron said. "Maybe had it out for Underdown, and once we brought 'em all inside, she waited for a chance and decided to get some revenge on Wren."

"Could be," Vye said cautiously. "I guess it's possible."

"Stretching. Outsider, I buy," Hondo added. "But personal vendetta? Pulled this off on her own? I don't see that."

"I have to agree," said Connor. "Whatever her motives, she's got all the marks of someone who grew up beyond the wall." *Beyond the wall.* A phrase Connor probably considered more diplomatic, but still managed to make sound demeaning. Another way to say outsider. Second-class. Other. Like Cass.

"Or someone went to a great deal of trouble to make it seem like she came from the outside," North said, and Cass watched his words ripple through the Council. Aron and Hondo exchanged a quick glance; Rae clenched her jaw; Vye just sat there looking at the pictures of the girl and shaking her head. Connor stayed very still. For a long moment, they sat in silence, the implications sinking in.

"How did she…?" Vye asked, unable to bring herself to say it.

"She killed herself," Cass said. She tossed the handle of the girl's knife on the table. Hondo picked it up, examined it, held it up for the others to see.

"It's a popper."

"A what?" Vye said.

"Shatter-blade," Aron explained. "Got a little charge in there, makes the blade explode in a million pieces and turns your insides to soup. Nasty business. Find 'em on outsiders all the time." He added the last bit as if it was proof positive his assumptions were right. Awfully convinced.

"Who would do such a thing?" Connor said, almost to himself. He shook his head. "Who could even *conceive* of such a thing? He's just a boy!" There was genuine despair in his voice. A rare display of emotion.

"Not to them," said Vye. Her voice was quiet but certain.

"And that's what I mean," Aron said. "Look. In here, to us, we know who Wren is. But out there, he's just a name. Or… or… or a king. Or a god."

"Or a devil," said Hondo. Cass held herself still, refused to react to the almost-familiar words. After a moment, she let her eyes slide casually across Vye to Hondo.

"That's not what I meant," Vye said.

"It isn't what you said, but it's what you meant," Hondo replied. "And what do you expect? He brought ghouls to live among us." Aron and Connor both reacted, and Vye actually gasped aloud. Hondo glanced at her, then turned and addressed Cass directly. "Look, don't take it the wrong way, Cass. I'm just trying to be honest about how some folk feel."

Cass waved her hand, casually dismissing any offense. She'd been called worse.

"There are certain segments out there," Hondo continued, "not me mind you, you know not me, but there are segments who just want things back the way they were."

Connor said, "Things will never be the way they were–"

"It doesn't matter, Connor, people will always want it anyway!" Hondo said, voice rising. "I got people out there still talking about going home one day! *Home*, Connor! What kind of home you think is left out there for anyone to go back to?"

"People are just afraid," Rae said. "Afraid of change, afraid of uncertainty. And when people are afraid, they drive themselves to do things. Crazy things."

Aron said, "And that's why I said we had to keep the gates closed!"

"Didn't we *just* agree we weren't going back there, Aron?" said Hondo.

Things were getting heated again. Cass glanced at North. He was still, expressionless, soaking it all in.

Aron replied, "But back there is the problem, Hondo. Back there is where too much changed, too fast. Look here, bringin' Wren to the people, makin' him governor, that was the quick fix. Underdown's son, heir to the throne. What he would have wanted. That's easy, people get that. But throwin' the gates open to the outsiders? And then this business with... you know. I'm sorry, Cass, but it's true."

She said, "No one here needs to apologize to me for anything. I know what I am."

"Again, Aron," said Rae, "we all appreciate your keen sense of problems, but why don't you try solving one for a change!"

He said, "We gotta get 'em off the streets. Bring 'em all here, or let me take 'em in at my place, I don't care. We just need a place for 'em to stay until people get used to the idea."

North spoke at last. "They're free people, Aron. Free *people*. Like you. Like me."

"No, North, they're not. Doesn't matter what we say, doesn't matter whether you like it or I like it. They're different."

"That's the problem, isn't it?" said a small voice from the entryway. The whole Council turned, and even Cass felt a jolt. There was Wren, standing near the door. Observing, for who knew how long. Just like his mama. Able hovered by the entrance, at once protective and unobtrusive.

Cass opened her mouth to protest but caught herself, closed it. *You shouldn't be here. You should be resting. You should be playing. You should be having a childhood.* Not in front of the Council. In here she was his advisor, not his mother. A war she constantly fought.

Wren approached, and everyone stood as he climbed up in his chair at the head of the table. A formality they insisted on, though Wren had often said it seemed silly. His

legs dangled freely above the floor, but his face was grave
with understanding well beyond his eight years.

The Council retook their seats.

"How are you, Wren?" Rae asked.

"I'm well, Miss Rae, thank you," Wren said. His words and
tone were kind, respectful, but Cass could tell the answer
had been more reflex than response. "It's the difference that
scares people so much. All the changes."

He said it like a statement, but it was a question. Looking
for confirmation.

"Change, uncertainty," Aron said, nodding. "Like Rae says."

"But that's not the whole truth," Hondo said, leaning
forward. "It's *them*, too. What they are. What they represent."

Cass felt anger rising, but checked herself.

"Tell us, Hondo," North said. He was speaking Cass's mind,
whether he knew it or not. "What do our friends *represent*?"

Hondo swallowed, licked his lips, glanced around the
table for allies. Maybe he'd pushed it too far.

"People think they could go back," Wren said. The
Council seemed surprised to hear him answer for Hondo.
"To the way they were."

Hondo nodded. For a moment, Cass lost herself hearing
her son give voice to the nightmare that haunted her
daily; the terrifying thought that she might ever... relapse?
Revert? Was there even a word for it?

"And some folk blame them for things that happened,"
Hondo added after a moment. "I know it's not fair. It's not
right, and it's not fair, but that's how it is."

"None of this moves us any closer to resolving last night's
attack," Cass said, reasserting control of the conversation.
"Unless you're suggesting that we've reached such a state in
Morningside that people would send someone to kill my son?"

Hondo shrugged in a way that suggested it was the only possible explanation.

"What purpose would that possibly serve?" Rae asked.

"It'd be the first step towards getting things back to the way they were, wouldn't it?" Hondo said. "Think about it. Wren dies by the hand of an outsider, what's the first thing everyone's going to want to do?"

"Send them all back outside," Vye said.

"Whoa, slow down now, slow down," Aron countered. "Ain't no reason to go makin' up conspiracies when it coulda been just like I said. Girl after revenge, on her own, cause of her own reasons."

"It makes sense, though," Connor said. "A terrible, terrible kind of sense."

Rae took over. She said, "Look, in the immediate, it's irrelevant. Whether she was crazy, or desperate, or a hired assassin, we're not going to figure that out sitting around this table. The question we're here to answer right now is – what do we *do*?"

It was quiet for a moment, as each Council member looked to the others.

"Nothing," said Wren. Hondo suppressed a condescending smile; Connor smiled what he probably thought was an encouraging smile, but that ended up more condescending than Hondo's.

"We can't do *nothin'* Wren," Aron said. "Once people find out–"

"If we don't do anything, then no one has to know anything happened," Wren answered.

"I think you're putting a little too much faith in your guards," Hondo said.

"Maybe someone *will* talk," Wren replied, "But if we

don't make any sudden changes, then who will believe it? It'll just be like any of the other rumors people talk about every other day of the week." Wren was sitting up straighter, leaning forward. Confident. And becoming convincing. "You've been saying it yourselves all morning. People fear change. So, we don't change anything." He paused for a moment. "Except maybe I'll sleep in my mom's room for a while." He said it with a smile that undercut the seriousness of the moment. Rae chuckled.

"I agree," North said, "If we don't respond to the attack, it becomes a non-event."

"Unless she really was sent by someone," said Connor.

"Then our inaction will speak more powerfully than anything we could do at this point. We will not be terrorized."

Aron shook his head. "No. We can't pretend it was nothin'. It'd be pure foolishness."

"We need to help people adjust," Wren said. "We need to help them get used to how things are now. It won't help anybody if you just lock up the compound."

"It won't help anybody if you're dead either," Hondo said.

Wren's gaze dropped to the table and he went quiet.

"Whatever else we decide, we need to identify the girl," Cass said. "Discreetly. What are our options?"

The other Council members all exchanged looks, waiting for someone else to offer an idea or opinion. Finally Rae sat forward. "I've got a few connections by the West Wall. I'll see what I can find."

"I doubt it'll be any use, but I can handle the business district," Hondo said.

"And I'll talk to the elders," said Aron. "Most of us are only good for gossip these days anyway; someone's bound to know somethin'."

"Secrecy is crucial," North said. "We shouldn't ask so many questions that others begin to wonder."

"Agreed," Cass said. "Use your judgment, but err on the side of caution. Let's see what we can find out, and reconvene in two days."

The Council members agreed and, after a round of formal goodbyes, began excusing themselves. Cass watched them intently as they departed, looking for any final hints or clues as to what any of them might be hiding. But nothing stood out, nothing out of the ordinary. Or rather, so much out of the ordinary that made it difficult to discern motives.

"Mama," Wren said. "Are you mad at me?"

The question caught her completely off guard. "What? No, baby, why?"

"Because I came to the meeting anyway."

"No, of course not. I just thought you didn't want to come."

"I wish I hadn't," Wren replied.

"You did fine, sweetheart. You made some very good points."

"Then why do I feel like they don't want me around?"

Cass's heart sank to hear those words.

"I don't know, Wren. But we'll figure it out, OK?" She said it with what she hoped sounded like certainty, knowing that if they didn't figure it out soon, neither of them would be likely to survive whatever came next.

THREE

Fletcher had been the first one to spot the man with the blindfold. He was the smart one, always had been. The one who always noticed things, and thought of things, and made good plans; and that's why he was in charge. And it was lucky for ol' Blindfold down there that Fletcher was in charge, else the boys would've cut him up and fed most of him to Nice and Lady, and probably ate some of the leftovers themselves. Especially Cup. Cup was crazy.

Nice and Lady was their dogs what they got off a crazy old woman who thought they'd be protection and was wrong, and Fletcher had named 'em because he said that they got 'em from a real nice lady, and the boys thought that was pretty funny, so that's what they named 'em. Right now, Nice and Lady was somewhere with Sloan being real quiet like good dogs. And they was good dogs. Better than some of the boys, but that wa'n't much of a compliment when you thought about it.

But Fletcher was in charge, because he was the smart one, and so Blindfold was still warm and breathing for now. At least until Fletcher could figure what they *was* going to do with him. Killing him and letting the dogs eat good was the easy thing, they done that plenty of times, but Fletcher

knew the easy thing usually wa'n't the best thing. And
there was something wa'n't right about this one, because
Blindfold, he was dressed weird in a coat too big and had a
blindfold on his eyes, and was just kneeling down there in
the street like that for an hour or more. That's how Blindfold
was when Fletcher saw him, and that's how he was right
now, and it been an hour or more. So Fletcher knew he just
had to figure what to do with him.

"Heya, Fletcher," Mull whispered. Mull was a good one
of the boys, real quick with the jittergun, like magic-trick
quick, but he wasn't real smart.

"Shhh," Fletcher said.

"Yeah, but – Fletcher. You figure what we gonna do yet?
I gotta leak."

"Well, go on," Fletcher whispered back. "I ain't stoppin'
ya. Just do it quiet."

"Why's he just sittin' there like that, Fletcher?"

"Because somethin' ain't right with him, Mull."

"You mean like he's dead or somethin'?"

"Yeah, Mull, I been sittin' here lookin' at a dead man
for an hour. Go take your leak before ya wet us both." Mull
grunted and started off to another corner of the roof. "And
do it quiet!"

Fletcher took another look around, looking for something
he hadn't seen yet, something Blindfold might be counting
on or waiting for. But it all looked like everything else. Broke
down buildings and roofs that all fell in and garbage in the
street. He looked back down again, down at Blindfold, and
he was still just setting there, on his knees all weird, not
moving or nothing. Fletcher looked at the sky. Couldn't be
more than another half-hour before the sun go down and
the howlies come out, and it'd take a good ten minutes or so

to take care of Blindfold and get him packed up and maybe another fifteen to get back inside and locked up. Fletcher looked back at Blindfold again.

Guess they'd have to do the easy way after all.

"Mull," he whispered across the roof. Mull was zipping up and he looked over, and Fletcher motioned with his hands to get down off the roof and around back to where the boys was waiting. Mull nodded, and they both went down the back where an old ladder was only half hung on, but they climbed down easy because they was both pretty good on their feet.

When they got to the bottom, Creed and Yeager was sitting around leaning against the wall and doing the things they did when they was bored; and Mags he was sleeping; and Cup, well, Cup was just setting there facing the wall – staring at it like he could make it fall down just staring at it – and if anyone could it was probably him. Cup was crazy.

"Hey, Fletcher, what's the plan?" Creed said, and he stood up and stretched, like he was ready to do some work.

"Where's Sloan at?" Fletcher asked.

"Around the other building with Nice and Lady."

"OK. Here's the plan," Fletcher said, then noticed Mags was still sleeping. "Wake Mags up."

Yeager kicked Mags pretty good, and Mags woke up mad and Creed laughed a little.

"Come on, Mags," Fletcher said, "we gotta do some work."

"What's the plan?" Mags asked, sitting up and rubbing his ribs where Yeager'd kicked him.

"Creed, you and Yeager, you're gonna go round to where Sloan is, and then you boys get Nice and Lady and come up behind him. Then me and Cup and Mull and Mags, we're gonna come up in front of him."

"OK," Creed said. "And then what?"

"Then I'm gonna ask him some questions."

"OK. And then what?" Creed repeated.

"Well, then I reckon we kill him."

"OK."

"OK," Fletcher said.

"OK," Creed said, and then he and Yeager went off to find Sloan and the dogs.

"Cup," Fletcher said. "You get that?"

For a second, Cup didn't do nothing, then all sudden-like he just sits up and headbutts the wall, and he sits back with a big smile – with blood coming down between his eyes – and then gets up and starts walking. Cup was crazy.

Mags and Mull started following him, but Fletcher caught Mull's arm and said real low, "Hey, Mull. I'm gonna ask him a couple questions, but if he acts funny, you don't wait. You just go on and shoot him, alright? I wanna ask him a couple questions, but I won't be mad if you gotta just shoot him, alright?"

"Alright, Fletcher, I got you," Mull said, and he patted the jittergun he kept in a holster right at the front where he could reach it real quick.

"Alright," Fletcher said, and he patted Mull on the shoulder because he was one of the good ones, and you could always count on Mull, even when Cup went crazy.

Fletcher walked out into the street with Mull just behind him and walked up a couple of yards from Blindfold. Cup and Mags was already there, but kind of hanging back, and then when Fletcher was there in the street, Sloan give a little whistle and come out of the alley behind Blindfold with Nice and Lady barking all a-sudden – because they been such good dogs to be so quiet so long – and now they was slobbering and pulling their leashes, and Creed and Yeager was right there behind them, laughing at how the dogs was dragging Sloan up the street. But the dogs they quit when they got close and started pacing back and forth like they was a little confused and a little excited.

"Hey," Fletcher said, once all the boys was in place. But Blindfold just sat there on his knees with his head down like he was sleeping.

"Hey!" Fletcher said louder. Blindfold didn't move or nothing.

Then for no reason Cup just let out a holler and threw a brick or something right at Blindfold and it went next to his head so close his hair moved, no fooling. But Blindfold he didn't move or nothing, not even like it'd been a fly buzzing.

"Knock it off," Mull said, kind of sharp-like to Cup. Then he leaned in. "I told ya, Fletcher, pretty sure he's dead." Fletcher shooed Mull away. He was quick on the trigger, but not so much with the thinking.

"Hey, old man, my friend thinks you're dead. You ain't dead, are ya?" he asked.

"Not yet," Blindfold said, and Mags actually jumped back two steps, and Creed and Yeager both busted out laughing at that. And Nice and Lady kept walking back and forth, back and forth, and Nice whined a little high-pitched whine, and Sloan jerked his leash to shut him up.

"Not yet. That's right, not yet," Fletcher said, chuckling and turning to look at Mull. "See, Mull, he ain't dead yet." Then he turned back to Blindfold and Blindfold's head was up, like he was staring right at Fletcher, even though he couldn't see nothing, and Fletcher felt something wasn't right. Blindfold's hair was long like a woman's and dirty grey, and his coat was worn-through pretty good, and his hands was flat on his legs, palms down, and Fletcher saw his fingernails was all cracked and black in places like somebody been digging. "What's your name, old man?"

"Today," Blindfold said. "I am Faith."

Creed laughed at that, and Fletcher thought Creed laughed too much, and Nice and Lady both started whining and turning circles on their leashes, and Sloan had to rough-talk 'em to get 'em to shut up.

"Faith, huh?" Fletcher said, smiling big and putting on a show for the boys, even though he didn't much like how things was feeling. He took a step back to get a little distance, but did it all casual so it didn't look like he was scared. "Didn't know people still had any of that these parts."

"I do."

Fletcher heard Cup grunt behind him, and then he heard something heavy smash something else, and whatever it was must've broke from the racket it made.

"Yeah? And what you got faith in, Mister Faith man?"

"I had faith I'd find you here."

Nice and Lady were whining bad now, like they did when storms come up, and they was getting Sloan tangled in the leashes, and he kicked Nice once and Creed wasn't laughing no more.

"Sloan, shut them dogs up, will ya?" Mull said.

"Shut yerself up, Mull!" Sloan said.

Fletcher licked his lips because his mouth was all dry and he was going to ask some more questions, but something just wasn't right, so he decided he was done.

"Alright, Mull," he said.

"Yep," said Mull, and Mull stepped up, and Fletcher wondered if it was good or bad that ol' Blindfold couldn't see it coming. But all sudden-like Blindfold come up on one knee and he was close, way closer than Fletcher thought he could be, and there was a quick noise like water, and Nice and Lady broke running, and Mull made a little coughing sound.

"Fletcher..." Mull said, and he was looking down, and Fletcher looked down, and Mull had his hand on the jittergun – but the gun was still in the holster, and there was a piece of steel through his wrist and up deep into his belly and out his back, and Fletcher followed the steel back to Blindfold's hand and realized it was a blade.

"Well..." said Fletcher, but he didn't know why. And then Blindfold took his sword back and Mull fell down on his knees.

"Fletcher..." Mull said.

Creed and Yeager both went for their guns then – and Blindfold went backwards like he was on a cord that got yanked, and went past Sloan and cut Yeager, then turned a little half circle, and Creed fell down screaming. Blindfold made a little circle in front of him with his sword like he was cutting air, but it made red spray up, and then Creed quit screaming.

Sloan was used to having the dogs, so he was still trying to get out his knife when Blindfold went past him again fast; and Sloan didn't make no noise, he just tip over.

Fletcher was backing up then, backing up past Cup and Mags, and Blindfold coming right at them. And Mags had got his two-gun out by then and he shot both barrels of it, and Blindfold went down in the street. But turned out he was rolling and Mags just hit Cup with all his shooting, and Cup fell down. And then Blindfold took Mags at the knees and did something else too fast to follow, and Mags went backwards making a sound like a whistle gurgling.

Then Cup went crazy.

He got up all bloody in the front and screamed, and picked up a broken chunk of street three times bigger than his head – and had it over his head like he was going to smash Blindfold, but Blindfold turned around real fast and Cup's hands come off, and the piece of street fell on him, and his face hit the ground real hard, and he moved some and groaned, but his head was broke.

And then Blindfold was on one knee in front of Fletcher, and he had a sword in his hand and it had red on it, and Fletcher hurt in the middle, and his shirt and pants was all warm and wet, and he realized his gun was still in his holster – and he hadn't even thought about getting it out until just now.

"I knew you wasn't right," he said, and his voice sounded funny, like he was talking out the bottom of a well. Maybe he could get his gun out now. "I knew it."

Blindfold didn't say nothing, he just stood up and slung his blade out to the side, and all the red went sliding right off it like it'd never even touched it, then he put it somewhere in his big coat. Fletcher realized he was setting down, but he couldn't remember setting down; and he kept thinking if Fletcher could ask enough questions, he'd figure out what ol' Blindfold was up to and maybe then he could get his gun out and kill him.

"You come all the way out here, just for us?" Fletcher asked.

"No," Blindfold said. "You were on the way."

It was going dark, and Fletcher wondered if it was just his eyes, but then one of them howlies made a cry somewhere not real far off, and that meant the sun was going down. Blindfold didn't seem to be in no hurry though, just buttoning his rag-man coat like he was on his way to a funeral.

"Way to where?" he asked.

"East. There's a city."

Fletcher felt real tired and he figured if he laid down on his side, it'd be easier to get the pistol out the holster, and he was going to need that for killing Blindfold, and then again when the howlies come, so he leaned over sideways on an elbow. Blindfold started walking away, and Fletcher never had no worries about shooting a man in the back so long as he didn't get too far off, so he called after him. It didn't hurt none no more.

"Hey! What's it got there worth seein'?"

Ol' Blindfold stopped for a second and turned over his shoulder, but not really looking at Fletcher, like he was thinking about it.

"Demons," he said.

Then he just walked off.

Fletcher never did get that gun out.

FOUR

Night had fallen over Morningside, and with it came an uneasy sort of quiet without any peace. The kind of quiet that made Wren think of waiting in the clinic – when everyone was just sitting there not talking, and he knew he had to get a shot – and the whole time it felt like nobody was talking because they were all too busy thinking about how much it was going to hurt. The whole city felt like that to him now, like all those people were just out there, waiting. Waiting and thinking about how much it was going to hurt.

When he'd first come, Morningside had seemed so clean and perfect. All clean lines and smooth curves, and room enough for everything, and everything right where it belonged. After just a few days inside the wall, it was hard to remember how broken everything was beyond it. Broken, and dirty, and never enough of anything – except the stuff you didn't want and too much of that; too much cold, too much hunger, too much fear.

But not here. Not inside. There were wide roads, all smooth without any cracks or holes, and lights all along the sides so you could walk from the governor's compound to the main gate and back without ever stepping on a shadow if you wanted. And shops all along both sides, where you could find just about anything you wanted. Places to get all kinds of foods, foods Wren had never even been able to imagine before he came here. Stores that only sold beds, with so many inside the first time he'd seen one he asked the owner if the whole city slept there. And the owner had just laughed and laughed and patted him on the head like it was the funniest thing anyone had ever said. And there were shops with clothes that were brand new that no one else had ever worn, and they'd make to fit you, no matter how small you were for your age.

Even the people, the people seemed like they'd been made with the city, at the same time, by the same hands. All clean and gracious and never touched by anything sad. At least that's how they'd seemed when he'd first come to Morningside. Now Wren knew how it was, though. He'd gotten a really good look for himself. People were still people, no matter how good they had it. They always brought the broken in with them.

Wren hadn't been out at night in a few days, and hadn't been outside the wall in, what was it... almost three months now? Not since the night he'd snuck out through the secret tunnel that ran from the compound to a hidden place outside. The night he'd felt like if he stayed in the compound another minute, his insides would've gotten all crushed down, and Wren would never have been able to breathe ever again. The night he'd woken Painter.

Mama had been mad about that; mad about him sneaking out, mad about the gashes he came home with, all along his ribs. Madder than Wren could ever remember seeing her. And North had just shaken his head and said he was disappointed, and that had hurt the worst. But they'd rescued Painter – Wren and Mouse and Able – and then, they'd gone back out and found him and brought him in, and that had made it all worthwhile. Painter was a good friend; kind and generous. Almost like an older brother. A good older brother. Not like the other kind.

And now Wren had to take him heavy news. It'd taken all of Wren's powers of persuasion, but he'd finally managed to convince his mother to let him leave the compound on his most solemn vow that he'd go only to Mister Sun's Tea House and come straight back when he was done. Only Able accompanied Wren, to avoid attracting the attention that his usual contingent of guards would've drawn; Able had done all the convincing on that one. Well, only Able was right there with him. There were others, others walking ahead and others walking behind – Mouse and Wick and Gamble, always watchful. And Wren was pretty sure that Mama was out there somewhere, keeping her distance and keeping an eye on them. She'd gotten better at hiding herself from him since… since she woke up.

Able had taken him in a meandering path, spiraling out from the governor's compound and throughout the city. There were fewer people out on the streets, as Able had said. Since the night of the attack. For the most part, those they passed nodded silent greetings or ignored them, and Able was cautious about letting anyone trail them for long.

After about twenty minutes into what was normally a ten-minute walk, they finally reached the Tea House. Wren felt Able's hand on his shoulder, turning him gently.

Five minutes, Able signed. *If he won't come, we leave without him.*

Wren nodded.

And don't take off the hat.

Wren nodded. He hated the hat. It was round and flat,

with a low brim and a stupid orange fluffy ball on top of it, but apparently a lot of kids his age wore them. Well, not his age. Kids his size. Younger ones.

Able held out his hand, and Wren took it, and together they went up the steps into the Tea House, hopefully looking to any casual observer like a father and son out for a quick cup of Mister Sun's famous Dreamtime Blend. Wren was nervous, knowing the coming conversation wouldn't be easy, and knowing no one else could have it but him.

But the instant they crossed through the door, Wren felt himself relax, like he was crawling back into a warm bed on a cold morning. Mister Sun's Tea House was just like that.

The main room was a little dimmer than Wren's eyes were used to, even coming in out of the night. It was lit mainly by little flickering lights placed all around that looked like something Mister Sun called candles, except real candles used real fire, he said. It was warm, but not uncomfortably so. And Wren's favorite thing: there was a wide pool with a little bridge over it, and real fish swimming in it. There was a fountain that fed the pool, made to look like a little stream, and another one going out the other side, so that the stream went around the entire central room – and the sound of it always gave Wren the impression of rain on a roof. It was a drowsy atmosphere, with a low drone of quiet conversation and the soothing scents of tea and herbs and honeyed cakes drifting through.

Mister Sun came over to greet his newest customers, like he did for every single one, hunched over with his crooked back and always his smile. "Hello, my friend," he said, beaming. Mister Sun called everyone *"my friend"*. "Hello, so good to see you, my friend!"

When he got close, he gave a little start as he recognized Wren, and his eyes went to Able, who shook his head ever so slightly. Mister Sun nodded, hardly missing a beat, and held out his good hand to direct them towards an empty table towards the back.

No one actually knew what Mister Sun's real name was, but Aron had told Wren that back a long time ago, when he first opened the Tea House, some woman had said he was the city's night-time sun, and eventually everyone just started calling him that.

He escorted them through the main room, his warm patter comforting everyone he passed, reassuring them that absolutely nothing out of the ordinary was going on. "We have seven teas tonight for special, only seven, I'm so sorry, my friend, but maybe tomorrow night you'll come earlier?" He chuckled. "Out past bedtime, yes? Does Mother know? Boys' night out, is it? Or, *ha ha* – boys snuck out while Mother has girls' night out, I bet! I bet so, my friend, I bet so!" Though Mister Sun was friendly with everyone, he was truly a friend to the Governor, and doing a masterful job of covering Able's silence with a rhythm of his own words that implied more than was actually there. A casual listener would've assumed there were two sides to the one-sided conversation, the soft-spoken father's responses lost to the gentle hum of the room.

"Here you are, my friend," he said, pulling a chair out for Wren. "Dreamtime as usual? Excellent, and for Father?"

We need to see Painter, Able signed.

"Two Dreamtime, very fine, very fine." Mister Sun nodded. He bowed slightly, smiling all the way, and drifted easily towards the back room. "My friend, drink up and go home before Wife comes to find you!" he said to some regular at another table, earning a good-natured chuckle. He disappeared through a swinging door.

Wren kept his eyes on the table in front of him, drawing little figure eights with his index finger on the smooth, polished surface. Trying to think of what to say, how to say it.

A few moments later Mister Sun glided up to table with a tray balanced expertly on the back of his withered left hand, a small pot and two matching handleless mugs upon it. As he arranged the items on the table with his other hand, he leaned closer to Wren, as if listening intently.

"To see how we blend?" he said. "Of course, my friend, of course, if it is OK with Father?" Able nodded, and held up five fingers. "Five minutes. Yes, yes, come with me." And Mister Sun stepped back, took Wren's hand, and led him casually back to the back room, conveniently shielding Wren from the other customers by bending in front of him, talking the whole way. "I think you will find it very interesting, my friend, very interesting, and you can surprise Mother with what you learn. Unless Mother isn't supposed to know!"

Mister Sun shepherded Wren through the swinging door and into a little side room, where Painter was already waiting for him.

"Thanks, Mister Sun," Wren said.

"Of course, Master Wren, anything and everything for you, always." He bowed a little, and then stepped out and closed the door to the room, leaving Wren and Painter together.

"Hi, Painter," Wren said.

"Hey, Wruh- Wruh- Wruh…" Painter said, struggling to get his mouth around the words. He shook his head once, hard, like he was trying to crack his neck. "Hey, Wren. How're things?"

Wren shrugged and looked at the floor. No reason to lie about it. "Not so great."

Painter nodded. "Because of that Council mmm-meeting?"

"Sort of. And other stuff."

Painter nodded again, and the two stood in silence for a moment.

"Painter, I have to tell you something."

"OK."

"But before I tell you, I have to ask you to promise you won't tell anybody else."

"Alrrr- alrrrr...," the word caught in his mouth. Painter stopped himself, took a deep breath, and tried again. "Alright."

"It's really important that nobody else finds out, OK? Like, *really* important."

"I won't tuh..." Painter fought another word out. Wren waited patiently. "...tell anyone."

"OK. Well. OK. The night before you and Luck... you know, before you came to visit. Something happened. At the compound." Wren felt a rush of adrenaline, the memory of the attack freshly renewed, now with new dreadful significance. Painter remained silent, attentive. "Someone got in. A girl. And she tried to... hurt... me." He couldn't bring himself to say what she was really there to do.

Painter's unnatural eyes widened in perfectly natural surprise. "She ah... attacked you?" he asked.

"She tried, but I heard her coming and I got away. But, she didn't. She hurt herself." Wren felt tears welling up again at the thought, and put a finger in the corner of his eye to try to stop it. "I guess she didn't want to get caught, and she hurt herself, Painter. And I wanted to help her, and Mouse – he would have if there was something he could've done, but she was too hurt. She died."

Painter reached over and put a hand on Wren's shoulder, and squeezed it. "I'm so sorry. That must have b- must have been terrible."

Now the hard part. "I think she was someone you know," Wren said.

"Me?"

Wren nodded. "We didn't know who she was, not until today. We were trying to find out, but everyone was trying so hard to be careful and not give anything away. We didn't find out until Miss Rae talked to some of people from the West Wall." The West Wall was where a lot of the folks who used to live outside had made their camp. "They think her name…" Wren struggled to force the words out. "They think it was Snow."

Wren saw the confusion on Painter's face, watched as he slowly made the connection and then started shaking his head in disbelief. His hand slipped slowly off of Wren's shoulder.

"No, it cuh – no, it couldn't be her," he said, not denying it so much as saying there was clearly a misunderstanding. "It couldn't be. Why would you think that?"

"Miss Rae went out and showed her picture around, asking about her, and a woman said she knew her, but hadn't seen her in a few days. A woman named Charla."

Painter's hand went to his mouth, fingers lightly touching his lips. Still shaking his head. "That doesn't make any suh-sense."

"Have you seen her since… the first time?" Wren asked.

Painter shook his head. "Nuh… nuh… no. She wouldn't…" He shook his head again, and looked off to the corner of the room. Remembering, maybe. After a moment, he looked back at Wren. "But I'm sure it's not her. I'm sure she's just off, you know… she used to go off on her own, some, some, sometimes for days. Probably just exploring. She luh-luh-luh… she loves exploring."

"Well, could you come back to the compound with me? Just to be sure?"

"I c-c-can't, I'm working."

"I'm sure Mister Sun would say it was OK. It's your sister."

"It's not my sister!" Painter said, sharply enough that Wren flinched. Painter softened. "It's not my sister, OK? I'm shh… shhh… sure of it."

There was a tap at the door, and it opened a crack. Mister Sun leaned his head in. "Master Wren, Mister Able says it is time."

He replied, "OK, I'll be right there, Mister Sun. Thanks."

Mister Sun nodded and smiled, but Wren could see the concern on his face as he withdrew.

"You won't come back with me?" Wren asked.

Painter shook his head. "Maybe luh… later tonight, after I finish."

"I don't think it's safe to come alone, Painter. Not at night."

Painter just shrugged. He wasn't going to change his mind. And Able was waiting.

Wren nodded. "OK. Well, I'm sorry. I hope we're wrong."

"You are, and it's OK." Wren nodded again and moved to the door. "I'll come by in, in, in, a day or tuh – two, OK?" Painter said.

"OK."

"And Wren?"

"Yeah?"

"Nice hat."

Wren smiled and tried to force a laugh, but it came out like a lie. "Thanks. See you, Painter."

"Yep."

Able was standing at the door when Wren stepped out of the room, looking like he already knew how it had gone. He nodded slightly and put his hand out for Wren's, and together they left the Tea House.

Wren cried the whole way back.

As they neared the governor's compound, their path led them by the north-eastern gate and though Wren's eyes were on the ground, he felt Able's stride slow and his hand tensed.

"What is it, Able?" Wren asked, out of reflex. Able wasn't looking at him, so he didn't respond. He didn't have to. When Wren followed his gaze, he saw what had caused him to react.

The remnants were strewn all over the street. The gate itself didn't seem to be damaged at all, though Wren couldn't tell if anyone had been trying to break into the compound anyway. But what once had been a memorial to those who'd been taken was now little more than a pile of debris smashed against the base of the wall. The wreaths had been pulled apart, the vigil lights stomped on and smashed against the concrete, the various articles of clothing and other personal effects were all torn, crushed, or shattered. And the pictures. The pictures were mostly pulled down and scattered along the street. Some swirled, caught in little eddies of the night air.

Able swung Wren up and carried him quickly towards the main gate. As they headed inside the compound, Wren wondered if his grand idea not to keep extra guards posted was another catastrophe in the midst of unfolding.

Painter stood at the window of his second-story room, biting a towel between his teeth to keep the fear and heartbreak and tears in check. He stared out at the street below, but only saw the look on Snow's face, with crystal clarity, the moment she had first seen him after he'd returned. The reunion he'd imagined shattered by the horror in her eyes, the stark disgust on her face. For weeks Painter had been telling himself he'd go downstairs to work, and she'd be there, sitting at one of the tables, and she'd apologize, and Snow would wrap her arms around him and tell him how glad she was that he was alive and OK, and they'd be together again. And now... what if it was true? What if Wren was right? What if his baby sister was gone?

His eyes refocused on the flexiglass window, his faint reflection there staring back at him, staring back with those hellish electric eyes. His hand flashed without thought, fist driving through his own image, through the plate, out into the night air. The flexiglass exploded outward with a sound like a thunderbolt, the sharp *crack* snapping Painter's attention back to the here and now. He pulled his hand back in through the window, stretched out the fingers, watched the black fluid welling up around the shards stuck in his knuckles and in the back of his hand. Sharp fragments of what should have been unbreakable. Black ichor that should have been blood. He tugged at the slivers, drew them from his flesh, and wrapped the towel around the wounds. There was pain, but not what he would've expected. It was sharp but distant, with a fiery tingle. Already his modified body was reconstructing itself. Modified. *Optimized*.

Painter inhaled deeply, letting his eyes fall closed, felt the cool night air across his face through the hole in the window. He had been unfair to Wren. Only now he realized how much trouble the young governor had gone to, how much danger he had exposed himself to, just to be the one to tell Painter about Snow. Even if Wren was wrong, he had still taken a risk for no reason other than kindness. If Painter hurried, he might be able to catch up with them.

He bounded down the stairs two at a time, nearly colliding with Mister Sun at the bottom. Mister Sun caught him by the shoulders, held him upright.

"Everything OK, my friend?" Mister Sun asked.

"Yes, fuh- fuh… yes, fine, Mister Sun," Painter said. Mister Sun held him fast, the old man's good hand surprisingly strong on his shoulder. Mister Sun's eyes searched Painter's. "Really. I just need to go. I'll mmm- make up the time tomorrow, pruh- prrruhh- promise."

The old man's eyes narrowed, but after a moment he nodded, and squeezed Painter's shoulder, and then let him go. Painter hurried through the Tea House, realizing he'd have to be careful chasing after Able and Wren. He couldn't draw too much attention to them, after all.

He was lost in thought as he leapt down the stairs in front of the Tea House, and couldn't quite stop himself in time as he hit the street and ran right into a trio of men, nearly knocking one of them down. Painter reached out instinctively and grabbed the man's arm to steady him.

"Suh – suh – sorry, I'm sorry, are you alright?"

"Yeah, I'm fine, just watch–" the man cut himself off as he looked up into Painter's face, snatching his arm away roughly. "Get yer stinkin' hands off me, deadling!"

Painter held up his hands, hoping to defuse the situation. "I'm sorry, s-s-sss, sorry, sir."

The other two men closed ranks, one on each side of Painter, as the one he'd run into drew himself up. He was a good four or five inches shorter than Painter, but about twice as wide, and he had a gap between his front teeth big enough to stick a finger through.

"S-s-s-s-sorry!" Gap-tooth mocked. "S-s-s-sorry, he says. You got a busted mouth, deadling?"

"No, sir—" Painter started to say, but before he could say more, Gap-tooth smashed a fist into his face, and Painter hit the ground, his head bouncing hard against the concrete.

"Ya do now!" Gap-tooth said, and his buddies laughed at that, and one of them took a big step forward and kicked Painter in the gut. The shock wave sent all the breath exploding out of Painter's lungs and made him choke. Then Gap-tooth was on him, a knee in his crotch, crushing but dull pain; a hand around his throat under his jaw, shoving his head back into the concrete. Gap-tooth's face was right in Painter's, his foul breath spilling like kerosene over Painter's mouth and nose.

He said, "You and yer kind better think hard about where you belong, cause it ain't here. It ain't nowhere close to here, you unnerstan'? There's a storm comin', there's a storm comin', and you and all yer kind are gonna wash away or twist in the wind."

Painter fought to breathe, his vision mixed with dark spots and bright flashes. And floating images, images of Snow, and his reflection, and the window shattering, and dark things. Dark things that he had done before – before Wren had found him. How easily they had come apart in his hands before.

Gap-tooth reared back and punched at him again, but it was badly aimed and little more than a glancing blow. The man spat and Painter felt the wet spatter on his cheekbone and eyelid and upper lip, and then the weight was gone, and the three men melted away, laughing in the haze of Painter's stunned and battered mind. After a minute, or five, or twenty, he managed to roll to an elbow and push himself up to a sitting position. The world reeled, then settled to a lazy swirl, and Painter felt bile in the back of his throat and realized his hands were cold and sweaty, and he was shuddering uncontrollably.

He held them up and looked at the palms, torn from the fall. Up his slender fingers. How they trembled. And there, at the ends, graceful glints of steel reflecting the yellow-orange street light and the blue of his eyes. The talons of the Weir, a scant half-inch long and sharper than any blade or razor ever honed by human hands. Elegant. Utterly efficient. Painter couldn't remember having extended them. But for a brief moment he stared at them, and let himself imagine a different outcome. The tearing of Gap-tooth – the gush and spill as the man's friends screamed in helpless horror.

No. That wasn't him. He wasn't like that. Painter watched as the claws withdrew, settling into their housing beneath his intact fingernails. He was better than that. Better than them. In every way. It was his mercy that allowed them to live, not his weakness.

He pushed himself up to his feet, just as a well-dressed couple emerged from the Tea House. The woman gasped when she saw him, and for a moment Painter took it as a sign of her fear. But her eyes softened with concern as they came down the stairs towards him.

"Oh, Painter," she said, "are you alright? Do you need help?"

"I'm fff-fff," the word caught. Such a simple word. *Say it!* "I'm fine, ma'am. Took the stairs too fast is all."

The man with her shook his head and produced a handkerchief from his fine coat pocket. The idea of anyone carrying a handkerchief struck Painter as supremely absurd.

"Here, son," the man said, handing him the handkerchief. "You've got some… something, there."

"Thank you," Painter said. He wiped the spittle off his face and handed the handkerchief back. As the man took it, they both noticed a dark spot on it, and the man hesitated.

"I'm sorry, I'll cuh- cuh-, I'll clean it."

"No, no," the man said, smiling graciously as he took the handkerchief. "It's alright. That's what they're for after all. You sure you're OK?"

"Yes, sir. Thank you, sir. Mmmm- ma'am."

"Alright. Well. You take care, Painter."

"You too."

They smiled again, a little sadly, and turned away towards their home. As they disappeared down the street, Painter reflected on Gap-tooth's posse and the couple walking away from him now.

And he couldn't decide which of them he hated more.

FIVE

Cass could feel the pressure building in the city, an emotional power grid straining under the load of fear, tension, and long-harbored mistrust never resolved. She looked out over Morningside in its troubled sleep, the night air around her almost brittle with cold. From her balcony she could see down the long, wide street, almost all the way to the western gate. The roadway was warmly lit by its innumerable lamp posts, though the walks were all deserted this deep in the night. It was still hard for her to sleep at any time, but most especially at night, the time for which her body had been rewired for optimal performance.

She had had great hopes once, in the early days of her Awakening. There had been horror from some, a hatred born of a lifetime of terror. That was to be expected. But kindness had surprised her, and compassion. And after she had taken to wearing the veil, she'd found more and more people were able to overcome their instinctive reactions and Cass had begun to believe that one day she might be accepted as human again.

And when Wren began rescuing others, a network of support had formed almost without any real effort; good, honest men and women of Morningside came forward and gave of their time and money to help the survivors build some sense of a new life, and maybe even come to terms with who they had become. People like Aron, and Mister Sun, and others throughout the city who'd offered places to stay, clothes to wear, jobs to do.

Of course it couldn't have lasted. One or two, maybe the city could've absorbed them, thought of them as poor, wretched anomalies. But there were nearly thirty of them now. Too many to be ignored. Now, in some circles, they were seen more like wild animals that had strayed into civilization; no longer just a handful of damaged people looking for shelter.

Damaged. Rae had called them that once, in passing. Funny. Cass didn't *feel* damaged. Different, certainly. But vibrant. Alive. Alive in a way she'd never felt before the change. Before the change, she'd relied on chems to speed her reaction times, to make herself faster, stronger. Now she felt all these things without needing the chemicals. Sometimes she wondered if the pathways that had been forged by her use of quint had been exploited by the Weir's tampering.

There had been adjustments to be sure, new normals to learn, like how to see the world through her new eyes – or how to process the way Cass felt the presence of the people around her, sometimes even through walls – or how they exploded in light and... and something she didn't even have a word for, whenever they accessed the digital. No, she didn't feel damaged at all.

Out beyond the wall, Cass heard a Weir cry; a howl somewhere between a scream and a burst of static through organic vocal cords. At one time she would've been able to interpret it. Now it was just noise again. Even so, the sound had a different quality that she noticed but couldn't quite identify. Another Weir answered the first, somewhere off to her left. But not far. And a third, closely following the second. Cass felt the hair on the back of her neck bristle, found herself alert. There was an attack coming. She knew it without knowing why.

As she turned back into the compound, her brain started peppering her with all the reasons she was wrong. There hadn't been an organized attack in almost a year, not since they'd brought everyone inside the wall. The Weir had been scattered. Without Underdown's control, they'd reverted back to their pack behavior; no longer a collaborative entity. They were more like scavengers than predators. They would never assault the city directly.

Except they would, and Cass knew it.

She streaked through her room and sprinted down the hallway towards the front entry, pimming Gamble, the captain of the governor's Personal Guard, as she ran.

"Gamble," Cass pimmed, sending the message through the digital directly to her, wherever Gamble was. "The Weir are at the west gate!"

She didn't wait for a response. Cass saw Joris, one of the night guardsmen, flinch from down the hall as she approached. He raised a hand, but she couldn't tell if it was to slow her down or to defend himself.

"Joris, the Weir are at the west gate!" she called. He still had his mouth open when Cass passed him. "Get the guard to the gate! The *west* gate!"

She called it over her shoulder, trusting that his training would kick in and Joris would know what to do. Out through the front doors, she leapt from the top stair and cleared the bottom one ten feet below without missing a step. Instinctively, she tried to boost before her brain reminded her she no longer had the implant, no longer needed the chemicals in her bloodstream. No longer had a *blood*stream, for that matter.

Down the wide, empty street she sped, breathing quickly but easily. The cries of the Weir came more rapidly now, growing in number, converging to a single point. It was maybe six hundred yards from the governor's compound to the western gate. Cass reached it in just under a minute.

There were stairs near the gate, leading up thirty feet above the ground to the top of the wall in a switchback. She took them two at a time and was almost halfway up when the first shockwave hit the gate. There was a sound like thunder, followed by scattered impacts, like rocks after a landslide. When Cass gained the top of the wall, she found one of the city's watchmen staring down below, open-mouthed, frozen in fear.

"Hey!" she called, without thinking. The watchman's head snapped around and, seeing her, his eyes went wide, and she saw him fumbling at his hip. "No, no, no, wait!"

But it was too late. He had the weapon up and pointed. It all seemed to happen in half-speed, but the distance was too great. As Cass closed the gap, she saw the leap of blue fire in the muzzle as she twisted her head and body, heard the snap of the round as it passed by. She spun, whipping a hand out and caught the watchman's wrist as he fired the second time, sending another wild shot out into the night.

"It's me, it's Cass," she shouted at him. The man stood paralyzed for the seconds it took for his brain to process what had just happened, and then his face melted from terror to pure dismay.

"Lady Cass, I'm so sorry, I thought–"

"I know! Did you hit the alarm?"

"The alarm?" He looked confused, like "*alarm*" was some word she'd just made up.

"Yes, did you hit it?" she asked.

"What?" he said. Cass could see the realization dawning in painful slowness. "No. I…"

Below, the gate boomed again, followed again by secondary impacts. Cass released the watchman's wrist and gave him a firm shove towards the guard post. "Go, do it now! Go!" The watchman stumbled backwards, and then the shock finally seemed to wear off.

"Yes, ma'am, I'm on it!" He raced towards the post, and Cass ran to the edge of the wall and looked over. What she saw stole her breath.

The Weir were massed against the gate, dozens of them, in a writhing knot of flesh and claw. And as she watched, they fell back, scattering away from the wall. Then they turned again, and charged once more towards the gate. As one they collided into it, the few stragglers following closely behind and throwing themselves into the crush. They were trying to break through.

Cass felt the alarm charge up, an electric tingle just before the alert went out across the network to the City Guard. There was no blaring horn or screaming siren, no citywide notification of danger. The last thing the Guard needed in times of crisis was the mad panic of frightened citizens. Best to keep the sheep in their pens and let the sheepdogs do their work. Help would come.

Below her, the Weir continued their maddened surge, a near-human tide, momentarily receding, before racing forward again to crash against the iron gates. Cass couldn't see the use. The gates were far too heavy, and securely barred besides. It was almost like watching a child throw a tantrum, a too-small fist landing meaningless blows. She wondered briefly if the other gates were also under attack, but footsteps on the stairs behind Cass caught her attention.

Gamble was the first to reach the top, jittergun in her hand and fire in her eyes. Her dark hair was in tight braids, and she pushed a stray aside as she jogged to join Cass.

"They coming through?" Gamble asked, breathing heavily from her sprint.

"No, gate's secure and holding."

Gamble leaned over the wall to see for herself. "What're they doing?"

"I have no idea."

More footsteps on the stairs, and Able appeared, followed closely by Gamble's husband, Sky. Able, focused and intense, flowed past Cass and Gamble and took up a position further down the wall. Sky moved to the women at the edge of the wall, his long rifle pointed skyward but ready to deploy in an instant.

"What we got, Ace?" Sky asked.

"Forty, forty-five, I'd guess," Gamble answered. "Not sure what they're up to though."

For a few moments, they just stood and watched in silence as the Weir continued their futile assault. *Boom*. Withdraw. *Boom*. Withdraw. A few Weir had fallen and lay unmoving at the gate, heedlessly trampled by each new wave.

"They sure hate that door, huh?" Sky said.

Swoop and Wick came up the stairs and fell in on either side of Sky and Gamble.

"You boys are getting slow," Gamble said.

"Pff, you been here, like, thirty seconds," Wick replied.

"Forty-eight. Where's Finn?" she asked.

"With Mouse."

"Well, where's Mouse?"

"On the way. Running slow on account of carrying the boy."

"Not *my* boy," Cass said, looking sharply at Wick. Surely Wren wouldn't be so reckless.

"Uh… well," Wick answered.

"Figured you wouldn't want him coming on his own, ma'am," Swoop said, his tone even, his face completely devoid of emotion. "And he wasn't stayin' put."

"On account of being governor and all," Wick added.

There was an awkward moment of what would have been silence, if not for the continued rage of the Weir below. Cass had to watch herself, to be careful not to undermine Wren's authority with her mothering. But she'd been his sole protector for so long, it was hard to break old habits. To remember how much had changed.

"You want me to drop a couple?" Sky asked. He had his rifle shouldered now, sighting in on a target in the crowd below with easy grace, tracking it with unmatched fluidity. His weapon was all angles: long and thin with a flat top and an optic attached; his left arm was almost fully extended as he held a fore-grip, while his right hand, tucked in close to his body, kept the weapon in the pocket of his shoulder and pressed against his cheek. A precise instrument of death in the hands of an even deadlier man.

"What do you think, Cass?" said Gamble.

Cass thought for a moment. The crushed Weir at the gate hadn't seemed to have any effect on the others. She didn't see how shooting a few would be any different. And now that she knew some of them might be able to come back, she was less inclined to slaughter them without cause.

"Wait for Wren," she answered. "We'll see what he says."

The watchman who'd nearly shot Cass a few minutes before finally returned and stood off to one side, stealing sidelong glances at Sky and Gamble and the others. It was rare for regular watchmen to get to see, let alone talk to, the governor's elite bodyguard, and Cass could tell the young man was trying to work up the nerve to say something.

"Lady Cass," he finally said. "The alert's been sounded. My men should be here in just a few minutes."

Cass smirked at his use of the phrase *my men*, as if he were an officer of rank. But she made no mention of it. "Thank you…?" she trailed off.

"Espin."

"Thank you, Espin. Good work." It hadn't really been good work, since he'd forgotten to do his job and nearly killed her, but she saw how it puffed him up and didn't mind the lie. Espin looked at Swoop and smiled. Swoop's flat expression didn't change. Espin quickly looked away and bowed slightly to Cass.

"I'll just uhhh… take up a position over here."

"Actually, Espin, sorry to do this to you, but you can cancel the alarm. They're not coming through."

His shoulders slumped, and for a moment Cass thought he was actually going to protest. But in the end, he just nodded and jogged back towards the guard post, obviously embarrassed. Wick let out a little laugh that he didn't quite cover with a cough.

Cass turned her attention back to the Weir. It was almost like watching a hand, spreading out its fingers and then sharply clenching them to a fist. Crazed. Or perhaps haywire. She wondered if any of the Weir ever short-circuited.

"Here they come," Wick said, and Cass looked over her shoulder to see Finn at the top of the stairs with Mouse close behind, carrying Wren on his back. Finn was Wick's older brother, though you could hardly tell they were related just by looking at them. Finn caught her eye and gave a little shrug.

"Hi, Mom," Wren said, sliding off Mouse's back. He said it a little too casually, the way he did when he knew he'd done something wrong and was hoping she wouldn't notice. His blond hair was matted on one side and sticking up in the back, eyes still clouded by sleep. "What's going on?"

"Well... since you're here," she said, hoping her look made it clear how displeased she was, "maybe you can tell us. Come take a look."

Wren came over to her side, and she went down on one knee, offering the other as a step for him. He climbed up on it, using her shoulder for support as he did, and his heel dug into her quadriceps with a dull ache. When had he gotten so heavy?

"What do you think?" Cass asked.

She watched his face as Wren studied them for a moment. She waited for the sound of the next impact. But it never came.

"Alright, this is starting to give me the jibblies," Sky said.

"What now?" Cass asked.

"They stopped," said Gamble.

Cass took Wren off her leg and stood up to take a look.

"I can't see, Mama."

She picked him up and held him as they looked down over the wall together. The Weir were in a loose crowd, as if they'd begun to scatter and then abruptly stopped. Now they were just standing there, looking up at the wall. No. Looking up at Wren. And then one made the strangest sound.

"*Spshhhh. Naaaah.*"

Like a burst of thin hissing static, followed by wave of white noise, somewhere between a violent exhalation and a whispered howl. Cass had never heard anything like it before.

"Spshhhh. Naaaah."

The same as before. Exactly the same, as far as Cass could tell.

"Spshhhh. Naaaah."

They came in an even rhythm, almost like a chant. Some of the other Weir began shuffling together, gradually closing in around the one making the sound, like a dark pool spreading in reverse. Their eyes remained fixed on Wren. An evil shiver ran down Cass's spine.

"That one's begging for it," Sky said, sighting in. "Ace?"

"Hold on," Gamble answered. She looked at Cass.

"What do you think, baby?" Cass asked.

"Something's not right, Mama."

"Can you wake any of them?"

Wren surveyed the group below, and then shook his head with a sad look. Too far gone. Gamble gave a sharp nod in Sky's direction. A half-second later his rifle hummed quick and low, and the chanting Weir fell violently backwards.

The other Weir didn't even react. Some just stood around aimlessly, but those that were moving continued to gather together, closer and closer. A little over half of them, maybe twenty-five, slowly pressed together.

"Spshhhh. Naaaah."

A new one took up the call now. And then another. Then a third. Sky's rifle hummed once and quickly again, and two of them fell. Still no effect.

"Looks like some of 'em are busted," Wick said. "Look at that one just turning circles."

Sure enough, one Weir, separated from the others, was turning a slow circle; turn thirty degrees, stop, thirty degrees, stop, thirty degrees, stop. It really did look like a system glitch.

"Is it just me, or are some of them missing?" Finn asked.

Now that he mentioned it, the crowd did seem smaller. Cass was just about to say so when Able tore past her and she heard Swoop draw his sword. She turned.

"Mama!"

The Weir were on the wall. On top of the wall. Rushing towards them. Cass dropped Wren to his feet, pulled him behind her, and the team switched on in an instant. Able and Swoop were already there, intercepting the first two. Gamble, Mouse, Wick, and Finn all snapped weapons up as they collapsed in a protective ring around Cass and Wren. Sky swung his rifle around, ready to drop any that got past Able and Swoop. To Cass's surprise, she heard Sky's weapon hum. One Weir fell further down the wall, a perfectly placed shot right between Swoop and Able.

It was over in almost the time it'd taken her to process it. Only three of them, quickly dispatched.

"How did they get up?" Gamble shouted. She leapt on top of the parapet and started leaning out, scanning back and forth, checking the wall. "How did they get up here?" Sky instinctively grabbed her by the belt with his left hand, still keeping his weapon shouldered, up and ready, with his right.

"Mouse," Cass called. Mouse came quickly to her side, his weapon down but shouldered in case any other targets presented.

"Yes, ma'am?" he asked.

"Take Wren back to the compound, please. Wick, Finn, you too."

"But, Mama–" Wren started to protest, but Cass wasn't having it.

"No buts, Wren. You shouldn't have been here in the first place." She pushed Wren towards Mouse. The big man drew

Wren in close, protectively. "Straight to the compound," she added. "Lock it up."

"Yes, ma'am," Mouse said. He slung his weapon, and gathered Wren up. "Wick, Finn, let's move it out." Only then did the two brothers roll fluidly out of formation and take up defensive positions on either side of Mouse.

"Don't worry, Cass, we'll get him there, no sweat," Wick said as he moved by.

"I know," she said. The three men departed swiftly with her son, and for a moment Cass felt an almost overwhelming desire to go with them. But Gamble let out a startled cry, and Cass knew she had to stay.

"Look at this!" Gamble said. "Sky, let go, I'm not gonna fall. You gotta see this."

Sky lowered his weapon and leaned out over the wall as best he could. He didn't take his hand off his wife. "Yep. Jibblies."

Cass climbed cautiously up on the parapet next to Gamble and followed the other woman's arm to where she was pointing with her jittergun, about thirty yards further down the wall. At first, Cass couldn't tell what she was seeing. It looked almost like an enormously thick rope dangling the wrong way, from the ground up and not quite long enough to reach the top. Then her eyes picked up an arm here, a leg there. With horror it all clicked in her mind. Some number of the Weir had piled on top of one another, clinging together to form something like a pillar of flesh; a grotesque circus act, or twisted sculpture of the dead. It might have been comical if it hadn't been so horrifying. Another Weir was climbing, using its claws and mindlessly shredding its companions as it made its way up.

"Cut it down," Cass said.

Gamble didn't even reply. She just pulled Sky's hand free and jogged down the length of the parapet. By the time she made it to the Weir-pillar, the climbing Weir had nearly reached the top. Cass heard the jittergun buzz as Gamble opened up with it. The climbing Weir fell back and plummeted to the ground, followed closely by its collapsing companions; their bodies *thumped*, dull and wet far below.

"I sure hope I wake up in a couple minutes and find out this was all a bad dream," Sky said. After a moment, he added, "*Real* bad."

Gamble's gun ripped the air in two more short bursts, and then it was quiet. It was only then Cass realized the Weir had stopped making their eerie call. She turned back to where the crowd had once been and found all but one had disappeared. The last of the three chanters now stood alone, utterly still and staring. Staring at Cass. As if it had been waiting for her attention.

"*Spshhhh. Naaaah.*"

Sky's rifle hummed again, and the Weir collapsed in a pile.

"I'm about done with that," he said. Cass couldn't help but agree. But she knew that sound would haunt her for a long time to come.

About halfway between Cass and Gamble, Able and Swoop were working together to dump the dead Weir over the wall, outside the city. They'd take care of it in the morning, if the bodies were still there. More than likely, other Weir would come and reclaim them, as was their way. Gamble, walking back along the top of the parapet, stopped and crouched by them for a moment and exchanged a few words.

"I sure wish she'd get away from that edge," said Sky.

"I think she does it just to make you nervous," Cass replied.

"She does. And it does."

Gamble hopped down off the parapet and returned to Cass and Sky. She slid in next to her husband, and wrapped an arm around his waist, looking softer. He kissed the top of her head in such a casual motion it almost looked like reflex.

"Bad news, Cass," she said. Sky leaned his rifle against the wall and dropped an easy arm around her shoulders. The two of them just seemed to fit together. "The kid at the post…"

"Espin?"

Gamble nodded. "They must've gotten him on his way back from shutting down the alarm."

Cass closed her eyes and drew a deep breath. That was on her. She'd sent him off by himself. Careless. More blood on her hands.

"Hey, no way you could've known," Gamble said, reading her thoughts. "For as long as this city's stood, I have never known them to top the wall. They just don't do that."

"Until now," Cass answered.

"Yeah."

Cass felt unspeakably weary. Heavy arms, heavy legs, heavy heart. There was still so much to do.

"Miss Cass, you go on back to the compound," Sky said. "We'll finish up here, and we'll take good care of Espin."

"No, I should handle that. He's my responsibility."

"Go on, Cass," Gamble said. "Go take care of your boy. You should be together right now."

Cass leaned around to check on Able and Swoop, but Sky put a gentle hand on her shoulder.

"We've got this."

Cass thought it over. It didn't feel right to leave these people here on the wall without her. But nothing felt right about this night anyway. "Alright. Thank you."

Gamble reached out and squeezed her arm, and then smiled, warm and understanding. Cass nodded to the couple, and then turned and headed down the stairs with leaden legs. The way back to the compound seemed twice as far, the air twice as cold, as she made her way through the still empty streets of Morningside. An entire city slumbering under an illusion of safety.

Her mind raced with the mounting threats she had to face, both within the city and without. They were no closer to solving the mystery of Wren's attacker, and Luck's murderers were still unidentified. The Weir were changing. The regular guardsmen had never shown up. Not a single one. Discipline had crumbled. No doubt that too would change, come morning. Morning. The whole way back, Cass couldn't help but wonder what new terror the dawn would bring.

SIX

Something had changed. And it was very, very wrong.

Wren could feel a heaviness about him, an impenetrable grey quietness that seemed to descend from the sky and envelop him as he sat on his mother's bed. It was an almost violent stillness, and full of dread. It reminded him of being woken in the night by a sound that he couldn't be sure if he'd heard or just dreamt. Reminded him of those long, sweaty moments, lying in darkness, straining to hear, and being met by nothing but an oppressive silence. It was almost a living thing, beyond hearing.

The Weir had changed. Wren had felt it the previous night, in the cold morning hours, before Mama had gone running from her room. Remembering it now, he wished he'd warned her earlier. But even now, in the light of day, it was still such a distant feeling and hard to put into words; like the hour before the fever comes when you know you're going to be sick, even though nothing hurts yet.

He couldn't just ignore it, though. Something was definitely different about the Weir, something dangerous and terrible. But Wren had no idea what that difference *was*. Not exactly. There was no doubt they had coordinated during last night's attack. And not just in the way they'd scaled the wall.

The others near the gate had been a distraction, and Wren couldn't escape the feeling that it had been deliberate; an organized misdirection, to enable the others' assault.

Then there was the call, or chant, or whatever it had been. Even as young as he was, Wren had spent more time than most out in the open, and had heard the usual cries of the Weir. As frightening and unnatural as they were, still they were not so unearthly as the sound they'd made last night.

A knock sounded at the door, with a gentle familiarity. Wren knew it was Able, so instead of saying "Come in," he just slid off the bed and opened the door himself.

"Hi, Able," Wren said.

Hello, Wren, Able signed. *You have a visitor.*

"Does my mom know?"

Able nodded. *She's with him now. It's Painter.*

Without knowing why, Wren felt a little jolt of anxiety, an unusual reluctance to see his friend. He found himself hoping to find an excuse to delay the meeting. "How long until the address?" he asked.

Half an hour, Able signed, and then added a shake of his hand afterwards to indicate the uncertainty... could be sooner, could be later.

Wren was already dreading facing the crowds. And he really did want more time to prepare. "Maybe I should tell him to come back another time?"

From Able's expression, Wren could tell he must've picked up on his own uneasiness. Able gave a slow shake of the head.

You should see him now.

Wren sighed before he could catch himself, and felt bad about it. "OK."

He stepped out into the hallway and closed the door to his mother's room behind him; *their* room, at least for the past few nights. Able turned and walked down the hall, and Wren followed behind with a flutter in his stomach. Why was he so reluctant to see Painter? Maybe it was just that he hadn't been prepared. An unexpected situation, while his mind was busy with other things. An unwanted interruption. And, he realized, he'd kind of forgotten about Painter. Just for the time being. He was still sorry for his friend, but he'd wanted to deal with it before. Now there were other things to worry about. Wren felt bad for thinking that way. But it didn't change the fact that he was annoyed by Painter's selfishness.

Able led the way to the eastern side of the building, down a flight of stairs, which suggested that Painter had probably come in through a side entrance. They found him in a side room, a sort of sitting room that had mostly gone unused. Cass was there as well, evidently keeping him company. Wren gasped when he saw him.

Wren asked, "Painter, what happened to your face?" His right eye was puffy and mottled with bruises, his upper lip split and swollen.

"Hey, I cuh-can't help it if, if, if – I was born uh-ugly," Painter said with a shrug and a strained smile. It made Wren feel terrible for being annoyed at him.

"No, really, are you OK?"

Painter nodded. "Took a tum – a tumble in the street. Caught myself with mmmm- my fuh- with my face." He held up his hands like it was no big deal, but behind it all his eyes seemed sad, even with their moonlight glow. Maybe a little angry.

"Painter came to talk to us about the girl," Cass said carefully. "He'd like to see her."

"Oh. OK. Does Mouse know?" Wren asked.

"He's all set. We'll go whenever you're ready, Painter."

Painter looked at Cass and drew a deep breath. His gaze

dropped to the floor as he absent-mindedly scratched his cheek and then ran his fingers over his mouth. Finally, he nodded. "I'm ready."

"Alright then. This way," Cass said. They all left the room and walked the long halls to the compound's clinic in a heavy kind of silence. It seemed awkward not to say anything, but it seemed like it'd be even more awkward to say something inappropriate. And Wren couldn't think of anything that seemed appropriate for such a time.

Mouse was waiting for them when they arrived. He had a kind expression on his face, and a quiet way of welcoming that seemed mismatched with his size, a gentleness that made Wren feel calm and safe.

"Mouse, this is Painter," Cass said. Mouse reached out his massive hands and shook Painter's hand with both of his.

"Painter," he said with a nod. "I'm sorry we haven't met before now."

"That's alright," Painter replied. "Wren's muh-muh-mentioned you en-en-nough, I forgot we hadn't."

"We're ready to see the girl," Cass said, her voice even and cool.

"Sure," Mouse answered. "Wren, why don't you wait here with Able?"

For a moment, Wren felt relief at the idea of avoiding seeing the dead girl again. But if it really was Snow, if it really *was* Painter's sister... it just didn't seem right to take the easy way out. He knew he'd regret it if he didn't stand there by Painter's side.

"No, I want to come too," Wren said.

"You d-d-don't have to, Wruh-Wren," Painter said.

"I want to."

"Alright," said Mouse. "She's this way."

Able waited in the front room while the others followed Mouse through the clinic and into a room in the back. Wren had never been in the compound's morgue before. It was small, and there were a couple of steel tables and some things that looked like tools, but not the kind of tools Wren would ever want to have to use. He didn't know what they were for and really didn't want to.

There was something under a white cloth on one of the tables, and Mouse moved next to it. He put his hand on the covering and paused. Wren took a deep breath, tried to prepare himself. Painter nodded, and Mouse drew back the cover.

She was there, the girl that had attacked Wren, looking calm and peaceful and lovely, and so very young. Apart from her absolute paleness, it was hard to believe she was dead and not just sound asleep. The breath caught in Wren's throat and everything came flashing back, and it seemed so impossible that such a beautiful and fragile creature could have ever tried to do him any harm.

Painter didn't react at all. He just stared at the girl, emotionless, expressionless. They waited in strained silence for him to identify her, to acknowledge it was his sister – or to confirm that it wasn't, to give some sign of recognition. Anything. But he just stood there.

Mouse watched him for a few moments, and then slowly slid his eyes over to Cass.

"Painter, sweetheart," she said in soothing tones.

He rubbed his nose with the back of his fingers, and then abruptly turned and walked out of the room. Wren could hear him sit heavily down in the room next door. The three others stood in silence for a moment, watching, and then Cass finally turned to look back at Mouse. He covered the body again.

"What do you think?" Cass asked.

"I think that's a confirmation," Mouse said. "But someone ought to talk to him."

"I'll do it," Wren said.

"We'll go together," Cass replied.

"No, Mama. Just me. To start."

She chewed her bottom lip for a second, the way she did when she was nervous, or thinking, or both. But finally she nodded. "OK, baby. To start."

Wren walked to the room next door, feeling hot and cold at the same time. His palms were all sweaty, and he felt a little bit like he might throw up. He didn't know if it was from having seen the girl again, or from fear of what Painter might say. Or do.

When he entered the room, Painter was sitting in a chair with his hands on his knees, looking at the floor. He didn't look up when Wren came in. Didn't show any signs of knowing Wren was even there. Wren stood in the door, wondering what to do next. An empty chair was next to Painter, so eventually Wren just went over and lowered himself carefully onto it.

They sat in silence for several minutes. Or at least what seemed like minutes. Finally Painter started moving again, just running his hands along his legs, back and forth, like maybe he was trying to dry his palms on his pantlegs.

"That's alright," he said. "That's alright. She'll be alright." And then he laughed, a short bark that made Wren jump. "I ffff-ffff… I forgot to bring her coat. I have a cuh-cuh-coat. She left it. I was suh-suh-ssss… supposed to give it back t-t-to her."

"I'm so sorry, Painter. I was hoping it wasn't her."

"It's not – it's nnn – it's not *her*," Painter said. He was still looking at the floor, still running his hands back and forth, back and forth. "Not r-r-really."

Wren felt a chill race down his back, felt vulnerable. He glanced at the other room where Mouse and Able were with his mama.

"That isn't your sister?" he asked.

"No," Painter answered, shaking his head, his voice calm and even. "No, Snuh-Snow's not... she's not... Snow dances, Wren. She's a duh-duh, a dancer. Best dancer you ever saw. She g-g-g-glides. That grrrr – that g-g-girl, she's just lying there."

"Painter..."

"Just luh-luh... just lying there," he said, still rubbing his legs. Wren looked down and inhaled sharply. Painter's pant legs had grown dark and torn, his fingertips blotched and spattered. Wren only now realized that Painter's claws were out and he was cutting into his own flesh.

"Painter, your legs..." Wren said, too terrified to move. Painter stopped and slowly lifted his hands, turned them over. He watched them as if they belonged to someone else.

"That's my baby sister," he said quietly. "My... baby... *sister*!" He flashed up out of his chair and in a single motion whipped it off the floor and across the room. The chair shattered against the wall, and Painter let out an inhuman howl of rage.

Mouse was there in an instant, grabbing at Painter, and Wren saw Painter's hands flailing, thrashing in Mouse's powerful grip. Able materialized seconds later and grabbed Painter from behind. Cass skidded into the room and put herself between Wren and the others, while the two men struggled to pin Painter's arms down and control him. Finally their combined strength overpowered Painter's, and he dropped to his knees, his fury giving way to bitter anguish. Able held on to him as he shook with soul-deep sobs.

"Snow," Painter said, "Snow, Snow, Snow."

Cass knelt next to him, and put her hand on his head, consoling him. Wren couldn't stop his own tears, and no one seemed to mind. Gradually Able released his hold. Painter slumped further forward until his face was almost on the floor, his hands slack in front of him. Cass gently pulled him over until his head was on her lap, and there she held him like a child.

Able remained crouched next to them, ever watchful, but all the fight seemed to have gone out of Painter. Mouse motioned for Able's attention, and when Able looked up, Mouse said, "If you've got this under control, I'm gonna get cleaned up."

Wren noticed the cuts across Mouse's arms, and chest, and face. Bright blood ran freely from a cut along his cheekbone.

How bad? Able signed.

Mouse shook his head. "Stings a little, but they're not deep. He wasn't trying to hurt anybody."

Able nodded, and Mouse disappeared. Painter's loud weeping eventually dwindled to an exhausted sort of despair, and he sat up with his hands in his lap.

"Sorry about… the, the, the, sorry about the chair," he said quietly. He wiped his nose on his sleeve and stared at the floor.

"It's nothing to worry about, OK?" Cass answered.

"Can I be a-a-alone for a few minutes?" he asked. "I woh-woh- won't go crazy."

"Sure, Painter. Whatever you need."

"Th-th-thanks."

Cass motioned to Wren and together with Able they left the room and returned to the front of the clinic.

"What do you think?" Cass asked in a low voice.

Keep him here for a couple of days, Able signed.

Wren collapsed into a chair in the corner by the door, exhausted and overwhelmed. Cass and Able carried on a quiet conversation, whispering and signing, but Wren didn't care to try to follow any of it. The scene that had just played out before him had been more terrible than he had imagined it would be. Death was nothing new to him, unfortunately, and he had seen the many different ways loss could affect the grieving. But Painter's unrestrained fury had surprised him. Since his Awakening, Painter had never been anything but softly spoken, humble, and kind. To see him tormented so fully broke Wren's heart.

"Do you think I should take him some water?" Wren asked across the room.

Cass stopped her conversation and looked over her shoulder at him. She smiled gently and then nodded. "Sure, baby. That'd be very thoughtful. I'm sure he'd appreciate it."

Wren rummaged around and found several empty steel drinking canisters in a cabinet. He took one and filled it with water from a nearby tap. The water ran cold and clear, drawing from a reservoir deep within the ground. Mouse had once explained how the compound's system worked, but all Wren remembered clearly was that it was a combination of natural water collected mostly from rainfall and water recycled from other sources. The fact that Mouse had stressed how many times the water was filtered and sterilized made Wren uneasy about what exactly "other sources" might have meant.

With the canister full, Wren walked carefully back to the other room, quiet so he didn't disrupt Painter, listening carefully to see if he'd started crying again. As Wren got close to the room, though, he heard Painter muttering. He leaned closer, straining to make out the words.

"I swear," Painter said. "I swear I will find them, Snow. I will find them and I will drain every last drop of blood from their veins for you. I swear it."

The words sent a shock of cold racing through Wren's body, like ice water through his veins. He stood frozen in place, unsure of what to do. Painter shifted in the room and sounded like he was standing up. Afraid of being caught in the hall, Wren crept slowly backwards, and then quickly made his way back to the front room. Too afraid to face Painter, terrified by what he'd overheard.

When he reached the front room, Mouse had joined the others. Wren's mind was flooded with emotion and thought. Surely he had to tell someone. Or did he? Was there anything to Painter's words besides the raw emotion anyone would feel in his situation? Had he even heard him right?

"Didn't want it?" Cass said. Her words called Wren to the moment, but meant nothing to him.

"What?" he said.

"The water. He didn't want it?"

Wren shook his head and paused, trying to figure out how much of the truth to tell them. But they didn't give him a chance.

"We need to get up to the Council Room," said Cass. "Everyone else is already there."

"What about Painter?" Wren asked.

"I'll keep him company," Mouse answered. His cheek had a sheen where he'd sealed the lacerations. Now they were just two thin red lines running along his high cheekbone, maybe half an inch from his eye. "And I'll walk him back when he's ready."

"Able thought maybe we ought to keep him here for a day or two. Make sure he's not going to hurt himself."

Or anyone else, Able added.

Mouse ran a hand along his jawline, scratched at the coarse stubble while he mulled it over. "I guess we could put him up on our floor."

Able nodded.

"Alright, I'll talk to Swoop about it. See what we can work out."

"Thanks, Mouse," Cass said. Mouse just dipped his head in something between a nod and a bow. She looked back at Wren. "Why don't you leave that with Mouse, sweetheart?"

Wren handed the canister of water to the big man, who in turn placed a huge hand gently on top of Wren's head. A momentary reassuring touch, like a priest offering a blessing. He didn't tousle Wren's hair, though, and Wren always appreciated him for that. Cass stretched out her hand to Wren. He reached up and took it, warm and soothing. But just as they were turning to go, Painter appeared in the doorway.

"Hey," he said, head bowed, staring down at the floor.

Wren was glad for that. He knew he couldn't have met Painter's eyes. "I'm suh-sorry... for all of th-th-that," Painter said.

"We all understand, Painter," Cass answered. "You don't need to apologize."

He shook his head. "I do. I do nnnn-need to." He raised his eyes, glanced around at them. Wren started to look away, but caught himself. Painter looked calmer, softer. More like his usual self. "I sh-sh-shhh... I shouldn't have l-lost control like that. I'm real sorry. Especially to you, Mouse."

Mouse walked over and laid a hand on Painter's shoulder. "All's well with us, son." He squeezed Painter's shoulder once, dipped his head in a meaningful nod, and then let go and propped himself against the nearby wall.

"We were just going up," Wren said, finding himself starting to feel better. "I have to give an address. Want to come with us?"

Painter smiled at him a little sadly. "Actually, if you d-d-don't mind. I was wuh-wuh, I was wondering if I could buh-buh..." his lips tightened as he fought to force the word out. He closed his eyes and took a breath. "...I'd like to bury my sister."

"Why don't you wait?" Cass said. "After the address, we'll all do it together."

Painter shook his head. "I'd like to d-d-do it alone, Miss Cass. There's a p-p-p-place we used to go as k-kids. Just us. Our secret place."

"Burying's hard work, son," said Mouse. "Harder when it's your own."

"I, I think… I think she would've w-w-wanted it, this way. And I'm a l-l-luh, I'm a lot stronger than I look." He added a little smile, but there was no humor in it. Mouse, Cass, and Able all exchanged looks, and all seemed to agree.

"Alright," Mouse said. "You all go on. I'll make sure he's got what he needs."

"Come on back to the compound when you're done, OK?" Cass said. "We'd like you to stay with us for a little while."

"Thank you, Miss Cass, b-b-but I'll be alright."

"I know you will be, but we still want you here."

"Maybe just a night or two," Painter said. "If it's n-n-n-not any tr-tr-trouble."

"No trouble at all," said Mouse. "We've got it all taken care of."

"Well… alright. Th-thank you." Painter's shoulders relaxed and Wren could tell he was really moved and relieved. It would be good for him to be surrounded by friends.

We need to go, Able signed, and Cass nodded.

"We've got to run, Painter. After you… when you're done, just come to the side gate again, OK? We'll take of everything."

Painter nodded. "Th-th-thanks."

"Mouse, you'll be on the wall after?" Cass asked.

"Yeah, Finn's covering till I get there. Shouldn't be long."

"Alright, see you in a few," she said. "Painter."

Painter raised his hand in goodbye. He looked at Wren. "Good luck, l-l-little buddy."

"Thanks," Wren answered. He almost said *"you too"*, but stopped himself. "See you later." It sounded too casual for the moment, but he didn't know what else to say.

Wren took his mama's hand again, and together they followed Able through the wide and empty halls up to the Council Room. His stomach churned the whole way, adrenaline and anxiety mingling together. He was still shaken from Painter's violent reaction, and the thought of standing in front of a crowd of people made his chest feel like it was buzzing.

They reached the Council Room where Aron, Vye, and North were waiting for them.

"Lady Cass," Aron said, bowing slightly when he saw them. "Governor."

"Hi, Uncle Aron," Wren said.

"The others?" Cass asked.

"Already outside," North answered. "The crowd formed earlier than we expected."

"Then we'd better get out there," Cass replied. An attendant brought her veil to her, and she began to put it on. Before she covered her face, she drew Wren to her and knelt in front of him. "Are you ready, baby?"

"Not really," Wren said.

"You'll be great. Just speak up, be confident. And see if you can spot Wick." It was sort of a game they played, though it had other purposes. Looking for Wick gave Wren something to think about besides all of those eyes staring at him. And Mama said it made it seem like he was talking to everyone in the crowd. And though no one had ever mentioned it, it didn't take much for Wren to figure out Wick was down there for security, too. He'd only managed to spot Wick once out of a dozen times.

Cass gave him a strong hug and kissed his cheek, then looked him in the eye. There were tears in her eyes, reflecting their hollow glow.

"What's wrong, Mama?"

"Nothing, baby," she said quietly. "I'm just so proud of you, and I love you so much."

"I love you too."

"Let's go get this over with."

"OK."

She stood and drew her black veil down over her face. Wren hated when she wore it. Hated that Cass felt like she needed to. She was his mama, no matter what she looked like, and she was beautiful.

He followed Cass out, with North and Aron coming on either side and slightly behind him. Vye trailed further back, and Wren had the sense that she wasn't going to join them on the wall. Something in her posture. He glanced back over his shoulder and caught her eye. She smiled quickly, but it felt false. He smiled back as best he could. She was nervous, but then she always seemed nervous. Maybe she was just feeling the same anxiousness that Wren was.

This wasn't the first time he'd had to address the citizens of Morningside. The people. *His* people. He'd done it maybe a dozen times by now. The Council agreed it was important, that his words reassured the city. Letting himself be seen, really. But it felt different this time. More dangerous. More at stake.

The hardest had been after the last big attack. Some people blamed Wren, of course, for not doing more. For not saving more. But the anger had been defused by his order to open the city to everyone – to bring all people inside the wall. And it had been *his* order. The first and only time he'd ever overridden the Council's vote. His right as governor.

Now it seemed like maybe a terrible mistake with delayed results. Too much change, too fast. Too many unintended consequences. And no way to undo it.

The doors opened and sunlight flooded into the hall through the main entrance. The tall steps seemed higher, the walk to the gate farther. And beyond the gate, a press of people – held at a distance by a thin line of guardsmen. When he stepped out onto the stone staircase, a cheer went up from the crowd. It made Wren feel sick to his stomach.

"Steady," North said behind him. "You'll be fine."

The cheering continued during his entire walk to the gate, and as he mounted the stairs to the top of the wall. Climbing the stairs was always the hardest part. The height made him a little dizzy, but it was the memory of the place that brought such disgust.

It was the very place that the previous governor had died, thrown down by a usurper. Governor Underdown, the father he never knew. The murderer Asher. Wren's half-brother. Him, he knew all too well. Now they were both gone, gone because of Wren.

And he was left here, in that same spot, with hundreds of people below just waiting to hear what he had to say. He'd never told anyone how horrible this place made him feel. Wren had been too scared to say anything the first time they'd made him give a speech. And after that, he figured since he'd done it once, they'd just tell Wren he could do it again. He climbed the final steps and tried to push the memories from his mind. Time to pretend he was someone braver and wiser.

As he crested the wall, Wren nearly choked. It wasn't a crowd below. It was a sea. He had never seen so many people gathered before: thousands of them, as if the entire city had shown up to hear his words. He turned back to Mama. She was there, smiling gently towards him, an expression he more felt through the veil than saw. North and Aron stood on either side of her. North looked unfazed by the enormity of the crowd, but Aron's eyes were wide as he scanned the multitude. And Wren noticed Vye was nowhere to be found. Three would've been proud that he'd picked up on that. It was small comfort.

The noise from the mass of people died down, and all the moisture left Wren's mouth. He glanced up and down the wall. Finn stood further down to his left, scanning the crowd with a grim look. On his right, maybe fifteen feet away, Gamble stood guard. That made him feel a little better, knowing Gamble was watching over him. She was great.

Wren stepped up to the edge of the wall, looking out over the crush of humanity below. He drew a deep breath and through his internal connection accessed the secure frequency that would broadcast and amplify his voice to the masses. There were so many. So many faces, so many smiles, so many fears. And throughout, oversized pictures dotted the crowd, held aloft in hopes that he would see. Held by women, mostly – mothers, though here and there a father, or brother, or child. Pictures of loved ones lost. Taken. Silent pleas for Wren to find them and bring them back. It was overwhelming, and Wren felt as though his legs would give way at any moment.

Find Wick, he told himself. *Just find Wick.*

He started slowly sweeping his eyes across the people, looking for that one face, and in doing so, the mass of individuals faded into scenery. Not men and women and children waiting for him to save them all. Just a backdrop for Wick to hide in.

"Go ahead, Wren," he heard his mama's voice behind him, speaking in low tones. Wren realized he had no idea how long it'd been since the crowd had quieted. He cleared his throat, and tried to remember to speak slowly.

"People of Morningside," he said, and the echo of his voice sounded thin and weak. He hated hearing his own voice. "My people. I don't want you to be afraid." Already it wasn't going quite as planned. Wren was supposed to say they had nothing to fear, because Aron said that was reassuring, and it didn't suggest anyone was a coward. Aron had said no one would ever admit they were afraid, and coming from a child it would sound even more childish. But it wasn't true. There were lots of things to fear, most of them they didn't know about. And Wren couldn't stand up here and lie.

He said, "Some things have happened these past few days. You've heard stories. Some of us are angry. Some of us are sad. Some of us are confused. I know, because I can feel it all myself." Where was Wick? It seemed almost useless to look for him in that mass of people, but not looking for him seemed even more daunting. "I can't tell you how you should feel. I just don't want you to be afraid."

For the most part the crowd was relatively still; as still as people ever are when they're standing close together. But there was some movement off to Wren's left that caught his attention. Some commotion; people being jostled. He tried not to let it break his concentration.

"Last night the Weir attacked the western gate, and we lost one of our guardsmen. But they were turned away. You can rest safely here in our city, because you have many men and women watching over you. We're safe here."

More motion off to the right, similar to the other side. A

couple of people made angry noises. And there in the center of the crowd, bodies shifting.

"Our walls are strong, and our people are stronger. There's nothing from the outside that can touch us. But inside our walls..." Wren trailed off for a moment, not sure how to say exactly what he wanted to say. And he could see now what was causing all the commotion. Several men were shoving their way forward through the crowd, quickly and roughly. They looked angry. *Find Wick. Find Wick.* "Here inside, we have to do our part. Each of us. The only thing that can harm this city is its own people."

A hand came down on his shoulder, grasping hard, and Wren felt himself being pulled back from the edge.

"Get him off the wall," Gamble said, right next to him. He never even saw her move. She was turning him, pushing him towards his mama. "Get him off the wall."

She wasn't shouting or anything, not really even raising her voice. But it was so controlled and direct Wren knew without a doubt something was going wrong. A murmur came up from the crowd, punctuated by a couple of cries. Finn was closing in, moving swiftly towards them, somehow without looking like he was rushing at all. Mouse was behind him, pointing down towards the crowd. How long had Mouse had been there?

"What about us?" someone shouted from below. "What about us?"

Wren tried to turn back to see who it was, what was happening, but he couldn't get free of the tide that was sweeping him from the wall, down the stairs. The crowd got louder then, people started shouting. As they got to the bottom of the stairs, Cass grabbed Wren's wrist and started pulling him along, too fast for a walk, but not quite a run.

Something thumped loudly, and there were screams, and the sounds of panic. Wren smelled smoke.

"What's happening, Mama?" Wren said. "What's happening?" he repeated.

"Just go, baby. Go."

Wren tried again to turn and see what was happening but North and Aron were right behind him, shepherding him back towards the building. There was another thump. He thought of the line of guardsmen that had been holding the people away from the gate, wondered if any of them were hurt. Or, from the sound of it, if any of them weren't.

"Back inside," Aron said, his hand coming down on Wren's shoulder, steering him along. "Up the stairs, quickly." Cass slowed her pace for a moment.

"Not through the front," she said, and she walked across in front of Wren, redirecting him. The pressure from Aron's hand made Wren twist funny, and he nearly tripped. They all stopped awkwardly.

"We need to get him somewhere safe," Aron said.

"Through the side," Cass answered.

"There's no time or reason–" said Aron, but Cass interrupted.

"Take your hand off my son." She said it low, but there was almost a growl in her voice.

"Cass…" Aron responded, like she was being unreasonable. But he didn't let go.

"Take your hand off or I will."

Wren didn't understand what was happening. There was so much noise, so much confusion, and the air was growing harsh with an acrid smoke. He stood off balance, stretched between his mama's grasp and Aron's. There was tension between them, and for a moment Wren thought Mama was going to do something to Aron. Something terrible. And just before it came, Aron let go and raised his hands. Cass didn't wait. She pulled Wren along around towards the side of the compound.

"Where are you taking him?" Aron called, but Cass didn't answer. Wren looked back to see that Aron was watching them go, with North's hand on his chest. He couldn't tell if North was comforting him or restraining him. They disappeared from view as Cass drew Wren around the corner of the main building.

He followed her silently through a side entrance, down a flight of stairs, and then another, and into a small maintenance room that accessed some underlying infrastructure to the compound. She shut the door behind them and locked it. Removed her veil.

"Mama?"

She didn't answer. Cass just took Wren by the hand and led him to the back of the room, away from the door. There, in the corner, she sat down, and brought him gently into her lap. The way she used to. When it had been just the two of them. When they had been on the run.

Wren sat quietly there, with his head on her shoulder and her arms around him, just letting himself be held. Something had broken in the city, and he wondered if it could ever be repaired.

SEVEN

The light rain pattered on the roof with all the comforting sounds of a leaky faucet. Boss was sore from a bad night's sleep, which meant he was cranky *and* tired. The numbers weren't making him any happier. They'd pushed out a shipment two days before, ahead of schedule, but the buyers still hadn't received the goods and naturally hadn't paid up yet. Which meant Boss was short on men, and worse, short on money to pay off the greasy dealer that was standing in front of him right now.

"Look," the dealer said, "I got places, so if you don't deal, I'm cut loss and head on, you know?"

"Relax," Boss answered. "I've got the points."

"So what's blockin' the stops, pops?"

The words made so little sense it made Boss's teeth hurt. "Waiting to hear back from Moneymath. Market prices, *you know.*"

"Deal's the deal, no time for chit-chat, take her at two hundred or we're gone."

Boss gave the dealer a good looking over. A gangly creature, with long stringy hair and blotchy skin like poorly tanned leather. His clothes were ill-fitting. His coat was surprisingly luxuriant and too big in the shoulders; the high collar of

his shirt was so wide, it looked like he could pull it off over
his head without unfastening it. But despite the disheveled
appearance and his terrible grasp of human language, Boss
recognized the keen look in the dealer's eyes. Here was a man
accustomed to walking into dangerous situations. And since
he was standing here, he was also accustomed to walking
back out of them. Boss was either going to have to come
clean with him, or kill him real quick.

"What's it, lawdog? Am I pricey or am I scoots?" he asked.

The *lawdog* caught Boss's attention, made his hackles
rise. He'd been a man of the law once, years ago, but he'd
left that far, far behind. The dealer had a sly grin on his
face, like he knew that'd get to him. Boss thought about
the two-gun he had hooked on a swivel under his desk.
That'd fold the dealer in half real quick and take his little
grin right with it.

But Boss couldn't help following the leash the dealer had
in his hands, right over to where it hooked on the girl's
collar. She couldn't be more than thirteen. Hands bound in
front of her. Pretty too, under the grime and bruises. The
two-gun wasn't the most precise of killing instruments.
Boss didn't want to risk damaging the goods.

"Stray, kin, or kidnap?" Boss asked the dealer.

"She's mine, don't mind you the why."

"My clients are the worrying sort. They expect details.
Where's she from?"

"The Six-Thirteen. She's mine, fair deal."

"I'm no one's but my own..." the girl said, looking up at
Boss. She didn't look as defeated as they usually did. The
dealer jerked the leash hard, and she immediately looked
at the floor again, but Boss could tell from the angle of her
head that she was watching the dealer out of the corner of

her eye. He didn't see any need for treating her so, and he started feeling a little better about killing this guy.

"No one's going to come looking for her?" Boss asked.

"Not without comin' up gravelike." The dealer smiled at that, like he was real pleased with himself. Probably stalked some poor family and murdered them in their sleep. For a brief moment, Boss felt a twinge of sympathy for the girl, which in turn made him feel more sorry for himself – for what he'd been reduced to. He was a good man caught in an evil time. But this was the hand he'd been dealt, the life of a once-lawman in a lawless world. Nothing to do but play it out as best he could. Boss sighed.

"Alright, finally," he said, smiling through the lie. "Moneymath says one seventy-three and some decimals is the going rate for pristine. She doesn't look quite pristine, though."

"Don't jerk, lawdog. She's all she is, unspoilt. Two hundred says the deal." The dealer's eyes narrowed ever so slightly, and his left hand edged a fraction of an inch closer towards the inside of his coat.

"She is real pretty," Boss answered. He pretended to think it over. Didn't really matter, since he couldn't afford it anyway. But supply was scarce lately, and he couldn't afford to lose this one either. "Call it one-ninety, no more questions asked."

The dealer rubbed the fingertips of his left hand together, either like he was already counting the money or he was getting ready to draw down. Boss leaned forward, like he was just shifting in his chair, and stretched his fingertips out to brush the grip of the weapon under the desk.

The dealer snorted something thick and nasty and made a little grunting noise in his throat, and then swallowed. Boss almost gagged at the sound.

"Fine enough, we'll call it."

"Excellent. I'll have one of my boys handle the transfer. You can leave her with me."

The dealer barked a laugh. "Not so, lawdog, spendies – then she stays."

Of course Boss had known that's how it'd go, but it was always worth a shot. The trick now was just figuring out which of his crew he needed in the room to keep things from turning into a bloodbath, and how to get them in without making him suspicious. Wing was a little faster on the draw, but Cauld was a deadeye who could shoot the flame off a candle and not even spill the wax. Probably couldn't get both of them in the room without tipping the dealer off, though.

Just then Wing poked his head in. "Hey, Boss, you got some guy out here wants to see you."

"He'll have to wait. We're in conference." Boss said. That made the decision for him. Wing was already here. He should stay and help with the dealer.

"Said it'd just take a second."

"What's he want?" Boss asked Wing.

"To see you, I reckon."

Boss dropped his gaze ever so slightly and clenched his jaw just a bit more. "Yeah, I figured that part. But what for? He selling or buying?" he asked.

"Beats me, Boss. Just said he had a message."

"Not the kind where he walks in and tries to kill me."

"Nah, Boss, he ain't gonna hurt nobody." Wing chuckled. "He's all old and beat-up lookin'. Beats all I ever seen. Got a blindfold and everything."

Boss scratched between his eyes with his thumb knuckle, but then it occurred to him that this might be just what he needed. A good distraction, an excuse to bring in both his guys. Just had to be careful not to give anything away. "You won't mind I hope. Shouldn't take long."

"Your house," the dealer said. "Just don't jerk."

"Alright," Boss said, and then added a heavy sigh, like he was doing everyone a favor. "Bring him in, but stay on him. Hey, and while you're at it, get Cauld in here so we can pay this man."

Wing scrunched up his face for a second, clearly trying to work out why Cauld would have anything to do with paying anybody, but then he figured it out. Thankfully the dealer was too busy watching Boss.

"Sure, Boss. What's the amount?" Wing asked.

"One-ninety."

Wing whistled, and then looked the girl up and down. "Yeah, I guess I could see that. Usual package or secure?"

"Secure." It was their internal code: The usual package was for when someone might have some use alive. Secure meant drop the hit fast and hard. Wing nodded and disappeared.

Boss raised his hands in mock exasperation. "Sorry for this. I have at times been overly kind to beggars. Guess word gets around." It was true. Boss tried to help the less fortunate out when he could. Just hadn't been able to all that much of late. The dealer didn't respond, except that he pulled on the leash and drew the girl closer.

A moment later, an older man shuffled through the door, his hand partially outstretched and head slightly bowed. Wing and Cauld followed him in. The dealer, wily as he was, slid over – slick as oil – and put his back to the wall, his eyes on the three arrivals while he kept the girl between him and Boss.

Wing trailed close to the old man and put a hand on his shoulder to stop him from getting too close to Boss. Cauld was a pure professional. He rolled in casually with a case in his hands and took up a spot next to Boss, one that just happened to have a real good angle on the dealer.

"You wanna handle the pay first, Boss?" Cauld asked.

"Best to keep that private, I'd think?" Boss answered, looking at the dealer.

"Fine that," the dealer said, his eyes roving smoothly between Boss, Cauld, and Wing.

The old man hadn't raised his head or stirred since Wing had stopped him in place. He just stood there, head bowed, hands folded in front of himself – like a child waiting to be punished. His hair was long and wild, a dirty grey, his face dusted with a wispy matted beard. He really did look pathetic, and Boss thought for a moment it might be kindest to just put him down. But Boss was a businessman, not a murderer.

"We're in the middle of something here, old man. What's the message?"

The beggar didn't raise his head or move at all, but his voice came out stronger than Boss expected. "An old friend seeks you."

"Oh yeah? Who's that?"

The old man was silent long enough that Boss opened his mouth to prompt him again. The old man drew a breath and said, "You were an agent once. A man of noble purpose and profession."

Boss snorted. "I was an agent, yeah. Don't know about all that other." He didn't care for how often that'd been mentioned today. Boss briefly wondered if maybe the dealer and this old guy were partners in something. The dealer was on edge, though. If they were in on it together, he was doing a masterful job of acting.

"You have strayed."

"Livin'll do that to a man. Do I know you?" Boss asked.

"You knew me once. Long ago."

"Yeah? What's your name?"

"Today," the old man said, "I am Honor."

Boss couldn't tell if he was joking or not. But Boss's name was Boss, so he didn't have much reason to doubt it. Still, it sounded funny, and so he let out a little non-committal chuckle that he hoped could be taken as either polite amusement, or simple acknowledgment. There was a too-long moment of silence afterwards.

"Look here," the dealer finally said, "clocks is spendies. Sum me out and chat after, or me and merch is scoots."

Boss was still trying to work out whether there was some connection between the two degenerates that stood before him – when all of a sudden the old man moved all easy and casual, like he was stretching after a nap. But in the movement he somehow covered the distance to the dealer and in the same motion, he swept his hand out in a graceful arc.

Maybe he touched the dealer; Boss couldn't tell exactly what happened. He just saw the dealer flinch. And just as smooth, the old man returned to his spot as calmly. And even as if he'd never moved at all, with his hands folded in front of him again. It'd all happened in less time than it took Boss to inhale. Everybody just stood there stunned for a second.

Then the dealer made a little gurgle, and he let go of the leash and reached up to his neck with both hands, and all of a sudden it looked like he was trying to tie a crimson silk neckerchief on, the way his hands were going, and all the red. Boss's brain wouldn't process what he was seeing because he couldn't comprehend what had just happened. The dealer fell on his knees and gurgled some more, and Wing said something that Boss didn't quite catch.

The old man was as still as if he'd turned to stone, even when the dealer went on over and fell, and leaked out everywhere. Standing there with his hands in front of him. But now Boss saw the blade; some sort of knife, though he had no idea where it'd come from.

"What'd you do?" Boss heard himself say. The old man didn't answer. Wing reached out and grabbed him by the shoulder, and Boss could've told him that was a bad idea if he'd just asked. It looked like the old man just kind of shrugged and brushed Wing's hand, but somehow the next thing anyone knew, the old man had Wing's hand flipped over palm up and bent the wrong way back, and Wing was howling like a woman with her hair on fire.

A sudden motion caught Boss's attention, and he saw Cauld had pulled out his little pocket popper, and almost had it aimed – when the old man flicked his other hand out. The knife came sliding out – flying straight like a dart – and stuck right in the middle of Cauld's chest. Cauld stumbled back, and tried to get the pistol up anyway, but he acted like it'd gotten too heavy all of a sudden.

Boss looked back in time to see the old man slam a fist into Wing's throat. Wing choked up and stopped screaming then. The girl was just standing there, watching the whole thing happen, and Boss knew if he pulled the trigger, he was going to hit her and probably Wing too. But at that point she didn't seem so valuable anymore, and Wing was probably dying anyway. He reached under the desk and grabbed for the grip of his short-barreled two-gun.

The old man took a funny little half-turn and kind of windmilled like he was doing a dance, and Boss realized the old man had produced a sword from somewhere and was bringing it down in a surprisingly fluid arc. He'd obviously misjudged the distance, though, and was coming down well short of his target. Boss almost felt sorry for him as he squeezed the trigger. Almost.

The two-gun thundered and Boss was caught off guard by the recoil. He completely lost his grip on the massive weapon, and his arm flew backwards with surprising violence. Strangely enough, the old man hadn't reacted at all. He was just standing there with his sword extended, having apparently cut Boss's desk through the middle. The girl seemed to be alright too. She just had her hands over her ears.

Boss noticed his hand had gone numb from the blast, and when he flexed it to check for damage, he noticed his hand wasn't there anymore at all. Just a ragged mess of bone and pulpy flesh hanging where his wrist used to be.

"What in the world?" he said. Then he saw under the desk where the two-gun was all mangled and blown out, and it dawned on him that the old man hadn't been so far off the mark after all. He'd cut clean through the two-gun and blown it up in Boss's hand.

The old man finally relaxed from his stance and walked casually but confidently around Boss's desk. He knelt over Cauld and whispered something.

"Who are you?" Boss asked. Or at least, that's what he'd wanted to ask, but the words came out slurred and with too many syllables. He tried again with the same result.

"You're going into shock," the old man said quietly. He stood, and Boss saw he was holding his knife again. "There isn't much time."

The girl, sadly, was stranger neither to the violence she'd endured, nor to that which she'd just witnessed. And she knew in this case, as in most cases, the very best thing to do was to stand very still and to be very quiet. She kept her head down, and watched carefully out of the corner of her eye. The old man with the blindfold was crouching in front of the big man behind the desk. The one that was going to buy her. She couldn't hear what they were saying, but it looked like Old Guy was talking and the buyer, well... if she didn't know better she would've said he was crying. He looked over at her once with wet eyes.

After a minute or so, Old Guy stood up with his hand on the buyer's shoulder. The girl had to see what was going on then. She dared to raise her head – just enough to get a better look. The buyer had Old Guy's knife in his remaining hand and was just staring down at it. Old Guy stood over him, head bowed a bit. Maybe it was some kind of honor thing... not wanting to kill an unarmed man. Or maybe Old Guy was giving the buyer one last chance.

From that close, the girl figured the buyer could stick Old Guy pretty quick. Either way, she was feeling pretty good about her chances of escape; couldn't be too hard to outrun a one-handed fat guy in the process of bleeding to death, or a blind old man – no matter how good he was with a sword.

She saw the buyer shift his weight and sit up a little straighter. He looked at her one more time and then nodded to himself. The buyer took a strong breath, exhaled sharply. He nodded again. And then plunged the knife into his own abdomen. In the next instant, Old Guy brought his sword up. The girl squeezed her eyes shut before it had a chance to come down again, but she heard the sound of steel through flesh and bone, and the thump of something falling to the floor.

That was the time to run. But the girl found herself frozen in place, not wanting to open her eyes and see what she knew she'd see. There were soft sounds she couldn't identify, and the next thing she knew, she could feel the old man standing in front of her. And then he was kneeling.

"Don't weep, child," he said. "You are safe."

His voice wasn't particularly deep, but it was warm and kind, like a grandfather's. She dared to open one eye. He was there, on a knee in front of her, his head tilted back slightly, looking up at her. Though he had the blindfold on, so obviously he couldn't be *looking* up at her.

His hands moved up and she flinched reflexively. In response, he held his hands open, palms out, for a moment, before reaching out for her wrists. With skillful fingers, Old Guy went to work on the cords that bound her hands together, and she wondered at how well he could apparently feel the knot.

"Will your parents be looking for you?" he asked.

"No, sir."

"Have you any family left?"

"No."

"Friends? Anyone to care for you?"

She said, "I take care of myself." Old Guy reached up and began gently removing the collar. "You're gonna let me go?"

"Of course, child. Do you have somewhere *to* go?"

The girl thought about that. It'd been three days since that man had caught her the second time, after she'd escaped the first. "Yeah, I know lots of places," she lied. She'd figure it out. Always had. She walked over to the corpse of the man who'd caused her so much pain and sorrow over the last week. His eyes were still open. "I appreciate what you done."

"It was necessary."

"Yeah, well," she said. She nudged the dead man with her toe, just to make sure. Then she bent and went through his coat pockets, taking back what was hers and some of what wasn't. She found her eight-kilojoule pistol and checked the cylinder. Still had all eight rounds. "I don't reckon you're headed back south?" the girl asked.

She flicked the cylinder shut with a snap of her wrist and slid the weapon into her waistband. When she looked, she realized she was alone with a bunch of dead men. Old Guy was just gone.

She sniffed once and thought about checking out what was in that case on the desk. But then she remembered what was behind the desk and thought better of it. Better not to push her luck. Better to move on and find a place before nightfall. For one final time, the girl looked at the man who'd tried to sell her.

The girl cleared her throat. Spat right on his face. And set out once more on her own.

EIGHT

Cass surveyed the weary faces around the table. The Council had gathered yet again, this time before dawn, and patience was thin. Though saying they'd gathered was misleading, since they hadn't ever departed after the chaos that erupted during Wren's address. That had been intended to soothe fears and tensions. Instead, it had ignited them. Or rather, certain elements had chosen that particular moment to ignite them. Looking around that table, Cass couldn't help but wonder who among them could be trusted. At the moment, she felt like there were none.

It took all the discipline Cass could muster to force herself to sit there, in yet another meeting, listening to these people talking to one another. That seemed to be all they ever did anymore.

She looked at Wren, seated on her right at the head of the table, his eyes vacant, ringed underneath with dark half-circles that gave him a bruised look. He sat staring, unfocused, at his hands folded in his lap, either listening intently or completely lost in his own thoughts. She hoped he'd at least be able to keep his eyes open.

"Bottom line is, we're losing control," Hondo said. He wasn't even bothering to try to sound diplomatic. "That little protest was just the beginning. We're lucky we were able to put it down so quickly."

"It's not luck to have a strong show of force prepared ahead of time," Aron said.

"Regardless. We don't want people to start thinking they can take matters into their own hands. Once that starts, it won't stop until the whole city's in ruins."

"What about a curfew?" Vye offered. "Just until things cool down."

"Too dangerous," Aron said. "We don't have the manpower to enforce it, not if it's challenged. The last thing we need is all these people figuring out we can't control them."

"I think a curfew is a must. At least a start. We could pull the guards off the wall," Rae said. "Use them to beef up the presence in the city, especially around the hotspots."

"And what about the Weir, Rae?" Hondo snapped. "You think they'll just wait till we get back before they try again?"

"There's no reason to think they'll try again," Connor said. Aron looked at Connor sharply.

Connor added, "I mean, not necessarily."

"I agree with Connor," Vye said. "The Weir haven't been a real concern for a long time. I don't think we should assume there's a reason to worry about them more now."

"You weren't there, Vye," Cass said. "There's reason enough."

"Maybe that's the problem," Aron said. The tone of his voice changed; lower, less sharp, more thoughtful. It made Cass uncomfortable. "Maybe they haven't been *enough* of a concern."

"If you've got a point," Hondo said, "make it."

"All this drama we got going on inside the walls of our city, over what? Some people don't like some other people.

So what? That's always been. But it's like people forget why we have the wall in the first place."

"And what?" Rae said.

"Maybe they need a reminder."

Hondo barked a humorless laugh. "What'd you have in mind, Aron? Leave a gate open overnight?"

"I don't know exactly. But something to shake these people up. Remind 'em what's out there. And remind 'em who it is that keeps 'em safe."

Rae shook her head dismissively. "This isn't even worth discussing, Aron. Out of the question."

"Well, hold on, Rae," Connor said. "There's no harm in talking it through."

"Just a means to an end," Aron said with a shrug.

Cass didn't like where the conversation was headed, but at the same time she felt like the longer she let it go, the more insight she could get. Wren hadn't budged.

"This is insane. You're talking about terrorizing your own people," Rae said.

"I'm talkin' about gettin' on top of a dangerous situation, Rae. I don't see any good choices right now, just a bunch of bad ones. And maybe keepin' people a little scared is worth it if it keeps 'em in line."

"If we don't do *something*, the city's going to destroy itself," Vye said quietly. "Drastic times, drastic measures."

"I'm not talking about doing nothing. I'm talking about not doing something we know is fundamentally wrong! And when have drastic measures ever turned out well?" Rae said.

"What about the machine?" Connor asked. The Council went quiet at that. Even Wren looked up at the mention of Underdown's device.

"What about it?" Cass said. Connor's eyes went to Wren. The implication wasn't lost on anyone.

"No, absolutely not," Rae said. "I can't believe you'd even think that was a possibility. We should've destroyed that thing long ago."

"Well, we didn't," Hondo said. "And I for one am not sorry. It might be useful someday."

"It might be useful now," Aron added.

"I can't believe this," Rae said, standing up. "Has it really come to that? Have we really come to the point where we're looking at Underdown's tyranny as a model for how to govern?"

"Argue with his methods all you want," Aron said. He was leaning back in his chair now, picking at a fingernail. Relaxed. Like his mind was made up. "One thing you can't argue is *results*."

"I'm not going to sit here and even pretend to entertain something as despicable as what you seem to be implying. Am I the only one in here who thinks this is crazy? Cass, surely you don't agree…" Rae said.

Of course Cass didn't agree. Of course she couldn't condone ruling by fear. Of course there were other options. But what were they? She didn't know, not immediately, but she did know that no matter what other course they might be forced to pursue, her son wasn't going anywhere near Underdown's machine. Cass opened her mouth to respond. But North raised a hand and stopped her.

"I would hear our governor's words before those of his mother," North said. "Let the boy speak."

Wren had been watching the discussion bounce around the table ever since Connor had mentioned the machine. He looked at her now, eyes searching hers for an answer.

"Your *own* thoughts, Governor," North said. He leaned forward and placed his hands on the table, focusing his attention on Wren and, in doing so, directing the rest of the Council to do the same. Now, Wren fixed his gaze on North. For a long moment, Wren sat silently. But Cass could tell from the look on his face that he knew what he wanted to say, he just hadn't figured out the exact words yet. Finally, he sat up a little straighter.

"I think anything built on a lie is bound to collapse eventually. Seems like the truth always finds a way to break out. That's why I'm governor now and my father isn't. And as governor, I can't be part of deliberately deceiving the people."

Pride swelled in Cass's heart. She still didn't know exactly how she would've answered, but she felt like Wren had said it better than she could have anyway. She quickly turned her attention to the rest of the Council members, just catching the tail end of a glance Hondo had thrown in Aron's direction. Aron either didn't notice, or didn't react. Connor had a little smile on his face. North, as usual, was unreadable, and Vye was just looking at Rae, who was still standing.

Rae nodded and drew a calming breath. She was just starting to take her seat again when Wren continued.

"But I know I've made some decisions that have caused a lot of problems. I've always tried to do what I think is the right thing for the city. But I know I've been wrong. So, if the Council can agree on what's best, I'm willing to do what you think is necessary. But I won't lie to the people. And I won't use the machine."

North sat back and placed his hands in his lap, impassive.

"Well," Hondo said, "that's all fine. But where does it get us?"

The Council as a whole sat in restless thought. From the look on Aron's face, Cass could tell he was still thinking it through, and she found herself wondering what he'd meant by *"something to shake these people up"*. Wondering if the attack on Wren was the kind of thing Aron had in mind.

Her thoughts were interrupted when the door to the Council Room opened and Able slid in. He stood by the entryway and motioned to her.

"Yes, Able," she said. "What is it?"

You need to come see this, he signed. He looked troubled.

"Can it wait?"

He shook his head.

"Ladies, gentlemen, I'm sorry, but I'll need to excuse myself for a moment–"

Able held up a hand, and then signed, *All of you.*

"Somethin's up," Aron said. They all rose and followed Able, who led them from the Council Room. By the entrance, a guardsman stood pale and sweating, clearly shaken. Cass guessed he'd brought Able the message.

Able took them out through the front entrance. The sun was just over the horizon, the air cool and damp and clean. A beautiful morning after so dark a night. The daylight overpowered Cass's sensitive modified eyes; she covered her face with her veil, filtering out the wavelengths that confused her vision. She could see a small crowd gathered at the main gate of the compound. The gate was still closed, and the knot of people seemed to be in a stir over something near the top of the wall. There was a large blackened lump there, suspended from the archway; a large bundle of rags, or a few bags of garbage, or some kind of–

No.

Cass grabbed Wren by the shoulder and turned him around. "Don't go any closer, Wren. Don't look, baby."

Vye cried out and covered her face with her hands.

"Well," Aron said, "I reckon that's gonna change things."

Bodies. Or what was left of them. They were black from burning, hacked, some missing limbs. Three, Cass guessed, maybe four of them, tied together and strung from the main gate of the governor's compound.

"Able," North said, touching the man on the shoulder. Once Able was looking directly at him, he added, "Help me cut them down." Able nodded, and together they scaled the gate.

Aron stepped forward and approached the citizens assembled on the other side. "Go on!" he shouted, waving the crowd away. "Ain't you got any respect! Get outta here!"

"Rae," Cass said, "would you mind taking Wren back inside?"

"Sure, Cass, I'll look after him." She didn't look at Cass when she said it.

"Thank you."

"Governor?" Rae said, playfully formal with a gentle smile. "Would you kindly escort me back to the hall?"

Wren nodded and started towards the main building, but paused and looked back over his shoulder. "Mama?"

"Yes...?" She managed to cut herself off before calling him *sweetheart*.

"I need to know who they are."

"I know."

He nodded and took Rae's hand. Cass watched them until they got to the top of the stairs and disappeared through the front entrance. She could trust Rae... she was pretty sure she could trust Rae.

When she looked back at the gate, Aron had climbed up on a crossbar to help North and Able. The crowd was mostly gone, with the exception of two or three stragglers who continued to stare, but from a greater distance. A few guards lingered nearby, some keeping watch, some waiting to receive the bodies. Vye was on her knees with her hands in her lap, glassy-eyed and staring at the sunrise. Hondo paced back and forth, giving orders no one followed – while Connor, pale and glistening with a sickly sweat, just stood below with his hands held uselessly in the air as if helping by projection.

With great effort the three managed to lower the remains to the ground in as respectful a way as anyone could. Hondo stood over them with his arms crossed, shaking his head. Connor went completely white and gagged, and then wandered off to a nearby planter to vomit. Cass approached and helped the others separate the bodies as best they could and lay them out next to each other.

Aron swore softly to himself, started to say something else, then just repeated the oath again.

There were four. So marred she couldn't identify who they were... who they'd been. Except for one. One she recognized, his body intact, his face untouched by flames. And not by accident.

She crouched next to him, smoothed back his hair, thick and tacky with blood. It was Luck. He had once been a Weir, like her. And like her, Wren had somehow brought him back. Restored his mind, though not his body. He was one of the Awakened.

And now, he was a message.

Wren sat on the end of the bed, too tired to cry anymore. He was empty. Totally and completely empty. He wanted to be sad. Wren knew he should be angry. He thought maybe he should be a little scared, too. But he didn't feel any of those things. Luck was gone, and all Wren could feel was responsible. It'd been his fault. Not directly, of course, he knew that. But he also knew that somewhere along the way he'd made a decision, or maybe a series of decisions, that ended here, with another person that he cared about dead.

"I shouldn't've luh-left him out th-th, out there," Painter said. He was sitting in a chair by the door of Wren's room. Or rather, of Cass's room, where Wren was staying now.

"It's not your fault, Painter," Wren said. "Whatever happened, I don't think you could've stopped it."

Painter shook his head. "Luck smiled tuh-tuh... he smiled too much. Always trying to g-g-get people to like him. He p-p-p... probably didn't even fight back."

"I'm glad you were here, anyway. I'm glad you're here now."

Painter nodded, but he didn't look at Wren. He was staring out through the flexiglass door that led to the balcony, out at the night sky. The moon had been up for a couple of hours. Wren hadn't seen Mama since that morning.

"I just don't understand," Wren continued. "I don't understand how anyone could do that to a person."

"Because we're not puh-people, Wren."

Wren wanted to tell Painter he was wrong – tell him that he shouldn't think of himself as anything other than a person. But whether it was because Wren was so tired, or maybe because he wasn't sure he believed it himself, Wren found he couldn't argue. If he had known this was how things were going to happen... it took so much effort, so much energy. It *hurt* him to wake them. If all it caused in the end was more pain, was it even worth it?

"Can I ask you something, Painter?" Wren asked.

Painter looked over to him. "Of course."

"Are you sorry that I brought you back?"

Painter seemed to think about it for a moment, but Wren couldn't read his expression. "Are you?"

"No."

"Then me nnn-neither."

"It's just… it's like when I made them let everyone inside the city. I thought it was the right thing to do. I didn't know it was going to cause so much trouble."

"That *was* the ruh-ruh-right thing, Wren. Trouble's got nnnn…" Painter struggled with the word. He snapped his head to the side in frustration. "Nothing to do with it."

"It's harder for you, though."

Painter shrugged and went back to looking outside. "They're affff-fraid of us."

"They shouldn't be."

"Yes, they should." He said it quietly, almost to himself. The door clicked and whirred, and Painter stood up quickly to face it. Wren got to his feet as it was opening.

"Mama!"

Wren didn't wait for her to get any further into the room before he wrapped his arms around her waist and pressed his cheek into her stomach. Cass kissed him on the top of the head and placed her hands on his back, squeezing him against her legs in an awkward kind of hug.

"Hey, baby," she said. She sounded exhausted. "Can I get in the door?"

Wren let go and backed up so she could enter the room. She closed the door behind her and then knelt down and held out her arms. "There, now let me get a proper hug." Wren stepped into her embrace and hugged her neck. She squeezed him so tight it was almost hard for him to breathe.

"Painter," Cass said. "Thanks so much for staying with him. Sorry it was so long."

"It was no problem, Miss Cass. Anyt-t-t-, any time. Any news?"

Cass gave Wren a final squeeze and then stood up. She took off her veil and tossed it in the chair next to the door, then unbuckled her jacket. "Curfew's in place, we've got a lot of extra enforcement on patrol."

"What about..." Wren couldn't bring himself to say the names. "...the bodies?"

"Turns out it was only two Awakened. Mez was the other."

Mez had been among the first few of the Awakened, an older man who'd spent most of his time outside the wall. He'd never really settled into Morningside, and hadn't kept much contact with Wren or Cass. Wren was still sorry for his death.

Cass said, "The others – we're not sure about yet. It's hard to get any information out of people after last night. What about you guys?"

Wren replied, "We've mostly been here. Just trying to stay out of the way."

Cass nodded. "Probably the best idea right now. Painter, anything I can do for you?"

Painter shook his head. "Pretty tired. Think I'm just guh-guh-going to go to b-bed."

"You're up with the team?" she asked him.

Painter nodded.

"They treating you well?"

Painter nodded again. "When they're around."

"Yeah," Cass said. "Been a busy few. Not sure when they'll be back tonight."

"Finn gave me his rrr-room."

"Oh, good. Won't wake you then. Well, thanks again, Painter. You've been a huge help."

Cass leaned forward and gave Painter a hug. From the look of it, Wren could almost imagine it was the first time Painter had ever been hugged. He stood there with his arms at his sides almost rigid, leaning slightly back. When she let go, he gave an embarrassed smile and then opened the door.

"See you tommm-morrow." He went out and closed the door behind him.

"I don't think Painter's getting enough hugs," Cass said. "What do you think?"

"Probably not," Wren said. He sat back down on the bed and scooted back so his feet were dangling. Cass plopped down next to him and put her arm around him.

"Tough day," she said. He nodded. "Did you eat anything?"

"A little."

"Hey," she said, turning his face towards her. "I didn't get to say this earlier, but I'm proud of what you said at Council this morning."

This morning. It seemed like a week ago. And what did it matter what he'd said? What Wren said hadn't stopped anyone from killing Luck. It hadn't even decided anything.

He said, "I'm tired, Mama."

"Me too, baby."

"Can you lie down with me?"

"Sure, sweetheart. Come on. Why don't we both get changed?"

Cass stood up and started pulling the covers down on the bed, while Wren tugged his arm out of the sleeve of his shirt. Even the idea of putting on pajamas seemed daunting, and Wren stopped when he got the one sleeve off. His arms felt like they were full of concrete. Maybe Mama could help. They were interrupted by a knock at the door. She sighed and walked over to it. "Probably Painter."

Cass opened the door more quickly than usual, and Wren could tell from her reaction it wasn't Painter. From his angle in the room, though, he couldn't see who it was.

"Gentlemen. You need me for something?" she asked.

"Can we come in?" said a voice in the hall. It sounded like Connor.

"Wren was just getting ready to go to sleep. Can we talk in the hall?"

"It's better if we don't," said a second voice. Uncle Aron. Wren put his arm back in the sleeve of his shirt. Cass stood her ground at the door, seemingly reluctant to let them in. Wren wondered if she was worried about him.

"It's OK, Mama," he said. "I don't mind."

She looked over at him, and Wren could tell from her expression that something else had been making her hesitate. Cass bit her bottom lip just a tiny bit, thinking it over.

"It won't take but a minute," Connor said.

"Alright," she said, backing up so they could enter. "Just for a minute. Otherwise it'll have to wait until morning."

"Thanks," Connor said as he came in. He gave Wren a little nod and smile. Aron followed after. He didn't smile. Cass closed the door. Aron remained next to it, with his hands folded in front of him. Connor came further in, between Cass and Wren, but closer to Wren. Wren got a bad feeling.

"What's this about?" Cass asked.

"Things are lookin' bad out there, Cass," Aron said. "We've got the entire guard turned out, and I'm not sure it's enough to keep the peace."

"Word's out about what we found this morning," Connor added. "We're trying to get everyone to stay inside, but there's been some scuffles by the West Wall already."

"Why there?" said Cass.

"Dunno," Connor said. "Could be something to do with the uhh, the Awakened that got killed. Could be just people thinking they can get away with anything now. Either way, it's not good."

Wren couldn't put his finger on it, but he felt really anxious. Something wasn't right. Something about the way Aron was looking at Cass, or something about the way Connor was talking. He seemed nervous.

"Mama," Wren said, "where's Able?"

She seemed distracted too. Maybe trying to figure out what he was trying to figure out.

"Able and his merry little band of hellwalkers are out there keeping the Weir away from the wall," Connor said. He didn't even bother trying to sound anything other than dismissive.

"You've got them stationed on the wall?" Cass asked. The governor's elite bodyguard was certainly capable of manning the wall, but that hardly seemed like the best use for them.

"No," Aron said. "They're outside."

"On whose order?" Cass asked.

"Mine," said Connor.

"Then who's guarding the compound?" she said.

"We've got our hands full trying to keep the city in one piece, Cass," Aron answered.

"Then maybe you should leave."

"Not yet."

Mama must've picked up on something because she managed to get a hand on Aron before Wren heard the *thump*, but the next thing he knew Connor had grabbed his arm and jerked him off balance. Mama had fallen backwards to the floor, but she was up on a knee, trying to get back to her feet – when Aron pointed a black box-like thing at her, and there was that *thump* again, and then two more *thump thump*, and Mama fell back and was still. And Wren tried to scream, but Connor had a hand over his mouth, and had his arms pinned to his sides; and no matter how much Wren fought, he couldn't get free, and the whole time Connor was in his ear. "Shhhhhh. Shhhhhhh. It's OK, Wren, it's OK, shhhhh."

But it wasn't OK, Mama was on the floor not moving and Aron was putting the box back inside his coat, and he looked angry.

"Don't fight, don't fight," Connor said. "Your mom's fine, she's just going to sleep for a while, OK? She's not hurt, OK?"

Wren felt like he couldn't breathe, and Mama was just laying there. And Aron was walking towards him now.

"She ain't hurt, kid," Aron said. "But we got a trace on Able and Gamble and the whole team, so don't you think about trying to call for help, or else we *will* hurt her, you understand?" Aron grabbed Wren's face and looked him in the eye. "Do you understand?"

Wren nodded, or at least did the best he could with Connor's hand over his mouth.

"Don't scream or fuss, you hear? We're not out to hurt anybody, but we will if we have to."

"I'm going to let you go, OK, Governor?" Connor said. "You won't scream or try to run away, right?"

Wren wasn't sure if he was supposed to nod or shake his head since Connor had asked him two questions, but he decided it was safer to nod. Agreement always seemed safer. Connor took his hand off of Wren's mouth, but didn't let him go.

"You said it yourself," Connor said, so close Wren could feel his breath. "You said it yourself, you said you'd do whatever was necessary, right? Right? Well, here it is."

Aron said, "You're gonna do just like we say, Wren. I know you don't understand right now, but you will. You'll see we're doin' the right thing."

"What'd you do to Mama?" Wren asked.

"She's just asleep," Connor said.

But Aron was pulling the box out of his coat again. He held it out for Wren to see. "It's just a dislocator, see? No permanent damage."

Wren had seen those before. A lot of the guardsmen carried them to deal with troublemakers. From what he knew, the projectiles they fired just spammed the target's datastream, overloaded it, made people shut down, and left nothing more than a deep bruise. But that was normal people. He had no idea what would they might do to someone like Mama.

"We're gonna take you somewhere now," Aron said. "Don't make trouble for us."

"I won't," Wren said.

"Everything's going to be fine, Wren," Connor said.

Wren wanted to ask why, if everything was going to be fine, they'd just shot his mama and were keeping such a tight grip on his arm, but he knew better. He'd been through something like this before, back when Asher had caught him and Three. And Able and Swoop had been training him for this sort of situation. Best to go along, until the opportunity presented itself. And it would.

Aron moved to the door and cracked it open, checking outside before committing to opening it all the way. He nodded to Connor and motioned for them to follow. The hallway was deserted, and that was a bad sign. If there were any guardsmen left in the building, they would probably be on Connor and Aron's side anyway.

It didn't take long for Wren to figure out where they were headed. They took him along halls that he hadn't been through in a long, long time. To a room he hadn't been in since... not since Three had died and his mama had come back. Aron led the way, and Connor half-dragged Wren along, apologizing the whole time, constantly telling Wren it was all for the best.

"We just want you to try, OK?" Connor said. "We just want you to see what you can do. It really is for the best. We all just want what's best for the city, OK?"

They took him through what was once a kind of throne room. The room where Wren's father had sat and held court and handed down his judgment. Already Wren could hear the faint hum. Wren wasn't exactly sure why they were making him come to the room itself. And it occurred to him that for all their plans and schemes, they still didn't even have a basic idea of how it really worked. Underdown's machine might as well have been magic as far as they were concerned.

Aron unlocked the door and stepped back. Connor pushed Wren inside. Even without the lights on yet, Wren could make out the shape of the thing. Underdown's machine. The device Underdown had constructed to tap into the minds of the Weir, or whatever it was. The way he'd called them, and forced them away. The way he'd controlled them, as a means to control his people.

Aron followed them in and activated the lights. The machine stood before them in the center of the room, emitting a hum that would've been soothing to anyone who didn't know what it'd been made to do. It didn't look like much. It was about Wren's height, maybe just over four feet tall and about half again as wide. Mostly smooth with a couple of panels and a few lights that were all darkened. Only now did Wren understand that the machine had never been shut down. Maybe they didn't even know how.

"We just want you to try," Connor repeated. He seemed more nervous now, even more than he had when they'd first come in Mama's room.

"Try what?" Wren asked. He was being honest. "I don't know what you mean."

"You know what your dad could do with this," Aron said. "We want you to do the same thing."

"I never even met my dad."

"Don't talk back to me, boy," Aron said sharply. "I helped make that wall. And I helped make your father. I'll make you too, if it's what it takes to keep this city alive. But don't you think for one second I'll hesitate to tear you down, either, if that's what it takes."

Wren had never seen the machine before, let alone tried to interface with it. But Aron and Connor didn't seem all that concerned with facts or excuses.

And he understood that if they thought he was doing anything other than what they wanted, there was no telling what they might do to Mama. So, for his mother's sake, Wren closed his eyes and put his hands on the machine, and tried to see what his father had seen. And he knew without a doubt: there was terror inside that box.

NINE

Painter lay awake on his bed, wondering if he'd ever get a chance to sleep. It was a constant battle, trying to maintain some semblance of a normal schedule during the day, knowing that his body was wired for the night. He'd adjusted to some degree, and somewhat better than others. But the early hours of night were always the toughest, trying to convince his body it was time to shut down, instead of wind up.

Not that it was really his bed he was lying on. It was Finn's. The man who had kindly given up his own room so Painter could stay among them at the governor's compound.

Why they'd given Painter a room on the same floor as the governor's personal guard, he didn't know. For protection, maybe. Though it'd be hard to guess whether they meant to protect him from others, or others from him.

Painter still felt bad about how he'd reacted when he'd seen Snow's body. Everyone had assured him there were no hard feelings, and that they all understood. But Painter couldn't let himself believe there were truly no hard feelings. And he was certain they didn't understand. But he'd taken care of her. She would be OK now. He'd done his part.

Except for repaying those that had taken her from him. That work still remained. Painter didn't blame Wren, or anyone in the compound. Someone had poisoned her mind. He knew that now. Poisoned Snow against him, and against everyone like him. Against Luck. And as much as her death had broken Painter, it had, in a way, also healed him. Her reaction to him, upon his return, it hadn't really been her. It'd been what she'd been taught. What she'd been told by others. It wasn't really her fault. He'd find out whose fault it was, and he would repay them in kind.

It was while Painter was lying awake, thinking through all that had happened to him, and around him, that something sparked in his mind and interrupted the natural progression of his thoughts. *Wren is in trouble.* He had no idea how or why he knew. But there was no doubt that his little friend needed help, and soon.

Painter sat up in bed. Was there any reason to think Wren was in danger? No. Surely not. He was with his mother, and she was more than capable of protecting him. And even if not, there was his personal guard. Able, and the rest of them. Finn. Surely those would be far more able to take care of the Governor than Painter ever could. It was a silly thought. Painter lay back down and tried to think of other things. But no matter what he did, he couldn't chase away the feeling that Wren needed him. *Him.* Painter. And so without understanding why, Painter got up and quickly put his clothes back on.

He'd never been much of a fighter. He believed he had the heart for it, just not the training or skill. But believing it was different to knowing it.

There was really only one way to know for sure. He crept to the door and opened it as quietly as he could.

Wren was focused on the machine. It was complicated. Far more complicated than anything he'd ever imagined, let alone seen before. If his father had used this to control the Weir, it was far beyond Wren's understanding. At first he'd just been searching for a way to connect, thinking that maybe if he showed he'd accessed the machine, it'd be easier to tell Aron and Connor that he'd really tried and couldn't do it. But once Wren had gained access, he'd become intrigued by the system. Though it was far more layered, far more intricate, Wren had once glimpsed something like it in a moment of uncontrollable fear and rage. It reminded him of what he'd seen just before he'd… whatever it was he had done to his brother. When he'd sent him away.

It was like that, multiplied by a thousand. Or ten thousand, maybe. Except less organized. Or maybe more so, but with a system too advanced and on a scale too massive for his comprehension. It was impossible to tell, because of the depth of it all. Wren felt himself drawn towards it. Sliding nearer. And for a moment, he thought he might be falling helplessly into it.

But there was a shout from somewhere far away. Somewhere in another world. And then Wren realized it was in his world. His room. Everything came rushing back and he saw everything again as it was. Aron was there. And Connor. And someone else. A Weir. A Weir had come from the machine.

No, not a Weir. Painter. It was Painter. Come to help him.

Aron was fumbling for something inside his coat, and Wren tried to warn Painter, but it was too late. Painter didn't need the warning. He leapt across the room, literally leapt, and struck Aron in a single motion. Aron's head snapped back and his feet came up off the floor; he crashed head first against the wall behind him before collapsing down. He landed heavily, and his skull bounced when he hit. It made an awful sound.

Connor was making some noise, yelling maybe, maybe calling for help, Wren couldn't tell. Everything still seemed like a dream at that point. And Painter – Painter was there, and his right hand flashed out and caught Connor by the neck or by the shirt, Wren couldn't see for sure. But his other hand, his other hand was a fist and it smashed into Connor's face. And again. And again. And Connor's knees buckled and he went to the floor, still screaming. Painter rode him down, and his fist kept smashing. Again, and again. Until there was a wet crunch with every impact, and someone was screaming: "Stop stop stop!" – and Wren realized it was him.

Painter stopped, his hand raised for another strike and bloody, and it was like he was waking up from a deep sleep, from the way he looked at Wren. He was straddled on Connor's chest. Connor was just laying there, still and silent, and his face was smashed in on one side and his eyes were open.

"Painter," Wren said.

"Wren. Are you OK?"

Wren swallowed and nodded, but he didn't feel OK. Connor was staring at him, and Wren could tell even from where he stood that there was no life left in those eyes.

Painter looked down at Connor and then stood up real fast, like he'd seen him for the first time. "What happened, Wren? What happened?"

"They came and took me. They hurt my mom."

"Is he dead?" Painter asked, looking down at Connor, and then at his own hands. His left one was spattered all the way up his forearm.

"I think so."

"What about the uh-uh-other one? Did I k-k-kill him too?"

Wren looked over at Aron, crumpled in the corner. He was

motionless, and Wren could see there was blood pooling under his head. "I don't know."

"I didn't mean to, Wren, I sss-sss I swear it. I thought they were hurting yuh-you."

"They might have. They wanted me to do something... something I don't think I can."

"What do we do?"

"I think we better go, Painter."

"I di-di-di... I di-didn't mean to kill them, Wren."

"I know, Painter, I know. Come on."

Wren led the way out of the room, and back through the halls towards his mama's room, his heart racing and his face cold with sweat. It all felt just like a nightmare, like waking up from a nightmare, except he knew he was awake and this was all happening, and all he wanted was to make sure Mama was OK. He could hear Painter right behind him, but Wren didn't want to turn around and look – because he'd seen what had happened, and he knew if he looked at Painter now he was going to lose it – so he just kept looking straight ahead, getting back to Mama.

They got back to her room without seeing a single person in the compound, and that seemed wrong. But so much seemed wrong now. Connor and Aron had betrayed them, and who knew who else on the Council had gone along with it. Had they really betrayed him? Connor was right, Wren *had* said he would do whatever was necessary, if the Council agreed. What if they'd all agreed, and this was what they'd agreed to? Now Connor was dead, and probably Aron too, and no matter what, there was no way to come back from that.

Wren tried the door and found it was locked, but that was nothing to him, not anymore. He barely even had to think about it, and the lock flipped open, and he swung the door so hard it banged into the wall. Mama was still there on the floor, right where they'd left her.

"Help me," Wren said, moving to her side, but even he didn't know what he meant. He just knelt next to her and touched her face. She was warm, but limp.

"What do we do?" Painter asked, kneeling beside him.

"I don't know," Wren said, "I don't know."

Painter put his hand on her upper stomach and held it there for a moment.

"Look," he said. "Look, she's buh-buh-buh breathing. I think she's... OK."

"Can you pick her up? Get her on the bed?"

Painter shrugged, but scooted around behind Cass and scooped his arms under her shoulders. He stood up, dragging her with him. Wren tried to help with her legs, but it seemed like Painter was doing all the work. They got her onto the bed, though once she was there, Wren didn't really know why he'd thought that was something to do. She was still out cold. Only now there was blood smeared across her shirt.

"Maybe you should go wash your hands," Wren said. Painter looked at his hands, and then at Cass's stained shirt, and then at his hands again. He nodded and went into the adjoining bathroom. Wren sat on the edge of the bed next to his mama and started stroking her forehead, her face, and her hands. Just hoping something would wake her. "Mama," he said. "Mama, can you hear me, Mama?"

But no matter what he did, she didn't respond. And he was so scared. So scared that she wasn't ever going to wake up, and that someone was going to come and take him away, and that this was the end of everything they'd tried to protect. And that thought, the thought that everything was coming undone, really and truly undone, that's when Wren felt it rising in him. It wasn't the first time. He just hadn't known what was happening before. But he was beginning to recognize the feeling now, when it started. And with it, Wren knew somehow he'd be able to do things he couldn't usually do.

There was something inside him that felt like it popped, deep in his chest, down in his very middle, something so deep it almost seemed impossible that it could be inside Wren at all. And it hurt, and it scared him, but it also gave him strength. Wren stretched out a shaking hand, forcing himself to touch Cass's forehead, and when he did, it seemed like he could see how she worked. Like a big complicated lock that needed opening. And, after a moment, he unlocked her.

Cass's eyes floated open, scanned the room, lingered on Wren, unfocused and distant for a heartbeat, then two. Then they went wide and fierce, and she sprang up on a knee and drew Wren to her so fast it made his neck hurt.

"It's OK, Mama, it's OK!" he said.

"Where are they? Did they hurt you?" she asked.

Wren wrestled his way free. "No, Mama, I'm OK. Are you OK?"

"I'm fine," she said. Her tone was sharp and certain, but Wren knew that it was more reflex than truth. "What happened?"

Now that she was back, now that he knew she was alright, he felt the surge of strength melt away, and he was just her son again and she was his mama, and only the fear remained.

"Something bad." Wren didn't know how much to tell her or even where to begin, and the tears came. He hated them, he didn't want to cry, but he couldn't help it. They just dripped out of his eyes and he kept trying to wipe them away. There wasn't time for crying.

"They came in the room. Aron and Connor. And Aron hit me with something... dislocator maybe?"

"I think so. He shot you. Four times."

Cass grunted as her hand went over her chest and stomach, probing the injuries. "No wonder everything hurts. Where are they now?"

"I killed them," Painter said, standing in the doorway of the bathroom. His arms were wet past the elbows and the skin on both looked raw, like they'd been scalded. "It won't cuh-cuh-cuh... come off." There were still little splotches of blood on his forearm, shirt, fist, and sleeve.

"What do you mean, Painter?" she asked slowly. "What did you do?"

"They took me to the machine, Mama," Wren said. "They wanted me to use it."

"I di-di-didn't mean to."

"They're dead? Both of them?" she asked.

Wren replied, "I think so. Connor is."

Cass put her hand over her mouth, but Wren could tell it wasn't from shock or disgust – she was thinking through everything, coming up with a plan.

"I th-th-thought... I don't even know wh-why. I thought Wren was in tr-tr-trrr-trouble."

"I did that," Wren said. "I called you."

"What about Able? Or Swoop?" Cass asked.

Wren shook his head. "Uncle Aron said they'd put a trace on the whole team. He said if I tried to call them, they'd know, and they'd hurt you." It felt weird calling him "Uncle" after what had just happened.

"OK," Cass said, getting up off the bed and grabbing her jacket. "OK. First things first. We need to get out of the compound." She looked at Painter. "All of us." Back to Wren.

"Who else is here? In the compound?"

"We didn't see anybody else."

"Not even guards?"

Wren shook his head. "Do you think it was just them, Mama? Just those two?"

Cass was already moving towards her closet. "I don't know, baby. That'll have to wait." She opened the closet door and pulled a small pack from the top shelf. "Is there anything you absolutely *have* to have? We might not be coming back here for a while."

Wren shook his head again. The idea of leaving seemed so strange. He'd thought about it a lot the past few months, but only as a dream, never as something that might actually require planning or packing or being prepared. He tried to think of what he'd need to take, or what'd he miss, but his mind was coming up blank.

Cass tossed a coat to Wren, and then threw the pack on the bed. While Wren put his coat on, she opened the pack and quickly scanned the contents. Wren couldn't see much, but he saw enough. It was Mama's go-bag. Back before they'd left RushRuin, really left, for pretty much as long as he could remember, she'd kept a bag packed. *Just in case*, she'd always say. He'd always thought it was for an emergency. Until the day they made a run for it. It was then he realized that back then, it hadn't been for an emergency, it'd been for an opportunity. Maybe old habits were just hard to break.

Cass looked down at her blood-smeared shirt. With a grimace, she ripped it off over her head, wadded it into a ball, and threw it in the corner. Her compression top didn't cover very much, and Wren could see two spiraling welts on her belly, one just above her left hip, and one on her upper chest, just above her heart. They were an angry red in the center, surrounded by spidery arms of bruising. Painter made a little sound, and when Wren looked at him, his face was all red and he was looking at the floor. Cass grabbed another shirt and threw it on, and then snatched a coat out of the closet.

A thought occurred to Wren. "Wait, there is something," he said. "In my room."

"You *need* it? Absolutely *need*?" She was already closing the bag back up.

Wren nodded.

"Alright, let's get it."

She crossed the room, slinging on her pack as she moved, and stood next to the door, hand on the handle. "Painter," she said. Painter was still just standing there in the bathroom door. He was just staring at the floor. "Painter, let's go."

His head snapped up and he looked at her, but it was like he hadn't heard her. "I didn't... mmmmean to, Cass."

"It's done, Painter. We need to move. Listen," she said, and then again sharply, "Listen!" His eyes focused, like he was finally really hearing her. "Wren and I are going across to his room. We'll come back to get you in a second. If you're not ready, we're leaving without you. Do you understand?"

"Yeah."

"Do you?"

"Yes, mmma'am, I'll buh-be ready."

"Wren, with me."

Wren moved to her side, and Cass placed a hand on his shoulder. Not for comfort, though. She gripped him firmly as she cracked open the door, ready to move him whatever direction might be necessary, depending on what she saw outside. After a couple of seconds scanning, Cass opened the door further and pushed Wren through, following close on his heels. He made a direct line across the hall, not even daring to look to either side. The door to his room was locked, but in the few steps it took to cross to it, he took care of it.

They slipped into his room in a smooth motion. Cass remained by the partially opened door, keeping watch. Neither of them turned on a light; Wren's little blue night light still glowed by the foot of his bed.

"Be quick," she said.

Wren went straight to the table across from his bed and slid open the drawer. It was there, where he always kept it, partially hidden under some clutter. His knife. The one Three had made for him. Mama had kept Three's pistol, kept it packed away in her room – but it was this knife that reminded Wren the most of the man. He took it out, rolled it over in his hand. Felt the weight, the balance, ran his thumb along the cool, simple lines. The blade was supremely economical. Efficient. Like everything Three had been pressed down into something Wren could hold. It hurt him to remember, but the pain was welcome, familiar. Simple, and real. Somehow things had become so complicated.

"OK, Mama," he said, returning to her side. "I'm ready now."

She nodded, and just as quickly as they'd come, they crossed the hall back to her room. Wren risked looking around that time, and just as they were passing through the doorway, his heart nearly stopped with dread. For a split second, he thought he saw a shadow at the end of the hall. Back in his mama's room, he gripped his knife a little tighter.

"Painter, let's go."

Painter appeared from the bathroom, mostly clean now, and looking much more in control. He just nodded and formed up next to them.

"Stay close to me," Cass said. "And quiet."

Wren held his breath while she eased the door open

again. But whatever he'd seen mustn't have been there now, because Mama slipped out into the hallway and pulled him along behind her. He was thankful that they were headed the opposite direction from the shadow. Wren was afraid to look back behind them, but he was more afraid not to, so he risked a peek. Nothing was following.

Cass led them around a corner and down a set of stairs to a lower level.

"What about the cuh-cuh-curfew?" Painter whispered.

"It's alright," Wren said. "They won't stop us."

"No, Painter's right," Cass answered. "We can't let anyone see us. If Connor was in on it, there's no telling which of the guard might be on his side. And we don't want anyone to know where we are, or where we're going, anyway. We'll have to be careful." She paused, and then added half to herself, "And maybe lucky."

They moved through a darkened hallway to a side entrance.

"Wren, door," Cass whispered. He didn't really respond, just flipped the lock. She eased it open. Checked for any guards – or anyone else, really. Then she pulled the door closed again, and turned back to them both. "We're going to move quickly, but keep your eyes open. We'll try to avoid patrols, but if we get spotted, just keep your heads down and keep moving. Stay with me, alright? Stay *right* with me."

Wren nodded, and then Painter did too. And with that, Cass pushed the door open once more, and the three of them moved out into the cool night air. For the first time, Wren felt that it was a far more dangerous thing to be trapped inside the wall than outside.

TEN

Cass kept the boys behind her at a corner, pressed against the outer wall of a darkened shop, waiting for the patrol to move further down the road. She counted three guardsmen, though from the way they were positioned, she got the feeling there were actually four of them out there. Or maybe she was truly *feeling* the fourth; those signals she was still learning to read. Yes, there. Trailing the others by a good thirty yards, holding himself to the far side of the street while they followed the center. Walking clean-up.

Cass waited until the guards had disappeared from view before she signaled the others to move forward. Wren clung close, a hand on her lower back, silently and fluidly adapting to her movement. They smoothly crossed the open stretch of ground and threaded their way through a narrow alley on the other side, turning right where it intersected in a T with another alley. At this rate, they'd make their destination in five, maybe seven more minutes. It hadn't been the most direct route by any means, but so far it'd been the right one. They stopped again at the mouth of the alley, pausing to assess. If the guard was running four-man patrols, they probably wouldn't be so close together. But now wasn't the time to risk *probably*.

Cass glanced over her shoulder at Wren. His eyes were

bright in the dim light, and focused. He still had his hand on her lower back; just enough pressure to be sure he was there, without pushing or hindering her movement. If he was feeling any fear, he was doing a masterful job of hiding it.

Painter was a different story. Cass looked up to check on him, and wasn't reassured. Ever since they'd left her room, his face had been a constant mask of utter desperation. His eyes never stopped roving, as if danger might leap out at them from every angle. It was like he'd already decided they were doomed and was just waiting for the proof. And whenever they moved, everything he did seemed loud to her. His footsteps, the rustle of his clothing, his breathing. Loud.

Whenever they stopped, Painter had a distracting way of clutching at Wren and at her. Completely different from Wren's touch. Wren's hand on her was a method of communication, a sign that he was with her, really *with* her, moving, stopping, and moving again as one. Painter, on the other hand, clawed at them like they were a raft for a drowning man. As if he was afraid they might push out into the darkness and leave him drifting behind.

Wren patted her lower back twice, quickly, and she returned her attention to the street ahead. It looked clear. But as Cass started to move forward, she felt Wren's hand clench, enough change to make her hold position. She scanned the street again, slower this time, looking for any sign of anyone, guard, citizen, or otherwise. But came up empty. She turned slowly back to look at Wren and when she did, he pointed. Across the street. And up.

Cass followed the line from his finger. Across the street. Up. The building directly across from them was three stories high. The windows were all dark, but there was a sign glowing orange along the top. Cass squinted against the glare, raised a hand to shield her eyes from the buzzing light. Nothing. And then. There. The scantest silhouette, black against a midnight blue sky. Shoulders, head, little more, with just a trace of soft halo where she detected his electromagnetic aura. How Wren had seen him, she had no idea, but for now it was enough that he had. She turned back to Wren and Painter, hunched low.

"Back," Cass whispered, barely louder than an exhalation. "We'll have to cut around the other side."

Wren nodded. Painter just looked scared. Cass noticed he had a hand on Wren's shoulder, and Wren's coat was all bunched up in his fist. She tried not to be annoyed. And for a split second she wondered if this was how Three felt about her the first time he took her into the open. Not now. She shoved Three from her thoughts and retraced her steps back down the alley.

But as they approached the point where the two alleys intersected, a chill gripped Cass and she stopped dead. Strained with all her senses. There was someone else in the alley.

She pressed back against the wall, and with her arm swept the other two against it as well. For a moment, there was nothing. But then, a soft sound from around the corner. An inhalation. And then without warning, a white light splashed on the wall across from them, illuminating them all in its glow.

"Someone down there?" the Someone Else called. A younger male, or a gruffer female. Trying to sound authoritative. There was uncertainty, but not fear. Cass felt Wren press in closer, and someone clutched her sleeve. Footsteps, now: slow and cautious, approaching. "Hello?"

Cass's mind raced through the options. Backing up again was out. The guy on the roof had that end covered. They could wait, hope whoever it was would just turn around. That seemed unlikely. She could announce herself. There was a good chance that a guard wouldn't try to do anything other than report her position. But they were close enough to their destination that if the guard called it in, it wouldn't take long for any other Council members to put the pieces together. If any other Council members were even in on it. Too many unknowns.

"I know you're back there, so come on out. Easy."

The footsteps were getting closer, and Cass heard the distinctive click and hum of a coilgun powering up. No way for one of those to be used for nonlethal means. Apparently they weren't taking any chances with the curfew.

She might have to just ambush the guard, avoid the weapon, go for the quick knockout. Cass was fast enough. But there was always the chance for that to go wrong and get noisy. And there was always the chance that this guard was on the right side of things, anyway. That was the trouble with betrayal... even the innocent became suspect.

None of them seemed like good options, but they were running out of time. She'd announce herself, and hope the guard didn't come looking far enough to see the others. That might leave some chance of a cover story, if they needed one.

"OK, OK," Painter called to the guard. "I'm guh-guh-gonna step out."

He'd cracked under the pressure. Cass whipped around to look at him. He still looked petrified, but he had a hand up. Wait. What was he up to?

"I'm ssss-sorry, I'm cuh-cuh-cuh... I'm coming out. But don't freak out, I'm A-a-awakened."

"Come out here real slow, with your hands up where I can see 'em!" the guard called.

Painter nodded to Cass and patted Wren on the shoulder gently, and then stretched his hands out and eased towards the corner. He showed his hands first, and then followed them out very slowly.

"Get down on your knees," the guard said, the light still blazing like a miniature sun with Painter's shadow stark in its middle.

"Yeah, sssss-sure," Painter said. But he didn't. He made a risky move and advanced a few steps down the alley, towards the guard – and away from Cass and Wren.

"Hold it, hold it!" the guard said, raising her voice. Not shouting, but heading that way. Cass was sure that coilgun was going to sing any second. "I said get on your knees!"

"Yeah, yeah, look, please, d-d-don't take me in," Painter said. Cass couldn't see him anymore, but judging from the shadow and the sounds, he was getting down on the ground. "Please, listen–"

"You're in violation of a hard curfew, as ordered by the governor–"

"I nuh-nuh, I know, please, ma'am," Painter pleaded. Female guard then. "Let me explain."

It was a dangerous game. The guard hadn't called for backup yet, but that was always a possibility. Maybe even a likelihood. With the noise they were making, calling for it might not even be necessary.

She said, "Talking won't matter, kid, I've got orders."

"Please, I'll luh-luh, I'll lose my job, ma'am, please."

"You should've thought of that before you violated the curfew. Lie flat, face down, hands stretched out above your head."

"I didn't mmm-mmean to, I lost tr-track of tuh-tuh-tuh, of time."

"It's not my problem, kid."

"Please, there's this guh-guh, there's a girl," Painter said. There was a pause after that.

"A girl?" the guard said. Her voice had lost the slightest bit of its edge.

"Yes, mmm-ma'am."

"She with you now?" the guard asked.

"No, ma'am, I was on my way b-b-back from her place. I'm sss-sorry."

Another pause.

"You're that one from Mister Sun's place, ain't ya?" She said *that one* with just a hint of emphasis. "Hunter or something."

"Yes, ma'am. Painter."

She replied, "Painter, that's right. And this girl. She worth getting shot over, Painter?"

Painter was quiet for a second. "Yes, ma'am."

"What about getting jumped and strung up by a bunch of thugs?"

"I rrrrr-, I reckon she's wuh-wuh-worth just about any kind of hell Mmmmorningside's got, ma'am."

The guard chuckled at that. "Just about, huh?" she said, with a hint of amusement.

"Just about. May-may-may… maybe not losing my job."

Cass heard the click of the coilgun, and it quit humming.

"Alright, kid. You got me. I might be just enough of a romantic to let you off once. *Once*, you understand?"

"Yes, ma'am."

"I'm gonna swing by Mister Sun's in ten minutes. If you aren't there, I'm gonna bring my boys down on you."

"Yes, ma'am."

"Get outta here."

There was scuffling in the alleyway as Painter got back to his feet. "Th-th-thank you."

"Don't thank me for something that never happened, kid. Get."

"Yes, mmma'am."

Painter's shadow gradually shrank on the wall and then he was in the intersection. Cass held her breath. But he did the right thing, and turned the opposite direction without the slightest hitch or glance their way. A few moments later the light switched off, and she could hear the guard muttering something to herself. Footsteps receded down the alley, and the unusual silence of Morningside returned. Cass felt Wren relax behind her, but still she waited a full minute before crossing the intersection, just to be sure.

Together she and Wren edged their way to the street, slow and steady. Cass surveyed the area. All clear. She checked with Wren anyway. He gave a quick nod, and they skittered down the street, keeping close to the buildings along the side, slipping into the shadows whenever they could.

Painter was nowhere in sight. Cass had intended to make one more loop before approaching their destination, both to scout the path and to make doubly sure they weren't followed. But after the close call it seemed like any extra time they spent on the street was the greater risk. They reached a storefront alcove, and Cass pulled Wren into its shadows and knelt in front of him, so close their noses nearly touched.

"We're going to make for the door," she whispered. "We're not going to run, but we're going to go straight there and in. If anyone tries to stop us, you hear someone shout or anything, just ignore it. Don't stop, don't look at them, just head straight inside, OK?"

Wren nodded, serious and focused.

"I just hope Painter got there first," Cass added as she stood. One more check, up and down the street. Deep breath. And they moved out. She drew Wren alongside her, held his hand, walked briskly. They crossed the street, more concerned now about speed than discretion. Thirty yards, and a left turn. Still clear. Just another fifty yards. Forty. Thirty. Twenty. The stairs were there on the left, the door closed, its windows darkened. Mister Sun's Tea House. Surely Painter had gotten here ahead of them and prepared the way.

They made it to the stairs, but as they were climbing them there was a flutter in Cass's peripheral vision. Someone coming around the corner at the far end of the street maybe. She didn't look, focusing instead on the door. It was inset slightly, providing a little cover. They gained the top of the stairs. Normally the motion sensor would've triggered the door by now. Cass pressed into the door, pulling Wren hard against her. Painter should've been here – the door should've been unlocked.

There were footsteps coming down the street, faster than a regular patrol would've been going. Cass drew Wren in front of her, squeezing him into the corner between the door and its housing, shielding him with her body. Hopefully whoever it was would just walk right on by without noticing them. Unless of course the whoever it was had already noticed them.

The footsteps grew louder, closer. Cass fought the urge to look over her shoulder, fearful that the motion or the glow from her eyes might give them away. But in the end she had no choice. The person was coming up the stairs.

Cass readied herself as she slowly turned her head to identify the approaching figure. "Painter."

Painter was looking down the street when she said his name, and he gasped and skidded backwards down two steps when she spoke, apparently never having seen them at all. He recovered and quickly made his way to the door.

"I th-th-think my heart stopped," he said. "Like, really st-stopped for a ssssecond." He held his palm up in front of a security panel, and the door *snicked* and started sliding smoothly open. Before it was even fully open, Cass pushed

Wren inside and followed right on his heels into the dark main room of Mister Sun's Tea House.

Not that the room was dark to Cass's eyes. She could see plainly the various tables arrayed around the room, with the chairs flipped upside down on top as they were when Mister Sun's was closed. Everything looked like it was bathed in the light of a strong full moon, though she knew that wasn't how it appeared to Wren. The fountain-stream burbled softly in the otherwise silent room.

"What took you so long?" she asked.

"I th-thought you were g-g-going around," Painter said as he secured the door. "I waited."

Cass couldn't fault him for that. She'd changed plans on the assumption that he'd head straight to the building, an assumption she'd made without even realizing it. Luckily it hadn't cost them anything more than a few tense seconds. She was just about to respond, to tell Painter he'd done the right thing, or to thank him, when the lights came on.

She hadn't heard anyone approach, and no one had said anything, but nevertheless there was Mister Sun, standing off to one side of the room, casually leaning against the doorframe of a private room. There was a stimstick between his lips, dangling at a forty-five degree angle like it might drop out of his mouth at any moment. His palsied left hand was curled up and resting on his belly, but Cass noticed he was holding his right arm close along his body and slightly behind his leg, hiding his other hand from view.

"Busy night, my friends?" he said. There was something heavy to his voice; a darker quality, and deeper. Not quite threatening, but Cass felt certain that Mister Sun wasn't just the easygoing, happy-go-lucky tea merchant he usually seemed to be.

"Mister Sun," Painter said. "It's me, Painter."

The old man squinted slightly and recognition came. He stood up from the doorframe, and his demeanor instantly changed.

"Governor Wren, Lady Cass," he said, taking a few steps towards them. "Come in, come in." He motioned for them to come in out of the entryway. "What brings you to Mister Sun's at so late an hour?"

Cass had chosen to come to Mister Sun's not because she trusted him, necessarily, but rather because she knew his was a place they could lie low – while they tried to figure out what was going on, and what they had to do next. As long as they weren't followed, it was unlikely anyone would think to look for them there. And he certainly didn't seem like the type that anyone would involve in secret plots. But she hadn't really had a chance to think through just how much she could tell him.

"Mister Sun," she said. "We need your help."

"Of course, anything. What is the trouble?"

"We're not sure," Cass answered. "But I don't think the compound's safe for us right now."

Mister Sun moved to a table near the back corner of the main room and directed the others to join him. As they approached, Cass saw him lay something across the table; the device he'd been concealing behind himself when they entered. It was a three-barreled weapon, a little over a foot in length and not particularly elegant. She didn't recognize it exactly, but it didn't take much to imagine the kind of damage it could deliver. Probably meant for crowd control. She'd never seen Mister Sun brandish a weapon before, but judging from the practiced familiarity he showed with it, she knew it was far from his first time.

Mister Sun started pulling chairs off the table, and Painter joined in.

"Breach in security?" Mister Sun asked. He flipped the last chair over and directed the others to sit.

"Not exactly," Cass replied.

He slid the weapon back off the table, carefully keeping it pointed in a safe direction without even seeming to think about it, and held it at his side while he gazed at her. Cass held steady, not wanting to say any more than she absolutely had to. After a moment, he seemed to understand all he needed to.

"My house is yours, Lady. I'll bring tea." Mister Sun bowed slightly and turned towards the back room, and then paused and turned back. "Or perhaps something stronger?"

"I could use ssss-something… fuh-fuh-ffff," Painter said, struggling mightily. "For my nnnerves."

Mister Sun nodded and then disappeared into the back room. A moment later a few smaller lights around the table blinked softly on, and the overheads switched off. It left their immediate area lit with dim warmth, while the rest of the room returned to darkness. Cass's first reaction was to scan the room again to see if someone else had come in, but then realized Mister Sun must've adjusted the lighting from the back room. Smart. From the street, the tea house would likely look all dark again and avoid attracting any unwanted attention at this hour. It also had a settling effect that seemed to put them all more at ease.

Cass surveyed the boys, Wren on her left, Painter on her right. Painter had his elbows on the table, face in his hands, massaging his temples. She got the sense that his entire world was coming apart and that he was doing everything he could just to keep it together right now. Wren was sitting forward in his chair, hands in his lap, eyes fixed on her. Calm, but serious. *What do we do now, Mama?* She had no idea.

Mister Sun reappeared with a tray that held a stainless-steel pot, an oddly shaped bottle, and three of his trademark handleless mugs. Ever the master servant, he laid everything out with a quiet efficiency that somehow seemed to leave their privacy completely intact.

"Thanks, Mister Sun," Wren said in a quiet voice.

He bowed slightly, and then indicated the pot and the bottle. "Both are special blends, and both should calm. I'll leave you to decide. But I think perhaps Master Wren should drink only from the pot."

"Thank you," Cass added. "Thanks for helping us."

Mister Sun inclined his head in acknowledgment.

"Aren't you going to join us?" Wren asked. Cass grimaced. She hadn't really noticed that there were only three mugs until Wren mentioned it. Now she wished she'd taken the opportunity while Mister Sun was away to tell the others not to involve him any more than they already had.

Fortunately, Mister Sun shook his head graciously. "I have no wish to impose, Master Wren."

Just then, three dull impacts sounded on the front door, startling everyone. For a moment, they were all frozen. Cass's mind raced. Had someone seen them enter the tea house after all?

Mister Sun motioned to Cass and Wren, put a finger to his lips, and then pointed towards the back room. Cass nodded and helped Wren out of his chair, grabbed her pack off the floor, and then together they slipped silently out of the main room. Cass pushed Wren ahead of her, but kept next to the door herself. Pressed against the wall, she slid low and peeked out. Mister Sun was saying something to Painter, who was still seated at the table, but it was too quiet for her to hear. Painter nodded, and Mister Sun started making his way towards the front door. Cass noticed he had his gun in hand again, carefully hidden behind his back.

Boom boom boom – three more heavy blows on the door.

"I'm coming, I'm coming," Mister Sun called. Just as he was reaching the entrance, Painter quickly grabbed one of the mugs from off the table and put it on the floor next to his chair. The door slid partially open. From that distance, Cass couldn't see who was there.

"Yes, my friend?" Mister Sun said.

"I'm sorry to bother you at this hour, Mister Sun," said the voice on the other side of the door. It was a man, but that was about all Cass could tell. "But we're looking for someone."

"And someone you've found. Well done."

"Is there anyone else here with you tonight, sir?"

Cass immediately started thinking through the options. There was a back entrance that led out to the alley behind the tea house, but surely they'd be covering that. She knew there were rooms upstairs, but she'd never been up there. No way to know what their escape options would be from that direction. Most likely, nothing subtle.

"Yes," Mister Sun answered.

"Could you identify them for us?"

"I'm always at your service, my friend."

There was a long pause, until it was clear that was all Mister Sun intended to say. "Who else is in there, Mister Sun?" the voice asked, sounding irritated.

"My associate Mister Painter and I were just enjoying a drink together."

"I'd like to verify that, if you don't mind."

Mister Sun stepped back from the door, but didn't open it further. Cass ducked back behind the wall. A chair scraped the floor in the main room. Painter standing, maybe.

And then...

"Alright, just had to make sure. We had a request come down the chain to check in on him. Sorry for the interruption."

"Glad to be of service, my friend. Good night. Stay safe."

"You too, Mister Sun. Night."

Cass heard the door slide shut again, but didn't move until Mister Sun poked his head into the back room.

"Strange," he said. "It was the guard."

"Because of befff-fore," Painter said from the other room. "The one in th... the alley. Said she'd come by. I f-f-forgot."

"Right. It's alright, Painter." Cass chided herself for having forgotten it too. It wasn't exactly a minor detail. "Thanks yet again, Mister Sun."

They returned to the main room and took their seats again. Painter retrieved his mug from the floor and promptly filled it almost to the brim with the cloudy milky-white liquid from the bottle. Cass poured tea from the pot into both her and Wren's mugs.

"If you have all you need," Mister Sun said, "I will retire to my room."

"Actually, Mister Sun," Cass replied, "why don't you pull up a chair?"

Painter was starting to feel quite a bit more relaxed and just a little pleasantly warm. It'd been, what, an hour, an hour and a half maybe? Whatever it was, they'd spent about two and a half mug's worth, anyway, bringing Mister Sun up to speed and discussing their options. Or rather, Cass and Wren had done so. Painter had mostly been drinking and listening. Talking wasn't really his thing, and he wasn't sure he had much to offer anyway. Everything still seemed so surreal and horrible. He didn't even want to think about it. But there really wasn't anything else he *could* think about. He truly hadn't meant to kill those men. It'd just been so easy. So terribly, terribly easy.

"I don't know what else to do," Cass said. Painter realized he'd tuned out and had no idea how much of the conversation he'd missed.

"What about Able?" Wren asked. Cass shook her head and bit her lower lip. There was something really attractive about the way she did that. It wasn't the first time Painter had noticed it, but it seemed like maybe it was the first time he had noticed that he'd noticed. Or maybe he'd had more to drink than he'd thought. Or maybe both.

"Too risky," she said. "If they really do have a trace on, we don't know who else might be running it. Unless you think you could slip it?"

Wren considered it, but then shook his head. "I don't think so, Mama. I don't know what to look for. And what if looking for it is the thing that sets it off?"

Cass sipped her tea and shook her head slightly. "And there's no telling what their backup plan is if that alarm gets raised."

"It might be raised already," Mister Sun said. He seemed more serious than usual. And he wasn't calling them all *my friend*, which somehow seemed odd. "They might already be looking for you."

"True," Cass said. "I really don't see any other way. I'll just have to risk it."

"Mama, I don't want you to go," Wren said. He looked really tired. And with good reason. It was after midnight.

"I know, baby, but I don't think we have any other options. Once I get outside the wall, I should be able to find at least one of them pretty quickly. If not Able, maybe Swoop or Gamble."

"I'll do it," Painter said. It seemed to catch everyone off guard, even himself a little bit. Maybe it was because he hadn't said anything in a while. Or maybe they weren't sure if he was serious. So he said it again. "I'll do it."

"Thank you, Painter," Cass said, and she sounded like she really meant it. "But I can't let you go back out there."

"You don't have to l-l-l-*let* me," Painter said. "I don't think I need your permmm-mission."

"I didn't mean it like that. It's just... it's really dangerous out there. With the curfew, and people on edge already. Never know when a jumpy guard might just start shooting. And if someone catches me out there, they won't try to arrest me."

"They might, Mama."

Cass glanced at Wren and for a moment seemed to be considering what he'd said. But she shook her head again. "I can't ask that of you, Painter. You've already done so much."

"You didn't ask," Painter said. For some reason the more he heard her tell him why he couldn't, the more he wanted to prove Cass wrong. Maybe she thought Painter couldn't because he'd been so scared on their way here. Or maybe his stutter made her think he was incapable. But he'd bailed them out in the alley with nothing but words. *Words*. His weakness. Imagine what he could do with his *strength*. Actually he didn't have to imagine it. He'd already shown that too, without even meaning to.

"I'll go, I w-w-want to," Painter said. It wasn't a discussion anymore. "What sh-sh-shhh, what should I say?"

They all stared at him for a moment. Cass seemed to still be trying to figure out how to dissuade him. Wren piped up.

"I think you should find Finn," Wren said. "If they really do have a trace, he'd know what to do about it."

"OK," Painter said, standing. He felt slightly light-headed and not even a little scared. Looking back on it, he wasn't sure why he'd been so afraid on the way over. Rattled from everything that had happened maybe. He felt calmer now, more sure of himself. Purposeful. It'd been a long time since he'd felt that.

"How will you get outside?" Cass asked. A hitch. Painter hadn't even thought about that.

"Climb down?" he offered. But even standing here feeling brave, he knew that wasn't really an option. The gates would be locked up tight, so those were out.

"He could use the tunnel," Wren said, and his mother looked at him sharply – as if he'd just blurted out a shameful family secret. He held her gaze, shrugged slightly.

"What t-t, what tunnel?"

Cass continued to look at Wren, but Painter could see now that she wasn't upset. She was thinking it through. Finally she said, "There's a tunnel, by the compound. It runs under the wall."

"It's secret," Wren added.

"Back to the… compound?" Painter asked. He lowered himself back into his chair. Sneaking from Mister Sun's to the wall didn't seem like such a stretch, but going all the way back to the governor's compound was a different story. Not to mention getting back *inside*.

"Yeah," Cass said. "It's alright, Painter. We'll figure something else out."

Painter felt deflated. In theory it had been a challenge, almost an adventure. But now all of the realities started flooding into his mind, all of the tedious particulars of what it would entail. Travel back to the governor's compound. Get back inside. Find the secret tunnel. And then what? Even if he didn't get caught on the streets, how was he even supposed to find any of those people outside the wall? And what would they do when they saw Painter skulking around looking for them? Shoot him dead before he ever even saw them, most likely.

Who was he kidding? He was just a kid, a useless dishwasher who'd had too much to drink. But then something else started to bubble up in his mind. Thoughts of the thugs that had beaten him up nights ago. And thoughts of what people like them had done to his friend, Luck. And thoughts of his sister.

And where alcohol-induced bravery had burned away, anger filled the void. These people had taken nearly all he had. No way Painter was going to sit around while they took the rest. He stood up again.

"How do I find the tunnel?" he asked.

There was silence for a moment. And then Cass laid it all out for him; where the entrance was, how to access it, where it led, and how to find his way back again. And as they talked it through, other hasty plans came together. It began to seem possible again. And by the end, it almost seemed inevitable.

They escorted him to the door, everyone giving him final words of caution, and thanks, and encouragement. Then Mister Sun was opening the door just wide enough for Painter to slip out, and the night air was cold – and full of a crackling energy that almost felt alive. The door slid shut behind him, and he drew a deep breath.

To think. Him. Painter. A messenger. He almost laughed as he stepped out into the street.

ELEVEN

For Painter, the first few minutes had been a strange mix of fear and giddiness. The fear had begun to melt away after he'd successfully crossed the first of the major streets in his path. The giddiness wore off soon after. And now, as he crouched in shadow a hundred and fifty yards from the compound, he found himself falling into something like quiet determination. It was almost shocking how familiar it was beginning to feel. Stealing through the night, probing for anyone who might cross his path. He'd done it so frequently before. *Before.* Only now he was avoiding them instead of hunting them.

A patrol moved down the street, just two guardsmen, and neither of them paying much attention. Painter watched them from his hiding place, his eyes lowered slightly to reduce their glow. The guards seemed soft, somehow. Sloppy. How had he ever feared them? How could they possibly be the ones charged with protecting their city? With protecting Wren? And Cass?

He had been afraid before, truly afraid, when they'd made their way to Mister Sun's. Borderline panicked. Fearing the consequences of his actions. Not knowing what would happen if they were caught, nor if they escaped. How long would Cass let him stay with them after what he had done? And he'd feared for them as well. For Cass, and for Wren. Painter had feared making another mistake, something that would give them away, that would cause harm to those two and leave him with nothing.

But now, here, on his own, it almost felt like this was what he was made for. His altered eyes could see in the dark, and he could sense the digital pulse of the unaltered. Now that he had calmed himself, it felt right. It felt good. Fear was still there, lingering around the edges, but at his center anger remained, cold and righteous. And as long as he held to that, he knew the fear had no place to enter in.

The patrol moved on out of sight, and Painter slipped from the shadows across a small thoroughfare and into another alley. He paused there, in a nook where the corner of the building protruded in an architectural flourish. Morningside was eerie in its stillness, and out from beyond the wall, he could hear the occasional calls of the Weir, cold and electric. Calls that had once filled him with utter terror. But those sounds had lost that power over him now and free from fear he could hear a melancholy, almost musical quality behind them. Painter couldn't help but wonder what might happen once he was outside the wall. He hadn't left Morningside at all, even during the day, since Wren had brought him back. Could he walk among the Weir now? Would they attack Painter, or ignore him? Or maybe even accept him?

For just a moment, he felt the slightest pang of regret. For all the horror, the loss of self – the black harvest – amongst the Weir there had been in some strange way a sense of belonging that Painter hadn't known before and was unlikely to ever know again. An involuntary shiver brought him back to the moment. No. No, there was nothing good or right about what he had been. But maybe now he could find a way to bring good out of what he had become.

Painter eased around the corner of the building and threaded his way amongst the structures that led towards the governor's compound. Random patrols were bound to be fewer, this close to a secure location, but that also meant an increase in stationed guards. He'd have to keep his eyes open and his wits about him. *His eyes.* He held a hand up in front of his face, and judged the moonshine glow cast upon it. He'd been careful to avoid looking directly at patrols. But it was going to be far more difficult to keep his gaze averted when Painter had to scan the walls to locate the guardsmen posted there. And all but the laziest would surely notice the telltale shine gleaming from out of the darkness. Maybe he'd have it figured out by the time he got there. Most likely, he was just going to have to get lucky.

The final fifty yards posed no difficulty, and Painter felt he covered them far more quickly than he'd expected. Undoubtedly it was because he'd been counting on that time to grant him some revelation on how to gain entry. Naturally, there hadn't been one. The compound stood twenty-five yards away across an open stretch of ground, well-lit and offering few places to find cover.

Cass had said the north-eastern gate was his best bet, since it hadn't been used for months, but that didn't guarantee it'd go unwatched. On the contrary, since one or more of Morningside's disgruntled citizens had trashed the memorial a night or two ago, there was good reason to think there might be an extra guardsman or two stationed nearby. Painter circled around that direction anyway, swinging wide to avoid street lights where he could, and occasionally putting a building between him and the compound whenever he thought he might be too exposed. When the north-eastern gate was finally in view, Painter crouched low and cupped his hands around his eyes to shield their glow as much as possible.

On top of the wall he could see a faint electromagnetic swirl that indicated a guardsman that he couldn't quite make out otherwise. Though he wasn't *seeing* it, exactly. It was another sense that detected the guard's residual signal, processed it into something Painter could interpret, and though seeing wasn't quite right, he always felt like it had more to do with his eyes than anything else.

This was the testing point. The moment that would decide whether he would succeed or fail. Playing hide and seek with the patrols had been one thing. Walking out into the open during the night would present a similar challenge. But infiltrating the compound was something else entirely. Something he'd never done before in either of his lives.

He sat back on his haunches and tried to think it through. Somehow back at Mister Sun's they'd skimmed over this part. *Once you're inside...* almost taken it for granted. Painter had never been much of one to call the shots. That'd always been more of Snow's thing.

Snow. Little sister, always in charge, always in control. She'd been the clever one, and confident. He smiled with bitterness at the memories. At first it'd just been easier to go along with her because she was such a bully. He pictured her as the chubby four year-old, full of fire – fearless and fearsome. Remembered the bruises on his own thin arms and shins. But Snow had changed after Dad had died. Still fearless and in charge, but tempered. Wiser, maybe, or at least less concerned about just getting what *she* wanted, doing it *her* way. But then doing it her way had gone from the easy thing to the right thing. At least most of the time. What would she have told him now?

You can't do it, her voice said in his head. And Snow would've been right. The old Painter could never have done it. But that wasn't him anymore. He was stronger now, faster. Surely there was *something* he could do.

You can't do it alone, her voice came again – correcting his initial thought as if he'd interrupted her before she'd finished. That's what she would've told Painter. It was a fault, Snow said, how much he took upon himself, how little he trusted others. And the beginning of a plan formed in his mind.

"Wren," he pimmed, whispering into the night air and speaking to his friend a half-mile away.

"Painter, are you OK?" came the reply a few moments later, Wren's voice somewhere inside Painter's own head.

"At the c-c-compound," Painter answered. "Do you know a wuh, a way to get the guards to… to… to broadcast?"

"Hmm… no, I don't think so. Sorry," he said. And then, "Hold on, let me ask my mom."

There was a long delay before the response came. Painter's calves were starting to burn. A pair of guardsmen wandered into view, and he shifted back.

"She thinks she can try something. Do you want her to do it now?" Wren said.

"Wait one sss-second."

The patrol moved counter-clockwise around the governor's compound, and didn't seem to be in a hurry about it. Judging from the looks of things, Painter guessed no one had found the bodies yet. The guards moved on out of sight.

"OK, go," Painter said.

Seconds ticked by. Ten. Fifteen. Thirty. Painter was just about to pim again when all of a sudden there was a shimmering flare on the wall, like mirage roiling off hot concrete. And then another. And another. One after the other, the guardsmen were responding to whatever Cass had done, actively broadcasting information through the digital and lighting up in Painter's vision with each burst.

"OK, is anything happening?" Wren asked.

"Yes," Painter answered. "Thhh-thanks. I see them now. Gotta go."

"OK. Be careful."

There were eight that Painter could see – four along the top of the wall, two by the gate, and another two somewhere deeper in the courtyard. It surprised him to see guards actually posted at the north-eastern gate, but it looked like they weren't taking any chances. There was a gap, though, along the wall. Two guards stood close together, apparently in conversation, and that left them spaced unevenly. His opening.

Painter surveyed the street once more, saw it was clear. He sidled his way along the edge, towards the darkest corridor he could find, where two lights overlapped incompletely. The first ten yards would be the greatest danger. But the closer he got to the wall, the less chance there was that someone would be able to see him from above. Assuming they didn't see Painter start his run. There were no guarantees, and sitting around any longer wasn't going to improve his chances at all. It was tough to judge, but as best as he could tell, none of the guardsmen were looking his way. Time to try. He inhaled sharply and launched himself out of his hiding place.

Ducking his head and leaning forward, Painter sprinted directly towards the wall of the compound, running lightly on the balls of his feet to minimize the noise. Panic rose up the instant he stepped into the light, but he gritted his teeth and pressed on. Five yards in. Seven. Ten. He passed from the brightest segment into partial shadow, chances of success improving with every step. And then he was at the base of the wall, pressed flat against it, heart pounding more from the fear of getting caught than from any exertion. Seconds stretched. But no sounds of warning came to him. He'd made it.

Now, the fun part. Painter had never tried any extended climbing before and he hadn't known what to expect. He was relieved to find that the wall wasn't nearly as smooth as he'd originally thought. It was composed of steel panels joined together and there were slight gaps between the plates, barely wide enough for Painter to jam his fingertips into. That alone wouldn't have been enough for any normal human. But Painter was no normal human. He extended his claws. And began to climb.

After a few test holds, he found that by angling his claws downwards into the seams he was able to hook in a relatively strong grip. It was his feet that caused him trouble. Cramming the toe of his shoe into a gap gave some help with balance, but was hardly enough to provide any push. His arms would have to do the work. He wrestled his way up four feet off the ground when his first slip came.

It happened so fast that he didn't have any time to try to catch himself. Painter just fell straight down. His body reacted instinctively, legs bending to absorb the shock of impact. He landed lightly, thankfully, and after a few stunned seconds of frantic listening, it appeared that he'd managed to escape detection. Climbing seemed like an even worse idea now than it had just a minute ago, and it'd hadn't seemed like such a great idea then anyway. But Painter couldn't think of anything else to do, and the residual signal was starting to fade on the guardsmen. There wasn't time to try something else.

On a whim, he pulled his shoes off, buckled them together, and jammed them down the back of his pants. It wasn't comfortable by any means, but when he started climbing again he was glad to notice he had a much better feel for the wall without his shoes on.

Painter took it slower this time, making sure both feet had some sense of stability before he tried to move a hand up. It was hard work, though, hauling himself up the wall using almost nothing but arm strength. He kept his body pressed as flat against the wall as he could, feeling his way up rather than looking. The gaps were regularly spaced and it didn't take long for Painter to get a rhythm established. Even so, every time he released one handhold to slide his way up to another, he felt at any second he could plummet right back down again.

His forearms began to burn, and it became increasingly difficult for Painter to keep his hands curled into the hooks that gave him the surest grip. By the time he was halfway up the wall, his claws almost felt like they were starting to tear away. But still he pushed himself. For Snow, and Luck, and Wren. For Cass. Hand up. Pull. Reach. Set feet. Hand up. Again and again and again. And then he slid his right hand up, looking for a seam, and found instead a corner.

The top of the wall.

Whether it was from surprise at having reached the top, or a sense of relief come too soon, Painter lost concentration for a crucial moment – and in turn lost his already precarious footing. He slipped sideways, dangling from one hand, and spun around backwards, wrenching his shoulder and elbow. For a sickening second, he felt his fingers sliding along the top of the wall. Losing grip. He was falling.

No.

Something broke deep inside him, and the glowing ember of anger he had been nurturing kindled into a rage. And with rage came strength. Without knowing how, Painter found himself flipped back around, facing the wall again. He simply refused to fall. He reached, stretched, willed himself up high enough to get hold of the ledge. Then he scrambled up, rolled over the parapet, and flopped ungracefully onto the walk.

Painter lay panting there for several seconds, adrenaline, or something like it, coursing through his veins. His arms trembled and he noticed when he tried to close his hands into fists, he couldn't do it. There was dark ichor around a couple of his fingertips where his claws had partially peeled back the nails. The buckle of one of his shoes was digging into his kidney.

And then Painter's brain caught up with him, and he realized he was inside the compound, lying on top of the wall where four guardsmen were posted. He quickly rolled to his stomach and scanned. The two guards who had been talking were separated now, and one was moving his way. But just behind Painter, a set of stairs led down to the courtyard. He slithered on his belly, moving backward, until he reached the steps, and then turned and hurried down them, crouched as low as he could go.

It was dark at the bottom of the stairs, and when he reached the courtyard, Painter doubled back and pressed himself flat against the side of the stairs. He slid along until he reached the corner where they jutted out from the wall, then tucked himself into the alcove it created. There he sat down and put his face in his hands, and tried very hard to suppress the nervous laughter that threatened to bubble out. Relief mingled with disbelief; the hardest part was over. He was going to make it.

Painter slipped his shoes back on, took a moment to gather his thoughts and focus, and then slipped out into the courtyard. Not far now. Not far to the tunnel, and from there, to the outside. The outside. At night. A smile spread itself involuntarily.

Sky was tired. Not that tired was new or different, necessarily, tired was pretty much part of the job. He was just noticing it again, the way he did when there was a momentary lull. He was lying on his belly, four stories up, keeping watch for Swoop and Mouse while they searched a cluster of buildings not far from the wall. It was a clear night, with less than half a moon, and long shadows stretched from the buildings. The optic on his rifle could be set to amplify ambient light, but for the time being Sky had left it off, preferring to keep his eyes adjusted to the natural level of light. He suppressed a yawn.

The team had been going almost nonstop since the night before, prepping for security for the Governor's big speech. And then afterwards, after the disturbance had threatened to turn into a full-blown riot, they'd sprung into action, plugging holes in the line and keeping a hard posture – to make sure anybody in the crowd that was thinking about firing that first shot knew good and clear they'd be dead before they got off a second.

Gamble and Swoop had done a masterful job of keeping the guard from breaking rank or popping off into the crowd, which was no small task. Fortunately the team's reputation was intact, if a little overblown. At least, no one seemed to be up for testing it. Once they'd regrouped in front of the gate, the steam had gone out of most of the crowd, and they'd dispersed not too long after. A couple of kids got knocked around a bit – those that got all their bravery from the mob and realized soon after that individuals could still feel pain – but luckily everybody got to go home. Situations like that were ugly, no matter what, and they didn't always turn out as well as that one had.

Still, something nagged at him about the way it had all unfolded. For all the reassurances of the Council, the disturbance hadn't felt as spontaneous as they seemed to want to believe. Sky had been up high on overwatch and though he couldn't point to any one detail as evidence, something about the big picture – the way the crowd had moved, or the number of simultaneous presentations of threat... it seemed coordinated. Orchestrated, even.

And they were out here now, instead of maintaining security for the Governor. Connor had been worried about another attack from the Weir, and most of the guard was busy enforcing the curfew. But sticking the team on the wrong side of the wall seemed like overkill. True, they'd ended up clearing one cell tonight already; three Weir had been prowling around close enough to Morningside that Gamble had decided to deal with them, just to be safe. But for the most part, the Weir were scattered and didn't seem to be making any attempts at the city. And if something flared up on the inside, it was going to be tough to respond. Orders were orders. But things weren't adding up the way they should've been.

"Sky, we're clear in here," Swoop said over the shared channel. "How's topside?"

From his elevated position, Sky scanned the tops of the buildings Swoop and Mouse were moving through. No sign of trouble.

"Looks good," he replied.

"Alright, check," Swoop said. "We're gonna push half a

klick due west, then walk it back on the curve. You wanna go check on the boys?"

Sky said, "If you guys are good."

"Yeah, we're good."

"Alright, Sky's moving. I'll be down for two minutes."

"You can stay put," Finn said, breaking in. "There's only two things going on out our way."

"Jack," said Wick.

"And squat," Finn finished.

"Keep the channel clear, gentlemen," Gamble broke in, stern, serious, always on point. "Sky, move."

"Yep, got it, Ace," Sky answered. "Sky moving."

Sky flicked his weapon to safe and got to his feet. He wasn't on the roof, exactly, but since the top half of the building he was in had disappeared some time ago, he guessed it was close enough to count. Sky was headed for the stairs when he caught a tiny motion in his peripheral vision. Down there in the street. He instinctively brought his weapon to bear and dropped to a knee, scanning with both eyes open wide to see if he could pick up what had drawn his attention.

"Stand by," Sky said. "Got some movement in the street."

"You got eyes on?" Swoop said.

"Negative."

"You need us to come out?"

"Negative."

Sky surveyed the area below, slowly sweeping from right to left, and then back again. Nothing was immediately apparent. Maybe he'd imagined it. Tired eyes playing tricks. But patience was critical to his line of work, as was meticulous attention to detail. There was something about the corner of one building that kept drawing his eye. A slight bulge, where the outer wall sagged. Only he didn't remember seeing it sagging before.

"Got eyes," he said. "South of your position, two buildings down, south-west corner."

"Can you ID?"

Sky adjusted the optic on his rifle, dialed the zoom in tighter. Even zoomed in, he couldn't tell what exactly he was looking at. Maybe he was wrong, and it really was just debris. But his gut told him otherwise. A moment later, his eyes confirmed his instincts. The lump shifted and two pin-pricks of blue light peered around the corner of the building.

"Yep, it's a Weir."

As he watched, the Weir slinked along the outer wall of the building, moving towards Swoop and Mouse. It was cautious in its movements, moving only a few feet forward before stopping again. The Weir was so still that whenever it turned its eyes away from Sky's direction, he had to keep blinking to keep it from melting into the background.

"Heading your way, real careful. Might have a read on you. You want me to take it?" Sky asked.

"How many?"

"Just one, as far as I can tell."

The Weir shifted forward again, halving the distance to Swoop's building. Sky tracked it, keeping the aimpoint steady on its center of mass. If they'd all been inside the city, safe behind the wall, it wouldn't have been such a big deal to take the shot. But it was at range, and if he didn't kill it instantly on the first shot, it was going to get loud. The team was used to running low profile, and they couldn't afford to draw any more attention than they absolutely had to. Of course, if the Weir in the street had a line on Swoop and Mouse, others might be on the way already.

"It's closing," he warned. It moved again, faster this time. Stopped again. It had to know they were in there. Sky flicked his weapon off safe but kept his finger off the trigger. For now.

"How far?"

"Twenty meters from the door."

The Weir scanned its surroundings again. It looked up, but not high enough. It didn't spot Sky. There was something unusual about this one; an uncertainty of purpose, a hesitancy in its movement. But their behavior had been growing stranger and stranger of late. Maybe this was just another malfunctioning stray.

"We're up a floor," Swoop said.

"It gets inside, I won't be able to track it."

The Weir slipped forward again, and paused at the corner of the building. Even as Sky calculated the distance and the wind, something prickled in a corner of his mind. Was this one of the Weir he'd seen the night of their attack on the gate?

"Three meters," Sky said. "I'm gonna lose it."

"Alright, take it," Swoop said. "Don't miss."

"Yep." Sky moved his finger to the trigger, drew in the slack on it so the slightest bit of additional pressure would fire. Just under four hundred meters. Easy. He inhaled smoothly. Exhaled. Held. Waited for the moment between heartbeats.

"Hold that," Gamble said. "I'm almost to your position."

Sky allowed himself a breath, let the slack back out of the trigger, but kept his finger in contact and the Weir dead center in his optic. "You sure, Ace? I got the shot."

"Yeah, I got it, babe. Ten seconds."

The Weir down below moved to the door, but paused. So strange. Sky dialed in further, magnifying his target. Something about the silhouette. Familiarity out of context.

And then – like lightning from a clear sky – recognition. Gamble flashed into view almost at the same time that Sky called out, "Hold! Hold! It's the kid! It's Painter!"

The collision lifted the Weir… *Painter* – up off the ground, Gamble's momentum rocketing him skyward and depriving him of any ability to counter her attack. Not a clumsy tackle; this was a relentlessly practiced technique to ensure a sudden and definite kill. Sky's optic was zoomed in too close to track the outcome, but he didn't need to see it to know what happened. He went numb. Why hadn't he realized it sooner? And what was the kid doing outside the wall?

"You sure?" Swoop asked.

"Positive," Sky answered.

After a few moments, Gamble said, "Yeah, I confirm. It's Painter." Swoop cursed. Sky backed his optic out and found his wife, crouched on top of Painter's sprawled form.

"Is he dead?"

"Oughta be," Gamble said. "But no, he's not dead. Ain't happy either."

"What's going on?" Wick asked.

"Hold on."

"We're on the way out," Mouse said.

"Check," Gamble said. "Able, I need you on security. Sky, sit tight."

"Alright, check," Sky said. The kid had been anxious lately, agitated, and with good reason. Seemed like a real bad time to be out stretching his legs, though.

There was movement in an alley near Gamble. Sky recognized Able's fluid stride as he moved into position about five yards behind Gamble. He dropped to a knee, facing away from her, his head up and scanning for threats. A few moments later, Swoop and Mouse appeared in the building's entryway. Swoop flowed out onto the street and mirrored Able, watching the other direction, while Mouse went directly to assess Painter.

It looked like the kid was sitting up now, at least. Sky

surveyed the surrounding area from his perch, watching for any sign of danger. Several minutes passed amidst the cold night air and the occasional croak or call from a distant Weir, but nothing seemed to be heading their way

"Finn," Gamble said. "Location." Her words were clipped, direct.

"Want me to ping it?" he responded.

"Negative, comms only."

"North-west of you, six hundred meters. About fifty meters east of the wall."

"Stay put, we're coming to."

"Alrighty."

"Sky, you OK to move on your own?" she asked.

Sky chuckled. If anyone on the team was used to moving alone, it was Sky. "Yes, *Mom*," he said. She hated when he called her that, but a little dig seemed appropriate after the question she'd asked.

"Alright, rally on Finn," she answered. Her tone was flat, all business, like Gamble hadn't even noticed the *Mom*.

Sky asked, "What's going on?"

"Just move, Sky."

Something was definitely wrong. Down below, Sky saw his wife helping Painter to his feet while the other three formed a protective triangle around them. As soon as Painter was up, they started moving as a unit. Sky kept watch over them until they disappeared down a distant alley. Once they were out of sight, he slung his rifle and headed down the exposed staircase. Down one flight, he drew his sidearm. Just in case.

The whole left side of Painter's face throbbed and burned, and any time he took too deep a breath, it felt like every muscle in his back went into spasm. He was sitting on the floor, trying to track Mouse's finger by moving only his eyes. The whole team had gathered and taken shelter in a nearby one-floor building, and Mouse had insisted on giving Painter a thorough once-over. Gamble had apologized five or six times, which had been nice. But it didn't make his body hurt any less.

"Well, that sly son," Finn said, almost to himself. And then louder, "Check this out. It's a siphon. They hid it in a co-routine, off our secure channel."

"For stupid people, Finn," Sky said from the door, where he was keeping watch.

"The kid's right. They've got a trace on. Never would've noticed it if I hadn't gone looking."

"Custom job?" Wick asked.

"Nah, it's really not that sophisticated. Only clever bit was where they stuck it, which makes sense if Connor's involved. Otherwise, it just looks like an off-the-shelf solution."

"Aww," Wick said, "and I was about to start feeling special."

"Can you kill it without anyone noticing?" Gamble asked.

"Sure, easy," Finn answered. "Now that I know it's there. I can spin it off, let it run isolated."

"What about following it back?" Swoop said.

Finn went quiet, eyes staring up into the corner of the room, as though he was seeing something else entirely.

"Alright," Mouse said, patting Painter on the shoulder. "I don't think there's any permanent damage. How do you feel?"

"Like I fell out a fifth-story window," Painter said.

"She must've held back on you, then," Mouse said, winking.

"Yeah," Finn said. "Yeah, I think I could follow it back, Swoop. Only problem is whoever's on the other end might be watching. Could tip 'em off."

"Any way to tell?" Gamble said.

Finn shook his head. "Looks like it's got two listeners running. I can run 'em back, but no way to tell what might be waiting until I get there."

"C-c-connor, and Aron, I bbb-bet," Painter said.

"Not if they're dead," Finn said.

"So, could've been as many as four, then," Gamble said.

"Yeah, I guess so," said Finn.

"Kill it."

"You got it."

Gamble approached Painter, and knelt in front of him. "How you feeling, Painter?"

"Still brrr, still breathing."

"We need to get back to Cass and Wren, and we need to do it quickly. If you don't think you can make it, I can leave a couple of the boys with you."

"I c-c-can do it."

"This isn't a time to tell me what you think I want to hear." Painter answered by getting to his feet.

"Alright, then," Gamble said, standing. "Pack it up, gentlemen, we're moving out. Finn, are we scrubbed?"

"Yeah, channel's clean."

"Then I've got point. Swoop, Mouse, you've got the cargo."

The team snapped into go-mode, wordlessly forming up. Swoop and Mouse took positions on Painter's left and right. And a few seconds later, they were pushing out into the open, headed from a known danger into one unknown.

TWELVE

Cass sat at a table right in the middle of the Mister Sun's main room, alone, eyes intent on the door. The lights near the entrance were turned low, all the others were off completely, casting the area in a dusky gloom. Painter and Wren were both upstairs in Painter's small room, hopefully getting some much needed sleep. Though she wouldn't have been surprised if they were both lying wide awake, listening for whatever might come. Mister Sun had retired to his side room. She was pretty sure he was waiting just on the other side of the door, just in case.

It'd been a gamble, sending a message through Able, but it was one she'd felt she had to take. If North was in on the plot, they would know soon enough. And they'd already done everything they could to stack the odds in their favor.

"One incoming," Cass heard Wick say over internal comms. "It's him."

A minute later, the front doors slid smoothly open, and a hulking figure stood in the entrance, silhouetted by the street lights behind him. He stepped cautiously over the threshold, out of the shadows and into the softer lights at the entrance. It was North. He looked off to his right as he entered, lowered his head and squinted, trying to force his eyes to adjust as he peered into the darkness. But as he scanned back to his left, his eyes quickly locked on Cass's, drawn no doubt by their soft electric glow.

"Lady Cass," he said, with a slight bow. North seemed surprised to see her. "I wasn't expecting to see you here." He stepped forward.

"That's close enough," Cass said as North reached the edge of the light, near the first row of tables. The doors slid closed and the locking mechanism clicked audibly.

"Front's clear," Wick said.

"Street's clear," Sky said.

"Rear's good," Finn answered.

Cass didn't answer. Just kept her eyes on North. He remained at the entrance, hands folded in front of him. Usually quietly confident, he seemed instead tense and uncertain. Maybe just a man awakened in the middle of the night. Or maybe a man fearing the unraveling of a plan. Cass let him wait in silence, knowing the less she led him, the more likely he was to reveal his own thoughts.

"A bit late for tea," North said. Cass held herself still, her eyes locked on his. An odd benefit of her altered eyes; he knew without a doubt that she was watching him, but couldn't read her expression.

"Are the others joining us?" he asked.

"We'll see," she answered.

"May I sit?"

"If you must."

Cass waited while North moved to the closest table and pulled a chair out for himself. He sat with his hands in his lap, under the table.

"Hands on the table," Cass said.

"What's going on, Cass?"

"Hands on the table," she repeated. His shoulders sagged and he sighed. Then he raised his hands slowly in an exaggerated motion and held them up and open, and then placed them flat on the table in front of him.

"You're usually more hospitable," North said.

"You never really know people, do you?"

"It's been a long few days, Lady. I have neither the energy nor the patience for games."

"No games," Cass said. "But I do have some questions."

"They couldn't wait for morning?"

"No."

"Enough, Cass. I assume from the time and location of this meeting that you've learned something significant. And I assume from the fact that we're the only two here that it's something you don't want the others to know."

"What makes you think we're the only two here?"

North's eyes narrowed and his head started to turn slightly, but he stopped himself, kept his eyes on hers. She wondered just how much of her he could make out in the darkness.

"Have you spoken with Aron tonight?" she asked.

North shook his head. "Should I have?"

"How about Connor?"

His brow furrowed. "Not since we were with him together. Did they discover something?"

"They're dead."

His face passed through a range of emotion in seconds, from confusion to disbelief to shock. It all looked genuine to Cass. "Who... what happened?" he asked.

"They tried to take Wren." Another wave of emotion.

"Tried to *take* him? Where? I don't understand."

"This is the first you've heard of it?"

For a brief moment, North didn't seem to understand the question. When he grasped the implication, he became visibly angry and stood up.

"I have pledged my life to serve your son," he said. "And I have served faithfully, at times to my own great pain."

"Easy there, partner," came a voice behind him. His eyes went wide, but he didn't turn. "Why don't you sit back down and keep your hands on the table like the good lady asked."

North slowly lowered himself back into his chair, revealing Gamble's petite frame behind him, her jittergun aimed squarely at the back of his head.

"I take this treatment as a great personal offense," he said. "I have been nothing but a friend to you and your son."

"You didn't answer the question," Cass said.

"If I had known anything about a plan to take Wren from you, I would've stopped it myself." He glowered at her from across the room, seemingly more angry at the questioning of his honor than over the deaths of Aron and Connor. "And if what you say is true, then I do not blame you for taking their lives."

"It is true. It's why I'm here, instead of at the compound. And it's why I asked you to come, North. I don't know who else we can trust."

"*This* is trust?" he said, waving his hand vaguely around and ending by pointing at Gamble behind him.

"No. But it's smart," Cass answered. Then, "You can bring the lights up."

A moment later, the lights came up in the room, and North's eyes darted first to the back corner of the room, then to the left, where Able and Swoop were standing.

"Seems excessive for one man," he said.

"We weren't sure you'd come alone."

"The message said to."

"Can I offer you a drink?" she asked.

"Are they really dead?"

Cass nodded. North looked down at his hands on the table, curled them into fists, and then stretched his fingers out wide. "Then yes, I would like a drink."

Before Cass could stand up, the door to Mister Sun's room swung open and he came out with a little bow, motioning for her to keep her seat. She chuckled at that, and suppressed a smile as Mister Sun disappeared to the back room. Gamble holstered her pistol and sat on a table, legs dangling like a kid.

A few moments later, Mister Sun returned, carrying a tray with cups and a pair of bottles, which he placed on Cass's table. Cass motioned to North, and he joined her. He poured for himself from one of the bottles, and offered some to her, which she declined. They sat in silence for a few minutes while North sipped and processed.

"What was their plan?" he said. "What were they hoping to accomplish?"

"They wanted him to use the machine."

North watched her for a long moment, and then took another sip of his drink. He shook his head as he set the cup back on the table.

"No. Before. Let's start at the beginning."

It started as a flutter in the corner of Painter's mind. Something alien and unwanted, like a nightmare he fought to forget, all the while feeling the more he struggled to ignore it, the more certain it seemed he would recall it in all its vivid horror. Yet worse. Painter couldn't quite find a way to describe it even to himself. It was almost as if it was *someone else's* nightmare was thrust into his own head. A flash of incoherent babble crackled through his mind, and he sat up violently on the floor.

But as quickly as it had come, it vanished, and his thoughts were clear once more. He checked the time. 01.47 GST. Maybe he'd started to doze off, and the turmoil of the day had bubbled through in an almost-dream. If there was another explanation, Painter couldn't think of one. Even so, the feeling it left behind made him uneasy.

He looked over to the bed he'd given up, where Wren was breathing in the slow even rhythms of undisturbed sleep. At least he hadn't woken his young friend. Hard not to envy the little king, sleeping peacefully despite the events of the day. Of the week. But then Painter shook his head. Who knew what burdens the poor boy carried? It seemed more like a life in prison than a life of power.

Painter fluffed up the bundle of clothes he was using as a pillow and then lowered himself onto his back carefully. His back and ribs still ached from his near-death experience with Gamble, but already the pain was less severe than it'd been, even just an hour ago. He reached up and lightly ran his fingers over his cheekbone, and over the gash that Mouse had had to seal up. Still puffy, and warm to the touch, but some healing was already evident there too. Funny, the way people treated him, like he was something lesser, something to be pitied. If they only knew... but then, even Painter still didn't know all the ways he was different. Better, even.

His thoughts turned to Snow. If she had only known, would she still have joined up with whatever gang it was that had poisoned her so? Her eyes haunted him. The look of utter horror as she stared at him, mouth open, as if Painter had risen rotting from the grave. If she had only given him the chance, could he have even explained it to Snow?

Not with his mouth, no. Odd that with all the other improvements the Weir seemed to have made, they couldn't fix his stutter. Improvements. Something within him revolted at that idea. They weren't improvements as much as they were *violations*. And yet, he couldn't deny that the Weir had in some way made him stronger. For so long they had been nightmare creatures, bringers of terror and death. His instinctual hatred was only natural. It was a challenge to even entertain the idea that maybe the Weir were in some way not completely evil. But if they *were* completely evil, then what did that mean for him?

Painter laughed at himself for trying to find reason in any of it. It all seemed meaningless. Useless attempts at philosophy by an untrained mind. Maybe life was just a series of accidents after all. Probably he was too tired to think. He lay with his eyes open, staring at the ceiling, and let his mind wander, heedless of its direction.

The room was dark except for thin orange ribbons cast on the ceiling by the street lights through the blinds. Not *dark* to Painter's eyes, but what he knew was dark for normal humans. *Normal.* Average. Common. *Unremarkable.* Painter closed his eyes and let himself smile at that. Yes, that seemed a better description. *Unremarkable* humans.

And just as he was finally drifting off into sleep, a soft but sudden sensation caught his attention. He lay still, holding his breath, searching for it again. A few moments later, yes, there. The merest trace of a new pulse of signal. It was hard for him to notice unless he really concentrated. Painter rolled over silently and pushed himself up. Crept to the window. Eased the blinds away from the window ever so slowly. Just enough to catch a glimpse of a shadow as it slipped into an alley.

Someone was in the street below.

"Straggler's back," Sky said over the team's special communications channel. This was the third time the figure had passed near Mister Sun's place; first might've been an accident, and the second a coincidence. But three times was as good as an enemy action. It was a tough call, though. The straggler was either really terrible at avoiding observation, or really good at looking like an amateur. Trouble was figuring out whether he was scouting the site, acting as bait, or just in the absolute wrong place at the perfectly wrong time.

"That's three strikes," Wick said. "If you wanna drop him, I'll work clean-up."

Technically, as a member of the Governor's personal bodyguard, Sky was authorized to take any measure he deemed necessary to ensure the boy governor's safety. It was a heavy responsibility to bear, though, and Sky was ever mindful of the cost every time he pulled the trigger, no matter how justified. And he was nowhere close to feeling justified.

"Finn, you getting any read off him?" he asked.

"Negative. He's not talking to anybody."

Sky shook his head. "What are you doing out here, man?" he whispered to the figure below. Straggler moved into the shadows along the building across from the Tea House. "Go home. Just go home."

"I don't like it, Sky," Wick said. Wick hadn't been blessed with Sky's patience, but he never went without the OK. Of course, he also usually had a really good read on people, and if he didn't like it, there was probably good reason.

Just as Sky was thinking that, the straggler darted across the street and towards the back entrance. Wick was nice enough not to comment.

"Trouble," Sky said. "Straggler just ducked behind the building. Did you pick him up, Finn?"

"No, I don't see him. You get an ID?"

"Negative. Pretty sure it's a dude, but never got a look at the face. Some kind of hood or something."

"I'm not seeing him," Finn said.

"You've got eyes on the back door?" Wick asked.

"Of course," Finn said. "But if the first time I see him is when he's at the door, that's bad things, man."

"Sky, you agree he's hostile?" said Wick. He was looking for confirmation, to OK the kill if necessary.

"Can't say for sure. But he's definitely shady."

"Alright, hang tight, bro," Wick said to his brother. "I'll swing around."

"Hold there, Wick," Finn said. "I'll loop Able, get him to come out."

"I'm already street level," Wick answered, and Sky could hear the movement in his voice. "And I'm almost there anyway."

From his elevated position, Sky saw Wick effortlessly flow across the street like a wisp of smoke. They were all highly trained professionals, but nobody really moved like Wick. He vanished around the same corner where the straggler had gone less than a minute before.

There was a long silence. Sky kept careful watch of the approaches towards Mister Sun's, but his eyes kept drifting back to that corner, wondering what was going on down there. What was taking so long? As he looked back up at the far end of the street, three figures came into view, and Sky cursed to himself.

"Patrol inbound; front side, three men, fifty meters," he said.

"Check," Finn said.

Wick didn't answer. Forty meters. There was a sudden sharp noise from the alley, quickly muffled. But not quickly enough. Sky saw the guards in the street react, their posture stiffening. Alerted. They fanned out slightly and started prowling towards the building.

"Wick, you alright?" Finn asked. No response. Thirty meters. "Wick!" Finn said again, more forcefully.

"Yeah, I'm fine," he answered in a whisper. "How close is that patrol?"

"Twenty meters," Sky reported. "One's splitting off." One of the guards was now moving to an adjacent alley, circling around towards the back of Mister Sun's house.

"I gotta to take Straggler in."

"Swoop'll be pissed," Finn said.

"Doesn't matter, they're too close. Tell him we're comin' in the back."

"Alright, check."

Sky heard the subtle click in the channel as Finn cycled it and looped Swoop in. "Swoop, Finn."

A moment later, Swoop answered, "Yeah, go."

"Problem. Wick's gotta bring a guest in through the back door."

Sky watched as the two remaining guards spread their position, one keeping to the front of the building, while the other cautiously tried to get an angle on the alley where Wick and Straggler had gone.

"And we've got a patrol sniffing around outside," Finn added.

There was a pause. There was almost always a pause with Swoop. "Check," he finally said.

The guards looked at each other, and one nodded to the other. The first entered the alley.

"Keep your head down back there, Finn," Sky said.

Cass heard a commotion on the stairs, someone descending in a hurry.

"There's someone outside!" Painter called as he came down, but Swoop was already in motion and just pointed for him to get back upstairs.

Cass barely had time to process what Painter had said, before she heard Wick come bursting through the back door. He appeared in the central room a few seconds later, forcing a hooded figure ahead of him. Painter finally seemed to realize what Swoop had meant, and quickly retreated up the stairs again.

"Sorry," Wick said. "Patrol's right outside. I told him to keep his eyes closed, his head down, and his mouth *shut*." He leaned in and put his mouth nearly against the side of Hood's head when he said the last part, for emphasis. Hood shrank away from Wick slightly, but the tilt of his head made it seem more from annoyance than fear. Wick forced Hood into a chair near the back of the room and stood in front of him, gripping his shoulder.

Swoop moved in next to Wick, and started asking questions in a low voice, in his steady tone. Somehow the lack of emotion made Swoop more frightening.

Able took a place about midway between Cass and Hood, positioning himself as an additional shield. Gamble kept her spot at the front of the room, but slid off the table to her feet, and casually rested one hand on the grip of her holstered jittergun. She caught Cass's eye, held a finger up to her lips, and then pointed to Mister Sun's side room. Cass nodded, and she quietly got up from the table and signaled for North to follow her. But before she reached the other room–

"What'd you do to Painter?" Hood blurted, a little louder than was comfortable. A woman's voice, vaguely familiar to Cass's ears. "I saw him with you. You beat him up."

"What do you care?" Wick said.

"You *people*," Hood said, with a strange emphasis on the word. "You think you can just do whatever you want to whoever you want. It's not right!"

"So you think we roughed Painter up, and then you thought it'd be a good idea to come here, and what?"

Hood didn't answer. Cass moved closer and motioned to Swoop to pull the hood back. He shook his head and pointed to his eyes with two fingers. Worried that Hood was going to see Cass. But Cass persisted. Swoop drew back the hood, and as he did, a cascade of wavy red hair tumbled out. Hood didn't raise her head though, just stayed hidden under her fiery mane.

Hood hadn't sounded scared, and neither did she look it. Cass thought she'd recognized the voice. Now she was sure of it.

"Kit," Cass said. Swoop glanced at Cass sharply for breaking security and revealing her presence, but Cass held up a hand indicating it was alright. The girl reacted by raising her head slightly, but she still didn't open her eyes. "Kit, it's alright, you can open your eyes. It's Cass."

Wick let go of Kit's shoulder and took a step back.

Kit opened her eyes slowly and raised them to meet Cass's. They shone softly with the light of the Weir and refracted in the tears that pooled at their base. "Miss Cass?" Kit looked around the room then. She was in her mid-twenties, and when she sat up straight, her muscular frame and broad shoulders were apparent. "What's going on?"

"What're you doing here, Kit?" Cass asked.

"I saw them with Painter."

"You shouldn't have come. It's very dangerous right now."

"I thought he was hurt. I thought maybe..." she trailed off, and her eyes darted to Swoop and then down to the floor. "I don't know what I thought. I just couldn't do nothing."

"Well, now that you're here, ma'am," Wick said, "we're going to have to ask you to stay for a little while." Kit glanced up at him, uncertain. "For security."

He squatted down so he wasn't towering over her anymore, and softened his voice. "And don't worry, Painter's fine, we didn't beat him up. Not really. I mean, I guess technically we did, but not for the reason you probably think."

"Wick, lock it up," Swoop said. Wick nodded and flashed a quick smile at Kit, reached out and patted her leg, and then stood again. He motioned with his thumb towards the back door and raised his eyebrows, but Swoop shook his head and held up a finger, telling him to wait.

"Sky, status," Swoop said. He waited for a moment, and then said, "Check." He subtly shook his head at Wick. Then he turned his attention to Kit. "Ma'am, I'm going to need you to move this room over here." He pointed towards Mister Sun's side room.

Kit stood, but didn't move. "You can't keep me here," she said. "I haven't done anything wrong."

"You broke curfew."

Kit shrugged. "Then I'll go outside and turn myself into the guard."

"Ma'am." Swoop said it with an even tone, but there was a warning behind it. Kit was strong, though, and not one easily intimidated.

"It's not about you, Kit," Cass said. "It's for me."

"Are you in trouble?"

Cass just smiled.

"Then how can I help?"

"For now, you can just do as we ask."

"OK, sure. If you just *ask*," she said, with a pointed look at Swoop. Kit started towards Mister Sun's room. Able automatically glided over to escort her, and Mister Sun followed closely behind.

"I'll keep her company," Mister Sun said.

"Thanks, Mister Sun," Cass said.

Kit and Mister Sun went into his side room. Able closed the door behind them and stood guard next to it. Gamble returned to her perch on the table in the front, and Swoop disappeared into the back room.

"She's got a little fire in her, doesn't she?" Wick said to no one in particular, with a little smile on his face.

"More than a little," Cass answered, as she returned to her seat. Wren had always said Kit had been the easiest for him to Awaken, that she'd just *"sprung open"* – like she'd been fighting it on her own already, and just needed a little nudge. For many nights afterwards, in the still, quiet hours, Cass had wondered if anyone could ever free themselves from the Weir – wondered if maybe she could've fought harder to recover herself. And if she had, if Three would not be dead now. But no, Wren had assured her there was nothing she could've done. No use dwelling on what might've been. Especially now, when there was so much else to do. "North, we've got to make some decisions."

North returned to his chair at the table, across from her. "The girl complicates matters."

"It was already complicated. And she won't tell anyone we're here."

"Not on purpose, perhaps."

"Well, I'm open to suggestions," Cass replied.

"I wouldn't have ever expected to say this, but I believe the safest thing for you... for you and the Governor." He paused and rubbed his chin with his fingertips. "The safest thing is for you to leave Morningside."

THIRTEEN

"And go where?" Cass asked.

"It would be better if I did not know," North answered. "No one can steal information I do not possess."

The concept struck Cass as both impossible and inevitable. How could they leave Morningside? And yet how could they stay? Members of the Council had gone from quietly attempting assassination and sabotage to a brazen assault. The only logical escalation was open revolution. And there was no telling how far or wide or deep the conspiracy had spread. Connor oversaw the entire contingent of guardsmen. Any one of them might be involved. *All* of them could be, for that matter.

And Aron. One of the few remaining elders. If he had *their* blessing, then Wren's was truly a hollow power in the city. She thought back to the conversation with her son in the courtyard, just a few days before. The idea of leaving the city had seemed like a fantasy then. How quickly life could change.

"We can't just leave. Wren most of all," Cass said. "If he disappeared, there would be utter chaos."

"Not if we conceal it. Security has already been tightened. We will simply spread word that the Governor must remain within the compound for his safety. No one need know otherwise."

Cass tried to think it through, though her mind was fogged with fatigue and stress. A week, maybe two. Just long enough to get clear of the immediate danger. So much would need to be rebuilt over the coming months, but North was right. Ensuring Wren's physical safety was their highest priority, and there was nowhere inside these walls they could trust for any length of time.

North leaned forward and touched Cass's hand. "I do not mean exile, Lady. Only a temporary retreat, until we can be certain of your safety again."

"Gamble," Cass called. "What do you think?"

Gamble hopped off her table and approached. She didn't sit at the table though, just leaned over it, with both hands on the back of a chair. "I think getting you out of the city is the smartest thing to do for you and your son. That's my one and only concern. All the rest of it, I can't say."

"It might not be a great plan," North said. "It might not even be a very good one. But I fear if we wait for a better one, it will then be too late."

"It's not really a plan, sir," Gamble said. "But I agree. I think we move you to a secure location, and figure the rest out from there."

"Gamble," Cass said. "You do understand I'm not asking you to come with us?"

"Doesn't matter if you ask us or not, ma'am," Gamble said. "We're coming."

"Look, I appreciate the sentiment, but this isn't what you signed up for."

"Cass, what we signed up for was to do whatever it takes to keep you both safe. There's not one of us that would let you walk out there on your own, whether you wanted us to or not."

"We spent a lot of time out there on our own before we came here, Gamble."

"And now you don't have to."

Cass didn't know what to say. The circumstances were so far outside the boundaries of their professional duties, she couldn't possibly expect them to stand by her side. But Gamble made it sound like she couldn't expect anything less.

"Once you leave, you'll have to assume we're all traced," North said.

"It's alright, we've got Finn–" Gamble said, but cut herself off. She stood up straight, and Wick and Able both reacted in the same instant.

"What is it?" Cass asked.

"Alert just went out over wide broadcast," Gamble explained. "They found the bodies."

Swoop appeared from the back room a few seconds later, looking even more intense than usual.

"You want me back out front?" Wick asked.

"Stand by," Swoop said.

"Do they know we're gone?" Cass asked.

"Didn't say, but we better get ahead of the curve on that," Gamble answered. Then she added, "Finn, Gamble… need you to bounce a message…"

"Sir, you need to leave," Swoop said to North.

"I don't think we're quite done–" North said.

"Right now."

North looked at Cass, but there really wasn't any question. Swoop didn't stand on ceremony and he certainly wasn't above throwing a Council member out in the street if he thought it was necessary. And even as big as North was, there wasn't much doubt Swoop could do it. North got to his feet, and Cass stood at the same time.

Gamble was still talking to Finn. "Let the guard know that the governor and Lady Cass have been moved to a secure location... yeah, wide net but scattered, I don't want anyone localizing it."

"Good luck, Lady," North said. "Give me three days, and then check in."

"Thank you, North. Watch yourself."

He bowed his head slightly, and then turned towards the front door.

"This way, sir," Swoop said. "We'll go out the back."

North nodded and returned, and Swoop escorted him into the back room. Gamble waited until they'd left the room to start talking again. "City's going into lockdown, no doubt about that," Gamble said. "If we're going to get you out of here, we need to do it soon."

"How soon?" Cass asked.

"Wick?"

"Depends on where we're headed."

Gamble looked at Cass.

"I think Wren knows a place," she said.

"Better go wake him then."

Cass nodded and went upstairs to Painter's room. She knocked softly on the door and then opened it and peeked in. Painter was sitting up on the floor, his eyes glowing back at her. Wren was snoring softly. Painter got to his feet and motioned her in.

"Sorry to wake you," she whispered. "I need Wren."

"Wasn't asleep any, ennnn, anyway," Painter whispered back.

Cass entered the room and sat down on the bed next to her son. He was asleep on his stomach, slightly sweaty, mouth open. She rubbed his back.

"Wren," she said softly. His eyes floated open immediately,

but otherwise he remained completely still. An old habit she had trained him in. "Baby, we need you downstairs."

He sniffed and rubbed his eyes and then nodded sleepily. He sat up and stifled a yawn.

"Do you want me to carry you?" Cass asked.

He shook his head and got to his feet.

"Should I come tuh-too?" Painter asked.

"Yeah," Cass answered. "I think you better."

They all returned to the main room together. Gamble had gathered Swoop, Able, and Wick around her in conference.

"What's going on?" Wren asked.

"We're leaving," Cass said.

"Back to the compound?"

"No, baby, we're leaving the city."

He looked up at her with his big sea-green eyes, still glassy with sleep. There was surprise on his face, but a little smile formed on his lips, one he tried to suppress.

"Where are we going?" he asked, and she could hear hope in the question.

"Somewhere safe," Cass said. "Where no one will find us. Do you know a place like that?"

Wren let himself smile then, and nodded.

"Then we need you to tell Wick where it is."

"I have it marked," he said. "Should I just ping it to you?"

"No, hold on," Wick said. And then he said, "Hey, Finn." He waited a moment, and then said, "I need to pull a grid off the Governor. Can you hook him in secure...? Alright, check." He looked back at Wren. "Finn's going to patch you in to our secure comms channel. Just to be safe."

Wren nodded and waited. A moment later his eyes lit up, and he said, "Yes, I hear you... OK... Just like normal, though...? OK."

Wren looked at Wick, who nodded. "Got it. Thanks, Finn." And then Wick's eyes rolled up slightly, almost like he was looking at the ceiling, and his brow furrowed for several seconds. "Whew, looks like that's all the way out on the edge of the Strand."

"It is."

"Not sure how safe that's gonna be."

"It's safer than you'd think. I stayed there for a few weeks. Before I came here."

"What do you think, Wick?" Gamble asked.

"Yeah… yeah, I reckon it'd work. Probably see trouble coming from a mile off out there."

"Alright, how long?"

"We did it in a day," Wren answered.

"But in a straight shot?"

Wren nodded. "I think so."

"Yeah," Wick said, "I could see that. Maybe eight hours or so straight. But we're going want to take a long way, I think."

"Agreed," Gamble said. She must've seen their confused looks, because she looked at Cass and Wren and added, "In case they send trackers out."

"Alright, I'll work it out," Wick said. "Gimme, I dunno, an hour?"

"You can have forty-five minutes. Less if someone comes knocking," Gamble said. Cass had always admired Gamble, but she'd never really seen her in this role before. Watching her bring a plan together was truly impressive. "Swoop, what about gear?" Gamble asked.

"How many days?"

"Pack heavy."

"Might be tough if the compound's all stirred up."

"You can take food and drink from here," Mister Sun said

from across the room. He was standing in the doorway of his side room. Kit was behind him, looking over his shoulder. "Take all you need."

"Thank you, Mister Sun," Gamble said. "That would make things a little easier."

"Anything is yours, my friend."

"Alright, Swoop, Able, get back to the compound, strip out what you can. You don't have to empty the cage, but think long-range profile."

"You got it," Swoop said.

"There's no telling how long we'll be out there. Where's Mouse?" Gamble asked.

"Out on watch," Swoop said.

"Round him up and take him with you. I want to keep Finn and Sky posted up until we leave." Swoop nodded. "And I don't think you should come back here. We'll have to rally up somewhere."

We'll take the tunnel, Able signed. *Meet you outside.*

"If you can do it without compromising it, yeah." Gamble held up one finger to her teammates and then said, "Sky, you have your linerunner with you? Alright, check." And then she was focused on the group again. "Alright, yeah, plan on that. If you're sure it's clear, take the tunnel out. We'll go over the wall and rally up. Wick will find us a spot, and let you know. Questions?"

Cass surveyed the team; they were all switched on, ready to move. It didn't seem to faze them in the slightest that they were talking about heading outside the wall for some unknown length of time. They were just focused on the job. Not a single one had asked why.

"Alright, let's roll it up. Check with Finn and Sky to see what they need, and then get out of here. I want to be outside the wall by… oh-three-hundred GST. Forty minutes."

"On it," Swoop said. He and Able swiveled and headed towards the back room.

"Thought I had forty-five," Wick said.

"Less every minute you fuss," Gamble replied.

"I'm just going to sit back there," Wick said, pointing to the far back corner. He moved to a table, and Cass saw him throw a little wave at Kit as he passed by. Kit didn't wave back, but she smiled a little and looked at the floor.

"Governor," Gamble said, "Painter, and Miss Cass, if you don't mind, I'd like to get your help pulling some supplies together."

"Sure," Cass said, "of course." Wren and Painter both just nodded.

"This way," Mister Sun said. He headed towards the back room and motioned for them to follow.

"What about me?" Kit said. "Do I need to stay?"

Gamble stopped and looked back at her. "Yes, ma'am, I'm afraid so. Just until we're gone."

"What do I do in the meantime?"

"Keep Wick company," Gamble said, flashing a smile.

Sky watched the streets below with an anticipation that bordered on nervousness. Patience usually wasn't a problem. But knowing they were planning to leave made every minute they had to wait seem that much more painful. Each extra moment they stayed inside the city brought a chance that they might be discovered, and the way things had been going lately, there was really no telling what might go down if that happened. He'd never had to hide from his own people before. And the thought of things going sideways, of having to shoot their way out… he shook his head. It wouldn't come to that. He wouldn't let it.

He checked the time, 02.48 GST. Gamble had said she'd wanted to be outside the wall by oh-three-hundred, and unless she was planning to make them all sprint to the closest point, they were running late.

"Sky, Finn," Finn said over the channel. "How's your angle on the east side of the building?"

Sky checked. He didn't have a full view, due to an overhang from another building. "Partially obstructed. What's up?"

"Maybe nothing." That didn't sound promising. "Just picked up a little traffic spike from somewhere out that way. I can't see anything over there though."

"Alright," Sky said, "stand by, I'll check it." He drew up his rifle and swept the area with his optic. As far as he could tell it was clear. Ever since the three-man patrol had quit poking around and moved on, they hadn't seen another soul in the streets. "I can't see anything down there from here, Finn. You want me to reposition?"

"No, that's alright. Just keep an eye out."

"Check." Finn was the cautious type, so it might very well have been nothing. But that didn't really make Sky feel any better.

They had reconvened in the main room, and laid out supplies in a few meticulous piles across several of the tables. It'd taken them longer than Gamble had anticipated, mostly because Mister Sun's storage room wasn't arranged with efficiency in mind. It was clear she was becoming increasingly anxious to get moving.

Cass had dumped the contents of her go-bag out to see what she could contribute. She couldn't help but feel a little proud when Gamble had complimented her on her preparedness. Cass didn't mention how much she'd learned from her first flight into the open.

"Alright, I think we're good enough," Gamble said. She was doing one final survey of the supplies. "Anything we don't have, we'll just have to make do without. Let's get all this loaded up and get moving."

Cass quickly repacked her go-bag and reorganized it so she could fit as many of the new additions as it could carry. Mister Sun had provided them with a couple of large storage sacks as a temporary solution until they could meet up with the others and redistribute everything more evenly. Painter and Wren were loading one, while Gamble worked on another.

"Wick," Gamble said, "we're out of time." Then to the others, "Don't worry about trying to keep it organized. The piles were just to make sure we had enough for everyone. Wick?"

"Yeah, I heard you," he answered from the back of the room. Cass noticed Kit had joined him at the table. She was sitting across from him, resting her head on her folded arms. "I don't have a full route worked out yet, G. It's a tricky run."

"You got us a place to stay for the night?"

"I think I found a spot, yeah, but–"

"Then figure out the rest on the way, we need to move."

"You know I hate that."

"You don't have to like it, you just have to do it." Gamble switched over to the team's channel. "Sky. Finn. We're wrapping it up in here, make ready to move."

Wick exhaled in obvious frustration, but he bounced up out of his chair and helped the boys finish stuffing the supplies in their storage sacks. Neither Wren nor Painter had spoken much since Cass had brought them downstairs. They both looked exhausted, though neither of them had complained at all throughout the entire process. The boys slipped their coats on, and Mister Sun buzzed around making last-minute gestures of good will, trying to be helpful and reassuring any way he could. Wick grabbed one of the supply sacks, and Gamble took the other, and with Painter they started towards the back door. Mister Sun lingered by the entrance to the back room, half in and half out, seemingly at a loss for what more he could do.

Wren came over to Cass and stood waiting for her. She saw him check something in his belt, realized it was his knife. He zipped his coat up over it.

Cass tossed her coat on, and made a final check on her pack. Everything seemed to be in order. She slung the single strap up over her head, onto her right shoulder, and then adjusted it tight across her body. She bounced up and down a couple of times to check it for weight and balance.

"We're really going to do it, aren't we?" Wren said. His smile was gone, but he didn't seem afraid.

"Yeah, baby," Cass answered. She put a hand on his shoulder, and then bent down and kissed the top of his head. "Like old times."

He reached up and placed his hand in hers. "Not too much like, I hope."

"Not too much."

They joined the others at the back door. Gamble lined them up against the wall, and stood in front of them, quickly scanning each of them head to toe, like she was taking inventory. Cass felt a surge of nervous energy. It'd been lingering in the background ever since they'd started making preparations. But now that everything that could be done had been done, now that they were standing at a door, ready to cross the threshold, it was like she'd given herself permission to actually feel the strange mix of emotions. Anxiety certainly, maybe some fear, but also an underlying sense of exhilaration. Maybe life inside the compound had taken more of a toll on her than she'd realized.

"Alright, listen up," Gamble said from the front of the line. "We need to stay light and fast out there. Wick's going to lead the way, then I want Cass, Wren, Painter, in that order. That clear?"

They all nodded.

"Just keep your eyes on Wick, go where he goes, don't worry about the people behind you. Whatever else happens, your job is always to stay with Wick. What's your job?"

"Stay with Wick," Wren said.

"Stay with Wick," Gamble repeated. "Once we walk out that door, I don't want any talking. We're going to cut straight across to the nearest point on the wall, and then follow it north to the first set of stairs."

"How will we g-g-get through the guh-, through the gate?" Painter asked.

"We won't," Gamble said. "We're going over."

"Over the wall?" Wren asked, with a little awe in his voice.

"Yeah. But we've got to get there first, so say your goodbyes, and let's get moving." Then, "Sky, Finn, we're thirty seconds to go."

Cass waved Mister Sun over and she and Wren both hugged the little man. Kit floated into the back room, tugging at her fingers and looking concerned.

"Thank you for everything, Mister Sun," Cass said. "We really have no way to repay you for all your kindness."

"Be safe," he answered, "and that will be payment enough."

"Kit, I'm sorry you got stuck in all this," said Cass. "I hope you understand."

"I do, Miss Cass, and I'm sorry for any trouble I've caused."

"You were no trouble at all. We'll just have to trust you to forget everything you saw tonight."

"Maybe not quite *every*thing," Kit said, and she looked at Wick then with a sly little smile. "But you can count on me, Miss Cass. You know I'd do anything for you two."

"How many?" Gamble said abruptly. It took a second before Cass realized she wasn't talking to any of them. And then she was. "Mister Sun, do you have any other exits besides this and the front door? Preferably something inconspicuous?"

Mister Sun shook his head. "I'm afraid not, my friend."

"What's up?" Cass asked.

"Guards in the street again," Gamble said.

"Same ones as before?" Cass asked her.

"Unknown. But there are more of them this time."

Wick set his bag of supplies on the floor. "Give me two minutes' headstart," he said. "I'll run interference, try to draw them away from the back so you guys can slip out."

"Negative," Gamble said. "I need you to get these people to the right place. I'll go."

"Wait," Cass said, "if it's the guard, can't you just go pull rank on them?"

"I wouldn't trust it, ma'am," Wick said. "If one of us goes walking out there to talk, they're gonna guess you're nearby. And if someone's looking for you…" He shook his head. "It's gotta be me, Gamble. No offense, but I've got a better chance of shaking them."

"I said no, Wick. I can't spare you. And I need Sky and Finn running the wings, so that leaves me."

"I'll do it," a quiet voice said. Everyone looked around. It was Kit. "I'll do it," she said a little more strongly.

"I appreciate it, ma'am," Gamble said, "but it's too dangerous."

"What do you need? Just some kind of distraction?" Kit asked.

"It's a little more complicated than that."

"Is it really?" Kit said. "Sounds to me like you just need somebody to make enough of a fuss – around the front door – to let you guys slip out the back."

"Ma'am, we don't know why those people are out there, or what they're looking for, or what they might do if they saw someone leaving. For all we know, they might shoot you on sight."

"So it's OK for you to get shot, but not me?"

"I've been shot before."

"Well, you can't afford to get shot now. And I'm faster than I look."

"It's true," Wick said. "She almost got away from me."

"*Almost*," Gamble said. But Cass could see it on her face already. If the girl was willing to try, it just might be the best option, and Gamble was considering it. "There are six of them out there."

"Let me help," Kit said. "Please. I can do this for you." She wasn't pleading. Just calmly stating a fact. "Maybe it'll make up for me stumbling in here in the first place."

"Understand this isn't something for you to *try*," Gamble said. "It's something you must *do*. If you go out there and get caught and bring down a bunch of reinforcements on us, it's going to go badly for a lot of people."

"They won't catch me." Gamble just looked at Kit with that level stare of hers, evaluating. "They won't," Kit said again.

Gamble clenched her jaw for a long moment. Then she finally dipped her head forward slightly. "Straight out the front, cross into the alley, don't look back. Do you know where you're running to?"

"Not yet."

"Pick a place. Somewhere away from the compound where you can get lost."

Kit thought for a moment, and then nodded. She said, "OK, I know one."

"And a backup."

"OK."

"The backup is only for if you get cut off. You got it?" Gamble asked.

"Yeah, I got it."

"If we had more time I'd have you pick two more."

"I won't even need the backup," Kit said.

Gamble kept looking at her, but said, "Sky, our guest is going to give us a hand... yeah... yeah, she can do it. Front door. Anybody tries to get a bead on her on her way out, you drop him." And then to Kit, "You sure you want to do this?"

Kit nodded with confidence, but she licked her lips as if they'd just gone dry.

"Alright," Gamble said. "Pull your hood up. And run like all hell is on your heels."

One of the trickier parts of Sky's job was keeping track of all the targets; not just how many and where they were, but how they were armed, their estimated skill level, who was in charge. If the team was ever forced to engage, it made everyone's jobs easier if they knew who the biggest threats were and where the bad guys were getting their orders from before the shooting started. Cleaning up the Weir was a lot easier. One was pretty much as good as another when it came to target selection.

"Finn, you still got two back there?" Sky whispered over their secure channel.

There were two clicks in the channel, the sound of Finn quickly opening and then closing his broadcast without speaking. The bad guys were so close he didn't want to risk answering.

"You in trouble? Gimme one for yes, two for no."

A pause. Then: *Click. Click.*

Right now, there were six guardsmen prowling around the perimeter of Mister Sun's Tea House, and Sky didn't recognize any of them from before. In fact, he didn't recognize any of them at all. He had eyes on four of them standing in a knot about thirty meters up the street from the Tea House. Two others had approached and disappeared around the back side. A few moments later, those two emerged from behind the building.

"Alright, I'm clear," Finn said. "I think those two were doing a quick high-low." Checking for entrances above or below street level.

"That's a lot of attention for the night."

"Might just be following up from before."

"That'd be nice. You think so?" Sky asked.

"No."

"Yeah."

Sky had already identified the head man in charge, which he just dubbed Headman; one of those close-crop haircuts, square-jawed, perpetually angry guys who was so emphatic he had to use a fully opened hand to point at things instead of just a finger. Two of the other guards had coilguns, small sidearm-style jobs that usually went to low-grade officers. And at least one was toting something heavier. The last two were a couple of grunt-level foot soldiers, each carrying a stunrod.

Three officers and a specialist meant something more than just the average foot patrol. This was a unit. And they were loaded for bear.

Sky adjusted his optic and scoped each target in order of importance; Headman, Heavy, Coilgun A, Coilgun B, Footie One, Footie Two. If they were a seasoned team, he'd have to drop half before they broke. If he was lucky, he might just have to take the first two. He never counted on being lucky.

The six guards broke into three teams. Headman and Heavy stayed back while each Coilgun paired up with a Footie and started spreading out on either side of the building. But they were keeping some distance. Sky got the impression that they might be there more for observation and containment than an assault. Or they might be an advance force, staging before the rest of them got there.

"Gamble, Sky," he whispered over comms. "I don't think this is gonna work, Ace."

"Nice timing," she answered.

Sky flicked his eyes to the front door. A split-second later it slid open, and he saw a figure standing in the entrance. Straggler. Kit. She had her hood back up. Gamble had updated him about her, but as he watched her come down the stairs, Sky stood by his original assessment; she definitely walked like a dude. Why was Kit walking?

Coilgun A and Footie Two were the pair of guards closest to the front, and they reacted almost immediately, shouting and gesturing at Kit, Coilgun A with his hand on his holstered coilgun. She just kept right on walking, head down, like she had nowhere in particular to be. Sky scoped in on the Headman. He and Heavy hadn't done anything yet, but they were intent on the situation. The other pair of guards had stopped in their tracks, but they were still far enough around to one side that there was no way Gamble and the others would be able to slip

out unnoticed. Sky looked back to find the guard had
his coilgun out now, pointed at Kit, and she had her
hands up.

"What exactly were you expecting her to do?" Sky asked.

"Run. Why, what's she doing?"

"Pretty much the opposite."

Kit lowered herself to her knees, and then placed her
hands behind her head. Footie Two had the stunrod out. He
eased his way toward her while Coilgun A kept her covered.
Sky was too high up to hear what was going on, but from
the body language it looked like they were talking back and
forth. Was she giving them up?

"She's talking, Ace. She's talking to 'em."

Footie Two had stopped about six feet away from Kit, and
he turned back to look at Coilgun A. Coilgun A turned back
and motioned towards the Headman. He and Heavy started
approaching. Sky started sighting in again. Headman,
Heavy, Coilgun A. Hopefully the grunts would just scatter
and at least *they'd* get to go home.

"Finn, can you get a bead on those two around the side?"
Sky said.

"Stand by," Finn answered. This was exactly how it
wasn't supposed to go. Both sides just doing their jobs, and
people ending up dead for it. "Yeeeah, I can get 'em if they
don't move too much more your way."

"Check, I'll pick 'em up last if I have to."

"We going?" Finn said.

"Not yet."

"Alright, on your shot."

"Check."

Kit laid back her hood, and then pointed away up the
street, back towards where Headman had been standing.

What was she doing?

"Sky, status," Gamble said.

"Bad, getting worse," Sky said.

And just as the last word was leaving his mouth, Kit was in motion. It was tough to follow exactly what happened after she closed in on the grunt, but somehow she ended up with the stunrod. There was a burst of shouting and commotion, and Heavy stumbled back a couple of steps. Sky snapped his weapon up and sighted in on Heavy, just as the guard was shouldering his weapon. But something made Sky hesitate, something almost reflexive, too fast to consciously process. If Heavy had wanted to fire, Sky had just given him the chance. But neither of them had pulled the trigger.

And now Sky saw why. Footie Two and Coilgun A were both on the ground, out cold, and Kit had an arm around Headman's neck, using him as a shield. She had the stunrod held up right in front of his face, and he'd gone real quiet. Heavy was tracking her with his weapon, but Kit was doing a good job of keeping the Headman between them. She started backing slowly up, towards the alley across the street from Mister Sun's.

"I'm losing 'em," Finn warned. He was losing his shot on the other two. But that was actually good news. It meant they were moving towards Kit, which meant they were moving away from the back door.

"I think she's actually gonna pull this off," Sky said. It wasn't going anywhere near according to Gamble's plan, but if Kit could just get clear...

"Sky, what's going on out there?" Gamble said.

"Get ready to move," Sky said. "On my call."

Kit was walking backwards slow and steady, maybe

fifteen steps from the alley. Twelve. Ten. Coilgun B had his gun out, but his angle was worse than Heavy's. Footie One just kind of stood there, slightly behind Coilgun B, looking lost. Headman must've been talking, judging from the look on Heavy's face, but Kit just kept retreating towards that alley. Sky was going to lose her once she made that corner, but he didn't want to risk repositioning at such a critical moment. He just kept on Heavy, watching the man's face through that optic. Heavy was intense, grim. A total pro. Just waiting for his opening.

"Let her go, man," Sky whispered. "Let her go."

If Sky could've talked to her, he would have told Kit to just keep backing down that alley until she could make a lateral move. Dump the Headman and take off before Heavy got a clean shot. Unfortunately, Sky couldn't talk to her.

The Headman went limp, and then violently ragdolled forward, straight at Heavy. But Heavy leapt sideways and dropped to a knee, and got two shots off before Sky could reacquire him.

"Sky?" Gamble called.

"Go, Gamble, move!"

"Moving."

The other two guards rushed over to the fallen Headman, and Coilgun B knelt beside him, checked for a pulse. From the looks of it, Kit had hit him with the stunrod and then tossed or kicked his body at Heavy. Heavy was still on one knee, at least. Kit was gone, somewhere down that alley. No way to tell from where Sky was whether she'd been hit or not. Judging from the fact that no one was chasing after her though, he had a pretty good guess.

"Sky, Finn," Finn said. "Precious cargo is away. We need to roll out, brother."

"Alright, check," Sky answered. He gave one last look at Heavy, still in his sights. It'd be so easy. But now it'd just be revenge. Heavy stood slowly and advanced cautiously into the alley, weapon still shouldered. "Sky moving."

Wren was trembling, but he couldn't tell if it was from the cold, or the nerves, or a combination of the two. He felt it mostly in his chest, and no matter how hard he squeezed his arms into his sides, his ribcage just kept on vibrating like he had some kind of machine stuck inside. He pulled the hood up on his coat. It made it a little harder to see what was going on around him, but maybe that was OK. Wren was just focused on keeping near Mama anyway. And Wick. His job was to stay with Wick.

He hoped Kit was OK. He'd heard the shots, of course. But everything had happened so fast after that, and no one had mentioned anything, and he wasn't supposed to talk or ask any questions. He'd always liked her, even though Wren didn't know her very well. She'd been one of the first he'd Awakened, even before Mez, and she'd been the easiest to help. And now Mez was dead, and Luck, and now maybe Kit too. It seemed especially cruel, to him; like life had been twice stolen from them. The hollow promise of a second chance, snatched away.

The heavy quiet still seemed eerie, like the silence that falls after some background noise everyone had grown accustomed to suddenly goes away. And everything they did seemed too loud in it. Their footsteps, the jangle of their gear, even their breathing. Wren found himself breathing through his mouth, just to try to keep quiet.

The air was cold enough that he could just see his breath every once in a while, if he was looking for it, and there was enough light to see. For the most part, though, Wick was leading them through back alleys and narrow passages where the street lamps were fewer and the shadows were darker. If Wren had ever been down any of these paths, he certainly didn't recognize them now. He wasn't even sure which direction they were headed, except he assumed they were getting steadily closer to the wall. Wren also realized he had no idea how long it'd been since they'd left the Tea House. It seemed like they'd been walking a long time, way longer than it should've taken. But he remembered traveling with Three, and how sometimes when you were scared and tired, a few minutes could seem like an hour. And right now, Wren was a little scared, and really, really tired.

He bumped into Cass without even realizing he'd lost focus. Apparently they were stopping. A few steps ahead, Wick was crouched low, whispering something that Wren couldn't make out. Wick turned around and motioned for them all to get low. Straight ahead looked like a brick wall, so they were either at an intersection of alleys, or a dead end. They waited in silence for several minutes, or what seemed like it anyway. Wren heard Gamble whisper, and then a few moments later Wick did too. Talking to each other, probably. It was strange, the way they communicated. Wick had called it their *secure channel,* but Wren didn't know how it worked. It wasn't like pimming, exactly, and somehow it didn't *feel* the same. It sounded funny; tinny, with static. Low signal, low profile. Maybe it was something they had developed to avoid attracting the Weir when they were out beyond the wall.

Gamble and Wick took turns, whispering back and forth a few times, and then Gamble came up from the back of the line and crouched down next to Wick. Wren couldn't help but wonder if something had gone wrong. They hadn't seen any patrols, or really anyone for that matter, since they'd left Mister Sun's. Whether that was because Wick was such a good pathfinder, or because Finn and Sky were out there somewhere helping guide them around, Wren wasn't sure. But this was the first time they'd stopped in one place for this long. Wren's legs were starting to go to sleep.

Finally, Wick moved forward and disappeared around a corner, but Gamble turned to face them and held up a hand, signaling for them to wait. She seemed to be listening intently for something. After another minute or two, she nodded.

"Alright, check," she whispered. "Wren first."

Wren didn't like the sound of that. Gamble pointed at him, and then motioned for him to join her. He walked to her bent double, and his legs were all tingly from the long wait. When he got to her, she put a hand on his shoulder and her lips right next to his ear.

"We're going to cross one at a time," Gamble whispered. "Wick's waiting around the corner. I want you to go first, OK?"

"OK."

"Here, look." She leaned Wren out a little so he could see around the corner. They were in a small T-intersection, and beyond it there was a wide stretch of open ground ending at the wall. Almost there. Gamble let him stand up straight again and then said, "Just run straight across. Wick's waiting right on the other side, OK?"

"OK. You want me to run?" he asked.

"Yep, the quicker the better."

Wren nodded.

"OK, Wick," she whispered, "Wren's coming across. Let me know when it's safe."

She smiled at him while they waited, but Wren wondered what she meant by *when it's safe*. Did that mean it wasn't safe now? Or were they just double-checking to make sure it was clear? He was still thinking that when she said, "OK, go, Wren!"

And the next thing he knew he was running, running out of the alley, and running across that wide stretch, and once he was in the open, it seemed a whole lot wider than it had before. And he knew he should just look straight ahead, but Wren couldn't help it. He glanced to the side, just for a second.

Just for a second.

Maybe there was a crack in the concrete, or maybe the surface wasn't as level as it looked. Maybe he was just too tired. Wren hardly had time to notice he had tripped before he felt his palms skid and his chin slam into the ground. The impact left him stunned and disoriented. There was a funny taste in his mouth, and Wren's hands felt like he was holding fire. Everything was completely dark. Why couldn't he see? And there was a funny drumming in his ears. It took him a few seconds before he realized what it was.

Footsteps.

Someone was running towards him. Wren was just lifting his head when he felt hands grabbing at his coat. Someone was picking him up. Running with him. He almost called out, but then he could see again, and Wren realized that his coat had gotten twisted and he'd been looking into his hood. And then they were at the base of the wall, and he was on his feet and someone was in front of him.

"Are you OK?" he whispered. "Wren, are you *OK?*"

It was Wick. Wick had come to get him.

Wren nodded. "I fell," he said.

Wick smiled. "I saw."

"I'm sorry, Wick."

"Yeah, he's fine," Wick said, and then, "It's OK, buddy. No harm done. Except maybe your chin there." Wren touched his chin and it stung. His fingers came away wet.

Wick said, "We'll get Mouse to take a look at you when we see him. You still got your teeth?"

"I think so." Wren checked the inside of his mouth with his tongue and found a place that felt funny inside his cheek, like there was a piece of food stuck there that wouldn't come off. "I think I bit my cheek."

"Yeah, that was a good tumble. When we get where we're going, maybe I'll teach you how to roll, huh?" Wick smiled again and clapped Wren on the shoulder once. "Hang tight while we get the others across."

Wick gently moved Wren closer to the wall, and Wren knelt down again, feeling stupid. He watched silently while Painter came across, and then Cass, and finally Gamble.

"Are you alright, sweetheart?" Cass asked.

He just nodded because he didn't want to talk about it, even though his chin really hurt and the place in his cheek felt gross.

"Wick, go," Gamble said, and then mercifully they were off again and no one had a chance to talk about the fall anymore. They moved along the wall and found a set of stairs that climbed in a switchback. Wren expected that they'd have to take them slowly, but Wick actually accelerated as they went up, and when they reached the top, Wren understood. Sky was already there waiting for them.

"Finn?" Gamble asked, and Sky just pointed over the wall. "Alright, good. Wren, come on, you're up."

Wren didn't know what that meant, but he stepped over to Sky like he was instructed. Sky had on some kind of harness that Wren hadn't seen before, and there was a loose loop of strap hanging off the front.

"Legs through here," Sky said as he crouched down. The next thing Wren knew, a couple of pairs of hands were helping him get his legs in the right place, and then Sky stood up, and Wren went with him. "Hold on tight, Mister Governor," Sky said. "And you might not want to look down."

Sky sat back on the parapet and swiveled around. Wren had figured out what was going to happen, but he was still trying to work out exactly how – when Sky lurched, and it felt like the world turned upside down, and Wren shut his eyes and forgot everything but hanging on. There was a whizzing sound that started high and then got lower, and it felt like they were falling in slow motion. And then there were hands grabbing at him again, and Sky chuckled and said, "You can open your eyes now, sir." Finn was there, and they were on the ground again, but outside the wall.

It took a few moments to get Wren unhooked from Sky. Once Wren was clear, Sky went back over and put a foot on the wall, and then all of a sudden went floating right back up, kicking off and bounding his way to the top. Wren watched him the whole way up, and he finally saw the thin cable that was connected somewhere high above.

"Oooh, what happened to your chin?" Finn said. "You bang it coming down?"

Wren shook his head. "I fell. Before."

Finn nodded. "We'll get Mouse to take a look at it."

Wren couldn't help smiling at hearing it again. "Wick said that too."

"Yeah, well… he manages to get things right every once in a while."

The whizzing sound started again, and Wren looked up. The others came down in a different arrangement, clinging to Sky's back with their legs around his waist and their arms hooked around his chest. It didn't look comfortable for anybody, but nobody said anything. Wren figured they were all just glad to reach the bottom.

Gamble came last, and once everyone was down, Sky had them move away from the wall. When they were clear, he fiddled with some kind of device near his waist where the cable was attached, and the line went slack and fell. The device whirred and the cable retracted into it. Wren didn't get to see exactly how it all worked, because Wick had already started moving out, and Mama had pulled Wren along to keep pace.

The group formed up with Wick leading the way; and Finn and Gamble slightly ahead and to either side of Cass, Painter, and Wren. Sky caught up and trailed a little behind, forming the final point in a protective diamond around them. It was a few moments before it really sunk in for Wren.

He'd been so intent on the danger they faced in escaping Morningside, he'd actually felt relief once they'd touched down outside the wall. For a brief time, he had forgotten what lay ahead. But not for long. As they moved together into the dead cityscape, and the great wall of Morningside faded behind them, it dawned on Wren that they were leaving the realm of men – and walking straight into the arms of the Weir.

FOURTEEN

People had lived here once, Cass knew, here in the shadow of the wall, and not all that long ago. Those that the citizens of Morningside called outsiders. Exiles from Underdown's city, still living under his "protection". As they moved through the now-empty ruins, Cass could still see traces of it; even though most of the personal belongings had been stripped out, the shells of buildings that had housed life showed signs of intentional design and structure – of maintenance. The further they got from the city, though, the fewer of those shelters she saw.

For the first mile or so, Wick kept them moving at a cautious but steady pace. The four bodyguards had their weapons out, held low but ready to bring to action in an instant. Cass had rarely seen the team running this heavy. Sky, of course, had his long rifle, and Gamble had her jittergun in a holster strapped to her thigh, but she was also carrying a larger weapon on a sling across her chest. Something about halfway between a pistol and rifle. Cass had never seen it before, but there wasn't much doubt about its purpose. Both Wick and Finn had short-barreled rifles hanging on slings in front of them.

Whether out of fear or just good instincts, no one spoke while they walked. Every so often a Weir would call in the distance with an unearthly cry, but their cries were scattered and sporadic. Thankfully, none ever actually came within view. It'd been so long since Cass had been outside when the Weir were abroad. Even surrounded by a team she trusted completely, the farther they got from the city, the more vulnerable she felt.

She was just starting to wonder when and where they were going to regroup with Able and the others when Gamble quietly called for them to halt and to gather up around her. They crowded in close, but Wick, Finn, and Sky kept their backs to the rest of them, maintaining constant security intently.

"We're getting into the outer limits now," Gamble whispered. "The Weir don't typically show up in numbers this close to the city, but that's going to change in the next couple of miles."

"Just tell us what you need us to do," Cass said.

"I need *you* to tell *me*."

"I don't understand."

"Until tonight, none of us had ever been outside the wall with an Awakened before. And definitely not this far out. We need to know what to expect. Do they notice you? Can they track you? Are you going to draw their attention, or will they ignore you?"

Cass honestly had no idea. She hadn't often been outside the walls since she'd been Awakened, and until the night they attacked the gate she'd never confronted them as one.

"It d-d-d, it depends," Painter whispered.

"On what?" Gamble asked.

Painter shrugged. "Sometimes I'd go out. I tried to be careful, but s-s-somet-t-times… one f-f-followed me once, for a little while." He paused and looked away from the group.

"And once I guh-got attacked. I didn't go b… back out after."

"Doesn't sound like you draw them any special way, though?"

Painter shrugged again.

Gamble's eyes narrowed and her mouth made an almost perfectly flat line. "Alright. We'll just have to take it slow. We don't want to kill any if we don't have to, that usually brings trouble. But if it comes to that, you just stay next to me, do what I tell you, and let us do the work."

"You don't have to protect me," Cass said. "I can fight."

"I know you *can*, but with all due respect, we've got a way we operate. Best if we don't throw something unpredictable in that mix."

Cass hated the idea of being treated like some kind of helpless citizen. But Gamble was right. Cass wasn't one of them. What she thought was helping might actually throw them off. This was no time or place to let pride get in the way.

"We need to run as low profile as possible," Gamble continued. "No pimming, no active broadcast, keep everything locked down while we're out here."

"What about your secure channel?" Wren asked. Gamble looked at him with raised eyebrows. "Is that OK?"

"It's real low frequency so we can use it, but we try to keep it limited."

"That's why it sounds funny," Wren said.

"Finn can tell you all about it later," Gamble said with a quick nod and a wink. Her way of gently but clearly ending any further discussion. "We've still got a couple of hours until sunrise, but we need to put some distance between us and the city. I'm not trying to scare you, but I want you to understand there's some danger out there. We're going to do everything we can to keep us all out of trouble. But there's a whole lot of trouble between us and our destination. It'll be helpful if you guys keep your eyes and ears open too. Stay focused, stay with us. Questions?"

Cass looked at Wren and Painter, who both shook their heads.

"We're good to go," Cass said. Gamble nodded.

"Wick," she said. "You got an ETA on the others?"

"Should've been here before us."

"That's what I thought. Finn, any word?"

"Negative. Want me to ping him?"

"I'll do it… Swoop, Gamble. What's your location?" She waited several seconds. "Swoop, this is Gamble." Another long pause. In the distance, a Weir gave a call. A few seconds later, another answered. Gamble and Finn traded looks.

"Swoop?" she asked. After a moment, Gamble's expression changed slightly, but Cass couldn't read it. "You guys need support? One for yes, two for no."

"What's going on?" Cass asked Sky.

He glanced back over his shoulder. "He's clicking at us. Something's close enough to him he doesn't want to risk talking."

"Weir?"

"Hope so. Otherwise they're not out of the city yet."

"Alright, check," Gamble said. "We're going to move to alternate. Can you make the alternate…? Check. See you there."

Gamble adjusted the shoulder straps on the oversized pack she was carrying. "We're going to have to link up with them at the alternate. I'm guessing we've got some Weir wandering around between us and them… Wick?" She nodded his direction.

"Yep."

They set out again, the pace slightly faster than the one they'd maintained earlier. As they proceeded, Cass noticed a steady degradation of their surroundings. More collapsed buildings, more exposed beams and rods, more brokenness. Soon it was clear they were completely beyond the borders of any power Morningside had ever projected.

They'd walked another twenty minutes or so before they saw the first Weir. Finn spotted it, off to their left. He made a soft hissing sound, shouldered his weapon, and then extended it slightly to point at the Weir. The group stopped. Cass followed his line and caught a glimpse of the Weir just as it was passing behind the shell of a two-story building between them. She felt Wren press against her leg, and she instinctively dropped her arm around his shoulders.

About thirty seconds later, the Weir emerged from behind the building. It was a fair distance from them, maybe fifty or sixty yards away. Finn and Sky both tracked it as it prowled around the abandoned structure, crouched low enough that it sometimes placed its hands on the ground in an almost crawl. It stopped every so often, swiveling its head slowly from side to side, almost as a man would if listening for a particular sound, or trying to identify a peculiar scent. It sat back on its haunches and slowly started turning its glowing eyes in their direction.

Cass immediately averted her own eyes, realizing almost too late that if she could see it, it could most certainly see her. She heard it squawk once, a burst of static. A few moments later, it made the same noise again. The second time didn't sound as full.

"Ace?" Sky whispered.

"Wait."

Cass held herself as still as possible, eyes closed, feeling that even the natural sway of her body might be too much movement to be safe. The Weir squawked a third time, but it was distant. Cass realized she was holding her breath.

"Alright, let's move," Gamble whispered.

Cass opened her eyes to see Wick already pushing forward, instantly responsive to Gamble's commands. As they moved, she glanced back in the Weir's direction, but there was no sign of it. They marched on in silence, following closely the edges and contours of the broken buildings that surrounded them. Wick never let them stray far from cover, never committed them too fully to any one path or direction. The cries, croaks, and calls from the Weir grew more frequent. On more than one occasion Wick quickly redirected them down a side street or narrow alley, though his reasons weren't always clear. Even so, no one questioned his decisions.

The wind picked up as they continued on, stirring up swirls and eddies of concrete dust. Had they not been keeping pace and loaded down with packs, the chill might have been cutting. Cass looked down at Wren, hoping to gauge his feelings, but his face was hidden in the deep hood of his coat. Painter lagged slightly behind them, his eyes downcast and his face grim. Cass hoped Wren was warm enough, but didn't want to risk asking. He kept near her, steadily matching her pace without falter or complaint. These still, quiet hours of the night were *her* time, the time she felt most alive and aware. But she knew her son must have been fighting with every step just to keep his eyes open.

Watching him, it was hard to remember he was only eight. Though in another sense, it was equally hard to believe he was *already* eight. Still so small for his age, and yet in bearing years ahead. At times he was just her little boy; quick to call when frightened, eager to be held. But other times deeply brooding and withdrawn. Her son was fast becoming more and more of an enigma to her. And Cass couldn't help but think of her other son, how *he* had changed, who *he* had become. Her mind revolted at the concept that Wren could ever be anything like Asher. Yet fear remained. If Wren started down that path, would she notice in time to try and stop him? Would she even be capable of stopping him?

A sudden motion from Wick snapped Cass back into the moment. He gestured for them to stop, and then waved them into a narrow alley they'd just passed. The team moved as if the whole thing had been planned.

Sky rolled in first, keeping to the right and covering the left with his weapon. He hesitated a second or two while Finn caught up, and Finn moved to the left wall, mirroring Sky's movements, to cover the opposite side of the alley. Together they flowed down the narrow route and stopped just shy of where it intersected with another. Both went to a knee, weapons trained on the corners.

Gamble quickly shepherded Painter, Wren, and Cass in and had them move to one side, about halfway down. They stopped maybe seven yards back from Sky and Finn's position, and then she motioned for them to crouch down. Once they were set, Gamble turned around to face the alley entrance and placed herself behind them, using her own body to shield them from anything that might try to follow them in. Wick came last, sliding in at the mouth of the alley, partially concealed, but positioned to maintain watch.

They all held as still as possible. After two, maybe three minutes, Wick looked back over his shoulder and held up three fingers, and then waved an open hand at about forty-five degrees, towards the right of the alley entrance. Gamble nodded, and then ducked her head and whispered into her hand. The group held position for another minute or so, and then Wick gave another hand signal – a fist with thumb and pinky extended. Cass had no idea what it meant, but Gamble whispered into her hand again, and a moment later there was the hint of a shuffle from the other end of the alley.

Cass looked back and saw Sky moving towards them in a low crouch. Finn slid smoothly over into the spot where Sky had just been, keeping his weapon up to cover the intersecting alley. Sky continued past Cass, scooted up behind Wick, and patted him on the shoulder. As soon as he did, Wick swiveled fluidly and swept back down the alley towards Finn. Wick looked intense, though he managed a quick wink at Cass, and lightly touched the top of Wren's head, as he passed them. When he took up Finn's original position, the two of them carried on a brief conversation that was some mix of whispered words and indecipherable hand signals.

Gamble sidled up next to Cass and leaned in close, so close Cass could feel her breath when she spoke.

"They're pretty stirred up tonight," she whispered. "Wick's going to try to take us around. We'll move soon."

Cass nodded and Gamble returned back towards Sky. When Cass turned to check on Wren, she found him peering at her from within his hood. His eyes were wide.

"You OK?" she asked.

"Mama," he said. "They're everywhere."

Cass nodded. "They'll get us through," she said, hoping to reassure him. From his expression, though, it didn't look like she had.

Wick motioned again. Gamble relayed the message to the whole team, and then came alongside Cass and the boys.

"Stay about six feet behind me. And be quiet as you can."

Wick disappeared around the corner. Finn stood but held his position, providing cover as Gamble led Cass, Wren, and

Painter past him, quickly following Wick's lead. They slipped into the intersection. Gamble let the gap between them and Wick stretch to maybe four or five yards. It'd give them a little more time to react if something happened to him. As they progressed, Cass realized they were in a twisting network of narrow corridors and alleyways, amongst some cluster of buildings several stories high. There were branches every few yards, and Wick led them at a quicker pace than Cass had been expecting. He took turns seemingly at random, but with such certainty and precision she had to believe he knew exactly where he was going.

The calls of the Weir were coming almost on top of each other now, from all directions. At least that's what it seemed like to Cass. With the way the walls carried the sounds and the echoes, it was impossible to accurately judge numbers, distance, or location. But Cass felt the hair stand up on her neck and knew they were walking a knife's edge. She could feel the Weir, in a way. A kind of wild pressure, like the tension in the air just before a violent storm.

Wick took them down a short side street and then ushered them quickly across a narrow gap between buildings and into a deep recess under an overhang. At first glance, it looked something like a concrete U, and Cass didn't much care for the idea of getting boxed in. But on closer inspection, she saw a narrow opening near the center. She didn't have time to see much more, though. With a single aggressive hand gesture, Gamble directed her, Wren, and Painter to crowd back into the left-most corner.

Cass obeyed immediately and instinctively crouched down, though she didn't really know why. It just seemed like the right thing to do whenever they stopped moving. Wren slid in next to her, and Painter flopped down beside them.

He leaned back against the concrete wall and closed his eyes.

Wick and Sky remained near the entrance of the alcove, each on a knee and weapons shouldered. Scanning for targets. Behind them, Gamble and Finn stood next to each other in conference.

"Swoop, Gamble," Gamble said in a low voice. "Status…? Check. We've reached the alternate rally. It's pretty sporty out here. How is it your way…? Got an estimate…? Alright, check. See you in a few."

She looked up at Finn. "Think they've got a line on us?" Gamble said.

"Good chance," Finn answered.

"Anything you can do?"

"Not from here. Wick and I can go out, try to draw them away."

"Negative, I don't want to get split up more than we already are." Finn waited in patient silence while she thought through the options. "We'll hold here and hope the others get here first. Check that hall, make sure it's secure."

Finn gave an easy nod and moved towards the opening Cass had seen on their way in. Out in the open, the moonlight had been enough to navigate by, but beneath the overhang it was much darker. It didn't bother Cass, of course, but she wasn't sure how Finn was going to clear the corridor. He had his rifle up, pointed down the hall, but he hesitated at the entrance. A red light flicked on from somewhere alongside his weapon, bathing the corridor in a sinister hue. Low intensity, enough to see by without disturbing night-adjusted vision.

A necessary risk, and minimized, but still it made Cass nervous, knowing how little they could afford to draw any more attention to themselves. She didn't bother to ask for permission. She patted Wren on the back, and then slipped down the wall towards the darkened hallway. Her motion caused both Gamble and Finn to look at her sharply, and Cass held up a hand to let them know nothing was wrong.

"I'll check it," Cass said to Finn.

"I'll take care of it, ma'am," he said, as Gamble joined them.

"Finn, I can do it without the light. It's safer."

"What's going on?" Gamble asked.

"I'm going to clear the corridor," Cass answered before Finn could speak. "I don't need the light."

Gamble just looked at her for a moment.

"Finn, kill the light." Finn grunted in disapproval, but he switched the light off and lowered his weapon. "Back Sky for me."

Finn grimaced, but he nodded and went over to take a position between Wick and Sky.

"Down to the end and back," Gamble said. "I want to be sure we can get through there if we have to."

Cass nodded. Gamble pushed something into her hand. Cass looked down. Her jittergun. "You know how to use it, yeah?"

"Yeah," Cass answered, glancing back up to read Gamble's face. She was focused and serious, but Cass thought she could see a hint of fear behind Gamble's eyes. Cass couldn't remember a time when Gamble had feared anything.

"Shouldn't need it, but just in case," Gamble said with a fleeting and unconvincing smile.

"Be right back," Cass said. Gamble nodded, and Cass turned to face the entrance of the corridor. She eased her way slowly around the corner, carefully scanning it for any sign of trouble.

It was a concrete tunnel, smooth-walled and only about ten yards long, wide enough for maybe three people to walk shoulder-to-shoulder. It looked like it opened out into a similar configuration on the other side, into an open space beneath an overhang. There were a number of unevenly spaced gaps on either side of the hallway, though, and Cass couldn't tell if they were shallow alcoves or additional corridors.

The weight of the jittergun and the texture of the grip was oddly comforting, and she looked down again at the stubby weapon in her hand. It wasn't the same model as the one jCharles had given her long ago, but all the controls were basically in the same place. Memories returned: the air-rending buzz as it fired, the rapid vibration in her hand. The last time she'd used one of these, she'd been trapped in the Strand with Wren and Three. She'd killed a lot of Weir with it that night. But not enough.

Cass took a breath and gripped the jittergun a little tighter. And started down the corridor. There was debris strewn all along the floor. But no tracks through the rubble and dust. At least, no *obvious* tracks.

The first opening was to her right, and she moved as far to the left as she could. She brought the jittergun up with both hands and worked around the corner with cautious steps, not wanting to expose any more of herself than she had to. If there was anyone or any*thing* in there, the first thing it was going to see was the muzzle of the jitter, followed shortly thereafter by its devastating payload.

It didn't take long for her to see the back of the alcove. Not a corridor after all, for which Cass was thankful. Still, she moved carefully, carefully, around in an arc, making sure both corners were clear. There was nothing there but a couple of piles of debris that the wind had swept into the corners.

Cass continued down the hall, checking each alcove in the same fashion, taking nothing for granted. But they were all essentially the same. She reached the end without uncovering any surprises and became aware that her fingers were aching. She lowered the jittergun and relaxed her grip.

As expected, the corridor emptied out into a sort of three-walled room, a mirror image of the one where the others currently stood guard. Out across from her was an open area leading into another cluster of buildings. She stood there for maybe thirty seconds, carefully scanning for any sign of the Weir, but saw none. Satisfied they were secure, Cass turned and started walking back towards the others.

About halfway down the hall, a faint scraping noise sounded behind her, and made her stop dead. A gust of cold air funneled down the corridor and swirled around her. Had that been all it was? She couldn't take any chances; she ducked into the nearest alcove and crouched down. Gamble was just at the end of the hall. Fifteen feet away. But Cass had to be sure.

She peeked out around the corner. There was nothing there. Not yet. Something in her gut told her to wait. And then sure enough, there – far out beyond the end of the corridor – a Weir crept into view. It croaked once as it moved down the open expanse between Cass and the buildings across from her. Fortunately, it didn't seem to be headed their way, and eventually it turned into another alleyway and disappeared.

Cass waited in her hiding place a bit longer, just to be safe, and then rejoined the others.

"Hall's clear," she said to Gamble. "A few alcoves, but they're not deep. I saw a Weir across the street, but it was moving away from us."

"Check," Gamble answered, as she did so often. It seemed almost reflexive. "Can you pull security on that hall?"

"You mean watch it?" Cass asked.

"Yeah."

"Yeah, I can do that."

Cass looked over at Wren, still tucked into the corner. He was hugging his knees, with his head resting on top of them, but he was still watching everything intently. "How much longer?" she asked Gamble.

"Seven to ten minutes."

Cass nodded and returned to the corridor, keeping watch. Under normal circumstances, ten minutes wouldn't have seemed like much of a wait. But in that moment, Cass wasn't confident they'd last more than five.

They didn't even make it to three.

FIFTEEN

Cass realised that Finn must've picked up on something, because he moved before anyone else did. He grabbed a handful of Wick's coat and dragged his little brother backwards almost into Gamble's lap. Sky tensed up and withdrew from the edge of the recess.

There was a brief exchange of whispers between Wick, Finn, and Gamble, and then Finn was moving again. He motioned emphatically to Wren and Painter, shepherding them towards Cass. When they reached her, Finn moved down the corridor with careful steps, heel-toe, heel-toe, his weapon at his shoulder and his eyes no doubt focused on his aim point.

Sky was the next one in, and once he was past them, he motioned for them to follow. Painter went first. Wren stayed locked to Cass's side.

Gamble came in behind them, and Wick was last in again. Cass instinctively started guiding Wren into one of the alcoves, but Gamble grabbed her shoulder.

"Stay where I can see you," she whispered.

Cass nodded and hunkered down against the right side of the corridor, with Wren in front of her. She realized they were in essentially the same formation as they'd been in the alley earlier in the night. But this time, once Wick was in position, he had whipped the strap of his pack over his head and laid the cumbersome bundle on the ground behind him, along the alley wall, and then brought his weapon up. Wren pressed into Cass, and she drew him close.

When the first call came, its volume and proximity shocked Cass. Without a doubt, a Weir was not far from where they'd been standing just moments before. The answer, however, was far worse. A second Weir responded from the opposite end of the corridor. Cass tightened her hold on Wren.

Wick shifted backwards smoothly, silently, perfectly balanced – almost like he was on rails. He looked back over his shoulder and pointed to his eyes with two fingers, then held up his index finger, and then finally pointed towards the right of the alley entrance. It wasn't difficult to interpret. He'd seen one, right around the corner.

Gamble bowed her head and held a hand in front of her face, and made a sound like an uneven exhalation or broken sigh. It took a moment before Cass realized she was whispering. Gamble looked back around Cass, and Cass followed her gaze. Sky was motioning with his hand; two fingers up, and then a signal Cass guessed meant *moving this way*.

Gamble gave an exaggerated nod, and then ducked her head and held her hand up again. She whispered something, but it was so low and breathy there was no way Cass could make out the words. The Weir on Sky and Finn's end of the alley called out again. Much closer. On Wick's side, Cass could actually see the shine from the Weir's eyes at the entrance.

Wick eased his weapon down and reached behind him with his left hand. With a slow but steady pull, he drew a long-bladed knife from a sheath along his lower back. In the heavy silence, Cass could hear the Weir breathing around the corner, an eerily lifeless sound like wind through rusting pipes. Gamble made a little noise. And then many things happened at once.

There was a shuffling sound behind Cass, and the electric howl of a Weir was cut short by the hum of Sky's rifle, followed quickly by a muffled burst from Finn's weapon. In the same instant, Wick launched out of the alley and intercepted the Weir on his side just as it reached the corner. His left arm pumped like a piston as he drove the creature backwards, out of view. There was a heavy impact, and Cass knew Wick had slammed the Weir to the ground. Gamble flashed up with her weapon at the ready, moving towards Wick – and covering the distance with such practiced intensity it almost looked casual, even in its terrifying speed.

Cass snapped her head around and saw Sky and Finn violently rushing the other corner together, moving as a single entity. Then, all was still and silent. For a brief few seconds, it felt like all the world was holding its breath.

And then a chorus of electric shrieks sundered the night from every direction.

Gamble came flying back around the corner and caught Cass by the arm, pulling her to her feet. Wick followed closely after. He slowed only long enough to snatch the supply bag off the ground and throw it over his shoulder, then swept past the rest of them towards the other end of the corridor.

"Swoop, abort alternate, alternate is compromised. We are moving to contingency," Gamble said, in an emotionless tone at complete odds with the chaos. She ushered Cass, Wren, and Painter all towards the far end of the alley where Finn and Sky were.

Cass grabbed Wren's hand. "I say again, alternate is compromised, proceed to contingency. Warpath, warpath, warpath."

Cass didn't know what "warpath" meant exactly, but she had a pretty good guess; they were in trouble. As they exited the corridor, Finn grabbed Painter and locked him close to Finn's side, controlling Painter's movement. Sky covered their escape, his rifle pointed back down the hall. Cass heard it hum once and then quickly again as they raced across the open space and into the alleys across the street.

No one was concerned about how much noise they were making now. Wick plunged into an alleyway and Finn was right behind him, dragging along Painter with one hand and keeping his weapon at the ready with the other. Gamble kept a hand on Cass's shoulder. Her grip was firm, and though it didn't feel like she was forcing Cass any particular direction, she left no doubt where she intended everyone to go. Cass squeezed Wren's hand in hers.

They weren't running exactly, not even jogging really, but they moved so aggressively that Cass found herself occasionally having to surge forward a few steps to keep up. Wren kept up as best he could, though he stumbled several times and would have fallen at least once, if Cass hadn't been holding his hand. After the third time, she finally just picked Wren up and carried him, doing her best to keep her gun hand as free as she could.

Further down the alley, a Weir hurtled around the corner and charged straight at them. Wick didn't even break stride. He fired three times, *pop pop pop*, and hopped over the Weir's body as it skidded towards his feet. Cass hazarded a glance over her shoulder and noticed Sky was nowhere to be seen.

"Eyes forward," Gamble said, her voice even but full of intensity. "Just keep moving."

"Where are we going?" Cass called.

"Wherever Wick takes us," Gamble answered, and then switched over to comms. "Swoop, we're in contact, what's your location?"

Wick disappeared down an alley to the left and Cass heard a flurry of gunfire. Finn stopped at the intersection and pushed Painter up against the wall.

"Easy!" Painter said, but Finn didn't seem to hear him. He braced his rifle against the corner of the wall and squeezed off two shots as Wick backed his way out, firing his weapon as well.

It happened so fast that they were already moving again before Cass reached them.

"Not that way," Wick said as he resumed their initial path, leading them on without hesitation. Cass hazarded a glance down the left turn as she passed and saw four or maybe five Weir sprawled there, and one clambering over the bodies.

"There's another–" she cried, trying to warn Gamble, but Gamble's weapon was already up and firing.

"Wick," Gamble said without missing a beat, "find us a place to button up."

Wren clung tightly to Cass with his arms and legs, and kept his head buried in her shoulder. Not out of terror, though, or not *just* out of terror. She could tell he was doing his best to keep himself stable, taking some of his weight off of her arm so she could move better.

Up ahead, Wick exited the alley and slowed. Finn caught up and forcefully guided Painter into position between the brothers, one on each side. They moved together then, covering opposite directions. Cass cleared the alley and found that they were crossing a wide street. For the moment, there were no Weir in sight. Across the street, there was another row of decaying buildings. Wick made for a squat two-story structure. It had only one door and a small slot window at street level, both yawning with darkness.

When they reached the entrance, Finn and Wick left Painter just outside and steamrolled in, snapping their weapons around in precise movements as they made sure the room was clear. Their red lights danced across the walls and made it look like a fire was burning low inside.

Cass caught up and Gamble quickly directed them all inside. The first room was large and open, with a wide and partially collapsed staircase running up the left side, and a doorframe in the back wall. There red lights played along the walls of a hall, where Wick and Finn were rapidly searching for any threats. Wick's pack was in the middle of the room, on the floor. Gamble slung hers there as well.

"Cass," she said, pointing at the base of the staircase. "Anything moves up there, kill it. Boys, over here." Cass moved to the bottom of the stairs and went down on a knee, aiming the jittergun up into the darkness at the top of the stairs. Painter and Wren followed Gamble's directions and moved to a corner in the back of the room, furthest from all the entrances.

"Floor's clear," Finn said as he re-entered the room, "but there's a back door in one of the rooms." He turned off the light on his rifle.

"Wick," Gamble said. "You've got the hall."

"I'm on the hall, check," Wick answered. He stayed in the front room, but crouched down near the back where he had a tight angle through the doorframe into the hall.

"Upstairs?" Finn said.

"Cass has it," Gamble said. "I need you guns front."

Finn moved closer to the front entrance, though he remained well inside and to one side of the door. Gamble slid over to the opposite direction, so they were covering opposing angles through the entrance.

"Where's Sky?" Finn asked.

"On the way. Wick, you bounce the location?"

"Yeah, they've got it."

"Check."

Cass couldn't see what was going on outside the building from where she was, but the Weir were making a lot of noise calling and answering. Their cries and howls filled her with dread. And out there, somewhere, Sky was alone. Cass couldn't imagine what he must've been feeling. Or what Gamble must've been going through. Not that she was showing any signs of concern.

"Swoop? Gamble, what's your situation...? We had to hole up. You get Wick's bounce...? If you can, yeah."

"Here he comes," Finn said.

"Understood," Gamble said, though Cass couldn't tell if she was responding to Finn or still talking to Swoop.

"Come on, come on," Finn said to himself. And then, a few seconds later, slightly louder, "Sky's coming in." He lowered his rifle, and Gamble pointed hers at the ceiling. Moments later Sky ducked in through the entrance. As soon as he was through, both Gamble and Finn brought their weapons back on target.

"Sorry, Ace," Sky said, breathing heavily. "Had to do some extra legwork."

"You bring any with you?" she asked him.

"Not immediately. Left a little trail for them headed the opposite direction. Might buy us a couple minutes."

"Check."

Sky slid in next to Gamble, taking over her position. "Glad you're safe," she said.

"Me too," he answered.

Gamble moved further back into the room, putting herself between the door and the boys.

"Finn is front," Gamble said. "Wick is back. Cass is stairs."

"Check," Sky said. Coordinating, Cass figured. So if Gamble told everyone to move to the back, they all knew which way she meant.

They sat in silence after that, tensely. Three minutes passed. Five. Maybe as many as ten. Cass's arms grew tired, and she lowered them to rest on her knees. If anything had been upstairs, it likely would've come down by now. Even so she stayed focused on the staircase, just to be safe. The stairs bent to the right, preventing her from seeing all the way to the top, but a portion of the upper steps had collapsed, which gave Cass a better view than she would've had otherwise.

After a time, unless Cass was mistaken, the Weir began to quiet. It was subtle at first. More pauses between calls. Longer delays. And then they started to seem farther away. Maybe they'd thrown them off the trail after all.

Finn made a soft hissing sound. Cass glanced over and saw him holding up one finger. She wondered if anyone else could see it in the darkened room, but Gamble's whisper answered that question.

"How far?" she asked.

"Thirty meters," Finn answered.

"Inbound?"

"Not yet."

"Hold fire. See if it moves on."

Cass hated not being able to see what was going on. The slot window wasn't far from her. But she knew Gamble was counting on her to watch the stairs, and she fought back the urge to sneak a peek.

"What's it doing?" Gamble asked after a minute.

"Just standing there," Finn said. "But it's looking this way."

And then it made a sound that sent chills racing down Cass's spine.

"*Spshhhh. Naaaah.*" The same noise they'd made the night they attacked the wall. It was shockingly unlike the Weir's typical cries. They were some unholy mix of electronic and raw animal sound. As uncanny as those were, this new cry was different, more disturbing; almost as if a piece of machinery were trying to form words.

"Not again," Sky said.

"Hold," Gamble said.

"*Spshhhh. Naaaah.*"

"Count?" Gamble asked.

"Still just the one."

Cass watched the others, trying to get a read on the situation. Everyone was focused, intent on their areas of responsibility. Wick might as well have been oblivious to what was going on through the front door, even though Cass knew he was completely aware; he just kept his eyes fixed on that back hallway. Wren and Painter were still huddled together in that corner. Cass noticed Wren had his knife out.

Some instinct kicked in, and Cass quickly looked back at the stairs and at the same time brought the jittergun up. There was a soft glow reflecting, and through the gap she saw clawed fingers closing to grip the top stair.

A Weir.

Cass did her best to emulate what she'd seen the others do. She hissed and held up one finger, keeping her eyes on the Weir's hand she could still see. What was it waiting for?

Wordlessly, Gamble glided over to her side, and Cass pointed at the hand. Gamble shook her head. She couldn't see it, unlike Cass.

"*Spshhhh. Naaaah.*"

It didn't matter.

"Back hall, back hall," Wick called, and then he was firing, and Cass saw the fingers flex on the stair.

She squeezed the trigger just as the Weir pounced down the steps, and caught it with a full burst before it touched the ground. It landed in a wet heap and slid down the stairs towards her, but in the next instant a second Weir was on the steps, and she fired again. It fell backwards, flailing wildly. Gamble fired a burst from her weapon and the second Weir went still.

Wick was sending a steady but measured stream of death down his hall, *pop pop pop pop-pop*, and Finn fired two shots out the front.

"Help on the hall," Wick called, and Sky was there in a second, standing behind Wick's crouched form and adding his firepower.

Gamble ducked under Cass's gun and moved up two steps. Then Gamble leaned forward and braced herself with one hand to get a better look up the stairs, and then fired off two quick bursts.

"They're coming in through the roof!" she called, and then bounded up four more steps.

"Help front," Finn said.

"Sky moving front," Sky called, and he dashed across the room. Finn was standing right at the door, calmly firing. Sky slid on his knees and started shooting.

"Cover," Finn said. He ejected the magazine from his rifle and smoothly replaced it with a fresh one. "I'm up." And he went right back to firing.

"Back hall," Wick called again. "I'm low."

"Cass, help Wick," Gamble said.

Cass flew across the room and took up a position just as she'd seen Sky do a few moments before, leaning over Wick so she could shoot over top of him without impeding his movement. There were several dead Weir strewn in the hallway, all in awkward positions, and three more were charging towards them.

It was a tight angle. Cass fired and saw the doorframe splinter as the burst from her weapon tore through it and into the first Weir. Wick fired twice, and Cass followed with another burst, dropping the last Weir.

"Cover," Wick said, "keep it covered, Cass."

"Covering," Cass answered. And she killed another Weir that tried to round the corner.

Wick swapped magazines on his weapon and had it back up and running in under two seconds. "I'm up." He emphasized the point by firing off four rounds and dropping another two Weir. There were enough bodies piled in the hall now that other Weir were stumbling and clambering over their fallen. But still they came, heedless of the death that awaited them.

"Gamble," Sky called. "Get back where we can see you!"

If she answered, Cass couldn't hear it over the shrieks of the Weir and the gunfire echoing in the cavernous room. The jittergun was starting to get warm in her hand. She wondered how much ammunition she had left.

"Gamble!" Sky shouted.

"Here!" Gamble answered. Cass glanced at the staircase and saw Gamble backpedaling down the steps, firing controlled bursts the whole way. "We're gonna lose the stairs!"

"Finn?" Sky said.

"Go!" Finn yelled.

"Sky, moving to stairs!" Sky called, and as he moved to help his wife, he let his rifle drop on its sling and transitioned to his sidearm. Cass couldn't tell what it was, but it was loud.

"Swoop, we're in the heat!" Gamble said, still firing her weapon. A Weir tumbled down the stairs and Sky shot it twice more. "Where are you?" Then to Sky, "Back, get back off the stairs!" And then "Swoop, say again!"

Since Cass wasn't dialed in on the channel, she had no idea what Swoop's response was. But there was a sudden eruption of gunfire from the front of the building, and Finn gave a little whoop.

"There you go," Finn yelled. "Get on 'em, son!"

"Check, we're rolling out front side," Gamble called. "Front side, watch my ping! Finn, stairs!"

"Finn moving to stairs!" he said, moving instantly and stepping into position as soon as Gamble was clear. Gamble strode across the room, snagged her pack off the floor and threw it over a shoulder. Pulled the boys to their feet, shepherded them towards the front door.

"Cass, with me," she said. "We're going out the front. We're coming out!"

Cass fired a final burst and then turned and closed in on Gamble, who was already ushering the boys through the front door.

"Run, boys, run," Gamble said as they made it to the street. She got them pointed in the right direction, and they both took off. She hesitated, waving Cass on, and then giving her a quick slap on the shoulder as she passed.

The street was littered with dead Weir. Three figures were rapidly approaching: Swoop, Mouse, and Able. Painter and Wren reached them first, but Cass wasn't far behind.

Able lowered his weapon and caught Wren, and swung him up to carry him. Mouse took charge of Painter.

"Stay right behind me," Swoop said when Cass reached him. "Right hand on my left shoulder, stand behind me and to my left."

"Check," Cass answered, and she slid around behind him into position exactly as directed. Back down the street Gamble was still standing at the entrance, directing the others in their evacuation. Sky was already out, heading their way. Then Finn backed out, but he stopped just outside and kept firing back into the building. A few seconds later, Wick came out backwards in a crouch, dragging his pack with one hand and squeezing off bursts from his rifle with the other. When he was out, both he and Finn went full throttle and unleashed a non-stop torrent of fire.

Gamble pulled something off her vest and tossed it underhanded through the entrance. Then the three of them broke in a full-out sprint towards the rest of the team. A few seconds later a lightning flash silently erupted inside the building, momentarily dazzling Cass's eyes. Nothing else came out afterwards.

"Get lost?" Gamble said when she reached Swoop.

"Bad directions," Swoop answered. "Worse neighborhood."

A Weir stumbled out from the building, wounded or dazed or both. Sky's rifle hummed and dropped it before it'd gone three steps.

"Cover our withdrawal. Peel back, Swoop's the anchor. I've got the cargo," Gamble said, and she matched her words with hand signals.

"Check," Swoop said. He hunched over and brought his weapon up, covering the building. Finn, Wick, and Sky jogged and quickly lined up on a diagonal behind Swoop with about five yards between each of them.

"Cass, you're with me," she said. Mouse and Able were already moving with Painter and Wren. "I'm not going to hold on to you, but I need you to stay right behind me."

"Got it," Cass said. She lined up behind Gamble, just off her right shoulder. Gamble started guiding her away from the building.

A few moments later, Cass heard Swoop open up with his heavy weapon behind her, a long sustained burst. She looked back and saw him get up and start towards them, and as soon as he had passed Finn, Swoop slapped him on the shoulder and Finn started firing, full auto. A few Weir had come out, only to get cut down by the gunfire. Even so, the sheer volume was disconcerting given how precise and methodical the team usually were with their weapons.

"Keep moving, Cass," Gamble said. And then she added, "They're bounding back. Should keep the crowd from following."

Then Cass understood. Swoop and his team were making a rolling retreat, with the front man providing suppressive fire for a few seconds, and then running to the back of the line while the next man took over. It gave the others time to put some distance between them and the concentration of Weir that had gathered around the building.

Gamble caught up with, and then passed, Mouse and Able, and took point. She kept them all moving steadily, but set the pace quite a bit slower and more cautious than when they'd been headed for shelter. Eventually the gunfire ceased behind them, and a minute or two later the rest of the team rejoined them.

"All clear?" Gamble asked when Wick caught up. She kept her voice low, but it wasn't a whisper. That seemed encouraging.

"Yeah, last couple of bursts were just for fun. I don't think we got them all, but I'm pretty sure the survivors finally got the hint."

"Get us back on track. And try not to run us into any more trouble."

"Yes, *sir*," Wick said, and he jogged up to the front. Gamble dropped back a little, putting Mouse and Able ahead of her, while Finn and Sky moved out wider to either side of the group. Swoop fell in next to Gamble.

"Left a big mess back there," he said. "Somebody comes lookin', there's not gonna be much doubt what happened."

"We'll just have to hope the Weir clean up after themselves," Gamble answered. "Or that nobody comes looking."

"Anybody hurt?" Swoop asked.

"Don't think so. But we better give everybody a once-over once the sun's up."

At the mention, Cass noticed that the sky was already growing grey above them. She guessed they had another forty-five minutes, maybe an hour at most, before the Weir would withdraw. After what they'd just survived though, that seemed like a lifetime.

"Be nice to get this gear spread out then too," Swoop added.

"You need me to carry something for you, cupcake?" Gamble said.

"Nah," Swoop answered. "I just worry about Mouse."

"What's wrong with Mouse?" Cass asked. Gamble and Swoop both looked at her, and then at each other. Gamble smiled with one corner of her mouth.

"Soul of a poet trapped in a barbarian's body," Swoop said.

Mouse looked back over his shoulder with a disapproving eye. It might have been their deadpan delivery, or maybe she was more tired than she realized. Or it might have been that Cass's mind couldn't comprehend any sort of light-heartedness so soon after the ordeal they'd just survived. Whatever the case, it took her longer than it should have to recognize they were actually joking around.

"Sorry," she said, shaking her head. "I didn't realize you guys got issued senses of humor."

Swoop actually chuckled at that, and Cass thought that might have been the first time she'd ever heard him laugh.

"Careful, Miss Cass," Sky said. "People might start thinking you're one of us."

"I might be tempted to take that as a compliment."

"And that's how we know you're *not* one of us," Mouse said over his shoulder.

"Alright, quiet time, kids," Gamble said. "Swoop, rear guard. Eyes and guns up. We'll break at sunrise."

Swoop gave a nod and dropped back, and just like that, everyone was back to being switched on. Still, the briefly playful moment stuck with Cass and took some of the edge off the silent march. Ahead of her, Able was still carrying Wren. Her son had fallen asleep with his head on Able's shoulder. Though there were still distant calls and cries from the Weir, Cass felt herself relax. For some reason, she felt safer out in the open with these people than she had in the days back inside Morningside.

Wick led them confidently on. They had a few sudden changes in direction, and on one occasion they'd all crowded into a narrow courtyard and waited silently for a number of minutes. But for the most part – as the sky grew ever lighter grey above them and the stars disappeared – they faced no great danger.

Gradually the grey shifted to pale hues and the sounds of the Weir lessened, until a thin line of orange heralded a new dawn, and with it the retreat of the Weir. The team pressed on in weary silence until the sun was fully up and the horizon was vibrantly ablaze. Cass dug her veil out of her pack and covered her face to take the edge off the sharp morning light. Soon after, at long last, Gamble called for a halt and the group moved into a small protected courtyard and shed their gear.

"Get some rest," Gamble said. "I'll take first watch."

The team piled most of their supplies in the center of the courtyard, and then found places to get comfortable, have some food, and maybe grab a little sleep. Able laid Wren gently down in a shaded corner. Wren woke up briefly, but Cass came and sat with him, and he fell asleep again in her lap.

"You take a break, Ace," said Sky. "I'm good for another few hours at least."

"Negative. I need you sharp... You're cranky when you're tired."

Sky stared at her like he was thinking of a reason to protest, but Gamble gave him a look that let him know he wasn't going to win.

"Wake me up in forty-five minutes," Sky said.

"Sure."

"I mean it."

"OK," Gamble said. He leaned in and kissed her on the cheek. When he turned away from her, Gamble gave him a swat on the backside. Sky stretched out on the ground by all the gear, using one of the bags as a backrest. It didn't take him very long to doze off.

Painter was curled up on the concrete next to the courtyard wall, sound asleep, with his head on his arm. Able was eating by himself. Cass wondered how tired his arms and back were; he'd carried Wren the entire way, despite multiple offers from others to take over for him.

Wick and Finn were rehydrating, talking quietly and occasionally laughing to themselves. Swoop had disappeared for the moment. Mouse moved around the courtyard, checking on everyone. When he reached them, he encouraged Cass to make sure she and Wren both got some food and water in them before too long.

"Easy to forget you can get dehydrated in the cold," he said. "And out here, everybody needs to take extra good care of themselves."

Cass drank some water to reassure Mouse and promised she'd make sure Wren was well looked after when he woke up. Once he'd done a quick evaluation of the rest of the team members, Mouse joined Able across the courtyard. Gamble wandered over to where Cass was with Wren, and crouched next to them.

"How you holding up, Miss Cass?" she asked, keeping her voice low so as not to disturb Wren.

"I'm doing fine, Gamble. Thanks. How are you?"

Gamble dipped her head in a casual nod. "Right as rain. We'll need to cover about another fifteen klicks today. Kilometers, I mean. But we've got about nine hours of daylight, so we can afford to rest for a while."

"Are you going to take a break?"

"Yeah, in a couple of hours maybe."

"Not in forty-five minutes?" Cass asked with a smile.

"Like I said… Sky's cranky when he's tired."

"I don't mind taking a shift, if you'll let me. I wasn't always a lady of the court, you know."

"Yes, ma'am, I know. But I think we'll be alright," Gamble said. "I probably don't *need* to stay up myself, but we don't leave things to chance. Plus, the boys won't sleep if they think no one is on guard. They'll all just lie there listening for trouble."

"You've got a good team, Gamble."

"The best. But you're a pretty good fit yourself, Miss Cass."

"I don't know about that."

"Well, you *did* forget a move call right there at the end. Otherwise, pretty tight for your first time out."

Cass almost said it hadn't been her first time out, but just smiled instead. She thought back on what it'd been like for her, back when she'd been part of a crew. "Is it hard for you?"

"What's that?"

"Well… six men, you're the only woman…"

"We'd have more," Swoop said from behind them. "But we're the only ones that can keep up with her." He was just re-entering the courtyard. "Perimeter's good. Doesn't look like anyone's been through this way in a while."

"Check," Gamble answered. "Go crash out. I want you on graveyard tonight."

"I'm good, G. I slept a couple of days ago."

"Get some sleep, Swoop, or I'll put Wick on graveyard with you."

"She's a cruel mistress," Swoop said to Cass. He moved off and found a spot to rest as ordered.

"He'll sleep maybe an hour, and then he'll insist on staying up all night," Gamble said. "Sometimes I'm not sure he's human."

Cass smiled a little sadly. "I used to know someone like that."

"You should rest too, Miss Cass. We'll be plenty safe."

"Thanks, Gamble."

Gamble nodded again and crossed the courtyard to exchange quiet words with Mouse and Able. Cass's eyes felt dry and a little too big for their sockets, and she thought she might just close them, even though she didn't feel all that sleepy. She didn't even notice when she started dreaming.

Wren felt something heavy on his back and gradually became aware of someone saying his name. It took conscious effort to get his eyes to open, but he eventually managed it. The brightness surprised him and made him squint. Someone was crouched next to him. Someone big. Several seconds went by before Wren remembered where he was and what was going on. Mama wasn't there, though. He'd been using her lap as a pillow, but now her bag was under his head instead.

"Wren, buddy, can you wake up for me?" Mouse said. It was Mouse's hand on his back. Wren forced himself to sit up, even though it seemed like gravity had tripled since he'd fallen asleep. "Sorry to wake you, but we're going to get started here again in a little bit, and I wanted to take a look at your chin before we do."

Wren nodded and yawned and rubbed his eyes. He thought about looking around to find his mom, but it felt better to keep his eyes closed, so he just sat there with them shut while Mouse looked him over.

"I'm going to clean it up, OK, bud?" Mouse asked.

Wren nodded again. A few seconds later, a cold shock made him grimace and pull away.

"Sorry, it's probably going to sting a little."

"It's OK." Wren clenched his jaw and tried to hold still while Mouse cleaned up the wound and assessed it. By the time Mouse had finished, Wren was much more awake but no more ready to start walking again.

"Seems like you've been getting roughed up a lot lately," Mouse said. "You keep it up, I might start making you do this yourself." He smiled and clapped Wren on the upper arm, knocking him a little sideways.

"Thanks, Mouse."

"Sure thing, bud."

It was about 11.00 GST by that point, and the morning had warmed pleasantly; still cool with the breeze, but good weather for long walks. They'd stopped for almost four hours, which seemed like a long time to be stopped, but not very long to sleep. Cass brought him some food and water, and Painter sat with him while he ate. Wren was glad of the company, even though neither of them spoke much. The rest of the adults were busy repacking the final bits of gear. They must've unpacked everything and redistributed it all while he'd been asleep, because everybody's loads looked a lot more even now, and the two storage bags from Mister Sun's were empty.

Once all the bags were prepped, Gamble came over to them carrying a couple of smaller packs. She set them on the ground in front of them. He'd never seen her so loaded down before. In addition to her pack, she was wearing a harness with multiple pockets across her midsection, along her hips, and even a couple of smaller ones that ran up the shoulder straps. They all bulged with hardware, though Wren didn't know what much of it was for. Except the ammo. Seemed like Gamble had a lot of that. Though when he looked more closely, he noticed a couple of the magazines were empty. Not as much as he'd thought. Her short weapon hung across her chest on a sling, her jittergun was strapped to her thigh, and a long heavy-bladed knife dangled from her belt. Wren hadn't noticed it until now, but all of them had blades of some kind, in addition to their other weaponry.

"You fellas about set?" she asked.

"Yes, ma'am," Wren answered. Painter nodded.

"OK. We've got a lot of ground to cover today. I know you're tired, but once we get where we're going, we should all be able to rest a good while. You up for it?"

Wren got to his feet. "Yes, ma'am," he repeated. Painter was a little slower to rise.

"Good. These are for you." She slid the packs towards them with her foot. Able came over and joined them while Wren and Painter picked up the packs and put them on. At first, Wren was surprised by how heavy his was when he lifted it. Once he got it onto his back, however, he was even more surprised at how comfortable it felt. There were clasps at the waist and across the chest that Gamble fastened for him. The weight was noticeable, but didn't drag at Wren the way he had expected. Then Able helped him adjust the straps to make it even more secure and evenly distributed.

"Each of you has a buddy," Gamble said, while they were adjusting their packs. "Painter, you're with Mouse. Wren, Able's yours, of course. While we're out here, your job is to stay with your buddy, OK? Go where he goes, do what he tells you to. Anything you do, you do with your buddy. Got it?"

"Yes, ma'am," Wren said again. Painter just nodded.

"Alright," she said. And then louder, "Alright, let's spin it up, boys." And everybody else started slinging their packs on with practiced fluidity.

Wren noticed there was a black tube attached to his pack that came over his left shoulder, with a funny looking knobby ending. It was clipped to the shoulder strap.

"Able, what's this for?" he asked.

Water, Able signed. He unclipped it and held it up in front of Wren's mouth. Wren took it. *Squeeze this between your teeth to drink.*

Wren put the knobby end of the tube in his mouth and bit down on it slightly. A surprising gush of water flowed out and made him choke and splutter. Most of it ended up down his chin. When he looked up at Able, Wren could tell he was trying really hard not to laugh.

It takes a little practice.

Wren wiped his mouth and chin on the sleeve of his coat and then clipped the tube back in place. After that, they joined the rest of the team in the middle of courtyard, and they all set off together.

The team spread out into its familiar formation. Wick led the way, Finn and Sky pushed out to the sides, and Swoop brought up the rear, forming an outer ring of defense around their protectees. They set a steady pace, but Wren found that it was not difficult for him to keep. He was thankful. Sometimes when he traveled with adults, they seemed to forget that he had to take two or three steps for every one of theirs. Most times.

The team maintained focus as they passed through the empty urban ruins, speaking rarely, eyes constantly scanning. Even so, it seemed to Wren like they were almost relaxed. Though once he thought it about it, it kind of made sense. They were used to being out at night when deadly things were literally out hunting for them. Probably walking through the ruins in the daylight was a pleasant change. And even if there were bad people out here, it didn't seem likely that anyone would be dumb enough to try to start something with a group so obviously well-armed.

As it was, they saw no one else the entire day. They took a handful of short breaks along the way, but for the most part they made good progress with very little trouble. Only once did Wick decide to change direction and lead them in a detour. Wren wondered how it was that Wick never seemed to be at a loss for which way to go. It was almost like following someone around their own neighborhood. He rarely stopped to think, and when he did it was never for long.

By the time the sun was sinking towards the horizon, they'd reached their destination: a burned-out, partially collapsed structure. Wren actually wouldn't have thought it was safe to go inside of if Wick hadn't strolled so confidently through the gaping hole in the front. Even though the ceiling sagged enough in the middle, enough to make Wren nervous, Wick took them all inside and then did something with his hand to a place on the rear wall. A few moments later, there was a clicking sound and what looked like one of the exposed concrete support beams swung gently open. There was a metal staircase leading upwards into darkness.

It was a wayhouse, cleverly hidden within the failing structure. Wren gave another look at the bulging ceiling.

"It's safe," Finn said, seeing his concern. "It's actually reinforced, though you can't really tell from here. Clever bit of work, really."

They all filed in. Wick came in last, closing the door behind him. The air was a little stale, but not foul, which was reassuring. Wren noticed the door made a rubbery sort of sound when it shut, like it was vacuum-sealed.

It turned out there weren't actually that many steps. Someone activated the lights, and Wren was surprised at the size of the room at the top of the stairs. From where he was standing, it looked far too shallow for all of them to fit, and

Mouse had to hunch down to keep from hitting his head on the ceiling. Swoop, Sky, Finn, and Mouse paired up and disappeared from view, two to the left and two to the right.

When Wren reached the top, he saw that the room was actually very wide, spreading out maybe four times wider than it was deep, with the staircase right in the middle. The four men had split off to check the wayhouse, he realised. Wren could see them moving quickly down the halls on either side.

There were no real rooms that he could see; just one long corridor with a few short walls jutting out every so often to form stalls. To his right, the feet of several sets of steel-framed bunk beds poked out from several of the stalls. Off to his left, the place opened out a little more, and Wren assumed that was probably where the dining area and bathrooms were. He hoped there were doors on the bathrooms.

"It's clear," Swoop called as he came back towards the rest of the group. "Looks like we've got the place to ourselves."

"Anyone been through recently?" Gamble asked.

"Doesn't look like it."

"Doesn't smell like it either," Wick said. Wren looked up at him. "That's actually a good thing. I've been in a couple that were *fuuunky.*" He held the word out for extra emphasis.

"Give it till morning," Swoop said. "We ain't exactly a bunch of sweet-smellin' petunias."

"Speak for yourself," Sky said. "*I'm* as fresh as a baby's bottom." He tossed his pack on the floor in the stall closest to the entrance. "I call top bunk."

"Just make sure it doesn't squeak," Finn said as he moved by, further down the corridor. Gamble kicked his backside as he passed. The others started making themselves at home, laying claim to various stalls by slinging their packs down. Gamble shepherded Cass, Wren, and Painter along the hall towards the beds. She stopped them at one a few down from the entrance.

"I'd like to put you two in here," she said, indicating Cass and Wren. There wasn't much to it. A set of bunk beds with thin mattresses, bare concrete floor, bare concrete walls. There was a single light fixture in the middle of the low ceiling. "And Painter, if you don't mind, we'll put you right next door with Mouse."

Painter nodded. He looked exhausted. His goggles were down around his neck, and Wren could see the dark rings under his eyes, so dark they almost looked like bruises. Wren realized he couldn't remember the last time Painter had actually spoken.

"Painter, are you OK?" Wren asked.

Painter looked at him and nodded. He inhaled deeply, like it was an effort. "Just r-r-really tuh-, really tired." He gave a weak smile, but Wren got the impression there was something else going on.

"You go right ahead and sleep if you want," Gamble said. "We're here until morning." Painter nodded again and wandered to the next stall over. "Same for you two. Rest and recover as much as you can, but feel free to do whatever you like. Just don't leave." She said the last part with a smile.

"Thanks," Cass said.

Swoop passed by, on his way further down the hall. "I'm gonna rack out for a few."

"Good," Gamble said, and then a moment later called after him. "Make sure you eat something too."

"You're startin' to sound like Mouse," Swoop called back.

The remainder of the day was unremarkable for Wren. He and his mother ate some of their rations together in the dining area, on a wobbly steel table with mismatched chairs. Afterwards, he was so tired he just wanted to sleep. Cass helped him get ready for bed, which pretty much amounted to taking off his shoes and spreading his coat out on top of the mattress. Cass said she didn't want Wren lying directly on that old thing. She kissed him on the forehead and then went and removed some things from her pack, so she wouldn't wake him later. As Wren watched Cass, he saw her partially withdraw something and look at it for a moment.

She didn't pull it all the way out of the pack, but he recognized the grip of Three's pistol. She'd brought it along, even though he knew she didn't have any ammunition for it. Maybe for her it was like his knife was to him. He didn't really expect to use it, but he was glad to have it.

Cass glanced up and caught Wren looking at her. She smiled a little sadly and pushed the pistol back down into her pack, and finished whatever it was she had been doing. Then she came over and kissed his cheek again, and then switched off the light in their stall.

Wren wondered briefly if all the other lights and activity would make it hard for him to fall asleep, and that was his last thought before drifting off.

Painter awoke with the distinct feeling that someone had just called his name. His heart was hammering in his chest, and his forehead was covered with a light sweat. He lay still with his eyes open, listening for whoever it was to speak again. The lights were all out. He could hear Mouse on the lower bunk below him, breathing deeply. All else was quiet, still.

But the feeling remained. As if someone had been there, whispering his name right in his ear to wake him. And it almost felt like someone *was* standing there. When Painter looked around the room he saw nothing unusual. But there was a sense of presence, of someone else, close. It filled him with a creeping dread.

His sleep had been troubled by dark and twisted dreams, though he couldn't remember any of the details when he tried. Maybe it was just a lingering sensation from those. His subconscious trying to process the unbelievable chaos and pain of the past few days. Painter tried to remind himself that he was safe here, that no matter what was going on outside, he was secure in here. He was with good people, people who were capable of protecting him, and who had even shown their willingness to do so. Even so, the darkness remained, clinging to his mind like an oily shadow.

There was a sudden flutter through Painter's mind, a black tide of rippling thought. Foreign, incoherent, forced into his brain. He instinctively clapped his hands over his ears and squeezed his eyes shut. Pressure grew, as if a band had been stretched around his skull and was being gradually drawn tighter, tighter, tighter until it was almost unbearable. Painter gritted his teeth and wanted to scream, but found he couldn't even draw a breath.

And then just as suddenly as it had come, Painter felt an almost physical pop inside his head, and the pressure evaporated. And in its place was a tiny, quiet thought.

They should fear.

Painter opened his eyes and took his hands from his ears. He found he could breathe again. Everything was the same as it had been just moments before. Even Mouse's breathing seemed completely undisturbed. And the feeling of a presence in the room was gone. Everything was fine. Except for Painter.

He sat up slowly in the bed, which turned out to be a good thing because his forehead touched the ceiling before he remembered how low it was. The room seemed smaller than it should have. A growing claustrophobia pressed in around Painter, almost to the point of overwhelming him. He slid off the bunk and crept out into the hall, trying to steady his breathing. There just didn't seem to be enough air.

It would be an easy thing, to sneak out. He could be quiet when he wanted. But he shouldn't. It might be dangerous. It might draw attention. And who knew how the others would react if they woke and found Painter gone.

Would they care?

Another stray thought that felt like it came from outside himself. But the question lingered in his mind. Would they? Protecting him wasn't their job. He was just a tag-along. An accidental burden. Maybe it'd be easier for everyone if he just slipped away.

He crept further down the hall towards the staircase with careful footsteps. Past Wren and Cass, past Wick and Finn, past Sky and Gamble. Painter wouldn't leave them. Not like this. But he needed to get out, out into the night air, where he could breathe and think – and get his mind back clear and under control. The night was drawing him, whether he wanted it to or not.

At the stairs Painter paused and looked back down the hall, wrestling with himself. It felt wrong somehow. But why should it? He wasn't their prisoner, no matter how much they treated him like one. He wasn't one of those weak citizens, either. They didn't know what he was truly capable of, none of them did. If they had any idea, they would fear him. Maybe they *should* fear.

"Trouble sleeping?" The voice came from behind him, startling Painter, and he felt himself jump. He turned and found Swoop standing there, leaning against the wall, staring back at him without expression. And Painter came back to himself, and all his dark thoughts dissipated.

"Y-y-yeah," he said. *Listen to yourself! You can't even speak!* What had he been thinking? He felt almost as if he'd been sleepwalking. "Weird dreams."

Swoop didn't react in any noticeable way. He didn't even blink. Just stared steadily right into Painter's eyes.

"Just needed to mmm-mmm, to move a little," Painter said. "But I'm OK now... I'm gonna, I'm gonna go b-back to buh-bed."

Swoop dipped his head in a hint of a nod. Then after a heavy pause, he added, "Night."

Painter turned and walked back down the hall to his bunk, feeling Swoop's gaze on him the entire way. He stole a sidelong glance once he reached the stall, and caught a glimpse of Swoop out of the corner of his eye. Still standing there watching him.

It was unsettling. Painter climbed back up onto the bunk and, as he tried to get comfortable again, he wondered if maybe he'd been wrong to think he wasn't a prisoner.

Swoop gave it another minute or so, after the kid had gone back to his bunk. Just to be sure. And when he was sure, and only then, he holstered the sidearm he'd been holding behind his back.

The sounds of people moving around drifted into Wren's consciousness well before he opened his eyes. For a time he lay there listening, half-pretending to be asleep – just to see how long he could get away with it. The bunk hadn't been particularly comfortable and he'd gotten cold in the middle of the night, but, knowing another long day of walking was ahead, it felt good to just lie there. Wren wished he could store up that feeling, so he could draw on it later after he'd been on his feet for hours, and still had more to go.

It would be hard work. Even if his legs hadn't still been tired and sore from the day before, it would've been tough. But he was excited about getting to see Chapel and Lil and all their people again. To finally show Mama the compound, and to eat real food, and to live in a community without walls, even if it was just for a few days. That excitement, though, was mixed with nervousness.

Wren had always meant to go back before now. But after Mister Carter had died... well, it hadn't seemed right somehow, for Wren to go back when that great man could never return. He didn't know how everyone would react. There was no doubt they would welcome him, and everyone with him. It was Chapel's way to be welcoming. But Wren wondered how different their relationship would be.

And Mama. He hadn't thought about that until now. How would he explain Painter and Mama to Chapel? Most likely, he'd have to go ahead of them and prepare everyone. He'd have to mention that to Gamble and Wick, to make sure they didn't get too close before they had a chance to announce themselves.

Wren opened his eyes and lay still. The overhead light was still off, though lights were on elsewhere in the wayhouse, enough for him to see. His mama was crouched down, quietly rummaging through her pack. He couldn't tell if she was putting things in or taking them out, but she was taking care not to wake him.

"Hi, Mama," he said. She glanced up at him and smiled.

"Hi, sweetheart. Did I wake you?" she asked.

Wren shook his head. "What time is it?"

"Early still."

"Is everyone else up?"

"Everyone but Painter. We thought we'd let you two sleep as long as you could. Did you sleep well?"

"I slept OK. Not as good as at home." It seemed strange to him that he thought of Morningside as home. He sat up and rubbed the sleep out of his eyes.

Cass nodded. "I always have trouble sleeping in new places. Hungry?"

"Yes, Mama."

"Let's see what we can find for you to eat." She stood and picked him up off the bed and held him for a few seconds. Wren squeezed her shoulders. "Want me to carry you?" she asked.

"No, I'll walk."

She gave him a final squeeze and then eased him to his feet. They walked together down the long corridor back to the eating area. Sky was sitting on the lower bunk in his stall, checking his rifle. He gave a little wave as they passed.

When they reached the dining area, they found Swoop and Gamble there talking in low voices. Wren didn't catch what they were saying, but he noticed they were quick to end the conversation and change the subject when he came in the room.

"Morning, Governor," Gamble said. "How're you feeling?"

"Sleepy."

"Sleepy?" she said with a smile. "You slept almost twelve hours!"

"Didn't feel like that much."

She winked. "I know what you mean."

"I'm gonna check on Wick and Finn," Swoop said. Gamble gave him a little nod, and he bent forward in a partial bow. "Governor. Lady."

Wren slid into a seat at the table and rested his head in his hands while Cass found some food and water. To eat, there was some kind of dark-colored bar that was tough to chew and slightly gritty, that supposedly was going to give him lots of energy for the day. It didn't taste very good. But Mister Sun had snuck one of his pastries in too, and they'd saved it for him.

"Do you want to split it with me?" Wren asked his mama. She was just sitting there watching him eat.

"Thanks, sweetheart, but no, it's for you."

"I don't mind."

"No, baby, you go ahead."

He ate part of it, and Cass kept sitting there, watching him with a little smile on her face.

"Are you sure? It's tasty."

"Oh, OK," she said. "Just a bite."

Wren held it up for her, and she took a bite off the corner of it.

"Save anything ffff-for me?" Painter said from the hall.

"Oh, hey Painter," Cass said. "No, sorry. We ate all our rations first thing this morning."

He stood in the hall staring with a slightly puzzled look on his face. Painter still had the circles under his eyes, Wren noticed.

"I'm joking," Cass added. "Are you OK?"

"Oh," Painter said. "Yeah. Just tuh, tuh, just tired."

"Here, have a seat," she said. She got up from the table and went to get him some food. Painter eased himself onto one of the other chairs, almost like it hurt him to do it.

"Sore?" Wren asked.

Painter nodded, but he kept his eyes on the table in front of him. Wren got an uneasy feeling. Painter seemed different somehow. Or he *felt* different. Wren couldn't figure out what it was, though. It'd been a tough few days for all of them, but maybe Painter most of all. Maybe that's all there was to it. Or maybe it was nothing more than Wren's own frazzled nerves, making him worry about things that weren't there.

"I think you're really going to like Chapel's place," Wren said. "It's different from anywhere else. And the people are really nice."

Painter nodded again. After that, Wren stopped trying to make any conversation. Cass reappeared with food and water for Painter, and then left them on their own while she helped the others prepare to leave. It wasn't unusual for Painter to keep to himself, but as they sat together in silence, Wren couldn't escape the feeling that Painter was purposely shutting him out.

It was only a few minutes after Painter had finished eating that Gamble popped her head in and told them to get ready to move again. The boys went back to their stalls and gathered their things. Within ten minutes, they were all heading back down the stairs together and back out into the open.

A heavy fog waited for them when they stepped outside. It was cool, not cold, but the mist seemed to go right through Wren's coat and straight to his bones. He pulled his hood up and drew it down around his face. Everything was shrouded in a gentle rolling grey and as they pushed out into it, Wren felt almost like they were intruding on some sacred ground. As if the broken city had finally found rest in the misted silence, and every one of their magnified footsteps threatened to disturb its peace.

The others seemed to sense it too. They hardly ever talked, and when they did it was in near whispers. Wick led them on, occasionally disappearing briefly from view in the swirling mist.

By midday much of the fog had melted away, but the sky remained grey and heavily overcast, in the all-day sort of way where it might rain any moment, or not at all. Mama wasn't wearing her veil, and Painter didn't even need his goggles. They stopped for lunch and a brief rest. Gamble had them up and moving again well before Wren was ready.

It was hard to keep track of time on the colorless march. But Wren guessed it was midafternoon when he found himself recognizing parts of their surroundings, without being able to remember ever having noticed them in the first place. A buckled overpass, a series of cracked and crumbling concrete pillars, a sunken building. Landmarks from some forgotten corner of his mind.

"We're close," Wren said. "I think you should wait here, Mama."

Gamble called for the team to halt and conferred with everyone. Wick guessed they had about a five-minute walk left to reach the compound. It was decided that Gamble, Wick, and Able would escort Wren to the compound to scout it out. Once they'd explained everything to Chapel, they'd notify the others to join them. The two groups split up and Wren's team headed towards the compound.

Wren was more tired than he could remember being in a long time, but he felt excitement the closer they got. He hadn't realized how much he'd missed Chapel, and Lil too – until the idea of seeing them again had become more than a dream, and was moments away from becoming a reality.

It was quieter than he'd expected. Much quieter. A distant sense of dread pricked his mind. Wren tried to ignore it. The compound was just ahead, beyond a little rise in the terrain.

Probably the wind was carrying the normal sounds of life away in the other direction. Chapel would be there. Chapel and Lil. Everything would be just as he remembered.

But as they crested the rise, even as his mind denied it, Wren's heart went sharply cold and he found himself running, running towards those low walls, with Gamble shouting after him to stop. And then Able caught him, but Wren barely felt it because he was screaming in wordless agony, with tears soaking his face and blinding his eyes.

It couldn't be. It couldn't be, but it was.

Chapel's compound lay before them in ruins.

SIXTEEN

When Cass heard the scream echo through the cityscape, she didn't hesitate. She knew her son's voice. Cass was off at a full sprint before anyone else had even reacted.

The others were only a couple hundred yards away. As Cass approached, she saw Wick kneeling and Gamble standing nearby with her hands on top of her head. Able was holding Wren. Gamble reacted to the sound of her approach, but Cass's only concern was for her son.

"Wren!" she called. "Wren, what happened?"

His face was buried against Able's shoulder, and he didn't answer at first. But as she drew nearer, she could tell he was sobbing.

Gamble intercepted her with a stony expression.

"Is he alright, is he hurt?" Cass asked.

"He's not hurt," Gamble said. But her face was grave.

"Mama," Wren said, racked with sobs. "Mama, they're gone! They're all gone!" Able carried him over to her, and Wren clung to her fiercely, with her coat balled in his fists.

"What? What do you mean, Wren?"

Gamble just pointed down the slope. At first, Cass couldn't tell what she was pointing at. Nothing caught her eye as unusual. Just more of the same broken and scarred urban landscape.

But then Cass noticed a low wall with gentle curves, and from there started picking up little details. Here a shredded bit of cloth. There some kind of tool, broken in two. The damage was more recent than the rest of the surrounding area. Much more recent.

The rest of the team came barreling up behind them and immediately moved into positions with their weapons up, scanning for targets. They were breathing hard from the sprint with all that gear, but every man was sharp and alert. Painter was the last to reach them.

"What's going on?" Finn asked. He was inhaling deeply through his nose and exhaling out of his mouth, trying to bring his breathing back under control.

"Place is wrecked," Wick said.

"That it down there? With the fence?" said Finn.

"Yeah," Wick answered.

"Weir?"

"Not sure yet."

"Better check it," Swoop said. "G?"

Gamble nodded. That was all Swoop needed. "Wick, Finn, you're with me," he said. "Sky, think you can find a room with a view?"

"Yep," Sky said. The four men started removing their packs and double-checking their combat gear.

"Rest of you hang here while we make sure it's clear," said Swoop.

"Keep your eyes wide open, boy," Gamble said. "And watch your step. If it was scrapers, they might've left traps."

"Heard, understood, and acknowledged," Swoop said. "We'll keep you posted."

Swoop led Wick and Finn down the hill towards the compound, while Sky went off on his own to find an elevated position.

"Scrapers?" Painter asked.

"The worst kind of scavengers," Gamble said. "They don't necessarily wait around for you to die on your own. We had more trouble with them than we did with the Weir, back when Underdown was around."

"They would r-r-raid outsiders," Painter said. "I remember. Never heard them cuh... called that though."

Gamble didn't respond, and the group fell silent. Even Wren. He'd cried himself out, and was now just lying with his head on Cass's shoulder.

Down below, Swoop and the brothers cautiously approached the low wall that marked the boundary of the compound, and then slowly worked their way through one of the gates.

"Might as well get comfortable," Gamble said. "It'll be a while."

The team didn't budge. Cass figured Gamble's comment was meant for her, so she carried Wren over to a nearby building and sat him in her lap while she leaned back against a wall. No one spoke much. Cass could tell the team was checking in at regular intervals from Gamble's occasional one-sided responses, but otherwise they all just waited.

It was over an hour before they got word that it was clear for them to join the others. Sky reappeared a few minutes after they got the signal, and then they gathered up the packs that had been left behind and moved to the compound.

From a distance, Cass hadn't really gotten a sense of how extensive the damage was. Walking through the compound made everything all too real. There was no doubt that people had been living here not all that long ago. Belongings were broken and scattered all across the grounds. It was almost as if some great wind had scoured the little village for every last person and blown them from their homes.

The walk was both heartbreaking and mind-boggling. Everywhere Cass looked, she saw lingering signs of a carefully cultivated existence. An outpost of human life, here on the border of the Strand. And at the same time, she couldn't fathom how in the world people had ever managed to survive in such a place.

There were no strong defenses, no high walls, no bristling gun towers. If Wren hadn't told her so many stories of the people he'd met, she would never have imagined anyone could've lasted here for more than a few days.

They met Swoop and Wick in front of one of the larger structures in the compound, at the bottom of a set of stairs. Wren sat down on the steps and just stared vacantly at what was left of the place. Fire had consumed portions of the surrounding buildings, and there were clear signs of battle. Dark splotches spotted the ground, especially around the area where they now stood.

"What do you think?" Gamble asked.

"Weir, definitely," Swoop said. "Too much stuff left behind for it to have been scrapers."

Cass sat down next to Wren and rubbed his back.

"A lot of 'em, too," Wick added. "Judging from all the tracks. I'd say sixty at least. Maybe more."

"Sounds like an awful lot just to be prowling around," Sky said.

"Yeah, that's another thing. Looks to me like they all came in the same way, from the north-east."

"Not from the Strand?" Cass asked.

Wick shook his head. "My guess is the people put up a fight near the wall, and got pushed back. Tried to make a stand here."

"I don't understand what people would be doing out here in the first place," Sky said. "They couldn't have thought those walls would do anything."

"We aren't animals that we should live in a pen," Wren said quietly. Everyone turned to look at him.

"What, sweetheart?" Cass asked.

"It's what Chapel used to say. The people were their own protection."

Sky started to make a comment, but a sharp look from Gamble shut him up. "Damage looks pretty recent," she said.

"Yeah, three days, maybe," Wick said. "I'd guess five at the most."

"There was an attack when I was here before," Wren said. "A big one. Some people died. But they won. I just... I can't believe they're all gone."

"Well, I don't know about *all*," Wick said. "I think there were survivors."

"Got a guess on numbers?" Gamble asked.

Wick shook his head. "Not many. But I don't know how many there were to begin with. Do you remember, Wren?"

Wren shook his head slowly. "Not exactly. Two hundred? Maybe? I don't know really, I never thought to count. There were a bunch of kids..." He trailed off and put his face in his hands. Cass pulled him closer and laid her cheek on top of his head. She wasn't sure how much more he could take.

"Think you could track 'em?" Swoop asked Wick.

He shrugged. "Probably. Not sure how much help it'd be."

"We're gonna need a plan here pretty soon," Mouse said. The overcast sky made it tough to judge exactly how late in the day it was, but it was pretty clear they didn't have much time to travel.

"Wick, what you got?" said Gamble.

"Nothing close, G. We could try to roll back east, but I'm not sure what kind of shelter we'd be able to find in short time."

"Then I guess we might as well make ourselves at home. Swoop?" she asked.

"Back across the courtyard, there's an L-shaped building," he said. "Still mostly intact. Probably the most defensible for us."

"Alright. Let's get to it."

"There's something I want to show you first."

"It'll save time if you just tell us."

Swoop shook his head. "You gotta see it for yourself. Finn's down there now."

Cass picked Wren up, and Swoop led them all through the village, towards the western side. They found Finn standing to one side of a rectangular plot, where a series of rods jutted up from the ground, some covered by tangled masses of something Cass couldn't identify. As she got closer, though, she realized what she was looking at.

Plants. More than that. Crops.

"Would you look at that…" Sky said, quietly. Almost in reverence.

It'd been years since Cass had seen real, out-of-the-ground grown fruits or vegetables. And she'd never seen so many all in one place. There were beans, and some sort of green leafy things, though most of what was planted Cass couldn't identify. Many of the crops had been trampled, and some she'd just never seen before.

"I had no idea anyone still farmed," Mouse said, reaching out to feel the green leaves of one of the taller plants.

"Doesn't look like enough to feed two hundred, though."

"They had other stuff too," Wren said. "But the growing things always tasted better."

"Heads up," Swoop said all of a sudden, and he moved to put himself between Cass, Wren, and the bordering wall. Finn and Wick reacted quickly, and fell in beside him.

A group of figures stood in the distance. For a long moment, the two groups stared at one another, unmoving. Cass counted nine of them. As she watched, though, a few of them broke off from the group and disappeared behind a cluster of buildings.

"What do you think they want?" Wick said.

"All the stuff that's scattered all over the place, probably," Finn answered.

"Scrapers?"

"Could be."

Gamble gave Sky a look, and tilted her head to one side. Sky nodded and slipped off.

The group started advancing slowly. Five of them. No sign of the other four.

"Keep your weapons lowered," Gamble said. "We're going to be polite and friendly." She stepped around in front of the others and walked forward a few paces. And then over her shoulder she added, "But be ready to kill every last one of them."

Cass let Wren slide down to his feet, and then put him behind her. Mouse and Able took up positions on either side of her and a few steps behind.

Painter stepped up on her left. "Do they have guh- guns?"

"I can't tell," Cass said.

"I hope not," he said. "There's nnnn-nowhere for us to hide."

Cass glanced around. Painter was right. They were exposed, and the closest point of cover was a small structure a good twenty yards back into the village. If it came to shooting, it was almost guaranteed someone was going to get hit. And where had those other four gone?

The group of others halted their advance about ten yards back from the boundary wall. Three men and two women, judging from their builds, though Cass knew that wasn't always accurate. They were all wearing long cloaks, and two of them had their hoods up. Cass didn't see any guns on them, but they were all carrying weapons of some kind or another. Blades mostly, though one of the men had a short spear. It was telling that those weapons were on display; the cloaks could've easily concealed them. The message was clear enough. Though if those were the weapons they were willing to display, Cass wondered what else they might have hidden.

"Afternoon," Gamble called.

"Ma'am," answered one of the hooded figures. A woman, judging by her voice.

"What brings you out this way?"

"We were wondering the same about you."

"Just traveling through. Thought we might find a friend here."

"You won't."

"Yeah…" Gamble said. She glanced back over her left shoulder and gave a little nod. Mouse and Finn both turned to face that direction. A few seconds later the four missing members of the other group came into view. Gamble looked back at the five. "Well, one thing we're not doing is looking for trouble."

"I wouldn't have guessed that, judging from all the hardware you're running."

"Trouble sometimes comes to us."

Wren stepped around in front of Cass. She grabbed his shoulder, but he tried to shrug it off.

"Let go, Mama."

"Wren, not now–"

"Let go," he said, jerking away from her. There was almost a growl in his voice. Cass was shocked by his tone, and she held up her hands. She watched as he squeezed between Swoop and Wick, and went to stand next to Gamble.

"Wren, what're you doing?" Gamble asked, but he stepped past her.

"We're looking for a man named Chapel," he called. "Do you know what happened to him? To the people that lived here?"

The group of five reacted, exchanging glances with one another. Then the hooded woman spoke.

"Wren?" She laid back her hood. She had long brown hair and pale blue eyes. "Wren, is that you?"

"Lil!" Wren yelled, and before anyone could stop him, he took off towards her. She hopped over the low fence and went down on her knees to catch him in her arms. He nearly knocked Lil over with his tackling hug. It was strange for Cass, to see her son so happy to see someone she'd never met.

"So," Wick said. "I'm guessing we don't have to kill all of 'em, then?"

"Looks like," Finn answered.

"Stay sharp," Swoop said. "Ain't over yet."

The two groups started moving towards one another warily, with Lil and Wren at the center. Cass trailed a little behind the main group. Mouse and Finn were a few paces behind her, keeping their eyes on the four-man group that had come around their flank.

"Mama!" Wren called. He'd let go of the woman's neck with one arm and turned back partially towards them. "Mama, it's OK! It's Lil!"

Lil was smiling now as they approached, and Wren was rapidly introducing everyone, pointing to each in turn as he spoke their names.

"That's Gamble, and Swoop, and that's Wick, and that's my mom–"

Lil gasped and shot to her feet. One of the men from her group gave a little shout. Weapons flashed; swords from sheaths, rifles to shoulders. Cass noticed Lil had a grip on Wren's arm, and had pulled him slightly behind her.

"Wait, no! No," Wren called, pulling away. He stepped between the two groups, waving his arms. "It's OK, it's alright!"

Cass held up her hands, palms out, trying to look as nonthreatening as she could.

"Lil," she said, keeping her voice calm and controlled. "Wren's told me so much about you. About you, and Chapel, and Mister Carter."

She could see the utter confusion on the other woman's face, the horror mingled with incomprehension of the words Cass was speaking. Cass berated herself for not wearing her veil. A stupid and careless mistake.

"I'm sorry, I know it's a shock," Cass said.

The tip of Lil's blade lowered slightly.

"What… *are* you?" she half-whispered, fear evident in her voice.

Cass tried to think of how to answer. How could she possibly explain it?

"She's my mama," Wren said.

After a long tense moment, Lil lowered her sword, though she still looked confused and a little frightened. The people behind her lowered their weapons as well, but not completely. It was clear they didn't trust the situation.

"I don't understand," Lil said.

"They took her, Lil," said Wren. "But I got her back. And my friend Painter, too."

"Are they... human?"

"Not exactly," Cass answered. "But we *are* ourselves."

Lil shook her head, and then did it again more forcefully. The second time almost as if she were chastising herself. She sheathed her weapon and approached with her hand out.

"I'm sorry," she said. "I'm sorry, I shouldn't have said that. It's just..."

"Please don't apologize. It was thoughtless of me. I should've let Wren warn you. All of you," Cass said as she shook Lil's hand. "My name's Cass."

"Lil. It's amazing to meet you. Really."

Some of the others kept their distance, but one of Lil's companions stepped boldly forward and introduced himself as well, a grim-faced man named Elan. After that, with the immediate crisis seemingly averted, the two groups carefully came together and made hesitant introductions. Gamble called Sky back in from his hidden position. Cass gave a brief account of their journey from Morningside, though she was careful to avoid mentioning any details about why they'd left. Lil dispatched several of her companions to carry out whatever business they'd come to attend to, and then with the remainder, escorted Cass and the others back to the large rectangular building.

They went up the steps together and into the large main room, but stopped just inside the entrance. Like the rest of the village, the room had been largely wrecked, but there were a few tables and long benches that were still intact. The group gathered some of the furniture and set it up near the entrance. Swoop, Gamble, Cass, Wren, and Painter sat around the table with Lil and her escort. The rest of Gamble's team spread out around the room, standing nearby or leaning against walls in various locations.

The first few minutes were awkward, but as they continued conversation, it started to become clear that these people were all cut from the same cloth. Cass had seen it before. Even when they weren't on the same side, there just seemed to be a natural bond between warriors.

"They came three nights ago," Lil said. "In overwhelming numbers. We mounted a strong defense, as we had many times before. But this time..." She trailed off, shaking her head.

"Something changed," Elan said. "The way they moved. And fought."

"It was like... I don't even know how to describe it."

"Like they were one?" Cass said.

Lil looked at her and nodded. "One being, made from many creatures."

Gamble and Cass looked at each other. "We've seen it too," Gamble said. "Once in Morningside, and then again the night we left."

"What about Chapel?" Wren asked. "Is he OK?"

Lil looked at him sadly, and reached over to stroke his hair. She shook her head. "We lost Chapel many months ago. He was taken not long after you left. I'm sorry, Wren."

Wren's shoulders went slack and he closed his eyes. His face contorted as he tried to hold back the tears, but little coughing sobs escaped. Cass reached over and pulled his head to her shoulder to hold him while he cried. She noticed Lil watching them with a sweet smile tinged with sadness.

"Where are your people now?" Gamble asked.

"About forty minutes north and a little west," Lil answered. "There's a refuge. We'd hoped never to need it."

"*Closer* to the Strand?" Wick asked.

"Slightly."

"And how many are you?" asked Gamble.

Lil shook her head. "Too few." For a moment, her eyes lost focus, and her jaw clenched. She lowered her gaze to the table and inhaled deeply, trying to regain her composure.

"Eighteen able bodies," Elan said. "About thirty old, sick, wounded, or children."

Lil put a hand to her brow. "The children…" Elan put a hand on her shoulder and squeezed. Lil gathered herself and continued. "We've made a few trips back, to recover what we could. We'll need to get under way again soon. Our numbers are stretched thin as it is. I assume you'll return with us?"

Gamble exchanged a quick look with Swoop. "We haven't made any decisions yet," she said.

"I see. I'm not sure what your options are, but I imagine they're few. And we could use the help."

Gamble gave a non-committal nod. "Understood."

The two women held each other's gazes for a moment, and then Lil bowed her head slightly. "We'll let you discuss your plans. But we leave in twenty minutes." She stood, and her companions rose with her. They moved to the stairs, but Lil paused at the entrance and said over her shoulder, "I hope you'll do the right thing." And with that, they headed out to join the others in the village.

Once Lil and the others had cleared the room, the rest of the team gathered around the table to discuss their options.

"Thoughts?" Gamble said.

"Gotta go our separate ways," said Swoop. "No question."

"How you figure that?" Finn said.

"You got fifty frightened, dying, and desperate people holed up in some reinforced area we've never seen before. All that gear we're carrying?" He shook his head. "I don't care how nice they seem now. That's not a good set-up for us."

"We could be a lot of help to them, Swoop," Mouse said.

"No arguing that," Finn responded. "Just not sure how good it is for *us*."

"Our principals are the priority," Gamble said. "The only question to answer is if we're more secure somewhere on our own, or if we need to bunk up with these people for a night."

In the midst of everyone talking, Cass gradually became aware of a growing sense that she had somehow completely lost all control of her own life. Even knowing that Gamble and her team had the best intentions, it grated on her that they were talking all around her, and no one was talking *to* her.

How had Cass come to a place where she'd allowed others to sit around and decide her fate without even acknowledging her presence? And the more she reflected, the harder it was for her to remember when she'd ever truly been in control. For so long, it seemed like Cass had just been trying to manage the impact of everyone else's decisions on her and her son.

"If they've got a safe place," Wick was saying, "I don't care how many people they've got inside. That saves us the hard work of trying to reinforce a position in the ninety minutes we've got until sunset."

Able was standing off to one side, observing, as was his way. Sometimes she wondered how he differently he read these situations in his silent world. He somehow seemed more aware than most, despite his deafness. Maybe because of it. Cass caught his eye, and he dipped his head towards her. Acknowledgment.

"We walk in there, I guarantee we walk out poorer for it," Swoop said.

"I'm sorry," Cass said, interrupting. All eyes turned to her. "Can someone please remind me at what point I turned over my authority?"

Wick and Finn exchanged glances. Sky dropped his gaze to the table in front of him. Swoop's jaw clenched at the admonishment. He didn't care for it, but he wouldn't challenge her. Wren sat up, moving his head off of her shoulder, and put his hands in his lap.

Gamble held up a hand. "All due respect, Miss Cass–" she started, but Cass cut her off.

"That sentence never ends with the amount of respect actually due, Gamble." She let it hang in the air for a moment. "I understand that you're in your element out here. You're not used to having us tag along. But I would appreciate it if you would at least show us a little *respect*... in considering that we're talking about the safety of *my* son, and that I might have something to say about it."

"Of course," Gamble said, but her words were clipped. "Lady Cass."

"These people rescued Wren before. They cared for him when I could not. Without them, neither of us would be here now. I owe it to them to do whatever I can."

"Is it worth your life?" Swoop asked flatly.

Cass chewed the inside of her lip involuntarily for a quick moment. Then she answered, "It's worth the risk."

"Then let's quit wasting time," Swoop said, and he stood up and headed for the door.

"But you're under no obligation," Cass added. "I know there's danger. None of you should feel forced to go with us."

"We had this conversation already, Cass. It's not even a

question," Gamble said. "Where you go, we go." Then she addressed her team. "Saddle up, boys. We'll move out when our friends do."

The team didn't argue, now that the decision had been made. They all got up and went to make ready to leave. Gamble stood up and turned her back to Cass as she watched her team exit, but she lingered until the others were gone.

"Thank you, Gamble," Cass said. "Sorry if I came across too harshly."

"You were right, you're the authority," Gamble said, at first without looking at Cass. But she took a quick breath and turned around, and Cass saw the glint in her eyes. "But in the future, I'd prefer you address your concerns to me directly, and not put that on my boys. It wasn't my intention to overstep my bounds, but we speak freely as a team. That's how we operate. If that's not your way, that's fine, but as you said, this is *our* element. It'd be best if you don't get our wires crossed out here. When it comes down to it, I can't have any one of my boys questioning whose order they're supposed to follow."

Looking into Gamble's eyes, Cass wasn't intimidated. A dark thought flitted through her mind about how easily she could take Gamble apart – if Cass wanted to. Gamble didn't know who she was talking to. Not really.

"I'll go let Lil know your decision," Gamble said.

"Sounds good," Cass answered. They continued to stare at each other for a second longer, and then Gamble turned and walked away. As soon as her back was to Cass, Cass felt as if a spell had broken and she was ashamed of the thought she'd had. Where had that hostility come from? Gamble had never been anything but a trusted friend and ally. Cass closed her eyes and pinched the bridge of her nose. She had to be careful not to let paranoia get to her.

"It might not be safe, Mama," Wren said, his voice interrupting her thoughts. She opened her eyes and looked at him sitting next to her, small and pale, with his shining green eyes. Too beautiful and fragile a thing for such a world. She reached out and stroked his hair and the side of his face.

"I know, but it's the right thing to do," Cass answered.

Wren shook his head. "No, I mean it might not be safe for *them*."

"I thought you'd want to go with them. With Lil, especially."

"I do," he said, looking back down at his hands in his lap. "I just worry. I don't want to bring any more trouble on them."

Cass leaned over and kissed the top of his head. "The world's full of trouble, son, whether we bring it or not. But we should do what good's in our power, however little it may seem."

Wren said, "I wish Chapel was here."

"Me too. I would've liked to have met him."

"I'm going to guh, to guh, go for a walk," Painter said, standing.

Cass looked at him, unsure if he was joking or not. "We're going on a pretty long walk here in just a few minutes, Painter. You can't wait?"

He shook his head. "Just need to be alone for a ffff-few minutes. Clear my head." He started off towards the courtyard.

"Don't go far," Cass said.

"I won't."

She watched as Painter descended the stairs and stopped at the base for a moment, looking left and right. Then he turned left and disappeared from view. He'd been awfully quiet since they left Morningside. Not that he'd ever been much of a talker. But he seemed acutely anxious. Maybe once they got somewhere safe, he'd settle down and be able to relax. It wasn't easy for any of them, but Painter probably least of all. He'd been a Morningsider his whole life, even if most of it had been outside the wall.

Wren leaned forward on the table, and rested his head on his crossed arms. Cass rubbed his back in a slow, even motion, as she used to do when he had trouble sleeping. They sat together in silence for a time, each lost in their own thoughts. Outside the simple building, the sky was growing darker, with the afternoon sun hidden behind a blanket of heavy grey clouds, and a steady breeze that carried with it the scent of coming rain. After several minutes, Mouse climbed the few steps and stood at the entrance.

"We're about ready," he said.

"OK, we'll be right there," Cass answered.

"Where's Painter?"

"Should be around nearby. Said he needed a little alone time to clear his head."

Mouse frowned a little at that. "Alright. I'll find him." He started back down the stairs.

"He went off to the left."

"Check."

Wren had apparently dozed off. His mouth was open and the sleeve of his coat had a dark spot where it was wet with drool. Cass gently woke him. He sat up slowly and smacked his lips, and then wiped his mouth with his hand. It seemed to take him a moment to remember where he was.

"Time to go?" Wren said.

"Yeah."

He nodded and got to his feet. "I hope they have a place for us to sleep."

"Me too, baby."

They gathered their things and went to join the others, hand in hand. A cluster of people had formed in the courtyard, off in the direction of the small crop field, a mix of the two teams. Several of Lil's people had bulky bags on their backs, filled no doubt with whatever still-useful things they could collect from their former home. Most of Gamble's team were there already, though Wick, Mouse, and Painter weren't there yet.

"Have you seen Mouse?" Gamble asked as Cass and Wren approached.

"Yeah, he went to get Painter."

Gamble furrowed her brow. "Where'd Painter go?"

"Just around the courtyard, I think," Cass said. "I told him not to go far."

Gamble sucked her teeth and made a little clicking noise. The wind gusted and a few small drops of rain spattered down. The last of Lil's people walked up to join the group.

"Are we almost ready?" Lil asked.

"Almost," Gamble said. "Missing a couple of mine."

"We'll need to leave very soon," Lil said. She glanced up at the ever-darkening sky. "The Weir may be out earlier tonight."

"Understood."

They all waited in impatient silence for another minute or two. Some of Lil's group shifted their packs and exchanged glances. The message was obvious.

"Did he say where he was going?" Gamble asked Cass.

"No," Cass said. "I just assumed he'd stay in the courtyard. I told him not to wander off."

"I should've left someone with you," Gamble said to herself. And then she started to message, "Mouse, Gamble…" but Mouse appeared from around behind a building, and she called out, "Any luck?"

Mouse shook his head, obviously frustrated. Raindrops started falling; it was light but steady. Gamble mumbled a curse.

"Why don't you go ahead and get started?" Gamble said to Lil. "No reason for you to get caught out in the open on our account."

"We'll help you look," Lil answered, but Gamble waved her off.

"No, ma'am," she said. "If we all get scattered, we'll lose even more time trying to get everybody back together. Get underway. We'll catch up."

"But you don't know the way," said Lil.

"I'll stay with them," Elan said. Lil gave him a concerned look, but he just nodded. "Go ahead. We'll be fine."

"I hate to leave you," Lil said. She was looking at Elan when she said it, but then she scanned Cass and Wren and the rest of them, too.

"We'll just be a few minutes behind," Cass said. The rain started to pick up enough that those with hoods started pulling them up. Lil wavered a moment more, and then nodded.

"Elan can pim me if you need us to come back."

"Thanks," Gamble said. "See you in a few."

Lil nodded and then motioned to her people, who started off towards the west from where they'd first appeared. Gamble immediately rattled off orders: "Swoop, Able, Sky, start searching. I'll help in a second." The three men dropped their packs at their feet and fanned out in different directions. "Finn, see if you can sniff out a signal, let me know if you get any hits."

"Will do."

"Mouse, mind the cargo, and *you*," Gamble said as she waved a hand over Cass and Wren, "wait *right* here." Then she looked up slightly and said, "Wick, we've got a delay. Lil and her people are moving out, we'll have to catch up... Painter's missing... No, sit tight. I'll update you in a few."

Cass almost offered to help look, but she remembered her earlier conversation with Gamble and decided to keep her mouth shut. Gamble had it under control. Cass just nodded. Gamble gave Mouse a quick nod and then went to join the others in the search. Finn sat down on the ground cross-legged, and his eyes went unfocused.

"I'm sorry," Cass said. "I shouldn't have let him wander off alone."

"It's not your fault," Mouse said. "He's old enough to know better."

The voices of the other team members echoed through the ruined village as they called Painter's name. But there was never an answer.

"I hope he's OK," said Wren.

Mouse got down on one knee in front of Wren, and was still about six inches taller. "I'm sure he's fine, buddy," he answered. "Just rattled, probably."

"He doesn't seem like himself," Wren said.

Mouse nodded. "It's been hard going. Not everyone's as tough as you and your mom."

Wren dropped his gaze to the ground, always embarrassed by praise. Mouse smiled and clapped him gently on the shoulder, and then got back to his feet.

"I don't think you'd remember me," Elan said. "But I remember you." Wren looked up at him. "You played with my son, Ephraim."

Wren nodded, and he opened his mouth to ask a question, but then closed it again, uncertain. Elan anticipated the question anyway.

"He's safe, at the refuge. I was fortunate." He smiled, but tears welled up in his eyes. After a moment he inhaled quickly and cleared his throat. "You've been in Morningside?" Elan asked.

Wren nodded.

"That's a long way to travel just for a visit."

Wren looked up at Cass then.

"We haven't always been cityfolk," she answered. "It can get overwhelming."

Elan held her gaze for a moment and then nodded. Whether he suspected there was more to the story or not, he didn't push, and for that she was thankful. "And the man you were with... um. I'm sorry I've forgotten his name."

"Three," Wren said. "He died." He said it so bluntly that it was almost shocking. Somehow it seemed even more dreadful to hear coming out of the mouth of a child.

"Oh, I'm so sorry. He was a good man."

Wren nodded again, and after that they all stood without speaking for a while. In the background, they could still hear the occasional call for Painter, though by this time none of them expected a response. Even with Mouse's reassurances, Cass felt increasingly foolish for having let Painter out of her sight. When they found him, it wasn't a mistake she would repeat. *If* they found him. It seemed all too apparent that Painter wasn't helping himself be found.

And then it occurred to her that they might have to make a tough decision if they didn't locate him soon. How long could they risk everyone's lives for the sake of one? And who would that be on, then? Would Cass make the call? Or would Gamble? Cass knew it'd be unfair to leave that decision to Gamble, after the fuss she'd made earlier.

"How much longer do we give them?" Elan asked quietly.

"As long as they need," Mouse answered. "We're not going to leave him behind."

"We might have to," Cass responded. Mouse and Wren both looked at her, each with different but equally questioning expressions. "But not yet."

Just then Finn stirred and sat up straighter. "They got him. They're on their way back now." He got to his feet and started gathering his gear.

"Who found him?" Cass asked.

"Able," Finn said. "Of course."

"I would've put money on Swoop," Mouse said.

"Yeah, well, Swoop might've killed him, so it's probably for the best."

Swoop emerged from behind one of the buildings and came towards them at an aggressive pace. He had a dark, smoldering look on his face.

"He still might," Mouse said.

When Swoop reached them, he snatched his heavy pack up off the ground and slung it with some effort onto his back. Sky and Gamble came quickly striding over. A few moments later Painter appeared from another direction, followed closely by Able.

Painter had his head down, and they weren't moving as fast as everyone else. Everyone had their gear up and locked in by the time Painter and Able reached them. Swoop started towards Painter.

"Hey! Hey," he barked, "you *ever* put us at risk again, I promise–"

But Able stepped around in front of Painter, putting himself between the two, and he held up a hand and shook his head. Swoop stopped and shut his mouth, but Cass could see the muscles working in his jaw. He glowered at Painter for a few more tense moments, and then turned away in disgust.

"Let's get moving," Gamble said. "Elan?"

Elan dipped his head and led them off in the direction the others had gone. Painter slipped in next to Cass and a little behind her, but he wouldn't look at anyone.

Wren dropped back to join him.

"Are you OK?" he asked. Cass glanced over her shoulder and saw Painter nod, though he still just kept his eyes on the ground. Mouse and Able trailed behind them, and though they had their heads up scanning the surroundings, it was clear they were mostly watching Painter.

As they left the compound, the rain settled into a steady shower of small drops and Cass found she didn't mind walking through it. Under other circumstances, she might've even thought it pleasant. But between the ruined village behind them, the tension around them, and the unknown that lay ahead, it was hard to feel any sense of enjoyment.

Wren rejoined her and she held out her hand, but he didn't take it. His hood was up and Cass couldn't see his face. From his posture she could tell it wasn't by accident. He didn't want her to see him right now. She leaned forward just enough to catch the glimmer of wetness on his cheeks. She straightened without saying anything.

They pressed on in silence, Elan leading the way with Swoop close behind. Gamble and her team maintained a loose ring around Cass and the boys as they moved. About ten minutes into the journey, they crested a little rise in the terrain and saw a figure standing to one side of their path. It was Wick, waiting for them. He fell in with them when they drew near and held a quiet conference with Swoop and Gamble at the front of the group as they continued on their way.

Thunder rolled ahead of them, a distant rumble dull and weighty, and a cold wind swirled the rain into their faces. As they walked, the buildings around them became shorter, the remains more jagged, like broken teeth thrusting up from a fossilized jaw. The sky grew a darker grey above them, ominous and brooding, though it was hard to tell whether it came from the gathering storm or from the onset of dusk. Possibly both. Their pace was quickening, and Cass began to feel the urgency of their journey more acutely.

The raindrops became heavier, more oppressive, and the wind more insistent. Lightning flashed in the heavens, momentarily illuminating the clouds from within with an unearthly glow. Thunder growled. Still they trudged on. Whether consciously or not, Cass noticed the group had closed in more tightly together. Everyone was stoic and determined.

Wick glimpsed her looking at him out of the corner of his eye, and glanced over at her. He was bareheaded, hair plastered and dripping, but he flashed a quick smile and winked at her. She got the impression he might actually be enjoying himself.

"Nothing like a good rain to remind you how nice it is to be dry, huh?" Wick said.

"If I didn't know better, I'd say you like it out here," Cass said.

He shrugged. "Out here just is. You gotta make it what you want."

"Why don't you make it dry and sunny, then?" Finn said from Cass's other side.

"Ehn, sun's bad for my complexion," Wick answered. He lifted his face towards the sky with his eyes closed, letting the rain splash over it for effect.

"Obviously haven't found anything *good* for your complexion yet."

"It's just ahead," Elan said from the front of the group. He pointed at a squat building. There was a pair of tall iron-barred fences around it, one inside the other, both with circular razor wire along the top. It looked exactly like a prison. As they got closer, someone darted out of the main entrance and opened the gates. "Wait here a second," Elan said. "I want to make sure there are no surprises."

The group stopped a few feet away while Elan jogged to meet the gatekeeper. An electric cry cut through the rain, distant but unmistakable – the first of the Weir.

"Cutting it close," the gatekeeper said as Elan moved in.

"Lil make it back?" Elan asked.

The gatekeeper nodded. "About ten minutes ago. She told us you were bringing guests."

"Did she explain? About the two?"

"She explained. Not sure I believe it."

"You will." Elan turned back and motioned to the others. As the group started towards the building, Swoop caught Cass's arm – just inside her elbow – and leaned in close.

"Don't let your guard down," he whispered forcefully. "We don't know these people. They're just as likely to tear you apart as they are to accept your help. Keep close to Mouse."

He didn't wait for a response. Swoop went through the gate with a sharp nod to the gatekeeper. As soon as he was through, Swoop started scanning the place.

Cass had wanted to believe he'd been unnecessarily concerned before. Now, standing just outside the gate, she understood what he'd been trying to tell her back at the village. Once they passed through, they'd be trapped inside, and they didn't really know how they'd be received. She'd said it was worth the risk. Looking at what she'd led them into, though, made Cass wonder. If things went bad... well, if things went bad, she'd just have to make sure they only went bad for the people inside, no matter who they might've been once.

"Mama?" Wren asked. He was standing a little ahead of her, about to go through the gate.

Cass took a deep breath. "Coming."

SEVENTEEN

When they got inside the building, Wren's first impression was that the walls were too close and too... *heavy*. It was almost like he could feel the weight of them bearing down on him, like they were squeezing the air tighter somehow. The entryway was darker than he'd been expecting, and warmer. There was a thickness to the air, and it had a faintly unpleasant smell, though Wren couldn't place it. There were few windows, and those were high and narrow slots, reinforced by steel grating.

They were all standing in an open room without furniture, waiting, as they'd been asked to do. Well, all except for Swoop and Wick, who had dropped their gear off and then insisted on going back out to walk the grounds. Neither of them liked to be anywhere without having a solid idea of the layout. Wren didn't know how they could keep at it. It seemed like it'd been days since any of them had gotten any real sleep.

As for him, he felt like he could fall asleep standing up if they had to wait too much longer. The idea of standing up any longer was pretty hard to face, though, too. Wren couldn't remember the last time he'd felt so completely wiped out. Mentally, physically, emotionally. He just felt totally empty. It was a strange, vibrating hollowness; like he was really nervous and maybe wanted to cry, except he'd already cried so much Wren didn't feel like he had any tears left.

Lil finally reappeared in the corridor that led off from the entry room.

"Sorry to keep you waiting," she said. "I just wanted to make sure everyone was aware of the situation. We have several rooms prepared for you. If you'll follow me?"

The group gathered their packs up off the floor, and Lil led them back down the corridor. They passed a few doors on either side, though most were closed. One was cracked open slightly, and Wren thought he caught a glimpse of someone peeking out as they went by. They reached an intersecting hall with branches leading left and right.

There were sounds of activity coming from the left, and a few people stood further down that direction watching them, but Lil led them off to the right. This hall was shorter and there was a cluster of six rooms at the far end, three to a side.

"We'll put you in here, if some of you don't mind sharing," Lil said. "We have more space back down the other way, but I thought you'd prefer to all be together."

"This'll be perfect, Lil," Cass said. "Thank you."

Gamble quickly designated rooms for everyone, keeping Cass, Wren, and Painter in the middle rooms, with her team members on either side.

"I'll give you time to get settled," Lil said. "When you're ready, come get me and I'll show you around and make introductions. My room is there, at the end of the hall." She gave a little nod and turned to go.

"One sec, Miss Lil," Mouse said. He ducked into his room for a few moments and then came back out with his medical kit in hand. "I'd like to go ahead and take a look at your injured, if that's alright."

Lil seemed surprised. "Um, certainly," she said. "Of course. If you feel up to it."

"I do."

"Alright. Come with me, I'll take you to them."

She took Mouse back down the hall, and the rest of the team went to their rooms to get their gear settled. Cass and Wren had the room on the left of the hall, across from Painter's. Gamble had given him his own room, but Wren guessed somebody would be keeping a close eye on it.

"I'm gonna dump my stuff," said Finn. "Then I'll go make sure Swoop and Wick know where we are."

"Yeah, check," Gamble said. Wren thought, they sure did say *check* a lot.

"Come on, baby," Cass said. "Let's get changed into something dry."

They went together into their room and closed the door. There wasn't a whole lot to it. Two metal beds, one on each side of the room. But they had been made with simple blankets and pillows that looked clean. Wren remembered those blankets from the time he'd spent at the village before: light and a little scratchy, but warm. There was also a small table in the corner, but no chair. The room was lit by a single light that shone orange-yellow and sat recessed into the ceiling.

Wren dropped his pack on the bed and started taking off his coat. Cass made a little clucking sound with her tongue and walked over to grab his pack.

"That's going to get your bed all wet," she said, running her hand back and forth over the blanket. She took the pack and put it down on the table in the corner.

"I wasn't going to leave it there," Wren said.

Cass opened his pack and dug out a change of clothes for him. Wren put his coat on the table, collected his clothes, and took them back to the bed. He slipped his boots off, thankful that they'd kept the rain out. Wet socks were the worst. His shirt was mostly dry, but his pants were soaked, starting from about midway down his thigh. They were hard to take off. He sat down on the bed to wrestle with them.

"Here, hold on, hold on," Cass said, walking towards him.

"I can do it," Wren said. His mama reached down to grab one of the pant legs anyway. "I said I can do it!" he said again, snatching his leg away from her. She looked at him sharply, but after a moment she held up her hands and then went back to their packs.

Wren fought his feet out of the clinging pants. It was frustrating when Mama treated him like he was just a kid. Sometimes it was like she completely forgot how old he was. He wasn't seven anymore. With a flurry, Wren kicked his feet free and his pants flopped to the ground with a wet slap. He slid into his dry pair and then put his boots back on. Cass was laying her own clothes out. Wren went to the door.

"Where are you going?" she asked.

"To see Lil," he said. Wren put his hand on the door, but didn't open it. He shouldn't have to ask for permission.

"OK," she said. "Don't go far."

Wren slid the door open and went out into the hall, and then shut the door behind him. He wasn't really mad at Mama. It was just… well, he didn't really know. Wren felt out of sorts and wasn't sure why. But after all they'd been through, Mama didn't have to treat him like he couldn't change his own pants.

He padded down the hall towards Lil's room. The door was partially shut, but cracked. Wren raised his hand to knock and then caught himself. He was nervous. Maybe he should just wait for everyone else. It'd been such a long time. He had so many questions, but standing here now he wasn't sure if it was the right time to ask them.

It didn't matter. The door swung open and Lil gave a little start when she saw him there.

"Oh, Wren," she said. "Is everything OK?"

Wren nodded. He wasn't sure what to say. She'd changed her clothes, removed her sword and cloak. Now Lil looked much more like he remembered her. But more serious than before; her eyes didn't have the same spark of life that they'd once had.

"You've grown," she said, putting a hand on top of his head.

"A little."

"It's good to see you again."

Lil's words were warm, but Wren felt a gap between the two of them that he hadn't expected. "It's good to see you, Miss Lil." His mouth was dry, and he couldn't think of anything else to say.

There was a noise from inside the room, and Lil turned back to address it.

"Are you hungry, sweet one?" she said. And then, "Come here, there's someone I'd like you to meet." There were more shuffling noises, and Lil pushed the door open a little wider. In the middle of the room, a little girl was standing – brown-haired, brown-eyed, and a little chubby. She had some soft thing clutched to her cheek. She didn't come any closer. "This is Wren. He stayed with us for a little while, a long time ago." The little girl just stared, wide-eyed. "Wren, this is Thani."

"Hi, Thani," Wren said with a wave. Thani returned the wave, but didn't say anything. Wren guessed she was probably about six years old.

"Was there something you needed, Wren?" Lil asked.

Wren shook his head.

"OK. I'm going to take Thani to get something to eat. Would you like to come with us?"

"I should wait for my mom."

"OK. Well, we'll be just down there," she said, pointing down the hall towards where it bent to the right. "Around the corner, and at the end of the hall. You can join us there when you're ready."

"OK. Thanks, Lil."

She nodded, and then turned and held out a hand to Thani. "Come on, sweet one, let's go find you some food." Thani took Lil's hand. Wren stepped back away from the door to let them out.

"See you in a little bit," Lil said as she closed her door. Wren nodded. He stood watching the two of them walking down the hall, hand in hand, until they disappeared around the corner. Then he walked back to his room and stood outside the door, waiting for Mama. And while he waited, he felt completely out of place.

Later that evening, after Swoop and Wick had come back in from their scouting, Lil had given them all a quick tour of the complex. It was larger than it had initially appeared, with several floors extending down below ground. Whatever its original purpose, the building was clearly built to hold more people than were there now.

Lil had originally told them that she'd put them up on the top floor so they could all be together. But as they'd gotten shown around, Cass couldn't help but get the feeling that Lil had wanted to keep them separated from her own people as well. Everyone they'd met was cordial, but Cass could feel the distance between the two groups. And no one quite seemed to know what to make of Painter and her.

Mouse had clearly gained some favor amongst the people, having tended to the many wounded and having made improvements where he could. Even though Elan had counted eighteen able-bodied among them, it'd turned out that most of them had injuries as well; they were just too stubborn to let their wounds be considered anything more than minor. Mouse had come away impressed, both by the quality of the people and the skill they showed in medicine.

Afterwards, the team gathered in the mess hall, where a number of Lil's people had prepared a meal. Cass recognized some of those that had escorted Lil, among the cooks. There were several rows of long steel tables with benches, and Lil directed them to seats. Though Gamble and her team had put up a lot of resistance, Lil's people insisted on feeding them from their own stores. This place clearly hadn't been some improvised shelter; it had been stocked well ahead of their need, and for more than had survived.

Two men brought trays over to their table, carrying bowls of stew on them. They placed these in front of everyone wordlessly, and then departed. For the most part, they were left to themselves, but Lil and Elan both joined them at the table, as did the little girl, who was introduced as Thani.

The stew was brown and thick, and though Cass couldn't identify much of what was in it, she was surprised at how delicious it was. She'd expected something more typical of a survivors' enclave: thin, watery, flavorless. Instead, the meal was hearty and nourishing.

"I have to admit, Lil," Cass said. "I'm a little overwhelmed at your hospitality. You've done far too much."

Lil shook her head while she finished the food she had in her mouth. "A poor reception compared to the welcome you would've received a week ago. We've suffered much.

I'm afraid it's made my people wary and suspicious."

"Everyone's been very kind."

Lil sighed. "I'm glad that's how it seems." She looked over her shoulder at the people gathered around other tables. "But you didn't know us before. We're a changed people. I fear this latest attack may have broken us."

"It's only been three days, Lil," Elan said. "We'll adapt, same as always. Just takes time."

Lil turned back and stirred the stew in her bowl. "I hope you're right, Elan." She looked at Thani, and stroked the girl's hair. "But it wasn't just the attack. We've been dwindling for a long time now. Once we lost Chapel…"

"Chapel was your leader?" Cass asked.

Lil smiled a little sadly. "He would've said 'no'. But Chapel was the heart of our community. He was the first to believe we could live without walls. The first to *show* it. After he was taken…" She paused and shook her head again. "It was a slow process, but hope started to drain away. Families left. I suppose it was only a matter of time before our little remnant would fail."

"How did it happen, Lil?" asked Wren. There was an edge to the question, a hint of anger. "How did they get him?"

"I still ask myself the same question, Wren. It seems impossible, doesn't it?" Wren nodded.

"One night they came, and we repelled them. It wasn't even that large an attack. Nothing like the one we suffered when you were with us. But afterwards, when we all gathered back together, he was just… gone."

"Lil pursued them," Elan said. "She never tells that part."

"Many of us did, Elan."

"Not like you."

Lil shrugged.

"After Chapel, Lil has led us in his stead," Elan continued. "She kept our community together. If not for her, it would've collapsed completely."

"Elan is being generous," Lil said. But Elan shook his head.

"No, I'm being honest. If not for her, I don't think any of us would've survived."

"What will you do now?" Gamble asked.

"Get well first, I hope," Lil said. "After that, I have no idea."

"You could come to Morningside," Cass said. "I'm sure we could find a place for you there. For all of you."

Lil made a little frown, but more from thought than displeasure at the idea. "I'm not sure how my people would adjust. That would be quite a shock."

"It's not like it used to be," Wren said.

"And yet you fled it?" Lil asked. Cass and Gamble exchanged a quick glance.

Lil smiled gently. "You looked too much like a war party for me to believe you were just out for a visit."

"It's temporary," Cass answered. "We'll be returning soon."

Lil dipped her head. She didn't press for more information, but her eyes suggested she knew more than they'd shared. "We need some time to recover. Then we'll see. It's been years since I've been to a city."

"We can exchange SNIPs, if you like. When it comes time to make a decision, you can always pim me."

Lil nodded. "I'd like that. And what about you then? How many days do you think you'll be with us?"

Gamble shook her head. "Not many. We don't want to be a burden."

"You're free to do as you wish, of course, but you're no burden to us."

"Just the same," Gamble said.

"I understand," Lil answered, and the tone of her voice suggested she really did.

They finished their meal together, with the conversation carefully directed away from any more discussion of future plans. Wren was finally able to provide some closure for Lil and the others, telling the full story of what had happened after he'd left their compound: of Mister Carter's death at the hands of Dagon; of Three's attempt to reunite Wren with his father and his sacrifice; and of Asher's terrifying domination of the Weir, and of Cass's return.

"It all seems so impossible," Lil said. "And yet here you are. When Mister Carter didn't return, we knew something terrible had happened, but..." She trailed off with a shake of head.

Both Lil and Elan had questions about the Awakened, which they asked diplomatically. It was clear they still weren't fully comfortable with the idea or the implications, but they seemed to be genuinely making an effort to understand and to accept this new reality.

Cass wondered how much of the distance kept by the others here had to do exclusively with Painter and her. The more they all talked, the more she felt the group would've been welcomed far more had she not been accompanying them.

There was some discussion of the change in the Weir, a comparing of notes, though that proved of little use. What had caused it or what it meant remained a mystery to them all. Only, neither Lil nor Elan recalled having heard the Weir make the strange noise; Wick managed a fairly good impression of the uncanny "*Spshhhh. Naaaah*" – but no one recognized it.

Soon after they'd finished eating, Wren began to nod. Cass acted, and escorted him back to their room, and Painter took the opportunity to excuse himself as well.

There were still things Cass needed to discuss with Lil and with Gamble, but Wren didn't want to be left alone.

"Can I stay with Painter for a little while?" he asked.

"I don't think that'd be a good idea, sweetheart," Cass said. "Painter might like to have some time to himself." She tried to couch it in terms of what would be good for Painter, but in reality, she didn't like the idea of leaving Wren alone with him. Not since his disappearing act.

"Just until you come back, I mean."

"I can stay with you until you fall asleep, if you want."

"He's not going to hurt me, Mama," Wren said. He looked at her with his big sea-green eyes, and they were steady and determined. "And I think it might help him. He talks to me sometimes."

Cass still didn't like the idea; Painter hadn't really seemed himself lately, not since he'd confirmed Snow's identity. But it was true he'd never shown any signs of doing any of them harm. On the contrary, he'd gone out of his way to aid them, and lost his home for it. And maybe he *would* open up to Wren. If it helped Painter get a hold of himself, it'd be worth it. Even if not, maybe it'd at least give them some insight into what was going on with him.

"We can ask," she said. "But it's his decision."

Wren nodded. They crossed the hall and Cass knocked lightly, half-hoping Painter would be asleep already, or at least wouldn't answer the door. But she heard him stir, and then the door cracked open. The room was dark, and he peered out with his glowing eyes.

"Didn't wake you I hope," she said.

Painter shook his head. "Not sleepy."

"Wren was just wondering if you'd like some company for a little bit," Cass said, wording it so it didn't sound like she needed him to watch her son. She tried to give Painter every out to say no. "I figured you might want to be alone, though, and Wren understands. But I told him we'd ask, just in case."

"No, sure," Painter answered. He opened the door a little wider and stepped back. "It'd be n-n-n, it'd be nice."

Cass gave it one last shot. "Are you sure? I know you're exhausted, and it's not going to hurt our feelings if you say no."

"It's no prrr-roblem. Really."

Cass nodded, hoping her disappointment wasn't too apparent. She turned to Wren and put her hands on his shoulders, turning him to face her. "Half an hour. Then to bed."

"How about an hour?" he asked.

Cass sighed. She'd often wished that Wren had been more assertive; now she kind of missed the days when he'd just do whatever she asked without arguing. "Forty-five minutes. I'll come back and check on you."

Wren nodded. She bent down and kissed him on top of the head. Wren went into Painter's room and sat on one of the beds, where Painter's backpack was.

"Make sure he stays out of trouble," Cass said.

"Yes, ma'am," Painter said. Then he asked Wren, "You want the light on?"

"No, that's OK. Unless you want it."

Painter turned back and stared at Cass. After a moment, he cocked his head slightly and his eyebrows went up. Cass finally realized he was waiting for her.

"Alright," Cass said. "I'll be back in a little bit to get him."

Painter nodded. Cass lingered a few seconds longer.

"I'm not g-g-going to rrrr-run off with him or anything," Painter said softly.

Cass felt embarrassed, as if he'd guessed her mind. She gave a little laugh. "No, I know, of course not. I'm just... being a mom, I guess. Have a good time."

"You too," Painter said.

"I don't know about that," Cass said with a chuckle, and then she waved at Wren, who gave her an emphatic *go away already* look. "See you in a little bit."

"Yes, ma'am," Painter repeated, and he closed the door. It clicked shut, automatically locking. It took an effort for Cass to turn away from the door and to start walking back down the hall. He'd be fine. Just being a mom, indeed.

Cass went back to the mess hall and found it mostly deserted. Gamble and her team were still seated at their table – but Swoop was standing and they all looked troubled.

"What's going on?" Cass asked as she approached.

"Have you been in touch with North?" Gamble asked.

"No, why?"

"Anybody from Morningside?"

"No, not at all. Not since we left. What's the problem?" Cass asked.

"Can you try to contact him?"

"Is it safe?"

"We'll see."

Cass didn't like the sound of that, but she opened the connection and sent North a quick pim. In a split second, she got the response: *refused*.

"That's strange," she said. She tried again with the same result. Immediate denial.

"Locked out?" Gamble asked.

"Seems like it."

Gamble nodded, grim-faced.

"Why would that be?"

"I tried to check in with some of my contacts back in Morningside. Same result. I had Finn dig into it. He skimmed some backlogs, found an executive order declaring us *persona non grata*."

"What? From who?"

"North."

Cass was thunderstruck. There had to be some kind of mistake. "That doesn't make any sense."

"Doesn't it?" Swoop said.

"Why would he target your team?"

"It's not just *us*, Cass," Sky said. "It's all of us... you, and Wren included."

Cass shook her head. "No, there's no way. There's no way he could just issue a decree like that. Not on his own. What grounds would he have?"

Gamble answered, "The murder of Connor."

Cass's legs felt hollow, and she slowly lowered herself onto the bench. Her mind raced to put the pieces together. The attempt on Wren's life. The tension of the Council meetings. The protests. The murder of Luck and Mez and the others. Was North at the center of it all? Or was the entire Council corrupted?

"Can't we just get Wren to rescind it?" Wick asked. "He's still governor, isn't he?"

"How would he do that, Wick?" Finn said, his tone sharp.

"There's gotta be somebody back there we can contact. Let 'em know what really happened."

"And who do you think they're gonna believe? The upright and pristine politician that's there in the city, bringing them hard news? Or the people from beyond the wall," Finn said as he flicked his hand at Cass, "that fled in the night with their bloodstained bodyguard?"

Finn's words stung, but he was right. North was a long-time citizen. No matter what Underdown had done for Morningside and what hopes the people had for his son, Wren would always be an outsider. Cass was forever Other. And the citizens had never been comfortable with the guard; no one liked to be reminded of the bloody cost other people paid to keep them safe.

Was this what North had planned? Get them out of the city, and then assume power for himself? Or had he merely taken advantage of the opportunity? *The safest thing is for you to leave Morningside,* he'd told them. It just didn't make sense. None of it did.

"I can't believe it..." Cass said.

"Believe it or not, it's what is," Swoop growled.

"No, I mean I simply cannot believe North would betray us."

"Sister, at this point it doesn't matter," Mouse said. He was calm, his tone of voice controlled, disarming. "However you slice it, our timetable's changed. Right now, we need to focus on our next steps."

"Next steps is I go back and burn him down," Swoop said.

"Sure," Mouse said. "We could do that, Swoop. And you know I'd be right there with you, dying in a hail of gunfire, if I thought it was the right thing to do. But I don't think this problem is one we can shoot to fix."

Swoop took a deep breath. "I didn't say it'd fix anything," he said as he sat down. "It'd just make me feel a whole lot better."

We still need to find a place to set up for a while, Able signed.

"Agreed," Gamble said. "Let's talk options."

The group fell into a frank discussion of what lay ahead, and how best to tackle the immediate problem of finding a place to stay, possibly for a more extended period of time than they'd originally planned. They were a team, and as the conversation continued, Cass found herself slipping gradually out of the exchange. This time, however, she didn't bristle at how little they asked her opinion.

They were in operational planning mode, and she was content to sit back and observe the unique capabilities that Gamble's team possessed in action. Everyone had their specialties, and that always colored their approach to problem-solving, but even when tension seemed to be running high, the process never slowed down. Cass had never really seen this side of the team before, and she couldn't help but be impressed. She let them carry on planning, trusting them in their element.

EIGHTEEN

Wren sat on the bed with his back against the wall, resting an arm resting on Painter's pack next to him. Across from him, Painter was lying on the other bed on his back, with his hands behind his head, staring up at the ceiling, his electric eyes casting the room in a faint and soft blue glow. Wren yawned so wide it made one of his eyes water. He shifted his position, sitting up straighter and crossing his legs in front of himself in an effort to keep from falling asleep.

They'd had a brief conversation after Mama had first left, but it hadn't been about anything important and it'd felt strained. After that, they'd just been sitting quietly together. Wren kept wanting to ask Painter if he was OK, or about what had happened earlier at the compound, but he just couldn't seem to find the right words. Or the courage. So they just sat together in silence, while Wren tried to figure out what was keeping him from just getting up and leaving.

"What are we d-d-doing, Wren?" Painter asked. His voice wasn't loud, but it startled Wren anyway.

"How do you mean?" Wren said.

"Out here. On the rrrr, on the run. With these people. Any of it."

"I'm sorry I got you into this, Painter. I really am. I was scared, and I didn't know what to do, and I didn't think. I didn't think about what might happen…"

"No, it's not that," Painter said. "I mean… it's juh, just strange. Like the wrong people had to leave."

"It wasn't safe for us to stay."

"Yeah, but it shhhh, it should've been. We're the good guys, right?" he asked.

Wren thought about that for a moment, wondering what Painter was getting at. "I think so. I try to be."

"I'm sorry about earlier," Painter said. "I just… I'm OK nnnn-now. I kind of fruh… freaked out."

"It's alright," Wren said. "You've been through a lot lately."

"So have you. And I'm ssss-still sorry," Painter said. He pulled a hand out from behind his head and ran it over his face, briefly bathing the room in darkness. He returned to his original position. "Are you g-g-glad you got to ssss-see these people again?"

"Yes," Wren said, though something pricked his heart. It had been a terrible shock, of course, to see the destruction and to find out about Chapel. But death and loss was nothing new to him, and he had already become numbed, somewhat. The grief seemed distant and faded. There was something else though, sharper, harder to understand. Disappointment. "I guess."

"Not what you were exp… expecting."

"Not at all."

"I know what that's like. To hope for ssss-ssss…" Painter paused, then took a breath. "To hope for something for so long. And then to fff-find out it's gone forever."

Wren nodded. "And… it's different than I thought it'd be. I thought…" he paused too, searching for the words. What had he thought? The memories he'd had of Chapel's village, and the way people had treated him then. The feeling that Wren had been part of their community. That he belonged, even if just for a little while. That was gone, too. "I guess it was stupid of me to think it could ever be like it had been before."

"It's not sss-stupid, Wren," Painter said. "It's human."

Wren wished that made him feel better. Instead, he kept thinking about Lil sitting with that little girl, Thani. He wasn't jealous, not really. But it bothered Wren for some reason, just the same. Like he'd been replaced. Like maybe all the memories he had of that time had been a lie.

"I just wanted th-th-things to be like before too. You know?" Painter said after a few moments. "I kept thinking maybe if I juh, just did nnn-normal things. Maybe normal things would mmm-make me feel normal again. And maybe... people would treat me like I was nnn-normal."

He said *people* but Wren picked up what he'd left unsaid. His sister, Snow.

"But then... when I c-c-came in that room, and I th-thought they were hurting you... I got angry. And..." He paused. And then, "...I felt alive. *Alive,* Wren." Painter turned and looked over at Wren then. "That's tuh, tuh... that's terrible, isn't it?"

A sharp electric chill raced down Wren's spine, and he shivered once, but violently. "No, it's not terrible," he said, but even as he said it, Wren felt that maybe it might be something very terrible indeed. Painter continued to look at him for a long moment. Wren sat very still. Then Painter finally returned his gaze to the ceiling.

"Before..." Painter said. "You know, when I was sssss-still a... you know. I only remember bits and puh, pieces. Little shattered memories. But one thing I remember, I had a p-p-p..." he stopped and shook his head, "a *purpose.*"

Wren got the feeling that Painter was building up to something. Or rather was trying to confess something, without actually having to say it.

"It's not like I... don't... I'm not ssss-saying I want to go back or anything. But, you know, sometimes... parts of it... I miss having a purpose."

Wren didn't say anything. But he felt something at work in his mind. Something just behind his conscious thought was nagging at him, threatening to find some kind of hidden connection between Painter's words that Wren couldn't identify – but even so, he knew he didn't want to make.

"It's unbearable, to have no purpose..." Painter said quietly. "And no hope."

Against his will, something in Wren's subconscious put the pieces together, and a sudden black thought erupted to the front of his mind.

"Painter..." he said slowly, fearing he knew the answer, and dreading even more the thought of hearing it confirmed as true. "Where did you bury your sister?"

Painter looked at him sharply. "What? What mmm-made you think of that?"

"I don't know," Wren said. He scooted forward on the bed, so he could put his feet on the floor. "Where did you bury her?"

"Why are you asking mmmmm-me this?" Painter leaned up on an elbow.

"Where is Snow?"

"I t-t-t-told you. Outside. In our sss-secret place." He said it forcefully as he sat up fully, but his eyes gave him away. Painter wasn't angered by the question. He was scared by it.

"Oh no, Painter..." Wren said. "Painter, no..." He stood up and took a couple of steps towards the door, though he didn't really know why. "Please tell me you didn't leave her out there for the Weir."

Painter opened his mouth to answer, but after a moment his eyes softened and he dropped his gaze to the floor. Wren felt sick, and he put his hand over his mouth. He backed up and leaned against the door.

"How did you know?" Painter asked, practically whispering.

"I didn't," Wren said.

"But you understand, d-d-don't you?" Painter said, looking back up at him. "If you had a ch-chance, no matter how small… what if you c-c-could bring your friends back? Wouldn't you try?"

Wren shook his head. He didn't want to think about it. Didn't want to even let the smallest hint of that idea into his head, it seemed so terrible.

"She's your sister, Painter," Wren said.

"Exactly," he said. "My baby sister. I would do anything ffff-for her, Wren. I know it's a luh, a long shhhh-shot. But what if, Wren? What if? If I could ffff-find her again, you'd bring her back, wouldn't you?"

Wren stared back at his friend. His poor broken friend, who had lost so much. Who had lost everything. But as terrible as it all seemed, almost too horrible to comprehend, Wren found he couldn't lie to Painter or to himself.

"I can't promise that," he said. He saw Painter's expression change, and realized Painter thought Wren was just refusing outright. How could he explain that if Snow had been dead for days before she'd been taken, there was no chance that he'd be able to help her find her way back? He didn't even know if that was completely true himself, no matter how much he suspected it. And Wren remembered all too well what it was like to live a life without hope. "I would *try*, Painter. But…" Wren trailed off.

"That's all I c-c-could ask, Wren," Painter said.

There was a light knock at the door, and Wren jerked away from it, with his heart hammering. Then, muffled through the door, he heard his mama gently call his name.

"My mom," Wren said.

"You won't tuh, tell anyone, will you?"

Wren just stood there, the words not really registering with him.

"D-d-don't tell anyone, OK? Please?"

"I won't," Wren answered before he had time to think it through.

"You undersss-, understand, right?"

The knock came again, a little louder this time.

"I have to go," Wren said. He turned around and opened the door. The light from the hallway dazzled his eyes, and he had to squint against the glare. The lights in the hall weren't that bright, but his eyes struggled to adjust after sitting in the dark for so long.

"Hey, baby," Cass said. "Hi, Painter."

"Hi, Miss Cass," Painter said. "Everything going OK?"

He wasn't usually one to make conversation, and Wren couldn't help but feel that Painter was doing his best to change the subject as quickly as possible.

"For now," she answered, with a slight smile. Wren could tell something was off from the look on her face. She looked down at him. "Did you sleep?"

Wren shook his head. Her expression changed. He never really could hide anything from his mama.

"Are you OK?" Cass asked.

"Just tired," he said. "I want to go to bed now."

"Alright," she said. She looked back up at Painter. "Thanks for letting him stay with you, Painter. I appreciate it."

"Ssssh-sure, no problem," he replied.

"Good night," said Cass.

"Night," Painter said.

Wren started across the hall, but Cass stopped him with a light hand on his shoulder. He glanced back at Painter, who was staring out of that dark room at him with those eyes. Wren found it was hard to think of him as a friend just then. "Good night, Painter."

Wren crossed the hall and went into his own room, followed closely by his mother. She flicked on the light. He went straight to his bed and started taking off his shoes.

"Are you sure you're OK, Wren?" Cass asked.

He nodded without looking at her. There was nothing he wanted more than to just crawl into his bed and hide his face from the world. He'd never wanted things to be like this.

"Did something happen?"

He shook his head and pulled the covers back.

"Is Painter OK?"

"He's fine, Mom," Wren said, and it came out more sharply than he meant for it to. "I really want to go to sleep." He climbed into his bed and lay on his side, facing the wall, pulled the covers up under his chin. Footsteps approached, and Wren closed his eyes so that he didn't have to look at his mama. He knew she'd be able to read him, and he just couldn't face the conversation. There was no telling how anyone would react if they found out what Painter had done.

He felt Mama sit down on the edge of the bed. She stroked his hair, and then rubbed his back in silence. Wren tried to even out his breathing and pretended to be asleep, hoping that would keep her from trying to talk to him anymore. He just needed some time to think through everything. Maybe it didn't really matter what Painter had done. Maybe it mattered very much.

"We've been here before, baby," Cass whispered after a few minutes. "We'll figure this out, too." She leaned over him and kissed the side of his head gently. Then she got up and switched off the light, and left the room. Wren was certain she thought he was asleep, and that made him wonder all the more exactly what she'd meant.

"Seems risky to me," Finn said, as Cass rejoined the team. They were still discussing their options, and it didn't sound like they were any closer to a decision.

"Risky's all we've got, Finn," Swoop answered.

"Yeah, but there's no way we could roll up there heavy as we are and think they're going to let us in without asking questions. And no way I'm going up there unless we're rolling heavy."

"Well, we can't stay here," Gamble said, "and it seems the best option of few. Question is can we make it work?"

"Why not?" asked Wick.

"Why not what?" said Swoop.

"Why can't we stay here?"

"This place is an emergency shelter, Wick, not a long-term solution. Every day we're here, we're pullin' on resources they can't spare. I don't care how friendly they are, that ain't good for them or us."

Wick shrugged. "Ninestory just seems like a stretch to me. Hard people up that way. Not likely to look too kindly on a war party coming up in their midst."

"Then again," Mouse said, "if there are people who won't think twice about a bunch of roughnecks wandering around, it's probably them."

"I'm sorry," Cass interrupted. "Ninestory?"

Gamble nodded. "Midsized enclave. Not the nicest place,

but it's hardened. Figure we could set up for a good couple of weeks there."

"If we can get in the door," Finn said.

"You've been before?" Cass asked.

"A few of us passed through once," Sky said.

"Didn't leave on great terms, though," Swoop added. He and Sky shared a meaningful look.

"I doubt anyone would remember us."

"Hope not."

"I think it's our best shot," Gamble said. "It's close; we have more firsthand experience with it than anywhere else. And they're the type that might actually appreciate having a few extra steely-eyed shooters around."

"Or, you know, they'll open fire as soon as they see us and strip our gear," Finn said.

"What do you think, Lady Cass?" Gamble asked.

"It's what you would advise?"

"It is."

Cass surveyed the others gathered there, intent on her. Hard men led by a hard woman. She had bristled at their dismissal of her before. Now it seemed foolish that she had ever doubted.

"When do we leave?" she asked.

Cass was up before the sun, checking and double-checking their gear to make sure nothing was left behind. She kept as quiet as she could to let Wren sleep as long as he was able. It felt strange preparing to leave so soon after they'd arrived, but Swoop had been right. They'd done what they could for the wounded. Any more time spent in the refuge was just a drain on people who couldn't afford it. She'd felt it was only proper for her to be the one to break the news.

As dawn was breaking, Cass slipped out and made her way to Lil's room. She tapped lightly on the door, uncertain if Thani was in there and not wanting to wake the child. Cass was surprised by how quickly Lil answered, fully awake and fully dressed. Lil stepped out into the hall and closed the door behind them.

Cass explained their decision, and though Lil listened patiently and seemed to understand, she nevertheless made every effort to convince them to stay.

"It wouldn't be fair to you," Cass said. "And as unlikely as it seems, there may be trouble following us. I couldn't live with myself if we brought danger to your door."

"We're still the same people you sought before," Lil said. "Fewer, perhaps. But the same."

"It's not that. Our situation's changed. And you've suffered enough."

"We've *all* suffered enough," Lil said. "If by lingering another day or two, you, your son, or any of those with you can gain rest or restoration, I would welcome your delay. We all would."

"I appreciate it, Lil. All of us do. But we have to move."

Lil dipped her head. "If you must go, you must. But if you should decide to return, you'd be welcome."

"And what about you? Where will you go?"

Lil looked off down the hall, back towards where the others from her compound were sleeping, and inhaled deeply. She shook her head. "I don't know. It may be another week before all my people are well enough to move. And even then, some may choose a different path."

"What about Morningside?"

Lil looked at her with mild surprise. "Is it safe?" she asked.

"I believe it would be for you."

Lil nodded. "Perhaps. Time will tell."

"Well, whatever the future holds, I'm glad to have met you at last. Wren has talked about you so much, I feel like I've known you far longer than a day."

Lil smiled. "Wren is very special. I have to confess… my reluctance to let you go has a great deal to do with him. I'd really hoped to get to spend more time with him. If I'd known you'd be leaving so soon, I would've made more of an effort."

"He's very fond of you. It's easy to see why," Cass said. She paused, feeling the full weight of the debt she owed this woman. Cass shook her head. "I never really thanked you for all you did for him. I'm not sure I even know how."

"Seeing him alive and well is enough. And knowing he is with his mother is more than I could've hoped."

Cass shared her connection information and personal encryption key with Lil, and Lil shared hers, enabling the two women to pim one another. Each promised to update the other on any movement.

"I'll see you out when you're ready," Lil said.

"Shouldn't be long," Cass said.

As Cass returned to her room, she found Gamble and her team making their final preparations. They exchanged a few words, and Cass let Gamble know that Lil would be waiting to let them out of the compound. When Cass entered her room, Wren was sitting up in bed, bleary-eyed.

"We're leaving?" he asked.

Cass nodded. "Yeah, baby. Gamble thinks it's best."

He yawned. "OK."

Cass was a little surprised. She'd been expecting Wren to put up some resistance, or at least to ask why. Instead, he slid out of his bed and started making it.

"Will we have to go far today?" Wren asked.

"A few hours."

"That's not so bad."

He finished straightening the covers on his bed and got dressed. Cass was hesitant to push too much after his response the previous night, but she still wasn't convinced that everything had gone alright with Painter.

"Everything go OK with Painter last night?" she asked, testing the waters.

"Yeah, it was fine," he said. He glanced up at her quickly, and then Wren focused on his boots as he buckled them on. "I think he's just trying to figure out how to deal with everything."

Wren still seemed to be avoiding eye contact for some reason, but his mood was much improved over the night before. Maybe he had just been tired after all, Cass thought.

They loaded up their packs and went into the hall together, where the rest of the team had gathered. Even Painter was there, though Cass didn't know who had roused him, or if anyone had.

Elan came to meet them, and though they initially tried to refuse, he managed to convince them to share one last meal together. They were joined by Lil and a couple of the others who they'd met at the village's ruins.

It was a simple meal, but good and filling, and the conversation was sparse but genuine. Elan tried once more to encourage the group to remain for another day or so. But Gamble held firm. Mouse did insist on making one final check of the wounded, even though after his work the previous night the caregivers had everything well in hand.

Afterwards, Lil and Elan escorted them to the gates, where they said their goodbyes. Lil held Wren in a lingering embrace long enough that Wren actually blushed with embarrassment.

The team passed through the two iron gates back out into the open and assumed their usual positions, surrounding Cass, Wren, and Painter. Broken clouds streaked the sky above, the last remnants of the storm that had passed in the night. The air was cool and damp, and everywhere the soaked pavement glistened under the morning sun, and shone in places pooled with rainwater. The sunlight confused Cass's vision, and she drew down her veil to reduce the glare. Beside her, Painter donned his goggles.

Wick led them off on yet another unexpected phase of their journey. Cass glanced back at the refuge and saw Lil and Elan still watching them as they left. She wondered if they would ever see one another again, and found herself hoping so. And at the same time, she doubted it very much.

NINETEEN

The morning passed slowly, and the view changed little as they marched east and maybe a bit to the south. They certainly hadn't intended for it to be quite so roundabout, but the path they'd taken from Morningside – to where they were now – would've thrown off all but the most determined of trackers. If nothing else, certainly no one would be able to anticipate where they were headed based on their previous movements.

As they walked, Cass mulled over all she knew about the situation in Morningside. No matter what she did, she couldn't get the pieces to fit together in any way that made sense to her. She might have misjudged North altogether, but it still didn't account for all that had occurred. There were too many threads dangling, too many unanswered questions. But then, maybe she was thinking about it all wrong. She'd been assuming there had been a single plan all along, perfectly executed. What if, instead, it hadn't gone to plan at all?

There had always been politics at play when it came to the Council. She didn't for one moment believe that they had agreed to elevate Wren to governor out of any sense of altruism. He had been largely intended as a figurehead, to quell the rising panic after Underdown's death, and she'd agreed, knowing it would secure their place in the city. But once Wren's abilities had become widely known, the people of Morningside had seemed to revere him even more highly than his father. Had the Council members truly been trying to unseat him? Or had something gone terribly wrong?

"Hey," Wick said from the front. "*Persona non grata*. What's the plural of that?"

"I reckon we are," said Finn.

"*Personae non gratae*," Swoop muttered.

"Oh ho ho," Wick said, looking over his shoulder at Swoop. "A gentleman *and* a scholar, huh?"

Swoop spat.

"What does that mean?" Wren asked, and it dawned on Cass that she'd never told Wren and Painter about the executive order from Morningside.

"It means an unwelcome person," Sky said.

"Like an exile?" Wren said.

"Pretty much," Sky said.

Wren was quiet for a moment.

Cass was still trying to figure out how to share the news when he spoke again. "Does that mean we can't go home?"

Gamble glanced at Cass and grimaced, only then realizing the situation.

"For now," Cass said. "But we're going to figure it out, OK?"

"Wait," said Painter. "What?"

"We found out last night, after you were asleep," Cass said. "The Council cut us off."

"What? Whuh-wh-why?"

"Because of what happened… to Connor and Aron."

"Actually," Finn said, "it didn't mention Aron. And it didn't mention Painter, either."

It took a moment for the implication of that to sink in for Cass. "They think *I* killed him?" she said.

"Or," Mouse said, "they want everyone else to think that."

They all walked on in thoughtful silence for a few moments.

Cass didn't know why it hadn't occurred to her before. Of course they'd think she was the one who had killed Connor. There were no witnesses, and no reason for anyone to suspect that Painter would ever have been involved. Maybe it'd been a mistake to bring him with them after all.

"Well," Wick said. "On the bright side, at least *one* of us can go home."

"We're all goin' home," Swoop said. "Just might get a little loud when we do."

"I hope Uncle Aron's OK," Wren said quietly.

They marched on, breaking every hour or so to rest, often while Wick and Swoop scouted ahead, behind, or around. Cass never was sure what exactly they were looking for, but the fact that they hadn't encountered any traps or other travelers thus far probably had a lot to do with their vigilance.

At every stop, Mouse made the rounds to double-check everyone's water intake, and he fussed mildly at both Wren and Painter for not drinking more. Both the boys had kept mostly quiet during the journey, which was fast becoming the norm.

Their progress was steady over the course of a few hours. The streaks of clouds overhead steadily thickened and drew together and eventually hid the sun from view. Around them the area began to open out; buildings were spaced farther apart, and didn't tower as high, rarely reaching more than three stories. The streets and alleys were wider here, and abandoned living quarters sat comfortably between deserted shops and empty taverns. Whatever the place used to be, its layout gave Cass a less rushed feeling, like it was once a community where it had been alright to take your time, and people had a little more room to live. In the distance, Cass caught a glimpse of a tall building towering above the others.

"We're not far now," Wick said. "How do you want to handle the approach, G?"

"I hate to split up too much," she answered. "But I don't think it's wise to roll up to the front gate with our Awakened friends without announcing ourselves first."

"What if they just keep covered up?" Swoop asked.

"Might draw more attention than we want. And questions."

"I don't see how we can escape that," Mouse said. "And I don't think any explanation is actually going to prepare anybody."

"Fair enough," Gamble said. "Miss Cass, what do you think?"

"I'd rather stay together if we can make it work," Cass answered.

"Then we'll make it work," Gamble replied. "Tighten up a little, keep the weapons casual but in plain view. I want to look threatening without having to threaten. And Sky, I want you on overwatch anyway."

"Yep, check," Sky said.

In another ten minutes or so, they came to a wide intersection, and Sky broke off from the group and went to find a position. Nobody said anything, but Cass could almost feel the sharpening of focus. Nervous energy built. She drew closer to Wren, and tried to calm her breathing. It felt very much like they were walking into a fight.

When the enclave finally came into view, Cass quickly understood how it'd gotten its name. The tall building she'd seen before dominated the area, nine stories high. It was actually about fifty yards outside the wall of the enclave, just to the right of it from their direction, looming over it like a headstone.

"Main gate's just around to the right," Gamble said. "Swoop, Mouse, with me. We'll take point. Wick, fall back and watch the rear. The rest of you stay about five meters behind me. If anybody starts popping off, just hit the ground until it's quiet again. Or until I tell you otherwise.

"Sky," she said, "you set...? No, we're coming up on it now... alright. Well, stay put, we'll check it out."

"That's weird," Wick said.

"Maybe they've loosened up," Gamble answered. "Still. Eyes up."

Cass wanted to ask what the exchange was about, but thought better of it. Everyone else was switched on, no need to distract them. They approached the enclave, which was surrounded by a hexagonal concrete and metal wall, maybe fifteen feet high. The wall itself looked fairly well assembled; clean welds held the obviously scavenged parts together. It wasn't the prettiest place she'd seen, but they'd constructed it with some skill. There were a few scattered watchtowers peeking over the top, though as they got closer she could tell the towers were actually constructed next to the wall on the inside, rather than on top of it. Maybe not ideal, but certainly functional. She got the feeling the place had been added on to over the years, rather than having been planned from the start.

Wren tensed up beside her.

"Mama," he said quietly. "It's not right."

Cass slowed her pace. He stared straight ahead at the wall, eyes wide, shaking his head.

Gamble was just turning the corner around the wall and getting a view of where the gate was. She stopped short, and Swoop walked up right beside her.

"You gotta be kiddin' me," Swoop said. He readjusted his weapon on its sling and started towards the gate.

The rest of the group gathered behind Gamble. Wren called after Swoop. "Don't go in," he said. "It's not safe."

Now that Wren brought it to her attention, Cass could feel it too. There was a weird energy there. Ethereal, evasive. Wild. Angry. But something vaguely familiar that she couldn't place.

"Not again," Wick said.

The gate had two doors, opening inward, and at first it just looked like the people of Ninestory had left it open. It wasn't that uncommon for towns to let people enter freely during the day. But as Cass drew nearer, it became clear something had gone wrong. Towards the center, the metal was bent inwards, as if it'd been struck by some great force. Near the top of both doors, the hinges had flexed and pulled away. Something had most definitely breached the gate.

"Mama, don't," Wren insisted. He was hanging back, away from the gate. Wick and Swoop moved into the enclave with cautious steps. Finn and Mouse followed after, and the four men began to fan out with their weapons lowered, but shouldered.

"Sky, bring it in," Gamble said. She and Able remained outside the gate with Cass and the boys. "You boys be careful."

"Wren, what is it? What are you feeling?" Cass asked.

"There's something in there, Mama."

There were a number of buildings visible from the main entrance, but they were all closed up, windows dark. For all intents and purposes, the place looked completely abandoned.

"I don't think there's *anything* in there, Governor," Gamble said.

Think they all left? Able signed.

"Could be. Seems odd, though. Ninestory's been around for years. Don't see why they'd pull up and head out now."

There was a noise behind them, and Cass turned to see Sky jogging up to join them.

"What's the word?" he said as he drew near.

"Dunno yet," Gamble answered. "Could be an attack. Could be they up and left."

Sky let out an exasperated sigh. "Didn't we just do this?"

"Pretty much."

"Wasn't that great the first time, you know."

Inside the enclave, the four team members were approaching the nearest building. Wick led the way, with Finn right behind him, while Mouse and Swoop held off a few yards and covered their flanks.

"Yeah, Wick, I got you," Gamble said. "...Check. Just be careful. You see something you don't like, you come right back out."

"Please," Wren said, "please, let's just go. Let's go back."

Cass went down on one knee and drew Wren to her. He was trembling.

"Gamble, I really think we should listen to Wren," Cass said.

"I hear him," Gamble said. "Don't worry, we're not gonna stay long."

Wick eased open the front door and flowed in with Finn in support. They disappeared into the darkened building. Mouse and Swoop waited outside, weapons up, casually scanning.

"Check," Gamble said, and then looking back at Cass and Wren, "Front room's clear. They're just gonna check the lower level."

The words had barely left her mouth when the gunfire barked from inside the building. Gamble cursed, and immediately the whole team switched on, weapons up, closing in on the building. Wren clapped his hands over his ears.

The gunshots continued, and a few seconds later Finn appeared in the doorway, firing his weapon with one hand

and dragging something backwards with the other. He was screaming for Mouse.

It took a moment for Cass to realize what Finn was dragging: Wick. He was on his back, and his legs were fishtailing along the ground, trying to help his brother propel him backwards away from the building. Wick still had his weapon up, firing.

Mouse and Swoop started advancing towards the door – right as the first of the Weir stumbled out into the daylight. They both opened up, and the Weir dropped, but it was quickly replaced by another, and then another. Cass's mind couldn't comprehend what she was seeing, as a stream of Weir came pouring out into the street.

"Back! Fall back!" Gamble shouted, and all guns were up and firing, cutting down the impossible wave that flowed out of the building. Finn went down hard, fighting to drag Wick further away, but no matter how many they killed, the tide of Weir kept gaining ground. Mouse ran forward and skidded to a knee beside Wick, firing into the advancing horde.

Swoop let out a howl of pure rage and walked forward, unleashing an unrelenting torrent of gunfire. Able sprinted towards his comrades. Sky remained at the gate, methodically firing shot after shot after shot, with barely a second in between to acquire a new target.

And just when Cass thought the team was sure to be overwhelmed, the tide broke and the last of the Weir toppled to the ground, mere feet from where Wick lay.

"Come on, get him up, get him up!" Finn shouted, but Mouse was already there, lifting Wick to his feet. Mouse wrapped one of Wick's arms over his shoulder and hauled him up, jogging away from the building and the mass of bodies that lay sprawled in the street. Even from where Cass knelt, she could see the dark stains soaking Wick's chest, and the paleness of his face.

The others kept their weapons up as they backpedaled towards the gate. Cass was still trying to process what had just happened when the sounds started. It was muffled at first, an indistinct mass of white noise coming from somewhere within the enclave. But as it grew in intensity, it also sharpened, and Cass realized she wasn't hearing a single sound, but rather some countless number of them blending together.

The whole enclave was full of Weir. And they were coming.

"Back, to the building!" Gamble ordered. "Get to the building!"

Cass didn't hesitate. She swung Wren up in her arms and took off, sprinting for the tall building just over fifty yards away. The indistinct sounds became clearer, and she recognized the telltale cries of the Weir echoing behind her. But there was no sound of gunfire. Yet.

As she reached the door to the nine-story-tall building, Cass realized she had no idea what was on the other side of it. If there were Weir in the enclave, was there reason to think they wouldn't also be inside the building?

She skidded to halt just in front. Gamble caught up and didn't slow down. With a stomping kick, she slammed the double front doors open and entered aggressively with her weapon shouldered.

After a few moments she called from the inside, "Clear, let's go!"

Painter was staring back at the gate, eyes wide, unmoving. Cass grabbed his shoulder and spun him around, and shoved him through the door ahead of her, following him in closely. The entryway was a small dusty front room that led to a narrow corridor. The corridor was lined with a number of doors on both sides, and there was a concrete stairwell at the far end.

"Come on, come on!" Gamble shouted.

Cass pushed into the corridor to make room for everyone else. Gamble waited by the door, motioning fiercely to the rest of the team, as if by waving them in she could propel them that much faster.

Mouse was the first one through, carrying Wick across his shoulders. Cass couldn't believe he was able to carry both Wick and all their gear, and still walk, let alone run, but he managed to cover the ground with impressive speed. The others must've been holding back to cover Mouse, because as soon as he made it into the front room, the others piled in quickly behind. Swoop was the last one in.

He and Gamble slammed the doors shut behind them, and Able grabbed something off the side of Swoop's pack. Cass's eyes took a moment to adjust to the relative darkness of the room; the only light now came in from two narrow horizontal slot windows, placed high and covered over with steel grating on the inside. In two seconds Able was at work, running a wide band of what looked like some kind of thick grey putty down the center of the doors, overlapping both where the doors met in the middle. When it was in place, he made a flicking motion and stepped back, and seconds later the strip let off a shower of white-hot sparks, dazzling in the darkened room, fusing the doors together.

Everyone seemed to be moving all at once, but there was no chaos in the motion. Gamble was barking orders that the team seemed to be able to respond to faster than Cass could process. They put three guns on the door: Swoop, Able, and Finn.

Gamble sent Sky to check the stairwell, and he pushed past Cass with such intensity it seemed like he barely registered she was even there. Gamble started down the hall, checking the doors on either side.

Mouse had Wick sitting down on the floor, propped against the wall at the mouth of the corridor. Wick's eyes were open and he seemed alert, but his breathing was labored. He had a hand pressed hard into the hollow where his neck met his left shoulder, just above the collarbone. Cass could see the blood burbling out around his fingers. After a moment she realized Mouse was calling her name.

"Cass, I need you!" he called. She snapped into the moment. Cass was still holding Wren, so she slid him to his feet and then went and crouched next to Mouse. "Help me get his pack off."

Mouse leaned Wick gently forward while Cass worked on the buckles. They were gummed with blood and were hard to work.

"Steady your breathing, Wick," he said. "Slow it down."

"You first," Wick said with a clenched jaw. He grimaced, and Cass saw blood on his teeth. They got the pack off his back and scooted him back against the wall.

"Hey," Mouse said as they were helping him move, "you didn't have to run all that way, haulin' you." He said it with a smile, but Cass could see the concern in his eyes. Mouse gave a quick tug to a pouch on his chest harness, and it fell open, revealing the neatly packed and secured contents of his trauma kit. He worked quickly to get Wick's chest rig out of the way so he could assess the wound.

"Talk to me, Mouse!" Finn called.

"He's busy!" Wick responded. "...And mind your business!" And then more quietly, he said, "Is it bad, man?"

Mouse moved Wick's hand and blood pooled in the hollow of his clavicle, but Cass didn't have time to see the wound before Mouse poured some kind of gritty powder over it and started packing it with gauze.

"Quit leaking everywhere," Mouse said, "and it won't be. Cass, put pressure right here, hard, even if he squeals."

Cass did as she was instructed, and Wick locked eyes with her.

"You're going to be fine," she said.

"You're just saying that."

"It makes me feel better."

"I'll be fine."

"You're just saying that."

"I know."

Outside, the Weir continued to squall, but they sounded scattered and didn't seem to be getting any louder or closer that Cass could tell. Gamble came back down the hall past them and grabbed Able's shoulder. He turned his head to look at her, but kept his weapon up and pointed at the door.

"Go help Sky on the stairs," she said. Able nodded and hustled down the hall and up the stairs. Gamble came and dropped to a knee alongside Wick. "Wick, how bad are you?"

"More scared than hurt," he said.

"Mouse?" Gamble asked.

"Couple of punctures, just behind the clavicle, some tearing," Mouse said. "Jugular and carotid are probably OK, but if it hit the subclavian, could be bad news."

"Can we move him?" she asked.

"If we have to."

"I want to get higher, rig the stairs."

Mouse nodded. "Gimme a few, see if we can make sure this clots up."

A sudden impact made the doors shudder, snapping everyone's attention to the front. Except for Mouse. He was intent on Wick, calmly evaluating him.

"Might not have it," Gamble whispered.

They waited in tense silence, waited for that next blow to fall. Ten seconds passed.

"What do you think those doors are rated?" Finn asked in a low voice.

"Nothin' like that gate was," Swoop answered quietly. Finn readjusted his grip on his rifle.

Thirty seconds. Sixty. But no more blows fell on the doors.

"Seal up the hinges, too," Gamble said, her voice lowered. "And rig a charge on the center. If we have to get out that way, we'll go out hard."

Finn kept the door covered while Swoop cautiously approached. He produced another strip of the same putty-like substance Able had slapped on the middle of the door. This time, however, Swoop drew a large knife from its sheath on his chest rig and cut the strip into quarters. These he placed on the hinge-side of the doors, two on each, high and low. He ignited them in succession, and they each rained sparks to the floor. Once they'd finished, Swoop dropped his pack and dug out a few components that Cass didn't recognize.

"When you say 'go out hard', how hard do you mean?" Swoop asked, as he started assembling pieces.

"Hard enough to kill everything on the other side," Gamble answered.

Swoop nodded and grabbed another two components out his bag, and then started affixing them to the doors.

Wren was still standing in the hall where Cass had left him, with his hands over his ears, just watching those doors with wide eyes. Jaw clenched, lips white.

"Any chance they didn't actually see us come in here?" Finn asked.

"It's hard for them to track in the daylight," Cass said. "Maybe they lost us."

Mouse patted her on the arm and shifted position to take over putting pressure on Wick's wound. Cass lifted her hands slowly while he slid his in underneath and piled more gauze on top of the wound. Cass's hands were tacky where the blood had soaked through the first layers of the dressing.

"They know we're here," Wren said from the hall. Gamble looked at him, and then at Cass.

"If he says they know, they know," Cass said.

Gamble nodded.

"Sky," she said, "we need some elevation... Understood... Can you check for roof access...? I *understand* that. I'm not asking to clear the whole thing... Alright, check." She shook her head. "Can we get Wick up nine flights?"

"He's lost a lot of blood," Mouse said. "I don't want him going into shock."

"I'm not dead yet," Wick said. "You don't have to talk about me like I am."

"Sorry, *you* lost a lot of blood," Mouse replied.

"I didn't really *lose* it, it's all right outside."

"Knock it off, Wick, this isn't a joke," Finn said.

"I can make it up some stairs," Wick said. "If someone can carry my pack."

"I'll take it," Cass said, before anyone else could respond.

Swoop finished rigging the charge on the door and dropped back. Outside the cries of the Weir had dropped off. Mouse had Wick hold the gauze in place and started winding a wide bandage over the wound and around under his armpit.

"What happened in there, Finn?" Swoop asked.

"I don't really know," he said. "We were clearing rooms, everything was fine. Come around a corner, and we're staring at a crowd of Weir packed into a little dark room in the middle. Just standing there, all packed in together. Tried to back out, one of 'em pounced. Wick went down and it was on top of him, and the rest started coming after us. Like walking into the middle of a hornet's nest."

"My fault," Wick said. "Took it too fast..."

"No way anyone could've anticipated that," Finn said. "It was like they were switched off, and we woke 'em up. I've never seen anything like it."

"I don't think anyone has," Swoop said. "Never gave much thought to where they went during the day."

"Alright," Gamble said. "I want to get up to the roof, get a good look at what we're dealing with. Swoop, Finn, rig the first two flights of stairs. If they breach that door, I want it to cost them."

"You want to drop the stairs, or just kill a lot of 'em?" Swoop asked.

"Both."

He grunted. "That'll take most of what we got."

"I'd rather use it all than die with it in your pack."

Swoop gave a little nod. "Check."

"Everybody else, we're moving topside," Gamble said.

"To the t-t-top floor?" Painter asked.

"No. To the roof," Gamble said. "We don't have time to clear the whole building, but we can control the roof. Get your stuff, and we'll move up."

Cass grabbed Wick's pack. It was a lot heavier than she'd anticipated, and she once again marveled at Gamble and her "boys". As far as she knew, none of them were modified or enhanced with chems, or gene splicing, or servorganics. Just raw humanity and determination. It made their skill and stamina that much more impressive. Cass looped the straps over her shoulders, backwards, so she could carry his pack in front of her. Then she took Wren's hand, and together they followed Gamble down the corridor towards the stairs.

Behind them, Mouse helped Wick to his feet, and looped Wick's right arm over his shoulders.

"Lean on me, let me do most of the work," Mouse said. "And try to keep that left arm as stable as possible."

"Alright," Wick said.

"You let me know if you start feeling weak, dizzy, or like you can't catch your breath."

"I feel like all that right now."

"Then let me know if it gets worse."

"Alright."

They all started up the stairs together, Gamble leading the way, cautiously leading with her weapon. Cass came right behind, with Wren by her side. Painter followed them. Mouse and Wick brought up the rear.

The stairwell was plain: bare concrete floor and stairs, a simple iron railing. Vertical slot windows were spaced every so often, lending enough light to see by, but they were too narrow to give any meaningful view of what was going on outside.

Down below them, Finn started laying out charges and some other devices Cass hadn't seen before, while Swoop went to work rigging them up on the first set of stairs. Cass had never been around so many explosives before, and she found it wholly unnerving, even as much as she trusted Swoop as an expert.

"Hey," Gamble said, calling back down to Swoop and Finn. "Make it good enough, not perfect. I don't want you fiddling around down here."

"Ain't the kind of thing you rush, G," Swoop answered.

"We're more spread out than I like already. I don't want you guys getting cut off."

"Go on," Finn said. "We'll be right behind you."

Gamble looked like she was about to say something else, but instead she just nodded and resumed leading them up the stairs. Once they got to the top of the second floor, she said in a lowered voice, "Sky, we're coming up."

She kept her weapon up and swept the angles as they presented themselves, constantly vigilant for any sudden threat. Each floor was virtually indistinguishable from the others. At each landing, the stairwell connected to a long, dark corridor with doors on either side.

As they passed each one, Cass tried not to think about Gamble mentioning how they didn't have time to clear the whole building. There was no telling who – or what – might be lurking down any one of those halls, or behind any one of those doors. The fact that they hadn't heard or seen any signs of danger gave some small comfort, but the memory of the cascade of Weir pouring out of that building was still too fresh.

They took their time climbing the stairs, not wanting to rush Wick, not daring to get separated. Though it wasn't really that far to climb, by the time they reached the top floor, Cass's legs were starting to burn from all the weight she was carrying, combined with the slower pace.

Beyond the ninth floor, the stairwell extended up in a fully enclosed corridor, like a toppled chimney. There were no windows, and Cass knew for the others it must have seemed an overwhelming darkness. At the top there was a single door, which she assumed led out onto the roof.

Gamble halted at the bottom of the steps, and flicked on the red light affixed to the underside of her gun. "Sky, we're coming out."

She led them up the final flight of stairs, and swung the door open. The flood of sunlight overwhelmed Cass completely, and everyone shielded their eyes. When they made it out onto the roof, Able was waiting for them there by the door. Cass drew her veil down. When her eyes finally adjusted, she saw Sky set up at the edge of the roof, facing the enclave.

The roof itself was flat, with a few industrial-grade vents – and large dormant machinery of unknown purpose – clustered near the center. Here and there were scattered broken remnants of once-useful things. Cass guessed anything of value had long ago been scavenged by the residents of Ninestory. Or rather, by the former residents.

The team piled their gear by the rusted machinery. Mouse eased Wick to a sitting position, leaning back against their packs and facing the door. Wick was pale, his face slick with a thin sheen of sweat. His breathing seemed shallower and more labored than it had before, and Cass hoped it was just from the exertion of the climb. Mouse knelt next to him and checked his vitals. He didn't look happy with the results.

Cass walked across the roof to join Sky and Gamble at the edge. The wind was up, chilly even in the full sun. She flipped up the collar of her coat to keep it off her neck. As she crossed, she was amazed by the commanding view the roof provided of the surrounding cityscape.

It was the tallest building for miles around, and even though it wasn't all that high compared to many places she'd been before, the unbroken urban sprawl that surrounded them made Cass feel like they were on an island mountain amidst a concrete sea. What she saw when she reached the edge, however, took her breath away.

Far below, what looked like hundreds of Weir teemed throughout the enclave and the surrounding area, swarming like insects from an overturned nest. Just in front of the building, however, a stationary knot of them had formed.

Most of the ones in motion didn't seem to be following any particular pattern, but whenever an individual drew near the cluster, it quickly diverted its path to join the group, like iron filings collecting around a magnet. Even stranger, they had all gone utterly silent.

"I just don't understand it," Sky said, as he watched the creatures scurrying below. "They wiped out the whole enclave?"

"Looks that way," Gamble said. "And then took it over."

"I've never heard of that happening before. Ever."

"Me neither. Like Swoop said, I hadn't really thought about where they went after dark. Never would've guessed that, though."

Everything about it seemed wrong. Even more wrong than usual. Cass thought back to the night they'd attacked the gate of Morningside. She couldn't shake the feeling that something about the Weir had changed. Something significant. Something dire.

"You think they can see us up here?" Sky asked.

"Tough to say," Gamble said. Then she looked at Cass. "What do you think, Miss Cass?"

Cass stared down over ninety feet. Even through her veil, the sunlight affected the details she could make out like a thin mist.

"I'm not sure if they *see* the same way I do," she said. "But I can make out the shapes fine, just not much detail."

"I didn't think they'd come out in the daylight," Sky said.

"They usually don't on their own. It isn't natural," Gamble said.

"Nothing about them is," Sky replied. He gave Cass a little look out of the corner of his eye right after he said it, like he hadn't meant to say it out loud, or he was afraid she'd take it the wrong way, but Sky didn't say anything else.

"I think Wren's right," Cass said. "They know we're in the building. But I have no clue what they're doing about it."

"Never known them to be much for planning," Mouse said from behind them. He came up and stood next to Cass, between her and Gamble.

"How's Wick?" Gamble asked.

Mouse shook his head. "I'm worried."

"You're always worried when someone's hurt," Sky said.

"Not like this," Mouse answered. "I think he's got some internal bleeding. Lots of ways for that to be real bad, and most of 'em I can't do anything about out here. Could go into hypovolaemic shock, might be fluid leaking into his chest cavity…" He shook his head. "Even if it stops on its own, things get too heavy, his blood pressure could drop to critical."

"So, what're you saying?" Gamble asked, and the fear was evident in her voice, no matter how much she was trying to control it.

Mouse wouldn't look at her. He just kept staring down at all the Weir below. "I'm saying we don't all get out of here without some kind of miracle."

"Finn know?" Sky asked.

"Not yet."

"How about Wick?"

"He knows he's in trouble. Pretending he's not."

They all stood in silent thought after that, each no doubt running through the scenario from every angle they could think of, looking for a good solution. Nothing was presenting itself to Cass. It'd never occurred to her that any of Gamble's team might not survive, not really. Up until now, they'd all seemed invincible. But now, in that moment, everything became entirely too possible.

And then the Weir broke the silence.

"*Spshhhh. Naaaah.*"

The call, or chant. Worse this time. A chorus in perfect unison from every single Weir in that cluster.

"*Spshhhh. Naaaah.*"

The Weir stood down below, packed tightly together, staring up at the roof. Stragglers continued to join the cluster. And as they did, they each took up the call. They were packed so closely together it was almost impossible to get a count on how many there were, but Cass estimated a hundred or so.

"What is going on down there?" Sky said.

"I don't know, but I hate it," Gamble said.

"Can I start shooting?"

"Not yet."

"*Spshhhh. Naaaah.*"

"I know what it is," Wren said from behind them. Cass hadn't even heard him walk up. They all turned and looked at him. He was standing just a few feet away, eyes wide and glassy, even paler than usual. "I know what it is, now."

"*Spshhhh. Naaaah.*"

"What is it, baby?" Cass asked, knowing in her heart whatever the answer was, it would be more frightening than the uncertainty.

He looked at her with absolute despair.

"They're saying 'Spinner', Mama. They're saying my name."

Cass involuntarily grabbed Mouse's arm. He in turn caught her arm in reflexive support, but she knew that he didn't understand what Wren was saying. None of the others did. But now that Wren had made the connection, she knew he was right, no matter how much she wanted to deny it.

"*Spshhhh. Naaaah.*"

She could hear it too, now. The electronic squall was no longer just bursts of white noise. Instead, inhuman voices mimicking human speech.

"What?" Sky said.

"What are you talking about, Wren?" Gamble asked.

Wren walked closer to the edge and peered down. "It's Asher. He's in the Weir."

TWENTY

Cass regained herself and let go of Mouse's arm, and his grip on her relaxed, though his hand lingered protectively. She went down on a knee next to her son, spoke in a low voice.

"It can't be, Wren," Cass said. "Asher's gone. You sent him away."

"But sent him where, Mama?" he asked, not looking at her. She didn't have an answer.

"I don't understand," Gamble said. "You mean your brother's one of them down there?"

Wren took another step closer to the edge of the building, but Cass reached out and grabbed his shoulder. He stopped in place, just stared down at the crowd of Weir still chanting below.

"No," he said, shaking his head. "He's *all* of them."

It was almost too much to comprehend, the very idea too much to bear. After the events in Underdown's throne room, when Wren brought Cass back to herself and Three lay dying, Asher had been there on the floor. At least his body had been. His eyes had been open, fixed and staring, but there had been no life in him. It hadn't been any use asking Wren what he'd done to his half-brother; he didn't exactly know himself. But as terrible as Asher had been, and as dangerous, Wren had still never really forgiven himself for taking Asher's life.

I just wanted him to stop, was all he would say.

Could it be that somehow, in some way, when Asher's mind had been cast out of his body, he hadn't truly been destroyed? Cass looked down at her hands, the slender fingers with their metal blades beneath the nails. There had been a time before that she could've believed it impossible. No longer. As shocking as it was for her mind to accept, she found she didn't need to fully understand it to find herself believing.

"*Spshhhh. Naaaah.*"

"What's 'Spinner'?" Sky asked. "What does that mean?"

"It's what Asher used to call Wren. Before," Cass explained. "They called us different names."

"So you're saying your dead brother is controlling those things down there?"

Wren nodded.

"How do you know?" Gamble asked.

"I can feel him," Wren said.

In the street below, the cluster of Weir remained pressed together. Others still wandered in and around the enclave, but no more joined the group. A number of them even seemed to be returning to the buildings from which they had come.

"He's different," Wren said, after a moment, "...but not."

"What does that mean for us?" Mouse asked.

"Nothing good, I'm sure," Gamble said. "But for now the situation hasn't really changed, has it? I mean, if we kill all of 'em, will that be the end of it?"

"I don't know," Wren answered. "I don't think so."

There was noise back behind them, across the roof, and Cass turned to see Finn and Swoop rejoining the team. Both went immediately to Wick. Finn crouched down beside his brother. Swoop remained standing and seemed to exchange a few words with Wick, before heading over towards Gamble and the rest of them.

"How we lookin'?" Swoop asked.

"Not good," Gamble said.

Gamble gave Swoop the rundown, as much as she could. There wasn't really any good way to try to describe or explain what was going on with the Weir. Swoop took it all in with his usual stoicism.

"What about the rest of 'em?" Swoop asked.

"What do you mean?" Gamble said.

"Looks like about a hundred or so down there. Why aren't they all together?" he asked.

"I have no idea."

"Maybe he can't control them all," Wren said.

Finn and Able joined the group.

"Who's on the door?" Swoop asked as they approached.

"Wick's got it," Finn said.

Swoop glanced at Mouse, but Mouse didn't say anything.

"I know he's in trouble," Finn said, replying to the look. "He's hurt, not dead. He's got the door. So what are we doing?"

Everyone looked at Gamble.

"If anyone's got ideas, now's a good time," Gamble said.

Swoop started off. "Blow the door. Shoot the rest. Make a run for it."

"We're not running," Mouse said. "Not with Wick in the shape he's in."

"We can start picking them off from up here," Sky said. "See how many we can get through."

Gamble shook her head. "We're not going to kill a whole town's worth. Not before sundown."

"I'm light on ammo anyway," Finn said. "How about you all?"

"Same," Swoop said.

Able waggled his hand, indicating he still had some, but not as much as he'd like.

"No chance they're going to leave us alone, I guess," Mouse said.

"Wouldn't count on it," Gamble said.

"We could go back in, start reinforcing floor by floor," Finn said. "Start at the top, work our way down. See how far we get before they come. Try to get them choked up in the tight spots."

"Take it to blade-work then," Gamble said.

Finn nodded. "Haven't had to reload one yet."

Everyone stood silently considering. It would be hours of work, clearing and reinforcing each floor. And there was no telling when the Weir might actually launch their attack. For now they seemed to be content to stand out front, but Cass didn't expect them to remain that way. Certainly when night came, the enclave would empty, and the full strength of the Weir would be upon them. And then they would have to fight until morning.

Images from the battle on the night they escaped Morningside flashed through her mind. They would never last.

"What about Lil?" Cass said.

Eyes turned to her.

"What about her?" Gamble replied.

"I could pim her. Maybe they could help."

"I don't see how," Swoop said.

"I know they don't look like much," Cass answered, "but they lived in the open – in a village without walls – for years. They're fighters."

The team exchanged looks. Cass didn't know what other options they thought they had. The sun was high, nearly noon already. "And they're the only ones close enough to do anything."

"Might not be time enough for them to get here and us to all make it back," Finn said.

"Then we should probably ask them to get started now," Cass said.

Can't hurt to ask, Able signed. *Maybe they know something we don't.*

Gamble gave a little nod. "Alright, do it."

Cass pimmed Lil. She explained the situation as best she could, hoping to impress upon her how much trouble they were in – without making it sound like she was inviting them to certain death. After hearing it all, Lil told Cass she would talk to her people and see what they could come up with.

"She's going to get back to us," Cass told the others.

Five minutes passed. Ten. In the street below, the Weir remained pressed together, but they had thankfully given up their chant. The others had disappeared. Cass guessed they'd all returned to the shelter of the enclave. Mouse went to check on Wick again, and the rest of the team split time between watching the Weir and standing around restlessly.

Fifteen minutes. Still nothing.

"They're not coming," Swoop finally said. "And we're losing on our own time here. I'm with Finn. Reinforce what we can, pull a staged retreat. Take as many of 'em as we can."

"Roof as a final fallback," Finn said. "Only one way up. Maybe we can choke the stairs with their dead. Make 'em change their minds."

"If we blow the lower stairwell, we might be able to hold them there for a while."

"How long do you think it'll take to set up?" Gamble asked.

"Pretty much as long as we have," Swoop said.

"Then let's get started. Sky, keep eyes on, let us know if there's any change. Mouse, stay close to Wick. Cass, Painter,

I'm going to need you to come help."

It was as they were crossing the roof back towards the stairwell that Lil finally pimmed Cass a simple message: "We're coming."

"Hold on," Cass said to the team. "She says they're coming. They're on the way."

"How long?" Gamble asked.

Cass asked Lil for an estimate, and communicated the reply. "Three hours."

"And what're they going to do when they get here?"

"Whatever you tell them to."

Gamble thought for a moment, while the others stood by. "Mouse." She waved him over, and they spoke together in lowered voices. "If we put him on a litter, can we move Wick out?"

"If we have to move him, yeah, that's our best bet. But that'll put us down three shooters."

Gamble nodded. "You've got one?"

"Collapsible, in my pack, yeah."

"You know when you whisper, I can tell you're talking about me, right?" Wick called.

"We're trying to decide whether to roll you down the stairs or just drop you over the edge," Finn answered.

"Either one's better than all this sitting around," Wick said. He was trying to keep it light, but his voice already sounded thinner than usual.

"Swoop," Gamble said, "how's downstairs rigged?"

"Trip on the door, thirty-second delay off that on the stairs, plus another trip at the top."

"How tough to rewire the door to a clacker?"

"Easy day... Unless they decide to come knockin' while I'm workin' on it."

"Alright. Change of plans, gentlemen," Gamble said. "We're going to do some blockade running."

"So, pretty much what I said the first time?" Swoop said.

"Yes, Swoop, you're very smart, we should always listen to you, et cetera. We've still got to hold out three hours."

Gamble quickly laid out the plan. Mouse, Sky, and the three principals would remain on the roof with Wick: Sky to relay information about the Weir and their movements, Mouse to keep an eye on Wick, and the others, Cass assumed, largely to stay out of the way.

Swoop, Finn, Able, and Gamble were all headed back down to the bottom floor to rewire the explosives. Or rather, the three of them would provide security while Swoop did the work. And if the Weir came while they were down there, they would try to make a withdrawal up the stairs while continually engaging.

"And if that doesn't work..." Gamble said, looking at Cass with a flat expression. "Good luck." She held out her jittergun to Cass.

"You keep it," Cass said.

"Won't do you any good if it's on me and we get overrun."

"Don't get overrun then."

Gamble extended the gun out further and bobbed it up and down, waiting for Cass to take it. Cass held her hand palm out, and then flipped it around. Her thin blades sprang from their housing under her fingernails with a *snick*. For a moment the two women just looked at each other. And then, with a sigh, Gamble returned the jittergun to her leg holster.

"I can come with you, you know," Cass said.

Gamble shook her head. "Better up here. Puts four shooters top and bottom. Well... three shooters and Miss Fancy Nails up top, I guess." She flashed a quick smile. "Back in a few."

The four of them headed towards the stairs, but Finn stopped and jogged back. He knelt down by Wick and put his head against his brother's, and whispered a few words. Wick gave a little nod and patted him on the cheek. Then Finn rejoined the others and they disappeared down the darkened corridor.

"What do *we* do?" Painter asked.

"I suppose we wait," Cass said.

"And hope the Weir don't get tired of just standing around," Sky said. He gave a little nod and returned to his position at the edge of the roof. Painter went and found a place near one of the large ventilation shaft covers, where he could be in the sun, but out of the wind. He plopped his pack down to use as a pillow and stretched out on his back, with an arm over his eyes.

Wick, of course, was still sitting, propped against some of the packs, with his rifle laid across another one where he could keep it aimed at the door. Mouse grabbed two of the packs off the ground, one in each hand, and lugged them over towards the door. Cass guessed they were a good sixty pounds each, but he didn't seem to have too much trouble with them. He swung the door shut with his foot, and then piled the packs in front of it, one on top of the other.

"Gamble, Mouse," he said. "Door's braced, let me know when you're on your way back up."

Wren had gone to join Sky by the roof's edge. He had his hood up, and was sitting cross-legged next to him. Cass walked over and sat down beside her son.

They all sat in silence for a time, watching the Weir down below. As terrible as they were, Cass found that the fear they inspired was diminished by the broad daylight. Surely the darkness of night lent them some greater measure of terror. Even so, seeing so many gathered as one force was daunting. The thought of the battle that awaited them was not one she relished.

But at the same time, if what Wren said was true, if Asher was alive in some measure, and exerting control over those creatures, something stirred within her at the idea of doing all she could to destroy them. Asher had hounded them long enough, had caused them more than a lifetime's worth of sorrow. Cass would do whatever it took to ensure that he would never reach Wren again.

And another thought hung like a black cloud in the back of her mind, one she didn't even want to acknowledge. The great dreadful unknown that had haunted her since her Awakening: the fear that she might somehow revert to a mindless thrall of the Weir. Now, a new possibility arose, more nightmarish than any previously conceived.

If Asher had found his way into the Weir, was there anything preventing him from reclaiming Cass as well?

"Hey, Governor," Sky said. "All those down there. Any chance you could wake any of them?"

Wren was still and quiet for a few moments – before he finally shook his head slowly.

"Yeah," Sky said. "Just thought I'd ask. Makes me feel better if I know that before I have to shoot them."

The comment lingered in the air, heavy with the imminent storm that awaited them all.

"Could you do it again?" Cass asked. "Could you send Asher away again?"

"I don't know, Mama," Wren said. "I wouldn't know where to start." She leaned forward so she could see his face beneath his hood, and his eyes were sweeping back and forth, as if searching for a solution. "It's him. I know it's him. But he's different somehow. He seems... bigger."

Cass didn't know what to make of that. Though it seemed that she so rarely knew what to make of anything these days. She put her arm around her son, not knowing what else to do.

"I wish Three were here," Wren said.

"I know, baby."

Surely it was pure coincidence. But moments later, the Weir below erupted in a truly appalling clamor, an evil cacophony of short barking bursts. Wren instantly clapped his hands over his ears and squeezed his eyes shut. Yet again, it was like no sound Cass had ever heard them make before. Even as she winced against the noise, her brain processed it all with the knowledge that Asher was behind it. And just as their strange call had become intelligible to her, this too she understood. It was the sound of a horrible mechanical laughter.

And she knew that Asher was mocking them. Taunting them. Toying with them, as was his way. Cass understood now. He wouldn't breach the building. Not while the sun was up. He was content to keep them contained until dusk, when the full force of the Weir would be available.

Rage kindled in her heart. Not an explosive, violent anger, but a cold, hardened wrath. And as she cradled Wren's head to her chest, she found herself no longer dreading the impending battle – but instead inviting it.

Sky was a patient man, but knowing his wife was downstairs with nothing but a couple of doors between her and all that trouble made every minute into a test of his will and focus. Everybody had their jobs to do. His was to watch all those Weir in the street below. It was *not* his job to worry. But, well, he *was* worried. He just had to trust his teammates to do their jobs the way they trusted him to do his.

When Gamble and the others finally returned to the roof, everyone huddled up near the middle, where Wick was. As he joined them, Sky hoped his relief at seeing his wife again wasn't too obvious. The team always gave him grief over it, but never as much as Gamble did herself.

"Gettin' close to go time," Swoop said.

"Yep," Finn answered.

It'd been about two and a half hours since Lil had sent her first message. They'd already gone over the plan multiple times, with multiple contingencies, but they talked it through again anyway. It all came down to basically the same thing. Swoop had rigged the fused front doors with a heavy charge, laid out to disintegrate a good portion of the entrance and turn it into a massive shotgun blast. After it detonated, Gamble, Swoop, Able, Finn, and Sky would kill as many Weir as they could, while Cass and Mouse carried Wick out, and Wren and Painter made a run for Lil and her people. After that, it was pretty much react and hope for the best.

Not much of a plan, really. But then Wick always said a plan was just a list of stuff that never happened anyway.

At that point, they'd all done everything they could to prepare. Now it was just sit and wait.

"I'm going back to my spot," Sky said.

"Don't get too comfy," Gamble answered, and then winked at him. He gave her a little squeeze and returned to his position at the edge of the roof, smiling to himself. The wink had given her away. He hadn't been the only one worried.

When Cass received Lil's pim a few minutes later, a swirl of emotion came with it; relief that help was near tempered by the thought of what it would take to reach it. Cass steadied herself with a deep breath, and then signaled to Gamble and passed the message along.

"They're about twenty minutes out."

The team all started moving at once.

"Finn," Gamble said. "They close enough to hook in to the secure channel?"

"Yeah, probably, I'd guess."

"Patch Lil in so we can talk to her."

"Check."

"And go ahead and loop our principals in while you're at it," Gamble said, glancing over at Cass. "This would be a bad time for communication to break down."

A few moments later Cass responded to a connection request and found herself tied in to the team's secure comms channel. Finn quickly talked her through it; it wasn't much different than pimming, though the voices were tinny and had a little static to them. Much lower resolution than normal, and significant compression. Standing next to someone, she could hear a tiny delay between their real voice and the one through the channel. Cass guessed it all helped reduce their signature in the open, and maybe had additional layers of encryption.

"Alright, let's get Wick loaded up," Gamble said. "We'll move into position in five."

Mouse had already assembled his emergency litter, and he worked with Finn to get Wick transferred and strapped into it. Wick didn't make any jokes about it, and didn't put up any fuss, which worried Cass a great deal. While everyone else was making ready, she pulled Gamble aside.

"Let me go out first," Cass said.

"Out of the question," Gamble replied immediately.

"Gamble—"

"Cass, it's not up for discussion. We've got a plan, we're sticking to it." Gamble turned to walk away, but Cass reached out and caught her arm. She gripped tighter than was strictly necessary.

Gamble looked down at Cass's hand and then back up into her eyes. "I thought we covered this, Cass. Out here, I call the shots."

"You don't know what you're up against, Gamble," Cass said. "And you don't know me. Not really." Cass released Gamble's arm, but she didn't back down. "Asher will come for me, no matter what. If I go to him, it'll give you time to gain some distance. You transfer Wick to Lil's people, and then you're back up to almost full strength. I can fall back to you then, and you can pick off the pursuit."

"They'll tear you to pieces, Cass. I can't allow that."

"I'm not going to let anyone else die for me," Cass answered. "Not anymore."

Gamble continued to stare her down, but Cass could see the wheels spinning.

"I'm not going to convince you otherwise, am I?" Gamble said.

"No."

"And you're not going to recognize my authority on this, are you?"

"No."

"Should I even bother to offer you the jitter?"

"And the knife," Cass said.

Gamble handed her the jittergun and slid the knife out of its sheath. It had a thick, heavy blade, nearly a foot long, and curving slightly forward. There were symbols etched along it, though Cass didn't recognize them. Gamble flipped the knife in her hand and held the hilt out towards Cass. "This has been in my family a long time," Gamble said. "I want it back."

"I'll deliver it myself," Cass said. "Though I might need to clean it first."

"See that you do."

"Change of plans, boys," Gamble called. She gave a curt nod, and then went to explain the new plan to the others.

Out of the corner of her eye, Cass saw Wren was standing off to the side, looking at her. She went to him, crouched down to his height.

"I thought you were going to carry Wick," he said.

"I'm going to help a different way now," she answered.

"I don't like it when you fight, Mama."

"I know."

"It won't be like usual."

"I know."

Wren looked at her with his fathomless eyes, weary and sad. But Cass saw no fear there. "I'll help you if I can," he said.

"You just run to Lil, baby. I'll come to you when I can."

He nodded, and then approached and wrapped his arms tightly around her neck. She hugged him back with everything she had. And hoped it wasn't goodbye.

Afterwards, they all gathered their things. Swoop had stripped out some of the weight from their packs. It seemed a shame to leave perfectly good supplies behind, on the roof, outside a Weir-infested enclave, where no one would ever find them. But it seemed far more foolish to risk someone's life over a couple of extra batteries.

They moved down to just inside the hall on the second floor. Gamble and the others had taken the time to check the rooms on that floor on their last trip down. Even that was closer to the blast than Swoop was comfortable with, but it was safe enough, and Gamble didn't want to risk giving the Weir too much time to recover after the initial explosion. If they got stalled trying to get out of the door, that would be bad news.

Painter had taken over Cass's spot carrying Wick, and Mouse had put him in the front, near Wick's feet. Whether that was because it was the light end or because it would be less risky if Painter dropped him, Cass didn't know. Able had taken charge of Wren, and would ensure that he made it safely to Lil.

Swoop and Gamble stood just behind Cass.

Lil called in and let them know they were a couple of minutes out. They were going to stay out of sight until the initial blast. No one was sure how the Weir were going to react once they showed up, and Cass wanted to make sure that the bulk of the fighting didn't fall on them. As far as she was concerned, they were here to get Wren out, and as much of the team as they could. If they all made it, she'd consider that a bonus.

"Ready?" Swoop asked.

Cass gripped the knife in her right hand and the jittergun in her left. She drew a deep breath. Focused her mind. Asher was out there. Waiting. However many of them there were, they were all Asher to her.

"Do it," Cass said.

"Fire in the hole, fire in the hole," Swoop said calmly, just loud enough for everyone in the hall to hear. He squeezed a device in his hand three times, and then hell itself seemed to shake the building.

Dust leapt from every surface, and bits of concrete crumbled down the stairwell. Even two floors up, the blast vibrated Cass's teeth and made her ears hurt. But there was no time to think. Swoop banged her on the shoulder with the palm of his hand, signaling for her to go, and Cass took off.

All anxiety melted away as she felt the surge of focus. She was on the ground floor without having registered taking the stairs.

Down the hall ahead of her was an opaque white and grey smoke, swirling where she knew a door once stood. Cass plunged through, heard the crunch of debris beneath her feet and knew she was through the front room and then out into the open. The smoke was dissipating in the steady wind, just enough for her to start making out the charred, twisted, and broken forms of the Weir who'd been caught in the blast.

For a brief moment, she wondered if – by some miracle – the explosion had killed them all. The hope was quickly dispelled by an electric scream from somewhere in the smoke ahead of her. They were coming.

The first Weir leapt from out of the smoke in front of her, just to her right, and Cass spun to avoid it and fired a burst from the jittergun into its back as it landed. A second lunged from her left, and she met it with a cleaving stroke from the knife, dropping it at her feet.

She could see them now, lurching through the cloud towards her, two here, three there, and a fury overtook her. She fired one burst, then another, and then leapt forward and drove her knee into the chest of an approaching Weir, before severing its head from its body. The knife flashed almost of its own accord, perfectly balanced, deadly with every stroke.

Weir closed in from the sides, and she met them head on, smashing her fist into one's face and then whirling to shoot another. To her surprise, they seemed to be moving at almost half-speed, and Cass found herself anticipating their movements. One crouched back as if to pounce, and Cass stomped forward, crushing her heel into its face before it even started forward.

A quick spin and she took a leg just below the knee, and then came up and caught another Weir in the throat with the muzzle of the jitter. She squeezed the trigger as it stumbled back and didn't even bother to watch it fall.

The smoke continued to clear as Cass pressed forward, cutting her way through the throng. Her thoughts flashed back, back to the night, long ago, in the Strand when she'd fought among them, with a different result. Now, her full fury and vengeance coursed through her and into the Weir who could not stand before her.

But still they came, and where one fell, two soon took its place. As the air cleared around Cass, she saw that the blast had killed many and left others stunned. But she had little time to count casualties. The Weir were gathering their strength, and unity of purpose.

Cass felt the sting of claws sinking into her left shoulder, followed by a heavy impact from behind that sent her stumbling forward. She allowed the momentum to carry her, rolled, came up in a crouch and drove her blade into a Weir. Fired a long burst into the mass that rushed towards her now. And when she released the trigger, still they fell.

She leapt to her feet and spun to take the arm from the Weir who had been behind her, and then on the backswing, crushed its skull with the pommel of her blade. Cass continued her spin and brought the jittergun up, knowing the other Weir would be nearly upon her.

She fired off a burst, and then another, and found herself with more breathing room than she'd expected. Then she understood. Gamble and her team were out now, assisting.

Cass plunged forward, throwing herself into the nearest pack of Weir, trusting in the team that supported her. But as she fought on, she found the Weir rapidly changing tactics.

They began to coalesce around her, feinting and falling back from one side, and instantly surging forward from another. Before Cass could react, she found herself being swallowed up and driven further away from her companions.

The Weir began landing more strikes, her cheek, her back, her thigh bled freely. Even as Cass adjusted, they now seemed to anticipate and counter her every move. Their shrieks threatened to disorient her. As they pressed in around her, she knew her only chance was to focus all her wrath on a single point, to drive through the crush.

Cass, fired her jittergun, slashing with her knife, forcing her way back towards the building, back to where Gamble and the team were. But in the churn, she'd lost her bearings, and the writhing horde blocked her view. She took a heavy blow to the left side of her head, and the world tilted, and Cass felt herself sliding, crashing through glass and barbed wire. She was on the ground. On her back. And for the second time in her life, she *knew* she would die.

With a roar, Cass squeezed the trigger and held it so hard she thought her knuckle might break as the jittergun spewed a stream of death into the tide of Weir that surged towards her. And then – above the demonic cries of the Weir and the buzzsaw scream of her weapon – Cass heard the strangest sound.

A single clear note, high and piercing, like the wind in a winter storm. A human voice. Singing.

And at its sound, the Weir checked their advance. Cass continued to fire into the Weir until she realized that the jittergun had ceased to buzz, and now made only a rapid clicking sound as it tried to feed from an empty magazine.

Strong hands seized her from behind as three forms swept past her and into the Weir. A swirling, almost blinding blue-white light emanated from the three as they moved among the Weir and cut them down with swords that seemed made of fire.

Cass felt herself slipping away, and everything grew smaller, and darker. And the last thing that Cass beheld was a terrifying vision. One of the three forms turned her direction, and its face was of lightning – with blazing coals for eyes, an avenging angel among ravaging demons. And Cass knew no more.

Cass felt herself floating. Or rather, it seemed more like she was falling, but upwards. Her eyelids weighed heavily on her eyes, as if the pressure from the speed of her movement was forcing them into the sockets. Memory fragments returned. Her right hand clenched, desperate to cling to Gamble's knife, the one that had been in her family a long time, the one Cass had sworn she'd return. But her hand was empty. They had grabbed her. Dragged her away. The Weir had taken her. Again.

Her eyes drifted open, blurred. Tongue too big in her mouth. Everything felt too heavy. She was on her back. A hulking figure loomed. It reached for her. Cass tried to withdraw, but her body barely responded.

"Easy, sister," a deep baritone voice soothed, the grip firm, heavy, but gentle on her arm. "You're safe."

She'd heard that voice before. A long moment. Then her mind processed.

"Mouse?" she said. It took more effort than it should have.

"I'm here," he answered.

Her eyes still hadn't focused. "I feel heavy."

"I had to dose you. Probably going to feel groggy for a while."

She inhaled deeply. It seemed to take a long time. "Why the dose? Am I hurt bad?"

"They carved you up a little, and you took a hard blow to the head. Nothing life threatening." He chuckled a little. "I had to dose you because you kept trying to fight everybody."

"Where's Wren?" Cass asked.

"Sleeping. It's the middle of the night. He's perfectly fine. Not a scratch on him."

"We made it?"

"We did."

"All of us?"

He paused. "Almost."

Cass closed her eyes. "Wick?"

"He's in rough shape, but he's hanging in there. Had to give him a fresh whole blood transfusion on the trip back. Got a little lucky there. Turned out Lil was a match."

She opened her eyes again, turned towards Mouse. Her vision was clearing some. She could see his features. He looked tired. "Wick's alive?"

"He is," Mouse answered. He clenched his jaw with passing emotion. "We lost Elan."

"No," was all Cass could say. Mouse didn't respond. There wasn't really any reason for him to. She had prepared herself as best she could, expecting to lose some of their own. But to cost Lil and her wounded community another life... it seemed unconscionable. And Elan. She remembered him talking with Wren back before they'd left the village, talking about his son. What was his name? Ephraim. Now fatherless.

"How?"

Mouse shook his head. "It was a battle, Cass." But something in his voice, or his expression – or both – said more. The last moments replayed in her mind. The Weir pressing in around her. Hands dragging her backwards, as angels met the advancing creatures. She'd thought she'd been hallucinating.

Now Cass knew she hadn't been. Not completely.

"He died saving me." It wasn't a question.

Mouse took a moment, searched for the words, and then just said, "It wasn't your fault. And if not for you, more would have died."

"That doesn't bring Elan back."

"Neither does feeling guilty." She just looked at him, saw pain there, but also grim acceptance. "He knew what we were up against, Cass. He wanted to come help. He *volunteered* to come help. I guarantee you, if he'd known for sure how it was going to turn out, he still would've come."

"You sound awfully sure for someone who didn't know him."

"I knew him. He was a warrior, same as me. And if you gave me the choice between staying behind while others went to war, or laying down my life to see my brothers and sisters safely home, it wouldn't even be a choice."

Cass looked up at the ceiling. It was a bond she'd witnessed before, but had never known herself, not outside of her children. "How's Lil?"

"Glad so many made it home."

They fell into silence after that. Cass still had many questions, but they seemed to slip through her mind before she could fully grasp them. And while she chased them, a deep and dreamless sleep overtook her.

TWENTY-ONE

When Cass awoke, she knew it was morning from the light streaming in from the high narrow window above her head. She was still on her back, but her mind was sharper, her vision clear. She recognized the room now. The same one she'd been in during their previous stay at the refuge. Wall on her right. And to her left, on the bed across the small room, Wren sat next to Lil. They reacted to her movement; Lil smiled at her, and Wren slid off the bed and timidly approached.

"Hi, Mama," he said.

"Hey, baby."

"How are you feeling?" Wren asked.

"Still trying to figure that out. But better, I think."

"Do you think I could give you a hug?"

"Absolutely."

Cass held out her arms to him and he came and sat on the edge of her bed. Wren leaned down, gently tested his weight against her. Cass pulled him in tight. He responded by sliding one of his slender arms under her neck and squeezing fiercely, and pressing his face into hers.

"How are you?" she asked. "Are you hurt at all?"

She felt him shake his head against hers.

"I was scared for you," Wren said. "Mouse said you would be OK, but it didn't look like it."

"Mouse was right. I *am* OK. You don't need to worry."

He turned his face into the hollow where her neck met her shoulder, and whispered, "I hate it when you're hurt, Mama."

"Well, I'm OK now. How long have we been here?" Cass asked.

Wren finally released her neck and sat back up on the bed. "Just the night. We got back a little before the sun went down. You've been sleeping."

Cass decided to test her strength. She pushed herself up, slowly, to a sitting position. She still felt weak and a little dizzy, but she managed. There were bandages wound around her torso and her right biceps, and covering her left shoulder. She worked her left arm, felt a hollow pang deep, so deep it almost felt like it came from *within* her shoulder blade. With her fingertips, she gently probed the side of her head, from her hairline backwards. There was a goose egg just above and slightly behind her ear. The skin didn't seem to be broken. Small comfort.

She drew her legs up tentatively. A burn stretched through her right thigh and made her breath catch. After a moment, she exhaled slowly and patted Wren on the side. He scooted towards the foot of the bed, giving her room to swivel and swing her legs over the edge. She gingerly moved back so she could lean against the wall, and then straightened her legs out again.

The pain was hard to define. It hurt certainly, but the raw edge was missing. Cass wasn't sure if that was due to the injection Mouse had given her, or if it was a new way her body processed injury. The bandage around her thigh was discolored, like a bruise beneath the cloth, where the wound had oozed, but not enough to soak through.

Once she settled into position, she held up her arm and motioned for Wren. He slid in next to her and cuddled up.

Lil sat across from Cass, watching them together. The smile was gone, but she had a pleasant expression on her face. There was a heaviness in her eyes, though.

"Mouse told me about Elan," Cass said. "I can't even begin to express how sorry I am…"

Lil's gaze dropped for a moment at the mention of his name. But then she gave a nod and looked back up at Cass. "We will all miss him very dearly." And something in her voice said more, and Cass knew then that there had been more between them than she had previously guessed. More than friendship. Lovers. Perhaps only in secret, or maybe only in their hearts, separated by some other circumstance.

"His son… did I make him an orphan?" Cass asked.

Lil shook her head. "Ephraim's mother is here with us."

"How is she?"

"It's a difficult time for her. Their relationship had been strained for quite a while, and I'm afraid they didn't part on the best of terms."

"And how are you?"

Lil hesitated. But she seemed to soften slightly, and after a moment, an unspoken understanding passed between them. "It's a difficult time for us all."

The emotions swelled within Cass, the sorrow, the anger, but most of all the guilt. "Lil, if I could go back–"

Lil raised a hand and shook her head. "Don't, Cass. We know our enemy; our enemy took his life, not you. The seven of us made our own decisions, and we did so fully expecting that some wouldn't return. That six of us did, with all of you as well… it's a triumph beyond what anyone would have imagined. If you must feel sorry, pity Mouse. I think he has taken it the hardest of all."

She dropped her gaze again, but a little smile crept across her lips. "He is something of a mystery. A valiant warrior, yet even more fierce a healer. 'A poet in a barbarian's body'," Cass said, recalling Swoop's earlier joke. Half joke.

"He fought relentlessly to save Elan. When it was clear we wouldn't be able to resuscitate him, we had to physically restrain Mouse."

"That couldn't have been easy."

Lil chuckled. "It was not."

"But you were able to bring…" Cass almost said *the body*, but stopped herself, "…him home?"

Lil nodded. They sat in silence for a time. Cass ran her fingers through Wren's hair, kissed the top of his head.

"Can you tell me what happened?" Cass said at last. "It's all confused in my mind."

Lil drew a breath and remained quiet a few moments.

"I'm sorry, you don't have to," Cass said, but Lil shook her head.

"When we arrived, we spread out just north of the enclave and remained hidden. I came closer than the others, to scout. I confess, I thought you had exaggerated how many Weir were there. If anything, you may have underestimated their numbers.

"After the explosion, the dust and smoke were thick, and I couldn't see much at first. But we closed ranks as planned, hoping to provide a front against the Weir, for you to retreat behind."

She paused, her eyes momentarily distant, unfocused. Cass waited patiently.

"You killed a lot of them, Mama," Wren said. "A *lot*."

Cass glanced down at Wren and then back up to Lil for confirmation. She nodded.

"I've never seen anyone move like that before," Lil said. "Even now, I can hardly believe that what I remember is true. The explosion had thrown many to the ground, but it killed only a handful. Fifteen, maybe. We estimate you alone killed over forty."

"It wasn't *just* me," Cass said. "Gamble and her team were firing from the building."

"No," Lil said, shaking her head. "That was before your team made it to the door."

Cass thought back to the moments before she first heard gunfire. The ground had been covered with the slain, but she'd thought most of them had come from the explosion.

"The Weir didn't seem to even notice the others until they were already behind us. We called to you then. But you didn't hear. The Weir…" Lil trailed off for a moment, searching for the words. She shook her head again. "It was like a human whirlpool. *In*human. That was when we feared for you, and came to get you."

"I think… I think that was Asher," Wren said. "He didn't want you to get away."

"After I fell, I must've already been losing consciousness. I thought I saw…" Cass said; it was her turn to trail off now. She was almost embarrassed to say it. "I don't know. Something like angels, I guess. And I could swear I heard singing."

"That was Lil," Wren said. "She sings."

"We learned long ago that when one is surrounded by unearthly screams, a human voice can sometimes reduce the terror."

"No one sings like Lil, though," Wren added. "It makes you brave." Lil looked at him with a warm smile.

"Well, that's reassuring," said Cass. "Good to know I didn't hallucinate the *whole* thing."

"You didn't dream any of it, Mama," Wren said. "They were doing their trick."

Cass looked at Wren, and then back to Lil for an explanation. Lil didn't seem to understand exactly what Wren was saying either, at first.

But then she said, "There's something Chapel taught us. He called it broadcasting. We're not sure what it really does, or why it works, but it seems to make the Weir more hesitant to attack."

Cass thought back to her last view of the battle, and though her final thoughts had been full of dread, her curiosity nevertheless won out.

"Show me."

Lil was initially reluctant, but after a moment, she drew herself up on the bed and inhaled deeply. She locked her eyes on Cass's. At first, there was no change. But after a moment, a faint glow started to gather around her, subtle and shifting, like a thin wisp of electric smoke. Lil closed her eyes briefly. The glow rippled. Where once it had appeared to be drawing from the air around her, it now surged as if emanating from within her. Her skin became as white as lightning, and when she opened her eyes, they burned with white-orange intensity, like coals in the heart of a fire.

She was terrible to look upon. Terrible, beautiful, utterly impossible to withstand. Even knowing that Lil was a friend and would do nothing to harm her, Cass felt her heart quail within her. And yet she felt unable to look away.

In the next instant, the angel of destruction was gone and only Lil remained. Cass realized she was holding her breath. She closed her eyes and exhaled, tried to force the tension out of her body.

"Can you teach me?" Wren asked.

"It was difficult to learn," Lil said. "But I can try, if it's OK with your mother."

Wren looked up at her.

"We'll see," she said. And then to Lil, "It was you. It was you that I saw. You came, ran into the swarm and saved me."

Lil dipped her head forward in acknowledgment, and said, "I was there, with Elan and Mei. Swoop, Finn, and Mouse as well. Together we were able to push the Weir back and scatter them. Then we ran."

"They didn't pursue?"

Lil shook her head. "I don't know why. We thought maybe the daylight made it difficult for them."

"Asher lost control," Wren said. "I don't think he was expecting that."

"Expecting what?" Cass asked.

"Any of it. For us to attack. Or to have help. I think it was too much for him. This time. I think he's still learning."

"I still don't understand it," Cass said. "You're sure it's Asher?"

"I'm positive."

"Do you know how he's doing it?"

Wren looked down at his hands, clasped in his lap. After a few moments, he shook his head. "No, I don't, Mama. I'm sorry."

Cass leaned over and kissed him on top of the head again. In her hazy state, she'd almost let herself forget. She wanted to forget. But if it was true, and she had no reason to doubt her son, then Asher was out there, somehow. And that meant that Asher would, one day, come for them.

She thought back to the attack on Morningside's gate. The destruction of Chapel's village. Chapel's village. Had Asher known that they'd sheltered Wren before he first came to Morningside? A sudden chill settled over Cass as the thought crystallized. It was exactly the kind of thing Asher would do. Scorch the earth of any and all who may have had a hand in his undoing. Or something else. Not even revenge. Just to destroy something beloved by his little brother. Pure malice.

It was too much to consider for Cass in that moment. Her thoughts were still scattered, hard to capture. As much as she hated to admit it, she was in no shape to do anything about Asher, or even to think about doing anything.

"You should rest," Lil said. She got to her feet.

"Didn't I just do that for sixteen hours or something?" Cass said. But even as she said it, she felt a hint of relief at the suggestion, as if it gave her permission to feel as exhausted as she did.

Lil chuckled. "A drugged sleep is rarely a restful one, and your body needs time. Are you hungry?"

Cass shook her head.

"I'll check on you in a couple of hours," Lil said.

"Thanks, Lil."

Lil bowed slightly and gracefully left the room.

"I think I need to lie down again, baby," Cass said.

Wren slipped off the bed and stood next to it while Cass gingerly repositioned herself. The mattress hadn't seemed all that comfortable the first time she'd slept on it, but now it seemed as good as any bed she could remember.

"Can I stay with you?" Wren asked.

"Of course."

Cass scooted over and started to put her back to the wall, but found there was no way she could lie on her back or left side that didn't cause her some measure of pain. In the end she moved to the edge of the bed, to lie on her right side, and let Wren slide in between her and the wall. He lay on his back, with her arm under his neck and his head on her pillow. The pressure hurt her biceps a little, but she found the comfort of his weight outweighed the pain, reassuring her that he was here and safe. She laid her other arm over him and nuzzled his soft, warm cheek, and let her eyes fall closed.

Wren lay alongside his mother, listening to her steady breathing. It used to help him relax, to focus on her breathing. Now it just made him feel worse. He had lied to her. He'd never lied to her before. But then, he'd never had need to before.

It had been hard to say it, to actually get the false words to come out of his mouth. But he'd done it, and even though he felt bad, he was still sure it had been the right thing to do. Pretty sure, anyway. He'd told her he didn't know how Asher had gotten into the Weir. But in truth, he knew exactly how he'd done it.

Asher had found his way into Underdown's machine.

Wren had spent hours running it through his mind, replaying Asher's final moments, still vivid in his memory. Even after all this time, he wasn't certain what he had done. He wasn't even sure what he'd meant to do. He'd just wanted Asher to stop, and to go away, so he'd told him to. And then. Then it was like Asher had just... dissolved.

And maybe he had, in some way. Because Wren had never sensed Asher again. Until yesterday, on the rooftop.

He'd wondered from time to time what might have happened to Asher, of course. And now, though Wren still didn't have the exact answer, he felt he had at least some clue. Whatever Wren had done to him, Asher had managed to undo. To reclaim his consciousness. Or reassemble it, maybe. Outside the bounds of usual storage. Unsecured.

Wren guessed Asher had interfaced with the machine plenty of times before. He might in fact have been connected to it in that last moment. And from there, it would've been a small thing for someone like Asher. A small thing to infiltrate the minds of the Weir, already slaves to some other purpose, and bend them to his will.

The first time, the only time, Wren had connected to the machine, what he'd seen had reminded him of Asher, but it'd never occurred to him then that Asher might really have been there. Wren wondered now what he could've done differently, if only he'd recognized it sooner. The system or systems that Underdown's machine created, or tapped into, had been overwhelming. Underdown's machine. His *father's* machine. His father's creation had given Asher a place to dwell, to grow in power, and Wren had sent him there. A dark legacy, his to bear, made darker by his own foolishness.

It was his fault. Really and truly. Wren had brought Asher to Morningside. And Wren had released Asher too. And now wherever Wren went, he was sure to attract Asher's wrath.

He had to fix it. He had to make it right. And that meant Wren had to get back to Morningside to shut the machine down.

Painter sat balled up at the head of his bed, hunched in the corner with his back against two walls and his chin resting on his knees. He'd been sitting that way since before the sun came up, and even though he knew everyone else was up and about, he couldn't bring himself to leave his room. Not yet.

His mind felt splintered. Not confused, but tangled, like Painter was holding too many contrary thoughts in his head at once. He'd seen the way Cass had moved. The way she'd carved through the horde of Weir. It had awed him. And horrified him.

On one hand, he'd been... what, grateful? Relieved? Emboldened? Some strange mix of emotions had filled him when Painter had come through the front doors of the building, expecting to see the Weir coming from every side. Instead, they'd been pushed back and, carrying Wick, he and Mouse had had a straight and clear path from the door to Lil's people.

But as they'd approached, Lil had changed. They all had. And they had taken on some new, terrible form. And then they'd gone among the Weir. That was when he'd seen it all from a new perspective. The Weir had ceased to be merely appalling creatures in his eyes; they'd become something more. A community defending itself from some unholy vengeance that had come upon them without warning.

And somehow they hadn't seemed so different from anyone else. Only a few months ago, he could've been among them. Even now, his sister could be. What if Snow had been there? Would Cass have hesitated to strike her down?

And yet. And yet. No matter what he thought, there seemed to always be some other thought alongside it, swirling, countering. Wren was good. Cass was good. Lil was good.

And yet.

The only thing Painter was certain of was that he didn't belong. Not here with them. Not in Morningside. Not even among the Weir.

Where was Snow? Where *was* his sister? He missed her more than he'd thought possible. He wished she'd never gotten caught up in whatever game was being played in Morningside. Even when she'd rejected him, at least he'd known she was out there somewhere, alive. There'd still been hope.

There seemed little of that now.

I can't promise that, Wren had said. *I'd try, Painter,* he'd said. A far cry from hope. And though Painter didn't understand what it meant that this Asher had been in control of the Weir somehow, he knew it was something dreadful. Could Asher jump from one Weir to another? Or was it that he could control many at once? Whatever the case, the thought that Snow might be out there as little more than a puppet for Asher's malevolence…

Maybe he should've just buried her after all. He finally realized how desperate it had been, how foolish. It seemed all too likely that now the only outcome would be that he'd never really know what became of her. He made a decision then, in his heart.

Whatever might come, whatever the consequence, he would return to Morningside. Whether Painter had to live inside the wall or beyond it, he would find her. And then he would do whatever it took to help Snow find her way back.

It was midafternoon before Cass found the strength to come out of her room. Lil had brought her food a little after noon, and Mouse had stopped in to check on her. Gamble, too, had visited for a short time. Cass was relieved to know that she'd managed to cling to Gamble's knife through the battle. Apparently Mouse had had to pry it out of her hand at some point.

Out in the hall, Cass heard Wren's voice in one of the other rooms and followed its sound to a door that was cracked open.

"…because the bridge cuts off this loop here, see," a weak voice was saying, "so it's actually faster. Just not the safest way."

Cass knocked lightly on the door.

"Yeah, you can come in," the voice said. Cass nudged the door open and found Wren sitting in a chair next to Wick.

Wick was propped up on some pillows in bed. He hardly looked like himself, his face was so pale, and his eyes were darkly ringed. An IV bag hung on a makeshift apparatus, the line running to his right arm. "Hey, Lady. How you feeling?" Wick said, smiling broadly. He tried to sit up, but she motioned for him not to.

"I'm good, Wick. How are you?"

"Milking it," he said. But his voice was thin and didn't have the same smooth timbre it usually did. "I don't remember the last time I got to stay in bed all day."

"Hey, baby," Cass said to Wren.

"Hi, Mom," he answered. He glanced at her when he said it, but then went to looking at his hands in his lap. It made her feel like she'd interrupted something.

"What's the prognosis?"

Wick shrugged about halfway and then grimaced. It took a second before he could respond. "Mouse says four or five days, but he worries like a grandma." He waggled his arm with the IV in it. "Got me all juiced up out of fear of infection. But I figure I'm up and about tomorrow, maybe day after."

"You just do what Mouse tells you to. He knows what he's doing."

"Likes to give that impression, anyway."

Cass paused a moment, looking at him there. Grieved by his pain, grateful he was alive. "You had me really worried there, Wick. More than grandma worried."

"Yeah. I'm really sorry about getting poked, Miss Cass. I'm better than that, I promise."

Wick seemed genuinely upset with himself, and his apology was sincere. Cass shook her head. "Don't apologize.

I'm just sorry it happened."

"It shouldn't have."

His expression went dark when he said it. Remembering.
She could almost read his mind, or at least guess at his train
of thought. If he hadn't gotten hurt, no one would've had to
carry him, and if no one had had to carry him, there would've
been two more shooters, and if there'd been two more
shooters, maybe Cass wouldn't have gotten overwhelmed...
Nothing she said was going to make him feel any better about
how things had gone. She decided to change the subject.

"Wren's not keeping you up, is he?"

"No, not at all. He's good company. We were just getting
the lay of the land, seeing where we are in relation to
everything else. Sharp kid. You should keep him."

"I plan on it," Cass said, smiling at her son. Wren seemed
down, or troubled. "You OK, sweetheart?"

"Fine," Wick answered. "Thanks, honey."

Cass gave a Wick a look, and he just smiled back.

"I'm fine," Wren said. "Just tired."

"I was going to see if I could find something to eat. You
want to come?"

"No thanks." He still wouldn't look at her. Which usually
meant he was either upset about something, or that he was
wishing she'd leave. Cass motioned with her hands at Wick
to see if he needed her to have Wren come with her, but
Wick waved her off.

"OK," she said. "Wick, want me to bring you anything?"

"No, ma'am," he said. "Thank you though."

"Alright then." Cass hovered at the door for a moment. "A
few more minutes, and then we'll let Wick rest, OK, baby?"

"OK," Wren said. There was a brief silence, but then Wren
looked over and asked, "Can Lil teach me that thing now?"

It took a second before Cass remembered what he was talking about, and when she did, she didn't like the thought of it. Seeing her son like that. And Lil had said it was difficult to learn. But there was no doubt they'd be facing the Weir again. Worse. Asher in the Weir.

"If she has time," Cass said.

Wren's eyes glinted in either excitement or surprise. Maybe he'd been expecting her to say no. He got to his feet.

"Thanks, Wick. I hope you feel better." Wren offered his hand. Wick shook it with kind sobriety.

"Thanks for keeping me company, Governor."

Wren came over and stood next to Cass.

"Open or closed?" she asked.

"You can close it, thanks," Wick said. "Gonna rack out for a bit."

Cass chuckled and shook her head. Wick just flashed his grin. She should've known better than to think he'd ever ask Wren to leave, no matter how tired Wick was. Cass pulled the door closed, and then she and Wren turned and went down the hall. It was disconcerting how unstable Cass felt on her feet. They walked together in silence.

They found Lil in one of the common rooms on the top floor, talking with Finn and another woman that Cass didn't recognize. Everyone stood when they saw her.

"Miss Cass," Finn said. "How're you feeling?"

"Well enough, Finn. Thanks," Cass said. "Are we interrupting?"

"No, not at all," Lil said. "Please, join us." She introduced Cass to the other woman there with them. "Cass, this is Mei. Mei, Cass."

They shook hands. Mei was a couple of inches taller than Cass and willow thin. Her hands were surprisingly strong.

"Mei," Cass said. "You came with Lil to rescue us."

Mei nodded.

"Thank you."

"Of course."

"What brings you out and about?" Lil asked, as they all took seats.

"Wren had something he wanted to ask you," Cass answered. Lil looked at him.

"I was wondering if you had time to teach me your trick," he said. "The broadcasting."

Lil looked back at Cass for confirmation, and Cass nodded.

"Sure, Wren," Lil said. "We can try. Here, come sit next to me." She stood up to grab another chair, but Finn got up and slid his closer to her, and then went and found another for himself. Lil scooted the chair right next to hers and then sat back down and patted it. Wren crawled up into the chair. It was oversized anyway, and seemed even moreso with his small frame in it. Lil angled her body towards him, and Wren mirrored her.

"Now," she said, "I'll try to teach you, but you should know that it can be very challenging. Not everyone can do it. So, you have to promise you won't be upset with yourself if you don't get it right away."

"OK," Wren said. "I promise."

"OK. Take a deep breath, and try to relax."

Lil walked Wren through some early steps and explained what Chapel had taught her about boosting her own signal. Wren listened patiently, soaking it all in. As she watched silently, Cass could sense a gradual change between them and could almost imagine the relationship they must have had years ago. Wren seemed more open and comfortable with her than Cass had seen him in days. Weeks, maybe.

After several minutes, Wren gave it his first try. He closed his eyes and scrunched up his face. Cass could tell he was really concentrating. But there was no sign of anything happening.

"Will I be able to tell if I'm doing it?" Wren asked.

"You will. You'll feel it," Lil said. "It's hard to explain, but I think you'll know."

Cass almost mentioned that she'd be able to see it, but felt like any comment from her might seem like an intrusion. She remained quiet, as Lil gave Wren some further suggestions. He tried again, with little discernible difference. They worked together for nearly half an hour. Wren became increasingly frustrated, with himself, not with Lil, but Lil picked up on it.

"Why don't we take a little break," Lil said. "We can try again later if you like."

"Can we try one more time?" Wren said. Lil nodded.

"One more."

Again, Wren closed his eyes, though this time not as tightly. His lips moved slightly, pursing as he focused. Several seconds passed without any noticeable change. And then, there, just at the outer edge of his body, Cass saw it. A thin aura, faint and shimmering.

"There," Cass said. "You're doing it!"

Immediately it stopped as Wren opened his eyes.

"Am I?" he asked.

"You were," she said. "A little bit. I could just see it."

His shoulders slumped, and he looked dejected. "I was trying really hard."

Lil put her hand on his shoulder. "That you can do it at all is amazing, Wren. I've never seen anyone your age do it before. Not even twice your age. You should feel proud." She gave his shoulder a little squeeze. "And you promised not to be upset with yourself."

Wren nodded and sat back in his chair. Lil stood up.

"I should probably make the rounds anyway," she said. "We'll try again tomorrow if you like, OK?"

"OK," Wren said. "Thanks, Lil." Lil nodded and started towards the door. The others stood as well.

"Guess I'll go check on Wick," Finn said. "But maybe next time I'll try it too, huh?" Finn knocked Wren on the shoulder as he said it, and Wren gave him a little smile in return.

"I could work with you," Mei said. "If you think it'd help."

Finn smiled at her. "I'd appreciate it. Whether it helped or not."

Mei actually blushed a little. If Cass hadn't known better, she might've suspected there was something brewing between the two of them. Finn held out his hand to let Mei exit first, and then followed her out. As he passed Cass, he winked at her.

"Glad to see you up, ma'am."

Cass nodded back. "Thanks, Finn."

She watched them as they went out. From behind her, Wren made a little noise like he'd found something.

"Oh," he said aloud, but almost to himself. "I wonder..." And then to Cass, "Mama, am I doing it now?"

Cass turned, and as she did, she had to squint against the radiance emanating from her son. But he didn't appear to be her son anymore. Gone was her little boy, replaced instead by an otherworldly being, blazing like a star. The room behind him seemed dim in comparison to his brilliance. Where Lil had retained her general form and size, Wren seemed to grow. And his face changed; it seemed to be constantly shifting like a reflection on waves, his eyes and mouth distorted. If Lil's eyes had been burning coals, Wren's now were molten ore. Translucent orange fire seemed to gutter from the eye sockets and issue from his gaping mouth.

"Mama?" the demon said. Cass felt herself taking steps backwards without having meant to.

"Stop," she said, and her voice came out in a whisper. "Please, stop."

The light seemed to gather in on itself and moments later it subsided, and there set her son, small, fragile, nearly swallowed by the chair he was sitting in.

"Did I do it?" Wren asked.

Cass nodded, inhaled, tried to calm her pounding heart. "Yeah, baby," she answered. "You did it."

"I think there's an easier way than what Lil said."

And then, unexpectedly, Wren hopped up out of his chair and came over to her. He wrapped his arms around her waist and nestled his head against her stomach. Cass draped her arms over his back and hugged him. She hoped he couldn't tell she was trembling.

"I really love you a lot, Mama," he said.

"I really love *you* a lot, Wren." The contrast was almost shocking. The suddenness of it had surprised her, but she wasn't about to question the moment. It warmed her to hear him say it first.

"I'm hungry," he said.

"OK. Let's see what we can find."

"OK."

She took his hand, and they walked together towards the mess hall. And the whole way, she tried to fight back the tears.

Cass had always known her son was special and capable of great things, things beyond her imagining. And she had been afraid for him countless times. Afraid of what others might try to do to him, or force him to do – afraid of what the world had in store. But for the first time in her life, she had to face the fact that she was afraid *of* him. She had glimpsed him in power, and Cass knew without a doubt that whatever lay ahead, Wren would one day be beyond any need, or want, of her help. And that day might be much, much sooner than she had imagined.

TWENTY-TWO

Wren lay on his bed, watching the dust particles float above him in the pale light that came in through the high slot window. The first rays of dawn. Almost time to go.

He had it all figured out. At least as best as he could. The night before, he'd carefully given his guardians some casually vague and different ideas about where and with whom he'd be spending his time that morning. As long as everyone thought someone else was watching him, it ought to buy him a little time. It wouldn't work forever, of course. At some point two of them would run into each other, each thinking Wren was supposed to be with the other. After that it would be just a matter of time for it to all fall apart. But there was a chance they'd think there had just been some kind of mix-up, and maybe they'd spend a little time looking for him before anyone guessed what he'd really done.

It was an old trick he'd learned from his time in the governor's compound, and though he usually ended up getting caught at some point, it'd almost always bought him at least an hour or two of peace and quiet. Wren hoped he could get that much of a head start, if not more.

Mama would be frightened, of course. And probably furious. The whole team would be. Wren didn't even want to think about what Swoop would say. Or do, if he ever caught him. But there was no other way. None of them would ever let him go back to Morningside on his own. And he couldn't let them come with him. It was too dangerous for them, though they'd never admit it.

He'd thought about talking to them about it. About telling them what he thought was going on and what he had to do to stop it. But he was afraid that once he mentioned it, not only would they not let him go back, they'd be extra careful and always be watching him. Or they'd delay him, and try to make plans they thought were best. And Wren knew without a doubt that Asher was searching for him, and that anywhere he stayed for any amount of time was in danger. Even now he wanted to convince himself that maybe if he just talked to the right person, they'd agree that he was right. Able, maybe, or Wick. But in his heart he knew he'd never convince anyone. They still called him "Governor", but it'd been a long time since anyone had treated Wren like he had any sort of say.

And so he'd decided to keep it a secret. Just long enough to get away. He had to. There was no choice. If Asher was in the machine, then someone had to figure out a way to get him out. And there was no one else that could do it but Wren.

He already knew the way. Wick had shown him where they were, and the fastest way to get back to Morningside. And he was confident he could make it in one day, as long as he started out early enough. The trickiest part would just be getting out.

His bag was already packed at the foot of his bed. It had still been mostly packed anyway, since he hadn't ever unpacked it after they got back from Ninestory. He tried not to think too much about how that had turned out. And yet, he knew it was just the beginning. Unless he did what he had to do.

He reached beneath his pillow and slipped his knife out

from under it. It'd become less of a weapon to him. More of a… well, Wren didn't quite know the word for it. There was strength in it, somehow.

It was time. Even just thinking about it, Wren's heart started pounding, and he felt a little like he was going to throw up. He slipped out of bed as quietly as he could, and started putting on his boots. He'd slept in his clothes, so getting dressed wouldn't be a problem. Carefully he moved his pack and coat right over next to the door. Now the tricky part. Saying goodbye to his mama.

Wren tucked his knife into its sheath on his belt, and wiped his hands on his shirt. He knew if he didn't wake his mother up before he slipped out, she'd come looking for him as soon as she woke up. But getting out of the room with his stuff once she was awake might be tough, too.

He crept to her bedside and for a moment just watched her sleeping. She was on her side, facing the wall, breathing deeply and steadily. Wren's throat went tight, and he clenched his hands into fists. He took a deep breath, exhaled through his mouth, hoping that would loosen the lump. Reached out and gently tapped her on the shoulder.

She didn't stir. He tapped again.

"Mama," Wren said, a little louder than a whisper, and his voice came out sounding like he was about to cry. Cass reacted instantly, twisting in her bed and sitting up partially, her eyes wide for a long moment. Then she settled back and turned more completely around towards him, supporting herself on her left arm.

"Hey, sweetheart," she said, voice heavy with sleep. She reached out and squeezed his arm. "You OK?"

"Yeah," he said, and his voice felt steadier. "I'm going to get something to eat."

She blinked at him through unfocused eyes. "It's early."

He nodded. "I can't go back to sleep."

"OK," Cass said. She rubbed one eye with the palm of her hand. "Let me get dressed."

"No, it's OK, Mama. I can do it."

She looked at him for a moment. "You sure?"

Wren tried to give a casual nod, like it was no big deal, but felt like he couldn't remember how to make a casual face. She yawned and blinked several times. Her left eye watered.

"You should sleep, Mama," he said. "I'll be fine."

"Alright, baby," she said. "I'll get up in a little bit. I think I'm still feeling the effects of whatever Mouse gave me."

"It's fine," Wren said. She looked at him again a little harder than he liked, but then she gave him a little smile. He leaned over and kissed her cheek, and gave her a big hug. He tried not to hold her for too long, but once he'd started, it was hard to stop. "I love you."

She kissed him back and held him with one arm. "Love you too."

With one final squeeze, Wren let go and stepped back. He stayed by her bed for a moment, waiting for her to lie back down, but she didn't. He turned and went to the door. Glanced back over his shoulder. She was still watching him. He gave her a little smile and a wave and opened the door. When he turned back to pull it closed, she was still up on her arm. He'd hoped he could slide his pack through without her noticing, but there was no chance of that now. He pulled the door to, but held on to the handle, and counted to ten. Then decided to make it twenty.

Then very slowly, he pushed the door back open, just wide enough for his pack to fit through. He leaned in and glanced around the edge of the door. Mama was back on her side again, facing the wall. Wren eased down and carefully caught hold of the top of his pack. Lifted it as slowly as he could. The sound of the material sliding up off the floor seemed far louder than it should have. Wren held his breath.

"You need something, baby?"

Wren froze. Then glanced up. Mama was looking over her shoulder again, right at him.

"Just forgot something in my pack," he said. It sounded weak coming out of his mouth, but it was the best he could come up with. She continued looking at him for the span of a long breath. And then nodded, and laid her head back down on the pillow.

Wren pulled his pack through and closed the door quietly. It hadn't gone quite as planned, but at least she hadn't seemed to notice he was taking his coat too.

It was deathly quiet in the hallway. As he slipped his coat on, the rustle seemed to echo. He didn't want to risk zipping it up, and he decided just to carry his pack by the handle on top, at least until he got out into the entryway. Wren crept down the hall as softly as he was able. He tried not to walk too quickly, but every step he got farther away from his room felt like the one that was going to get him caught, and he couldn't help but pick up the pace. The turn towards the entrance was just ahead on the left. Once he made that turn, he'd almost be home free.

As he came around the corner, though, Wren was surprised to see another figure at the far end of the hallway. He tried to jerk back before the other person saw him, but it was too late. His sudden motion must have drawn attention. Wren hovered at the corner of the hall, trying to figure out what to do, what to say. Careful footsteps were headed his way. Just going to get something to eat, he'd say.

"Wren?" the person whispered. "Wren, it's mmm-me."

Painter. Wren peeked back around the corner to find him standing about halfway down the hall, hunched over like he was trying to hide a little. Painter had his coat on too, and his pack was on the floor. Wren eased all the way around the corner.

"What're you doing?" Painter asked, still whispering.

"Just… I was going to get something to eat."

Painter's eyes flicked to the pack in Wren's hand and then back. "Outside?"

"No," Wren said, "I just…" His words ran out. He set his pack down. Painter came closer and knelt down in front of him.

"I'm g-g-glad you're up," Painter said. "I wanted to say goodbye. To you, I mmmm-mean."

"What? Where are you going?"

"Back to Morningside." Wren stared back at Painter, not sure what to say. "D-d-don't try to talk me out of it, my mmm, my mind's made up."

"Why?"

"For Snow, Wren. I need to fffind my sister."

Wren nodded, but he couldn't decide whether this was good news or bad. He'd anticipated having to set out on his own. He'd tried to prepare himself for it. But the idea of having someone go with him made the whole thing seem so much more possible. Yet, at the same time, he didn't know what complications it might raise. If he and Painter were both missing, how long would it be before the others came looking for them?

"You've always buh… been great to me, Wren. Whatever happens, I hope it all g-goes well with you."

Wren still hadn't figured out what to say. Should he just let Painter leave, and then sneak out behind him? Painter nodded and got to his feet.

"See you again ssss-sometime," Painter said. "I hope."

"OK," Wren said.

Painter nodded again and smiled a little. He turned and walked back down the hall with careful steps. As he passed his pack, he snagged the straps and slung it up onto his back. He was just about to the end of the hall when Wren finally made his choice.

"Painter," he whispered as loudly as he could, "Wait." Painter stopped and turned partially around to look at him. He picked up his own pack and walked quickly down the hall. "I'm going back too."

Painter actually flinched at the words. Maybe he'd been expecting Wren to try to convince him not to leave, or just to say a better goodbye.

"No, Wren," Painter said. "I appreciate the thought, but I can't l-l-let you do that."

"You're not letting me do anything, Painter. I have to go back. Because of Asher."

"What are you tuh, talking about?"

"It's my dad's machine. I have to get back to it."

Painter's expression changed at the mention of the machine, and Wren couldn't blame him. The memories of that machine, that room, were still too fresh and far too vivid for Wren's liking. He could only imagine how Painter must've felt.

"Your mmmm-mom is going to freak out."

"That's why I have to go alone," Wren said. "Or with you." Painter shook his head slowly. Wren felt something rising up within him, born of frustration. "I'm going, no matter what. I know the way. You can come too, or you can go on your own. But don't get in my way. There's too much at stake." His voice came out louder than he meant for it to, but it seemed to have the effect he wanted. Painter stopped shaking his head.

"They're gonna come after us," he said.

"I know."

"Your mom will k-k-kuh... she'll kill me."

"I won't let her."

Painter looked at Wren for a long moment, and then finally nodded. "OK."

They both shouldered their packs, and Wren led the way cautiously towards the front entry. It was darker there. The lights were off, and the morning light was weak and pale through the high grated windows. Wren didn't know how Painter had been planning to get out on his own, but he felt pretty sure that he'd be able to unlock the door and gates himself. Hopefully there weren't any alarms on any of them. They crept through the front room.

"You boys are up early," came a voice from one corner behind them. They froze in place. Swoop. Wren turned around slowly, and saw him sitting there, propped against the far wall. "Goin' somewhere?"

Wren's mind went completely blank, and all the bravery he thought he had leaked right out. It seemed like the kind of time that a brain might go into overdrive and come up with a good excuse, or even a bad one. But in this case, Wren couldn't think of a single thing, couldn't even think of thinking. He just stared.

"We're g-g-going back," Painter said. "And you can't do anything to ssss, to stop us." Wren was surprised at the edge in Painter's voice. He actually sounded like he meant it.

Swoop chuckled. "That's probably not true." He got to his feet. He seemed bigger than usual. "Today's not the day, buddy. We'll get back to Morningside eventually."

"We're going now," Painter said. Swoop's expression changed. He'd seemed amused before. Not so much now.

"You sound pretty sure."

"I am."

Swoop just stared Painter down with that look of his, the one that kind of made you feel like you were lucky that he was still allowing you to live. And then his eyes slid over to Wren, like Painter wasn't even part of the conversation anymore. Or even in the room.

"What's going on?"

Painter had already blown any chance they had of convincing Swoop they weren't really planning to go anywhere further than the gate. And there was no way Wren could come up with a lie that Swoop would believe. So Wren sighed and did the thing he didn't want to do. He told the truth.

Wren did his best to explain what he believed was happening with Asher and Underdown's machine, the path he planned to take, and why he didn't want the others to try to come back with him. If everyone returned, Wren was sure there'd be a fight. The guards might even attack them on sight. But if it was just him, he felt sure that they wouldn't do anything worse than lock him up somewhere, probably in the governor's compound. And maybe once he explained what was happening to the Weir, they'd understand their own danger. If not, well, at least he'd be close enough to the machine to try to do what he needed to. And if Asher came for him, at least Mama would be safe.

Swoop listened to everything Wren had to say without any noticeable emotion. When he was finished, Swoop continued to look at him for a long moment.

Then, "You really think there's something you can do." It sounded like a statement, but it was a question. Wren nodded. "It's a terrible plan."

"Wick says a plan is just a list of stuff that never happens anyway."

Swoop cracked a half-smile at that. He actually seemed to be thinking about what Wren had said. That was more than Wren had hoped for. He decided to push.

"If you've ever thought of me as your governor, Swoop, please believe me now. I have to go back. Let us go."

Swoop worked his jaw. "You givin' me an order?"

"I'm asking you."

Swoop shook his head. "Are you giving me an *order*, sir?"

It still took Wren a second to understand what he was saying. And then he got it. "Oh. Yes. I order you to let us go."

Swoop nodded.

"Gamble, Swoop," he said. "...No, everything's fine. Just wanted to let you know Painter and the governor are with me... Yeah, check. I'll explain later."

He'd said it so casually Wren wasn't exactly sure what he'd meant. "So, you're going to let us go?"

"I'm gonna take you there myself."

"No, Swoop, you can't..." Wren started, but Swoop raised his eyebrows and gave him a look that made him stop mid-sentence.

"Give me five minutes to gear up."

"Swoop, I don't know what they'll do to you if you go back. And I don't think I'll be able to stop it."

He shook his head. "That's *my* home," Swoop said. "Earned in blood. I don't reckon *any*body has say over whether I get to keep it." He held up his hand with all five fingers up. "Five minutes."

Swoop headed out of the entryway back down the hall with his aggressive pace. Painter and Wren stood awkwardly waiting, neither really sure what had just happened or what it would mean. Wren had to admit he felt a lot better about the trip, knowing Swoop would be along too. And maybe he'd be able to convince Swoop to hang back as they got closer to Morningside, at least long enough for Wren to get an idea of what might happen.

It didn't even take a full five minutes before Swoop was back and all geared up.

"Governor," he said. "After you."

Wren led the way out through the door of the building. As they stepped outside, the morning air chilled Wren almost instantly. The sky above was steel grey and heavy with clouds, and there was a stillness to the air that made Wren think of snow. Their breaths came out in cloudy puffs. Wren pulled up his hood and jammed his hands in his coat pocket.

"Your mama's gonna kill me," Swoop said.

"And me," Painter said.

"I assume you got a plan for the gates?" Swoop asked.

Wren nodded and stepped towards them. They were large and heavy, but the locks that held them fast were simple encoded devices, easy to see. Wren stretched out through the digital and unlocked them. Painter pushed the first open, and then closed it behind them. Swoop got the second.

"Make sure you lock 'em back," Swoop said as they passed through. Wren didn't even need to turn around to do it. Together, with Wren leading the way, the three of them set out into the cold grey dawn.

TWENTY-THREE

Once they'd gotten a few minutes out from the refuge, Wren shared the route information he'd learned from Wick with Swoop. The path took them almost due east for a number of miles, to an old bridge called the Windspan. Wren didn't know why it was named that, just that it was supposed to be big. Swoop didn't like the idea.

Wick had mentioned that it wasn't a good area, but he hadn't specified why, and Wren had been too afraid to ask what he meant. After Swoop explained why, Wren was even more relieved that Swoop had come with them. The northern end of the bridge, where they'd be starting their journey across, was apparently a known thoroughfare for scrapers and other kinds of people that none of them wanted to meet.

Swoop wanted to find a different route, but it didn't take long for him to realize the Windspan really was the best option. At least, in the sense that it seemed to be the *only* option if they wanted to make the trip in a single day. After that, they didn't spend much time talking. Swoop took over leading the way, and Wren was glad to have someone else to follow.

Even though he had done his best to prepare himself for what the day would bring, Wren couldn't stop thinking about having left Mama behind. He'd had to say goodbye to her once before, but he hadn't had any choice back then. Now, with each step taking him further and further away from her, his throat and chest tightened. At least she would be safe, or safer anyway, apart from him. He guessed he himself would be the target of Asher's fury, and maybe that would make everything OK for Mama. He was glad he had his hood up, so the others couldn't see him cry.

And he hated himself for the tears. They made him feel stupid and weak. He wanted so desperately to be brave, and to never show emotions, like Swoop. Like Three. For all his ideas of returning to Morningside and fighting some battle against Asher, the reality of the cold, and the walk, and the growing loneliness were all so much harder to face than he'd expected. They'd only been gone maybe twenty minutes. Already he couldn't believe he'd ever thought he could do it. It had seemed so much easier to picture his brave return when he'd been warm in bed, with Mama close at hand.

His weakness appalled him. Now he knew without a doubt that if he *had* been able to sneak out on his own, he would've turned back. But he wasn't on his own. And if he wasn't brave enough to go on, at least he was too ashamed to quit in front of Painter and Swoop.

He kept his head down and his eyes focused on Swoop's feet in front of him.

Still they continued on in silence. Swoop set a hard enough pace that Wren didn't feel like he'd be able to talk a whole lot while he tried to keep up anyway. But there was something else, too. The heavy sky, the stillness of the morning, the chill air that bit cheeks and fingers, all of it made speaking seem out of place. It was gradually becoming lighter, though the sun never appeared anywhere Wren could see it.

For the first hour or so, Wren kept thinking his body would warm up to all the walking and he wouldn't feel so sluggish. But after a while he started to realize that he wasn't feeling any better, and wasn't likely to any time soon. The first journey out from Morningside had been tough enough. The trip out to Ninestory and back, with all of its fresh terror, was another matter. The anxiety and adrenaline of the fight, the flight back to the refuge under constant fear of pursuit, the death of Elan, and the close call with Wick. It had left Wren feeling completely empty.

And then there was Asher – he was like a great black storm cloud haunting Wren's every thought. Wren still didn't know what exactly he was going to do when he got to Morningside, what he expected to find inside the machine, or how he would even begin to challenge Asher. But Three had told Wren that whenever he didn't know what to do, he should always trust his gut. And his gut said he should go to Morningside.

Even while everything else in him was screaming to turn around and go back.

Cass woke with a start and sat up, gasping for breath, heart hammering in her chest. She had no idea what had woken her. A dream maybe, though she couldn't remember it. It took her a moment to recognize her surroundings and get her bearings. Once she did, though, she settled onto her back and tried to gather herself. She took a deep breath and let her shoulders relax and waited for her head to clear.

Everything felt just a little off. Soft around the edges. Blurred. Her vision, her thoughts, even her movement. Whatever Mouse had dosed her with had had plenty of time to clear. Maybe her injuries had been worse than Cass had initially thought.

A sudden paranoid thought leapt to her mind. What if that was how it began? What if Asher was already at work, trying to gain control over her? *Re*gain control. He'd had it once. Would that make it easier for him to do again? She shuddered at the thought.

No. Her mind was her own. It was true that Asher had once directed her, when she had been enslaved by the Weir. But Wren had freed her. That connection had surely been severed. She closed her eyes for a few moments, steadied herself.

Lil had graciously offered to let them stay at the refuge as long as they cared to, though she'd made no comment as to how much longer her own people were planning to stay.

Cass had decided they'd remain until Mouse was satisfied with Wick's condition. Hopefully that would give them enough time to figure out their next move. There was little doubt they would have to confront the situation in Morningside at some point. But she didn't want to walk blindly back into it.

When the news had first come of their exile, it had seemed earth-shattering. Now, in light of their uncovering of Asher, it was by comparison a petty distraction. A squabble in the face of doom. But Cass knew Asher far too well to pretend that Morningside would be safe from his vengeance. It had been the place of his destruction. He would bend all of his will to see pain revisited upon its populace, whether she and Wren were there or not.

Cass opened her eyes and then, with a deep breath, eased herself up to a sitting position and dropped her legs over the edge of the bed. The concrete was cold under her bare feet. She rolled her neck around, tested her shoulder. Every muscle felt tight. She'd probably spent more time in bed in the past two days than she had in the weeks previous.

The room was still gloomy in the weak morning light, though the sun had been up for a good couple of hours by that point. Cass got up and dressed. Might as well go see what everyone else was up to.

She opened the door and, just as she was about to pass through, something made her stop. She glanced down at the spot where Wren's pack had been earlier that morning, before he'd taken it. There'd been something else there with it. Something Cass hadn't paid attention to before, something that now seemed important.

His coat.

Cass glanced around the room quickly, at his bed, under it, on the table in the corner. There was no sign of anything of Wren's. And her heart skipped.

"Wren," she pimmed. Waited for a response. Tried again. "Wren!" Seconds ticked by. Plenty of time for a reply, if one was coming.

"Gamble," Cass called as she stepped into the hall. "Gamble!"

A few moments later a door opened behind her, and Mouse poked his head out into the hall.

"Hey, Cass," he said. "What's going on?"

"Have you seen Wren?"

"Not this morning, no."

"Where's Gamble?"

Mouse shook his head and shrugged. "Something wrong?"

"Wren's gone." A flood of emotion hit her, as if her words had transformed it from suspicion to certainty.

"What do you mean gone?"

"I mean, *gone*, Mouse. He left." Cass crossed the hall and knocked loudly on Painter's closed door.

"I'm sure he's around here somewhere..." Mouse said, coming out into the hall.

"Painter, you in there?" Cass said through the door. She didn't really wait for a response before she threw it open. The room was empty. Even the bed was made.

"Gamble, this is Mouse. You got a sec?"

Cass's mind started putting little pieces together that confirmed her fears. His comment the night before about how Wren might not see her much because he was going to spend some time with Elan's son, Ephraim. The long hug he'd given her when he'd woken her this morning. The conversation she'd interrupted between him and Wick, discussing their current location relative to other places. She raced through the scenarios. Knowing Wren, knowing the situation... Cass left Painter's room and went to Wick's, swung the door open. He was still lying propped up on a pile of pillows, and his eyes sprang open when Cass came in.

"Did you plot a route to Morningside out for my son?" Cass asked. It sounded angrier coming out than she'd meant for it to, but given the circumstances, she didn't really care.

Wick blinked back at her. "Do what now?"

"Did you give Wren a route to Morningside?"

He shook his head, confusion clear on his face. "No, of course not. Why? What's going on?"

Cass couldn't decide if that should be a relief or not. If he wasn't headed to Morningside, that was better than she'd feared, but it also meant she had no idea where he might be going.

"She thinks Wren might've left," Mouse said from the doorway.

"He's with Swoop," came Gamble's voice from outside, somewhere down the hall.

"Well, he *was* asking about where we were..." Wick trailed off as he thought it through. "No, wait." He looked up at Cass with sudden concern. "I thought he was just making conversation, keeping me company."

"And what?" Cass asked.

"I did tell him the fastest way. Over the Windspan."

Cass moved back towards the hall and found Gamble standing there with Sky and Finn. Mouse hovered nearby.

"Where's Swoop?" Cass asked.

"I just talked to him a little bit ago," Gamble said. "Wren's with him and he's fine. Painter's with him too."

"*Where*, Gamble?"

Gamble held up her hand as if to calm Cass, and Cass knew then without a doubt that Wren was making his way back to Morningside. It seemed to Cass that Gamble and her team were ringing her in on purpose.

"They left early this morning," Gamble said. "Wren thinks there's something he can do to stop Asher. Something with Underdown's machine."

That was a twofold blow. Not only was he returning to the city without her, he was going back to the governor's compound, back to the very heart of all the madness in the city. All to confront his brother, no less.

"And you let him go?" Cass asked.

"We didn't have a choice, Cass. By the time Swoop called it in, they were already miles out."

"You should've woken me!"

Gamble shook her head. "There was no reason to."

"No reason? I'm his mother! I would never have let him go!"

"Exactly. But he had to."

"That's not your decision to make!"

"It's not yours either," Gamble answered, with force. Her voice was becoming harder, more direct, but no louder.

"He's just a boy!"

"No, Cass, he's not. He's the Governor. Like it or not, you don't get to ignore his authority just because you're his mother." The words stung.

"You're telling me he ordered you to let him go, and you allowed it?"

"He was trying to sneak out on his own. Swoop went with him. He's thinking about you, Cass. He's worried for your safety. And so are we."

Cass started forward into the hall. "I'm going after him."

"Cass, no, you can't."

Gamble put her hand on Cass's shoulder to stop her. In a flash of rage and reflex, Cass snatched Gamble by her vest – using both hands – and flung her. She didn't mean to throw her that hard.

As it was, Gamble's feet left the ground as she catapulted into the wall. Her back impacted flat, her arms spread to catch herself, but she was tilted at an awkward angle and off balance, and crashed down hard on one knee. In a blink Gamble was on her feet and headed straight at Cass – but Mouse caught her, and Finn grabbed Sky, who looked like he was about to take Cass's head off himself.

"Whoa, whoa, whoa," Mouse said. "Let's not eat our own here. We're all on the same side."

"Are we?" Cass asked. "Your job is to protect my son, our governor. And you're all here – doing what?"

"Protecting you," Finn said.

"Well, I don't need it."

Gamble controlled herself, and Mouse released her, though he kept himself angled between the two women.

"We're not going to let you go on your own," Gamble said.

"You're not letting me do anything," Cass answered.

"But I *am* going. I doubt you'd be able to keep up anyway."

Gamble stared back at Cass for a long span. Cass held herself ready, uncertain about anyone else's intent at that point. If anyone else grabbed her, though, she wasn't going to hold back. Gamble's shoulders finally lowered, and she took a step towards the wall, clearing the way for Cass to pass by. Cass pushed through to her room without another word.

Wren felt a soft touch on his cheek just under his eye that made him flinch and brought his attention back to the world around him. He'd lost himself in the rhythm of their ceaseless steps, for some unknown amount of time. It took him several seconds to figure out what had touched him, but as he glanced around at their surroundings, he finally got a glimpse of something drifting on the meager wind.

A snowflake.

Once he noticed the first, it was easier to see the others, like dust or ash, gently settling around them. The flakes were small and widely spaced at first. Even when he looked directly up into the grey sky, it was several seconds before he felt another flake fall to his face.

Now that his awareness of his surroundings had been reawakened, however, he was startled by the marked change. Wren had traveled enough of the open to understand that most of the sprawling urban wasteland looked like a bad place to be. But somehow the shattered former city around them now made him feel powerfully threatened far beyond the usual.

"Swoop, where are we?" Wren asked, and his voice seemed harsh, though he'd barely spoken louder than a whisper.

Swoop's head snapped around and he bounced his index finger off his mouth, motioning for Wren to keep quiet.

They stopped moving and Swoop swept his eyes across the space around them. Then he bent low and put his face beside Wren's head, so close Wren could smell the sweat coming from him. "About five klicks from the bridge, if we go straight through," he whispered. "Gettin' into the badlands now."

He glanced up at the sky, watching the snow fall. The flakes were already bigger than they'd been a minute before. Swoop shook his head, and then looked back to Wren. "Eyes sharp, OK?"

Wren nodded. Swoop straightened again with one more look at the sky, and then turned and led them onwards.

Cass had stripped everything out of her pack and was reloading her smaller lighter slingpack. She didn't know what, if anything, she'd need for this trip, and she wasn't in much of a planning mood. She grabbed what looked best and tossed it in her go-bag.

"Some of us can come with you," came Mouse's voice from the door. Cass shook her head without looking at him. "Wick still needs a couple of more days, else we'd all be coming along, whether you wanted us to or not."

"I'll be moving fast, Mouse."

"I'm not going to try to change your mind, Cass, but I hope you know we're trying to do the right thing by you and your boy. All of us are."

Cass just focused on her packing. Good enough. She closed it up and slung the strap over her shoulder. Cinched it tight against her body. She turned and faced the door, where Mouse was standing.

"Let us know when you get there," Mouse said.

"I will."

Mouse nodded and backed out of the door reluctantly. "Watch yourself out there," he said as she passed by. She stopped next to him.

"This isn't how I wanted things to go," Cass said.

"I know."

"Take care of yourself."

"You too. We'll catch up when we can."

Lil was waiting for her by the front entrance. They exchanged a few brief words, warm but hurried. Lil led her out through the gates and, unexpectedly, embraced Cass before they parted ways. Cass thanked her a final time and started off at run, trusting that her body would perform what she demanded of it. East to the bridge, and then south.

The snow was falling steadily in big wet flakes, coating the ground in a thin layer of slick grey slush. Just deep enough to leave footprints. It looked pretty as it fell, though, and made everything feel more peaceful to Wren. It seemed somehow less likely that anything bad could happen when it was snowing.

"Alright, check," Swoop whispered. He stopped walking and turned towards the boys, motioned them close. "Mama's on the way."

"I thought Guh, Gamble was going to keep her there," Painter said.

"Said she'd *try*."

"Is she mad?" Wren asked.

"I'd count on it."

"Are we going to wuh, wuh… to wait for her?"

Swoop shook his head. "We can't sit in one place for long. She'll have to catch up on her own."

He paused and scanned their surroundings, intensely, like he was looking for something in particular. He'd been leading them in a fairly predictable path for the first several miles, mostly straight ahead. But for the past half hour or so, Wren had noticed a change in their pace and their pattern of movement. Their progress had been inconsistent, with more pauses, and they'd taken to winding through different alleys, sometimes even doubling back.

Wren knew they weren't lost, but it almost felt like that. For all the walking, they hadn't made nearly as much progress towards the bridge as Wren would've expected. Wren was briefly tempted to check their location, but he'd decided it was too risky. If Asher was out there looking for him, he might be able to locate Wren's signal.

Swoop lowered his head and leaned towards them again.

"Look," he said. "I don't want to scare you, but it's best if you know. We picked up a couple of stragglers. Been trailin' us about fifteen minutes now."

"Who are they?" Painter asked.

"Nobody we want to meet. Keep your eyes up."

They nodded, and then Swoop turned and led them forward. As they moved, Wren glanced behind them, looking for any sign of the people Swoop had seen. He didn't notice anyone, but he understood in a flash why Swoop had been shaking his head at the sky earlier. Their trail was clearly marked; three sets of slushy footprints, highlighted by the edges with crusted white. The snow would cover it up eventually, but definitely not soon enough to hide their tracks from their pursuers. He hoped they wouldn't have to fight anyone. But he checked his knife in his belt anyway.

Swoop took them through narrow streets and alleys, hemmed in on both sides by sagging tenements with holes through the walls. The amount of debris and rubble in the streets was more than Wren could ever remember seeing.

It was almost like someone had picked up each of the surrounding buildings and shaken their contents out all over the street. Most of the junk had been transformed by the snow into white lumps with the occasional jagged edge or frayed cable poking out. Wren could hardly believe that anyone would be living out here. But he couldn't escape the feeling that others were around them. And not just behind them. He felt sure they were on all sides.

The snowfall had lightened, the flakes smaller and swirling on the wind. But it was starting to accumulate in a thin sheet of white, almost like frost on top of the slush. Wren glanced to his left as they passed an alley and caught a glimpse of two figures at the far end. They seemed to have just been standing there, and Wren got the feeling that maybe they'd been waiting there.

Off to his right, a loud squawking call went up, echoed through the side streets. Further ahead on their left, it was answered by a screech. They sounded more like animal noises than any kind of human.

Swoop halted, and quickly scanned the narrow street ahead. Further down on the corner, a five-story building had collapsed in the center, looking as if some titanic fist had smashed the roof all the way to the foundation. Somewhere near the third or fourth floor, Wren could see a red door frame with the door still intact, right at the edge of the gaping hole. It was a strange detail to notice just then.

Swoop turned and grabbed Wren by the shoulder, and dragged him into a narrow space between two buildings. Not really an alley, it was barely wide enough for Swoop to walk down without his broad shoulders touching both sides. When they reached the midpoint, Swoop stopped and dropped to a knee.

"I gotta get out in front of these guys, see how many we're dealin' with. Wait here, stay low."

"What if th-th-they find us?" Painter whispered in a harsh tone. "What do we do?"

"Fight. With everything you got. Be right back."

Swoop continued down the alley and disappeared to the right. Wren drew his knife and gripped it tightly.

"Lean back against me," he whispered to Painter. "You watch the way we came, I'll watch this way."

Painter scooted closer, so their backs were touching. It was some comfort knowing his back wasn't completely exposed, but not much. There was a sharp noise from above them, like sheet metal falling flat – and then quickly silenced. It sounded like it came from a rooftop somewhere, but the way the noise carried made it impossible to pinpoint.

They waited in that narrow space for three terrible minutes. Wren's heart leapt in fright when a silhouette appeared at his end of the alley, but it was just Swoop coming back. He only came part of the way towards them, and then motioned with his hand for them to follow quickly.

Wren reached back and patted Painter's arm, and they rejoined Swoop.

Swoop bent close and whispered, "Looks like eight, maybe nine total. Trying to ring us in. We need to keep movin'."

"Can't you just shoot 'em?" Painter asked.

Swoop shook his head. "Last resort. Real low on ammo, and there's no telling what else that much noise might bring. Come on."

He didn't wait for a response before turning back around and leading them out. They paused at the end for a second while Swoop scanned, and then he stepped out and grabbed Wren's coat again.

"There," Swoop said in an intense whisper, and he pointed across an open stretch to a wider alley on the other side. "Run there." He gave Wren a little shove, and then walked out into lane with his weapon up and ready. Wren ran to the alley as he was told, with Painter right behind him. As he ran, he noticed there were already footprints in the snow. A bunch of them.

They made it to the alley and stopped. A few moments later Swoop followed them in, and then passed by.

"Come on, with me," he said.

They kept moving like that, leapfrogging from alley to alley. Every time Swoop wanted them to start, stop, or reposition, he'd grab some part of Wren or his coat and drag him around: an arm, a shoulder, once behind his neck. It hurt a little. But Swoop knew right where he wanted everyone to be, and he had no problem putting them there. Wren still hadn't seen who was chasing them, but he could hear their strange calls back and forth.

Swoop held them in place for a moment, and leaned out weapon first to check if it was clear. He kept his gun up and shouldered, but he let go of it with his left hand to reach for Wren. Just as he did so, there was a funny *tonk* sound, and Swoop grunted and fell back hard against the wall of the alley. He slid part way down, but caught himself, and managed to push Wren and Painter back away from the entrance. He motioned for them to go back the way they'd come.

But Wren noticed Swoop wasn't standing up straight, he was kind of hunched over to his left, and when Wren looked down, he gasped. There was what looked like a six-inch-long steel rod sticking out of Swoop's middle, about two inches below and to the left of his heart.

"Go, go," Swoop said.

They backtracked, but as they came out into the open space, there were three figures further down the street. Scrapers. One of them let out a high-pitched whoop.

They were too far away for Wren to make out many details, but he saw enough to know he would rather fight to the death than be caught by them.

Swoop forced Painter and Wren to cut to their right, but as they crossed the mouth of another alley, they saw two more scrapers heading their way. Swoop drove them towards another gap between buildings, but when they entered it, they saw the far end was blocked by a wall of debris.

Instead of turning around, though, Swoop pushed them further in. Wren didn't understand why, unless he was just trying to get distance between them. He was going to have to gun them down as they entered. But then Wren understood. He hadn't seen it from the other end, but as they got closer, he saw a gap in the ground.

It was a stairwell that led down to a door a few feet below street level. Swoop shepherded them down the steps.

"There, back against the door. Make yourselves as small as you can."

Wren did as he was told, and balled himself up in the corner. Painter squatted down beside him.

Swoop sprawled on his back in what seemed like a terribly uncomfortable position on the stairs, with his legs kicked wide for support. Across his body he laid his weapon, pointed back down the alley and braced on his right fist, which he rested on the lip where the ground met the stairwell. Very little of Swoop would be visible from the opening of the alley, but Wren had no doubt that Swoop had a clear and deadly view. The rod was still jutting out of his ribcage, and it made Wren feel sick to see it, but Swoop didn't seem to be paying any attention to it.

Wren pressed his hands over his ears, knowing at any second one or more of their pursuers would round the corner, and Swoop would open fire. Every pounding heartbeat seemed like the last one before the fight would start. But Swoop didn't shoot.

Wren uncovered his ears and listened. Painter was panting next to him. Swoop might've been holding his breath for all the sound he was making. And there was the soft patter of snow falling. There was a cry from one of the scrapers, and another several seconds later. And then all was still.

They waited ten maybe fifteen minutes there in that alley, waiting for the end to come. But nothing ever happened. Swoop finally took the time to glance down at the thing sticking out of him. He grunted again, like he was unimpressed.

He sat up part way, and shifted position so he was seated on one of the stairs, with his weapon still pointed at the entrance. He transferred the grip back over to his right hand, and then with his left, he took hold of the rod and waggled it back and forth with a grimace. It didn't budge.

"Well," he said. "Don't that beat all. Painter, come gimme a hand here."

Painter looked at Wren with a pained expression, but he reluctantly went to Swoop.

"Get a good hold on the end there," Swoop said, indicating the rod. "And pull it straight back. Pull, don't yank. And *straight*. Nothin' side-to-side, alright?"

Painter nodded and took hold of the tail end. "Ready?" he asked.

"Do it."

Painter strained for a moment, which made the wound seem even more terrible to Wren, but then it came free with a metallic pop.

"Figures," Swoop said. "Of all the places it could go."

Wren looked more closely and could see now that whatever the thing was that had been sticking out of Swoop moments ago, it'd actually gone through one of the magazine pouches on his chest harness first. Whatever was inside was surely destroyed, but it'd very likely saved Swoop's life.

"So we're real low on ammo now," he said, taking the damaged magazines out and looking at them briefly. "But I'm only a little nicked." He pulled his harness away from his body and Wren saw a wet crimson spot on the garment beneath.

"Guess that's a good tr-trade?" Painter said, still holding the rod. Some kind of projectile, though Wren didn't know what kind of weapon it had come from. It was about eight inches long, cylindrical, and sharpened to a stake-like point. About an inch of the point was bloody.

"Would've rather taken the hit and had the ammo," Swoop said.

"Are you OK?" Wren asked.

"Yeah. Burns a little, but I'll be fine."

"What happened to the scrapers?" Wren asked Swoop.

"Let's go see." Swoop got to his feet, and started moving cautiously towards the end of the alley, weapon up and ready. "Stay close behind me."

Wren fell in behind Swoop and put his hand on the man's back. Painter came along right behind Wren, with his hand on Wren's shoulder. Together the trio edged their way to the end of the alley.

"Well, that's something," Swoop said. He paused and lowered his weapon. Wren peered around Swoop, and then immediately wished he hadn't.

Two of the scrapers were lying in the street. One on his back, the other face down. Both in puddles bright red upon the snow.

"What h-h-happened to them?" Painter whispered.

Swoop shook his head. "No idea. Don't think we want to find out, either."

He didn't waste time moving out. There were several more scrapers lying in the snow in both directions, and as they made their way towards the bridge, they came across yet more. More than eight or nine, though Wren wasn't really keeping count by then. He mostly tried not to look at any of them.

It was another half hour or so before they came within sight of the Windspan. Calling it a large bridge had been a massive understatement. It didn't seem especially wide, no more than maybe two normal streets side-by-side. But it looked like it was miles long. And now that he saw it, Wren understood why it was so much of a time-saver on the way to Morningside. And too, he guessed at how it'd gotten its name.

The Windspan actually climbed up and over the sprawling urban ruins. There'd be no twisting or turning alleyways, no navigating unfamiliar territory. Just a long, straight shot to the other side.

Swoop halted for a moment, maybe fifty yards from the bridge.

"There it is, boys," he said. "The Windspan."

Wren noticed he kept pressing his arm into his side, and he seemed a little unsteady on his feet.

"There's s-s-suh, someone on it," Painter said.

"What?" Swoop said.

"There," Painter answered, stepping forward and pointing. Sure enough, there seemed to be someone on one side of the bridge. Just sitting there.

"Do you think he's dangerous?" Wren asked.

"Dunno," Swoop said. "But I wouldn't trust anyone just sittin' around out here." Swoop blinked a few times and squinted, like he was trying to clear spots out of his eyes. "What's on his face?"

Wren looked as carefully as he could. It was tough to make out from this distance.

Painter answered, "I th-think it's a… a… blindfold."

TWENTY-FOUR

Runners were a rare breed. Even under the best conditions, with a well-known route cleared ahead of time, it took a certain kind of person to risk all the dangers the open offered at that pace. A bad step, a rolled ankle or a twisted knee, and runners could find themselves a dozen or more miles from their destination when night came. And that didn't take into account the number of traps that evil or wretched people sometimes laid for the unwary. A shortcut through the wrong alley, or even the right one taken too fast, could lead straight to the grave.

Some called runners bold. Others, reckless. Cass had a new term for them.

Desperate.

She'd managed to keep her pace steady – despite the snow, which had made the terrain even more treacherous. Her lungs ached from the chill air, and her legs were increasingly leaden, but still she pushed herself. The wound on her thigh had seeped through her pant leg. About the only positive to the situation was that the route itself hadn't been a difficult one to follow.

Cass got the impression that the remains of the city around her had grown more broken and jagged. The snow

now enshrouding it covered but did not hide what lay beneath, a white sheet draped over a corpse. Surely this was a deadly place. But she refused the warning thoughts that tried to pry into her mind and force her to slow.

She wasn't far from the Windspan now, and she felt confident that she could overtake Wren and the others there. If she could reach it. If *they* had reached it. Cass hadn't really considered what she'd do if she'd overshot them, if she reached Morningside before they arrived. Wren was masking his location again, and there was no way she'd be able to track him if he didn't want her to.

A fork led her to a narrow street and as she saw the scene that lay ahead, fear pierced her heart. She slowed and slid to a stop. There was a man lying face down, frosted with a thin layer of white, surrounded by a sludgy pool of deep maroon. Part of her wanted to rush to him, while the other told her to stay away. Cass lingered, panting, afraid of how she might react if she discovered the body was Swoop's. She glanced around for any signs of combat, but saw none.

After a moment she crept towards the body, keeping her eyes up and watching in case it was some kind of trap. About eight feet away she stopped, and saw enough to know it wasn't Swoop. The relief was tempered with the anxiety of not knowing what had happened. There was a good chance that Wren had passed this way, but no way to know whether they had encountered the dead man. She considered checking the corpse to see if she could determine how the man had died. It didn't seem to matter though. He didn't look like he'd been shot, at least not by Swoop's weapon. Maybe the poor man had fallen victim to some unseen device.

Cass didn't like the implications of that thought – that she might be running through a minefield, literally or figuratively. She set off again, doing her best to ignore the anxiety that tried to beset her mind and the fatigue that dragged at her body.

Swoop led the way to the bridge, and Wren could tell from his stride that something was definitely wrong. Usually his stride was aggressive and direct, but now, every so often, his feet seemed to splay to the side.

"Swoop, are you OK?" Wren asked.

"Fine, Governor," he said.

They were coming up on the bridge now, and the man ahead was still just sitting there. Or maybe he was on his knees. Wren had assumed it was a man, though he supposed it could be a woman. It was hard to know for sure. The person's hair was long and grey and swirled about his face. If it was a he, his eyes were definitely covered by a blindfold.

Swoop stopped, and Painter and Wren came up next to him.

"When we get close, you boys stay behind me," Swoop said. "Ten feet or so. Until we know what he's up to."

"Can we just guh, go around him?" Painter asked.

Swoop shook his head. "I don't want him behind us. Not until I'm sure. Maybe even after I'm sure."

"OK," Wren said. "Be careful, Swoop."

"Yep."

They closed the final distance to the man on the bridge, and Swoop motioned with his hand for the boys to stop while he continued on. Wren and Painter held their place. Swoop advanced towards the man, but stopped about fifteen feet back from him. The man's head was bowed, and he did not stir as they approached.

"Sir," Swoop said. "Everything OK here?"

The man didn't move.

"Sir?" Swoop said again, and then a little smile appeared on the man's lips.

"All is well," he said. "Forgive me, it has been long since anyone has called me 'sir'."

Swoop swayed on his feet, and Wren saw him widen his stance. Something definitely wasn't right.

"Tough neighborhood," Swoop said. "Plannin' on stayin' long?"

"Not long."

For an old man sitting alone in the snow in the middle of dangerous ground, he seemed completely at peace. It frightened Wren terribly.

"You headed across the bridge, or did you come from that way?"

"I had planned to cross. Now, I wait."

"Waitin' for…?"

The old man raised his head then, as if he was looking at Swoop. "You."

Swoop's head lowered a little, and his shoulders came up, like he was getting ready for something to happen.

"Well," Swoop said. "Here we are."

"There are stories in the west," the old man said. "Stories of a king in a great eastern city, who raises the dead."

Painter looked at Wren.

"Raises, and enslaves," the old man continued. "You know this city."

"I know *a* city," Swoop said. "Don't know any king like you say."

"Yet you travel with him."

The old man's words filled Wren with dread, but there was something curious to them, something in the way he spoke, the way he formed the words, that pricked at Wren's mind.

"Look, fella, I don't know where you get your news, but I can tell you it's bad. And if you're thinkin' about makin' trouble, I got nothin' for you but worse."

"The king should be expecting me."

"Morningside has no king," Wren called as he came forward. He walked closer, but stopped a couple of steps behind Swoop. "But I am its governor. Or was. But I've never made a slave of anyone, and I don't think I was expecting you."

"You *should* be."

It was a mild correction, the old man reemphasizing what he had already said, as if he had been misunderstood. His face was still turned towards Swoop.

"Could you tell me your name, sir?" Wren asked.

"Today," the old man answered, "I am Justice."

It happened so fast, Wren couldn't really tell who moved first. Swoop knocked Wren backwards and brought his weapon up in a flash, but the old man was a blur. Wren fell. There was a clash of metal, and Swoop was thrown violently backwards. He crashed into the snow and skidded backwards on his back.

Somehow the old man was standing where Swoop had been moments before, as if he'd teleported. He stood sideways with his left shoulder towards Swoop, front leg bent and the other locked straight behind. A sword had materialized in his hands, though Wren had not seen him draw it. This he held vertically, close to his body.

Swoop sat up, momentarily dazed. He held up his weapon, but it was useless now. The old man had sheared the end of it off, just ahead of where Swoop usually gripped the front. It didn't seem like the old man had cut Swoop at all, though, only knocked him down with his charge. Still, Wren couldn't believe how far the old man's attack had thrown Swoop. Swoop was a good eight feet back from where he'd started. Which meant there was now no one between Wren and the old man.

The old man turned his face towards Wren. "You," the old man said.

But that was his only word before something streaked past Wren from behind. The old man spun just in time to avoid the impact, but the Thing that had pounced at him redirected and was on him in an instant. The two exchanged a lightning fast barrage of blows and then separated for a moment, long enough for Wren to identify the Thing.

Mama.

Wren wanted to call out to her, but fear seized him – fear of fatally distracting her. They stood facing one another, Mama panting for breath, and the old man called Justice still as a stone. The snow swirled gently around and between them, crackling softly as it met the frozen ground.

And then, like hammer and anvil, they clashed.

It was nearly impossible for Wren's eyes to follow what unfolded before him. The speed was terrifying to behold, almost as if time had been compressed. Time and again the old man's sword sang, and time and again his mother twisted away, only to snap out a deadly strike of her own. But neither fist nor blade found its target, so quick were they to dodge and counter.

Hands grabbed Wren's arms and lifted him out of the snow. Swoop was pulling him backwards, away from the fight. Painter was there, watching the fury in shocked silence.

The speed was frightening on its own but it was made all the more mystifying by how precisely the blindfolded man judged Cass's actions. Cass seemed far faster than the old man, but the old man's movements were so efficient and fluid he was surprisingly able to match her. His quickness was unhurried.

Though it was too fast to see exactly what happened, for a moment Cass seemed either to grab or strike the old man's forearms, and in the next instant his sword catapulted from his hands and tumbled into the snow several feet away. Yet the old man wasn't disrupted. In nearly the same motion, he grabbed Cass with both of his now-empty hands and quickly spun, throwing her over his hip.

Cass flipped headlong, but somehow managed to arch her back enough to get her feet on the ground first. With her body parallel to the ground, she clung to the old man's arms and launched a kick back over her head. Wren couldn't tell if she connected or not, but the old man came free and collapsed backwards into the snow. He rolled like a shadow spilling across the ground and in the next instant was back on his feet, blade in hand.

Cass twisted into a low crouch. A moment later, the old man closed the gap between them with a single lunge and attacked with a downward slash, followed instantly by an upward stroke. Cass evaded both, and closed in tight, once again inside the range of the sword.

He fought to trap her hands, but her elbow flashed upwards and snapped his head back. The old man stumbled backwards, skidded in the snow, but as he did his blade flicked out and Cass flinched. For a tense moment they stayed separated by about ten feet. Cass was breathing hard, her hands held up in front of her to guard against the next assault. A thin black line welled from cheekbone to jaw.

The old man's sword tip was pointed straight at her, steady and calm, like a knife in the hand of a surgeon. He seemed as relaxed as they'd found him, as if the combat had been no strain at all. He straightened slightly and gradually allowed his sword to lower, so low it nearly brushed the ground. And then he turned sideways and shifted his stance so the blade was pointed behind him, away from her. The two held their ground, each seeming to wait for the other to make a move.

And in that moment, something about the old man's silhouette – the way he stood, the way he held the sword – came together with the way he had spoken, in a flash completing the picture that had been struggling to form in Wren's mind. Before he'd even had time to process the thought and doubt it, he called out, "Chapel!"

It was impossible. Utterly impossible. And yet his heart was sure. The old man remained completely still, and Cass held her ground. Wren tried to run forward, but Swoop snatched at his coat and stopped him in place.

"Chapel, stop, please, it's me, it's me Wren!"

Still neither of them dared move. But the old man spoke.

"Chapel," he said, as if some distant memory was awakening within him.

"Wren," Cass said, despite breathing heavily. "What are you saying?"

"It's him, Mama." Wren managed to yank free of Swoop's grip and he raced between the two fighters. He stood right in the middle of them with his hands up and out to his sides, facing the blindfolded man he'd once known as Chapel. Now that Wren could see him up close, even through the blindfold, grime, and wild hair, there was no mistake that it was indeed Chapel. But something was far different about him.

"Chapel, don't you remember me?"

"Chapel," he said again, more certain this time. "Yes. That was once my name." He stood straight and relaxed his grip on his sword, but did not sheathe it. "I was at a place of refuge then. You were there for a time."

"I was," Wren said. "You saved me. From the Weir. You, and Lil, and Mister Carter."

"What is going on?" Cass said from behind him.

"I don't know," Wren answered. "I don't understand. They said you were gone. Lil said you'd been taken."

"Taken, yes," Chapel said. He stood silent for a moment. And then he sheathed his sword in a fluid motion, and it disappeared within his large shabby coat. "For a time, I did not know myself, and was lost."

Painter cautiously approached. Swoop wandered over and picked up the missing chunk of his rifle.

"What happened?" Wren asked.

"I strove. And I again became master of myself."

Wren couldn't understand what he was saying, how that could possibly be.

"You're Awakened?" Cass asked.

"I do not know the term."

"You were once a Weir? And now you're not?"

"That is true."

"You were going to kill me," Wren said.

"If I had determined the stories to be true, yes." He said it without any hint of remorse.

"But you're not gonna try that anymore," Swoop said. He came by Wren's side and stood just a little in front of him, with controlled menace. There was no doubt that Chapel was a foe far beyond Swoop's skill, but it didn't seem like that would keep Swoop from giving it a try anyway.

Chapel made no reply, and didn't even react to Swoop's voice.

"We came to find you," Wren said. "At the village. Everyone thought you were dead."

"Not yet," Chapel said.

"Are you really yourself, Chapel? Now?"

The old man inclined his head towards Wren and paused before responding.

"I am who I am meant to be," he answered after a moment. "Perhaps no longer who I was."

"So, are we friends or what?" Swoop said. "Because if we got things to settle, we oughta get it done. We're losin' daylight."

"These Awakened," Chapel said. "Who are they?"

"They're like you," Wren said. "Except they needed help. To get free."

"And you helped them?"

Wren nodded.

"And then?"

"And then what?"

"What becomes of them?"

"We live our l-l-l-lives," Painter said. Chapel turned his face towards him for the first time. "As best we can. Wren ssss-saved me. And others."

"And you are free?"

"As much as anyone," Painter said.

"We're going back to Morningside, Chapel," Wren said. "You could come with us and see for yourself. Or we could tell you where Lil is. She'll be so happy to know you're alive."

"Lil," he said. "...I had forgotten."

Wren wondered exactly how much of Chapel was still Chapel. For a moment, he thought back to Jackson, the young man he'd met at the Vault, who had had the trouble. The one whose mind had temporarily left his body, only to return with others. But no, Chapel didn't feel like that. There was stillness about him, where Jackson had been wild. Chapel was controlled, not full of chaos. Still, it almost seemed like there was a piece of him missing. Or maybe just out of place.

"I will consider," Chapel said. He bowed his head to them and then walked away towards the bridge and returned to the spot where they'd first found him. There, he knelt.

"We need to move on," Swoop said. Wren noticed there was a small, dark stain at the top of his pants, where he'd bled from under his vest.

"Not yet," Cass said. "You've got some explaining to do. All of you." Her breathing was more controlled, but hadn't fully settled yet. Even so, the anger was evident in her voice.

"Still got a long walk."

"Then you go ahead," Cass said. "I'll deal with you later."

Swoop's eyes narrowed. "Don't reckon I'm the kind to get dealt with, *ma'am*."

"I need a moment with my son," she answered. "We'll catch up."

"We'll wait on the bridge. Be quick."

Swoop nodded at Painter, and the two of them moved off to the Windspan, giving Cass and Wren some space. But not too much. Wren hated watching them go, because he knew what was coming.

Cass turned Wren to face her. She crouched and put both her hands on his shoulders. The cut on her cheek was bleeding freely, but she didn't seem to care.

"What were you thinking? How could you sneak off like that? How could you do that to me, Wren?" Her voice was low but intense. She looked angry, but there were tears in her eyes.

"I'm sorry," Wren said.

"Sorry? What if something had happened to you? What if I hadn't gotten here when I did? Did you think about what that would have done to me? Did you even think at all?"

Wren stood silent before her. He'd seen her this upset before, but not often. The last time had been when he'd snuck out of the governor's compound. The night he'd woken Painter. But this time was different. Different for him. Before, the harshness of her voice had frightened him, and the guilt for having done wrong had brought him to tears.

But this time he didn't feel sad, or scared, or guilty. Something had changed inside, and he saw her anger was misplaced, and it did not move him. He saw her fear, and he felt sorry for her.

"Why, Wren?" she demanded. "Why did you do this?"

"To protect you, Mama."

"No, Wren. No. That is not your job. I am your mother. It's *my* job to protect *you*."

"Not anymore."

Cass almost looked stunned at his words. She just stared back at him. But even as she did, some of the anger seemed to melt away.

"Asher wants *me*, Mama. He's always wanted to get to *me*. I thought if you were somewhere far away, maybe you'd be safe from him. But I have to try to stop him. I have to go back to Morningside…" He didn't want to say it at first. But then he realized there was no consequence he feared from her now, and no further pain he could cause her. "I have to go back to the machine."

For a moment she just stared into his eyes, searching. Her breathing was back to normal.

"Why didn't you just tell me?" she asked, and her voice had lost its edge.

"Because you wouldn't have let me go."

She shook her head as he said it, but she didn't reply. Wren could see she knew he was right. Tears finally dripped from her eyes, and she embraced him. He put his hands on her back to comfort her as best he could. She was squeezing both his arms though, so it was hard to do much. After a time she released him, and pulled away.

"You're hurt," he said, and he touched her cheek. Cass wiped the tears and… whatever her blood was now, away, and looked at her hand. Then she wiped her hands on her pants and stood.

"Swoop's right. We better get moving."

Wren shook his head. "Mama, I don't want you to come."

"I don't want you to go," she answered. "So we're both going to be disappointed."

She held out her hand. Wren looked at it. This wasn't going anything like he had planned. Not anywhere close. But he knew he'd never convince her to let him continue without her. And though there was a part of him that had wanted to be a noble warrior, he couldn't deny that he would be glad to be with her again. At length he took her hand, and together they walked to meet Swoop and Painter on the bridge.

The snow had dwindled to a light flurry of dust-like flakes. The wind gusted and Wren became aware of how wet his pants had become from being thrown down in the snow.

"Set?" Swoop said as they approached. Cass nodded, and without another word Swoop swiveled and started up the Windspan. Painter hesitated, but not quite long enough for Cass and Wren to catch up to him. He kept a few steps ahead, though Wren couldn't judge whether it was because he was still trying to give them some privacy, or if maybe Painter was afraid of what Cass would say to him.

Chapel remained kneeling as they neared and Cass didn't seem to have any intention of talking to him. Wren slowed his pace slightly, trailing behind his mother as she moved wordlessly past the old man. Wren stopped walking, but held on to his mother's hand. She halted a step or two ahead when she felt him pull against her.

"Have you decided what you're going to do, Chapel?" Wren said.

"I have," he answered. "In my haste, I deprived your guardian of his weapon. In recompense, I will lend my protection until you reach your destination."

"And will you stay with us when we get there?"

Chapel stood with such grace and ease it almost looked like he was falling in reverse. "After, I will go where I am led."

Wren didn't know what he meant, but he assumed that it was probably a no. Cass tugged Wren forward and they started on again. Chapel stayed in place for a few moments while they moved away, but in his own time he followed after them.

There was no conversation as they walked. Wren was still trying to process everything that had just occurred. It had been an utter whirlwind. Pursued, escaped, attacked, rescued, reunited. And completely confused.

If it had been anyone else, Wren would never have turned his back on the old man who was now following them. And he wasn't certain how much of the man behind him was still the man he once knew. But one thing that hadn't changed was the strength of Chapel's word. Even with the strangeness, and the unbelievable nature of his tale, there was some comfort in knowing Chapel's sword would be on their side. At least as far as Morningside.

Swoop had started out about ten yards ahead of everyone else, but he slowed his pace and let them close the gap to five yards or so before he picked it up again. The heavy cloud cover made the day seem later than it actually was. The degree of the bridge's ascent hadn't seemed too severe when Wren had just been looking at it, but as they continued upwards, he was surprised by the toll it took. And the Windspan was aptly named. The higher they climbed, the harsher the wind grew. They walked on in silence, hunched against the bite and bitter cold.

The group kept mostly towards the middle of the bridge, though from time to time Wren glanced out to one side or the other. From the Windspan, the city below looked like a circuit board coated in dust, running for miles in every direction. After about half an hour of walking, the snow had disappeared from beneath their feet, and the concrete was merely wet. They were still climbing up, though it was hard to tell if the angle of incline had lessened, or if Wren had just become used to the rise. Another half hour passed and a chilling fog descended upon them. He wondered briefly if they'd actually wandered up into the clouds.

Eventually the bridge seemed to level off, and the journey became a mere test of will; one foot in front of the other, with no end in sight – and cold to the bone. Swoop let them take a brief break, though it didn't provide much rest.

Wren had thought he couldn't possibly get any colder. Once they stopped moving, he quickly discovered he could. Cass and Swoop drew aside for a few minutes and spoke in low whispers, but Wren couldn't make out what they were discussing. They didn't halt for long, and though Wren's body screamed with fatigue when they started off again, he was at least thankful for the warmth the effort generated, meager as it was.

"Only about four klicks to go," Swoop said as they resumed their march.

"Only?" Painter said. "How mmmm-many were there to sss-, to start with?"

"Twelve," Swoop answered. "Give or take."

Wren tried to console himself with the thought that they were over two-thirds of the way across, but it wasn't much use. He knew all too well that the end of the bridge wasn't the end of their journey. And he didn't know nearly well enough what the end held in store.

Painter's whole body ached with the cold. *Ache* maybe wasn't quite right. The sensation wasn't exactly pain. It was more like a deep fatigue. *Depletion* seemed more accurate. But there was no doubt he was feeling the strain and discomfort of their bitter journey. He wondered now what would have become of him if he had come alone. Though, if he had come alone, he wondered if there would've been any need to make the journey in a single day.

He had been out among the Weir on his own before. Not often, but enough. Only once had he been attacked, and though he hadn't mentioned it to anyone when they'd asked before, he felt certain he had provoked it. He had pushed the boundaries, testing his own limits. Though he hadn't been bold enough to spend an entire night outside the wall, he felt stronger now than he had before. Stronger than he'd ever felt. And the closer they got to Morningside, the less certain Painter was that he would actually enter the city.

Painter started thinking through the scenarios likely to greet him upon his return. Would they arrest him for traveling with Wren and Cass? Or shoot him on sight? Finn had said Painter hadn't been named in the order. Maybe if he showed up separately, everything could go back to normal.

But what then? Was there any reason to believe he'd face anything other than persecution? Would he be free to come and go as he pleased? It seemed doubtful that the situation in Morningside had changed for the better in the short time they'd been away. More likely it had worsened. Which meant that the best outcome Painter could reasonably expect was a return to a life of meaningless service to people who despised him.

Why, when you could have power?

The thought rippled through his mind, like rings of water after a stone has disturbed its surface. The thought was his, but what had instigated it seemed to have come from somewhere else. Within his mind, but not of it. And for the first time since that had started happening, he didn't shy from the question it had stirred up.

What kind of power, he didn't know. But he felt it within himself. Something else for him, besides a life of lurking – and merely hoping to escape notice. Something more concrete than vaguely wandering the open in search of his sister.

Not just survival.

Purpose.

The sky must have been darkening overhead for some time, but the lateness of the day struck Wren suddenly. Now that he'd noticed, he couldn't understand why he hadn't seen it earlier. They'd left the Windspan behind some hours ago and taken only two brief breaks since. Their pace had slowed noticeably. At first, Wren had thought that maybe Swoop was trying not to run them too hard. But now, watching the man ahead of him, he wasn't so sure.

Swoop's stride wasn't as smooth as it usually was, and he seemed to be swaying from time to time. He'd been keeping ahead of them the whole time, saying it was safest to keep some distance between the point man and everyone else. Even when they'd stopped, he'd continued on a little ways to scout ahead, and then waited for them to catch up. But

Wren couldn't remember how long it'd been since he'd seen anything other than Swoop's back.

Cass had, more than once, asked him if he was alright. His answer was always the same, sometimes over his shoulder, sometimes without even turning his head in their direction... He'd say, "Fine."

At least there was some comfort in the look of the landscape. Wren didn't exactly recognize where they were, but he recognized the feel of it. Home couldn't be too much farther away now. If he could still call it "home".

He had told Chapel that he was the governor of Morningside. Now he wondered if that had been true at all. Maybe he'd never really been governor because he'd always had the Council. He'd always had Mama. He'd always had Able and Swoop and Gamble. He'd always been surrounded by other people who could do the hard work when he couldn't, who could make the hard decisions. And though Wren had always tried to do what he thought was right, he realized he could only remember one time that he'd made a decision that put himself in a tough position. Most of the time, he'd just been trying to find the compromise that made everyone happiest, or upset the fewest people.

That wasn't governing. That was managing. Maybe it was the difficulty of that final stretch that had made Wren recognize the difference. The level of effort it took just to keep moving forward, just to keep pushing one step further. Whatever it was, he realized that more times than not, as governor, he had avoided situations that made him feel this way. He'd quit pushing when there were other options on the table. Like the time he'd overheard the guards at the governor's compound talking badly about his mama. He'd walked right up to the brink then, and when it had been time to meet the challenge on his own, he'd shrunk back.

But maybe now, for the first time, he was actually doing something worthy of the title. Even if he'd already lost it. Maybe now he was thinking like a governor, and acting like one, whether he was or not.

And strangely, Wren didn't feel any braver or smarter or wiser than he had before. In fact, he felt very small and afraid. But he knew in his heart that he was doing what needed to be done. He was doing what he had to. And even if he failed, which he thought was probably going to be the case, at least he knew he'd be losing for the right side.

"There," Swoop said, and he stopped walking. The others caught up to him. There, up ahead, the top of the wall of Morningside peeked up over a rise. "Decision time," he said. His breathing seemed shallow.

For a time, they all stood next to each other in silence, looking off to the city shining in front of them. Then Wren felt moved and he stepped in front of them and turned to face them.

"I had planned to come back alone. I know now that I could never have done it. So, thank you for bringing me here. But now I think I can finish it on my own."

Swoop shook his head. "Not what I meant." He grimaced, and drew a breath before continuing. "Not a decision whether I'm going back. Just wanted to know what the plan was." Wren noticed now that the front of Swoop's left pant leg was dark and wet, almost all the way to the top of his boot. His wound was still bleeding.

"Swoop?" Wren said, staring at the stain.

"I'm gonna make it home, little man," he said. But even as Swoop said it, he swayed. Cass stepped around and looked him over.

"Oh, Swoop," she said. He just looked at her with that flat expression. "How long have you been bleeding?"

"Little while."

"When did it start up again?"

"Never stopped."

"What?" Cass said. "You told me it was fine!"

"Said it *would* be fine."

"How is it still bleeding?" Cass asked.

Swoop shrugged. He didn't look like he cared much. But he didn't look well either.

"There is a poison," Chapel said. "It prevents the blood from clotting."

Swoop looked over at him then. "Poison?"

Chapel nodded once, but he didn't turn. His face remained angled towards Morningside.

"Any other effects I oughta know about?" Swoop asked.

"There could be a number. Pain. Paralysis. Death." Chapel paused, but then he added, "Those beings who prey on their fellow man are evil creatures."

"Well," Swoop said. He took another deep breath. "Might as well finish the job." He started off towards the city again. Cass tried to make him stop, but he shrugged her off and kept going.

Whatever lay ahead for Wren, he knew he wasn't going to let Swoop wander off on his own. He turned and followed, but after a moment turned back. "Chapel?" he said. "Will you stay with us?"

Chapel remained impassive. "I will consider."

Wren nodded. He had hoped Chapel would remain with them, but he knew it was a long shot. "I hope you'll stay," he said. Chapel didn't reply.

Cass turned and started walking towards Wren. "Come on, Painter," she said over her shoulder.

"I'm not g-going," Painter answered. Cass stopped – and both she and Wren looked at him, surprised.

He said, "I'm not going back."

"Painter, you have to," Wren said. But Painter shook his head.

"I don't have to do anything I ch… I choose not to do," Painter said.

"But where else would you go?" Cass asked. "Why come all this way, if not to go back to the city?"

Painter looked off to the side, more avoiding eye contact than looking at anything in particular.

"I need some time," he said. Then he looked back at Wren.

Wren could tell by his expression that he'd made his decision. Painter didn't look sad or confused or anything. Wren hated to leave him behind, but Swoop was getting farther away, and Wren couldn't think of anything he could say that might change Painter's mind. He'd assumed that Painter had been planning to come back to Morningside to try to get some of his old life back. But he saw now in Painter's eyes that he had something else in mind.

"You know what I c-c-came to do," Painter said.

"I don't think it'll work, Painter," Wren said.

Emotion flashed across Painter's face, sudden anger, but Painter checked himself and merely said, "I have to try."

He had his own plans. Maybe Painter was expecting to try and track Snow down himself. Maybe he was just having another one of his moments, and he'd come around on his own.

But as much as Wren wanted to tell his friend he *had* to come with him, it had been only a few hours before that he'd told Chapel that Painter was no one's slave. Painter was a free man, just like everyone else in Morningside. Free to make his own choices, even if they hurt him.

"Bye, Wren," Painter said.

"Bye, Painter," Wren answered.

Cass shook her head, but seemed to sense Painter's determination as well.

"Take care of yourself, Painter," she said.

He nodded. Cass turned and walked over to Wren, and together they headed off to catch up with Swoop. It didn't take long for them to overtake him. He was clearly on weak legs, and when they reached him, Cass took hold of his arm and put it over her shoulder. The fact that Swoop didn't protest told Wren all he needed to know.

The city loomed before them, growing larger – and more ominous – with each step. As they came into view of the nearest gate, Wren could see there was activity stirred up just beyond it. A crowd had gathered inside. Or, perhaps, had been gathered. There were more guards at the gate than Wren had ever seen posted. And they were mostly facing inwards towards the crowd, rather than outwards.

And now that the moment of his return to Morningside was at hand, Wren felt anxiety. His whole body trembled with nervous energy, and his chest grew tight. But while his body flooded with emotion, Wren found it somehow didn't touch his mind. In the midst of the swirling chaos, he was able to find peace.

One of the guardsmen finally noticed their approach and, after a flurry of conversation, six of them came forward out of the gate to greet them. Or to bar their way.

The ranking officer held up his hand as they neared. He looked nervous.

"By order of the High Council," he said in a loud voice, "you may not enter the city of Morningside."

Cass and Wren stopped where they were, about ten feet

away. But Swoop took his arm from Cass's shoulders and
drew himself up.

"I look forward to you keeping me out."

He didn't stop, or really even slow his pace. He just kept
walking straight towards the officer.

"Sir, we're authorized to take any necessary action…"
the officer said. Swoop was only a few steps away from him.

"Swoop," Cass said. "Don't."

"Sir, please," the officer said. He put his hand on Swoop's
chest. A mistake. Swoop's hands flashed up, shoving the
officer, but before the officer could fall backwards, Swoop
caught the man's jacket and jerked him. As the officer
whipped forward, Swoop tucked his chin, and his victim's
face met the crown of Swoop's head with an awful sound.
The officer flopped awkwardly to the ground. Swoop
stepped over him and kept moving through the gate.

The other guards stood stunned for a moment, but
then one of them lunged and caught Swoop by the sleeve.
Swoop turned with the motion and buried his fist in the
side of the guard's face. The guard went down to a knee, but
that seemed to wake the others from their inaction. They
collapsed in on Swoop.

Cass launched forward and threw two of the guards to
the ground. The situation erupted into an all-out brawl. If
Wren didn't do something quickly, there was no telling how
many of them would end up injured – or dead. He rushed
into the writhing knot of people.

"Stop!" he cried. "Stop!"

Swoop had been knocked to the ground, and Wren threw
himself on top of him. "By order of the Governor, stop!"

The guards fell back a step, still poised to attack, but
apparently reluctant to risk hitting Wren.

"This man is my guardian and protector!" Wren said. "I demand that no harm should come to him."

"You no longer hold any authority here," said a voice behind him. Wren glanced back to see the officer getting to his feet. The poor man's nose was crooked, and blood ran freely and dripped from his chin. Wren stood, and tried to straighten up, to make himself seem as tall as he could.

"I never surrendered that authority. Who claims it now?" Wren asked.

"The High Council," he answered.

"It was just a Council when I left."

"Things have changed."

"Then take me to them," Wren said. "And see that no one harms this man or my mother."

"It's not like that, sir. We're going to have to arrest you all. It's orders."

"Orders given by an invalid authority based on a false accusation. My mother had nothing to do with Connor's death, and Swoop has only ever loyally protected and obeyed his governor. The only thing either of them are guilty of is remaining faithful where others faltered."

The officer glanced around at the other guardsmen, clearly uncertain how to handle the situation. And Wren understood his advantage now. While they were unsure, he was certain of his purpose, and that certainty gave him confidence.

"I can't..." the officer said.

"You will," Wren answered. He held out his hands. "I'll allow you to bind my hands, if it will help you."

"Wren, no," Cass said, but Wren ignored her. Now wasn't the time. The officer's eyes flicked to Cass and then back to Wren.

"I *am* still your governor," Wren said. "Regardless of what you've been told."

After a moment of hesitation, the officer took out a pair of binders and clamped them around Wren's wrists. Even when he had tightened them fully, they nearly slid down over Wren's hands. Wren was pretty sure he could have pulled free if he'd wanted to.

"What about these others?" one of the guards asked the officer in a low voice.

"I don't know, just… just keep an eye on 'em," the officer said. "Until we get this straightened out."

The officer and two other guards formed up around him, careful not to get too close to Swoop, who had worked his way up to his hands and knees, but hadn't made it much further.

Wren looked at his mama.

"Take care of Swoop," he said.

The officer placed his hand on Wren's shoulder and guided him forward. It was only as they started away from the gate that Wren realized the crowd had gone nearly silent. They were almost all watching him, some with concern, some with confusion, some with contempt. The guards cleared a path through the people as the officer kept a tight grip on Wren's shoulder. Murmurs swept through the crowd as they passed through.

Wren risked one last look over his shoulder, and saw Mama helping Swoop to his feet. There was a figure standing behind them in the distance, still outside the city: Chapel.

Wren smiled inwardly, as he quietly let the guardsmen lead him away to his uncertain fate.

TWENTY-FIVE

They had stripped Wren of most of his belongings; his pack, his coat, his knife. It was the knife he missed the most. At least they'd taken the binders off too. And it felt good to be warm again. Now he sat in a small, dim room within the governor's compound, waiting to hear what would become of him. For some reason they'd thought it necessary to blindfold him when they brought him inside, so he wasn't sure exactly where he was. He didn't recognize the room. But there were lots of rooms in the compound that he'd never seen. Wren guessed he was somewhere on one of the lower floors, below the main council room. There were two chairs in the room, with a low table between them.

For all the seriousness of the situation, there was a dark humor in it. He had been here before. It wasn't the same room, nor were circumstances the same. But not all that long ago, a year and a half maybe, he'd been captured, isolated, locked away so someone else could decide his fate. At least this time he'd chosen to be captured. And he hoped this time his fate would be his own to decide.

Night was closing in on Morningside. It was still his city. He was responsible for it, whether anyone recognized it or not. So, while Wren sat and waited for someone to come and take him before the Council, he closed his eyes and stretched outside of himself, searching for a way to connect to the machine.

It had been easier before, when he'd been able to touch it. Wren didn't know why, but that always seemed to be the case. Things were clearer somehow when he could touch them. But having had contact with the machine once before, at least he knew what he was looking for. He tried to visualize it, remember what it had been like, what it had *felt* like.

Somewhere in the ether he found a thread. He focused on that sliver of signal and traced it back to its source. But as he tried to follow it, it seemed to unravel. He tried again, but each time the signal dissolved before he could establish a solid connection. He hadn't often connected to complex systems, and certainly he'd never faced anything as complicated as Underdown's machine before. But even so, something felt different. It was almost as if the machine itself didn't want him to connect. Like it was resisting him.

The door to his room opened, startling Wren back to the physical world. Joris, one of the compound watchmen, stood in the doorway.

"It's time, Gov–" he said, cutting himself off before he finished the word. "Uh, they're ready for you."

Joris smiled sadly. He had always been one of the nice ones. Wren could see the reluctance in his face. He was following orders, but his heart wasn't in it.

"Thanks, Joris," Wren said.

There were two other guardsmen waiting in the hall, but Wren didn't recognize either of them.

"This way," Joris said. He led them down the corridor. The other two guards stayed close behind Wren, one at each shoulder. Wren's nerves started running wild as he pictured what he might be walking into. And he didn't know why they thought they needed three guards. They were treating him like an enemy who might try to escape. As if there was anything he could do to one of these stout men that would enable him to get away, let alone three of them.

They climbed up two flights of stairs and came out into a hallway that Wren recognized well. Joris wasn't leading them to the Council Room as he'd expected. They were heading towards the old throne room. The room where Underdown and Asher had each once sat. Where Wren had Awakened his mama, and where Three had died. A year and a half later, and Wren was back to where his life in Morningside had started. Maybe it was fitting that it should end here, too.

It had taken everything in Cass not to pursue the guards when they had led Wren away. But he had seemed changed somehow. Unafraid. Sure of purpose. In control. He had spoken to the guards in a tone she'd never heard from him before. And his words to her had been heavy with the weight of command.

Take care of Swoop.

And so she had. She'd taken Swoop's pack and had managed to get him back on his feet, but it'd taken a lot of effort to get him there. The guards that had been left behind had seemed reluctant both to let them go or to make them stay, so in the end they had just stood around doing their best not to interfere in any way.

The people gathered near the gate had mostly kept clear as well. They'd been largely content to stare at her, most impassively, some with anger and hatred upon their faces. But as she and Swoop had made their way through their midst, Swoop had stumbled and gone down hard on his knees. When Cass had tried to help him up, she'd been surprised to find two other pairs of hands there to assist.

Two women, both in shabby clothes, took it upon themselves to support Swoop the rest of the way, each with one of his arms over their shoulders. Together they had made their way to Mister Sun's Tea House. Cass hadn't known where else to go.

And as they approached, Cass noted a number of men and women arrayed around it. Some had swords, some knives, but most of them seemed to be wielding whatever they'd had on hand that might double as a weapon. At first Cass thought they were planning to attack the Tea House, but as she got closer she realized that wasn't it at all. They were guarding it.

When they saw her coming, they opened a gap in the line for her to pass through, and one of them jogged up the steps and opened the door for them. The inside had changed significantly since the last time Cass had been there, the night they'd fled the city. Some of the tables remained in the middle of the room, but many had been pushed to the corners and stacked. Now the main hall was segmented by folding screens and blankets hung on cords. And there were people everywhere – sitting at tables, sitting in their makeshift rooms, sitting on the floor. Others seemed to be milling around aimlessly. It had all the look of a refugee camp. Many Awakened were among them. Most, in fact. But Cass didn't see Kit anywhere.

Mister Sun quickly brought them through the main area and after a brief exchange, he took charge of Swoop and led him back to his own room. Mister Sun helped Swoop remove his clothes and then assessed the wound. To Cass's surprise, Mister Sun seemed to know quite a lot about cleaning and stitching up such injuries. After sealing the wound, Mister Sun applied some kind of salve and dressed it in a layer of bandages.

Once they made sure Swoop was as comfortable as they could make him, they left him to rest and returned to the main room. It was only then that Cass realized the two women who had helped her get Swoop to the Tea House were gone. She never even got their names.

"Mister Sun," Cass said. "What happened when we left? What's going on?"

He shook his head and slid a stimstick in his mouth. It activated, and he took a drag before he answered, "Trouble, Lady Cass. Much trouble."

He led her through the main area and then up the back stairs to a small room on the top floor. Painter's old room. They went inside and he closed the door.

"There was a riot, after you left," Mister Sun said. "Many were injured. Some killed."

"What started it?"

"Who can say which pebble caused the landslide? It had been building for weeks," he answered. "Citizens of old resent those brought in from outside the wall. Both despise the Awakened. When it was announced you had slain Connor and fled, there was outrage."

"I didn't kill Connor, Mister Sun."

He shrugged. "You were not here. It was convenient to believe what they said, for those who desired the same outcome."

"What outcome?" she asked.

"They're rounding people up," Mister Sun said. "Preparing to move them out of the city."

"That's why all those people were gathered at the gate."

Mister Sun nodded and took another pull on his stimstick.

"They can't," she said. "They can't do that. Those poor people will get slaughtered by the Weir."

"They claim the guard will patrol to protect them. Some have resisted. Most have not."

"And the people downstairs?"

"There was backlash against the Awakened," he replied. "We brought some of them here."

"What about the others?"

"With Aron."

The mention of his name shocked her. "I thought he was dead."

Mister Sun shook his head.

So, they were forcing the non-citizens back outside the wall. The pure foolishness of it struck her. Particularly now, with the danger that lay ahead.

And logistically, she didn't see how they could possibly expect to pull it off. There was no way the Council could have put together such a plan in such a short amount of time. Unless of course, they'd been planning it for much longer.

"I need to see Aron."

Joris opened the door to the throne room, and the first thing that struck Wren was the fact that there were now three throne-like chairs on the dais instead of one. No one was sitting in them yet, which somehow seemed worse than facing whoever was supposed to be there. The room was cleaner than it'd been the last time he'd seen it. The night that Connor and Aron had dragged him through it. Only a few days before, though it seemed like weeks in his mind.

They closed the door behind him and, when Wren looked back, he saw that only Joris remained with him.

"What's going to happen now?" Wren asked.

"The High Council will be here in a moment," Joris said without looking at him.

"But what will happen?"

"I don't know," Joris answered. Then his eyes flicked to Wren. He lowered his voice. "But try not to be scared." He tried to give a little encouraging smile.

But just then the door opened, and Joris snapped to attention. Three people strode in, followed by several guardsmen. The guards moved into a semicircle, half on each side of the dais with the chairs in between, while the three moved to sit upon the thrones: Hondo, North, Vye. The new High Council. Hondo sat in the middle, though from the arrangement of the thrones, it was hard to tell if that was meant to be a more important seat or not. It was farther back on the dais than the other two, which were angled slightly inwards. From where Wren stood, it felt more like he was at the focal point of all three. But there was still something inherently more intimidating about that center seat – where Hondo now sat. Vye was on Hondo's right, and North to his left.

Wren tried to remember everything Swoop had taught him about commanding a room. He pulled his shoulders back, widened his stance. Looking at the three of them seated there, Wren was surprised to find he wasn't intimidated. Before he had left, he would've frozen at a time like this. After what he had seen, after what he had learned, these three people seemed somehow lesser than he remembered. The adrenaline was coursing through his body, but he found it within himself to bend that nervous energy to his purpose.

"Wren," Vye said. "We're so glad you're alive. We've been worried."

Her kind voice took Wren completely by surprise. He'd expected an immediate confrontation.

"Where is your mother?" North asked.

Wren paused before answering. Swoop had always encouraged him to take a breath before he answered a question. "I don't know," Wren answered.

"You can tell us, Wren," Hondo said. "It'd be best for everyone."

"I don't know," Wren repeated. "I left her at the gate. With Swoop."

"And the rest of your guard?" Vye asked.

"We came back without them. Because of the order," he answered. Then, before they could ask another question, Wren pushed back. "Where are Aron and Rae?"

"They no longer serve on the Council," North said.

"By whose direction?"

"Aron by choice, Rae by vote," Vye said.

"And so you decided to steal my rightful authority?"

Hondo exhaled through his nose, a dismissive sound. It annoyed Wren. Hondo seemed small.

"You abandoned your post," Vye said. She said it with a hint of sadness, like she was explaining to a child why he was about to be punished.

"At this Council's direction," Wren answered.

"At one member's *suggestion*," Hondo said. "You have to understand our side, Wren. Connor was dead, Aron hurt. You ran away. You left the city in chaos. So while you thought only of yourself, we had to take measures to ensure the security of *every*one."

Wren felt anger rising at the accusation, the twisting of facts to suit their purpose. But he knew there was no use in arguing. Truth would change nothing here. "Then why exile? Why didn't you just call for us to come back?"

"To prevent further chaos," North said. "Trust has all but disappeared within Morningside. If we took control and then handed it back to you whenever you returned again, the citizens would never know what to expect. They'd never know who was in charge or why. It was a difficult decision, but it's for the best of the whole city."

There were so many things that seemed wrong with what had happened. Unjust. But Wren had to remember why he had come back. It wasn't to reclaim his seat, or even to understand what had occurred.

"I never gave up my authority as governor," he said. "But I didn't come back to claim it, either. I came back to try and save the city."

Hondo let out a laugh. "From what, little boy?"

"My brother."

"Your brother is dead," said North.

Wren shook his head. "I don't know how to explain it, but Asher is alive. I have to try to stop him. I need to use the machine."

Vye and North exchanged looks, but Hondo sat forward on his throne. "Certainly not," he said. "We know what your father could do with that machine. You will not touch it again."

"Hondo, Asher's gathering an army of Weir. I've seen it myself. And I believe he's going to bring them to Morningside."

"There is no such army," Hondo said sharply. "Unless *you* bring it. There are serious charges against you that must be answered. You can't escape them by trying to frighten us with children's stories."

"Is this supposed to be a trial?" Wren asked.

"It's not a trial, Wren," Vye said. "But we do have a decision to make."

"Connor and Aron attacked *me*. They attacked my mom."

"What happened with Connor and Aron was unfortunate. It was a mistake, to be sure," Hondo said. "But was it a mistake worth their lives?"

Wren was at a loss. He hadn't really expected the Council to welcome him back, but he had thought that maybe when he'd explained the situation they'd at least have treated it with seriousness, rather than dismissing it outright.

"It's a difficult time, Wren," Vye said. "We think it'd be best for everyone if you stay here in the compound."

"You're imprisoning me?" Wren asked.

"It's not prison, no," North said. "It's for your good and for the good of Morningside."

"It will be confusing to the people if you're out with them," Hondo added. "And it may not be safe for you. You are to remain within the compound until such time as we deem appropriate to release you."

Wren stood in stunned silence as two guards came forward. They ushered him towards the doors where Joris was waiting. Joris opened the door, and they joined the two other guards who were still waiting outside. And the five of them escorted Wren away to his prison.

Painter sat on the flat roof of a two-story building, with his legs dangling over the sides, and watched as the final traces of dusk seeped out of the horizon. Night would soon be fully upon them. The air was cold and damp, but the clouds had begun to break apart overhead, and here and there he could glimpse stars flickering and glittering in the heavens above. He was deeply weary from the journey, but his mind was active.

Tonight he would just observe. He knew better than to let himself hope that he might catch a glimpse of his sister on this first night. Instead of going out to hunt for her, he had decided it would be better to watch the Weir first. To get a feel for how many there were, and how they moved. They had rarely shown up in numbers of late, nor did they regularly approach the wall of Morningside. But perhaps here on the outskirts, he would be able to study their movements and discern any patterns.

He didn't have to wait long. There was an electric cry away to his right, not terribly far away. It sounded mournful and lonely to him, then. After a while he began to see them moving throughout the dark streets and alleyways below. Those were few in number, and if they had any plan or pattern, it was beyond Painter to decipher.

As the night wore on, Painter grew drowsy, and after a time, he scooted back on the roof so that his legs were no longer over the edge, out of fear that he might doze off and fall. He dragged his pack in close behind him and leaned back against it. He was still looking up at the sky when sleep overtook him.

Soon afterward, Painter began to dream that there was a shadow on his rooftop. Only it was darker than a shadow, and there wasn't anything there to cast it. As he watched, it began to spread towards him, like oil pooling in only one direction. The closer it drew, the more it rippled and seethed, as if the shadow were actually a living thing. Painter was frightened and tried to crawl back away from it, but found he couldn't move, couldn't even cry out.

Something seemed to grow from the middle of the inky surface, a bubble, which became a horn, which became a pillar twisting itself towards the sky. And then it was neither pillar nor shadow at all, but just a man in a long black coat. The man was young, no older than Painter, and perhaps even younger. His features were sharp, handsome, and he had a wide smile. But Painter saw the smile was not in the young man's eyes. Those were dark; dark and cold and full of malice. He came and sat next to Painter.

"I'm looking for someone," the young man said. "I wonder if you are him."

Everything within Painter told him that there was danger, but the young man's demeanor was patient and calm. Disarming.

"I need someone to go before me. To tell of my coming." He leaned forward, as if revealing a secret in confidence. "I need someone to be my voice."

Painter found that he could speak, could move freely. And while part of him cried out to flee, there was something engaging about this young man that made him want to linger. Surely it couldn't hurt to sit and talk.

"I d-d-don't think that's mmmm, that's me," he said.

The young man smiled.

"I can help you," he said. "I *will* help you. And your sister. If you'll allow me."

The young man held up his hand between them, and his expression was one of waiting for permission. How the young man knew about Snow and what he intended to do, Painter didn't know. But he felt in his heart that a crucial decision lay before him, one that once made he could never unmake. An opportunity once missed, that would never come again. For a moment, he struggled against himself.

But what, in reality, would he be giving up? Here was someone who had need of him. Someone who could help him. Someone who could help Snow. Looking at the young man, still patiently waiting for his decision, Painter felt reluctance. But he couldn't find a reason for it. Fear, unfounded. And Painter was tired of being afraid.

He nodded, and the young man extended his hand to touch Painter's mouth. And then he smiled again and stood, and walked to the edge of the roof. He turned back to face Painter.

"When the sun rises, tell them," he said. "Tell them I'm coming."

And then he stepped backwards off the roof and instead of falling, he shattered into a hundred fragments, which in turn became some kind of winged creatures, black like crows or ravens. They scattered in every direction, and Painter awoke with a start, his hands shooting out reflexively.

It took a moment for him to recognize where he was. And when he did, he quickly turned this way and that, searching for the young man. But there was no one to be seen on the rooftop. He rubbed his eyes to ensure he had actually awoken from his dream. The words still echoed in his mind.

Tell them I'm coming.

Painter touched his mouth, ran his hands over his face. And then he became aware of a strange sound, like a quiet popping or soft crackling. Or like the flapping of leathery wings. Painter glanced around again to look for the source of the noise. And when it occurred to him to look over the edge of the building, his breath caught in his throat.

The streets below were teeming with Weir.

Moving through the city after dark had become more dangerous than Cass had anticipated. The curfew was still in effect, and it seemed like the number of city guards had swelled in her short absence. On top of that, there were here and there pockets of rough-looking men and women skulking in the shadows. Whether they were working in league with the guards, or just out on their own accord, they certainly weren't operating in any official capacity. Cass wondered if these were the same kinds of people that had slain Luck and the others. But there was no time for questions now, and fortunately moving unseen had become almost second nature to her, particularly when she was on her own. The fatigue from the day's journey slowed her some, but not as much as she would've expected.

Cass found her way to Aron's shop on the eastern side of the city, in the outer ring of buildings set closest to the wall. His was one of the larger establishments in Morningside and had actually been two separate buildings at one time. The lower floors were dark, but light shone around the edges of the curtains pulled across the upstairs windows.

There was no one out front that she could see, but given what she'd seen at Mister Sun's, Cass had every reason to expect there were guards at every door. She had no idea what kind of reception she might get, she didn't want to risk a violent confrontation. She crept around the building looking for alternate ways in.

On the backside of the building, there was a balcony on the second floor. There were no obvious ways to gain access to it from ground, but the building next door had a decorative trellis that was easy to scale. Cass gained the roof of that building and paused there, watching for patrols. She saw only one guard on the wall. Too many in the city, too few on the walls.

When she was sure it was clear, she ran and leapt the gap between the two buildings and landed lightly on Aron's roof. She crept to the edge and lowered herself down to the balcony. Inside, she could hear voices. She tried the handle to the door, but of course it was locked. That made her think of Wren, and she paused for a moment, wondering where he was and what was happening with him. She took a deep breath and steadied herself.

She couldn't imagine that anyone on the Council would do him any harm. Not now. Not when he had returned so peacefully.

Actually, she could imagine it. But she refused to let herself do so. She would find Aron and, with him, answers.

Cass looked around on the balcony to see if there was anything she could use to open the door; a hidden key, or secret panel. And while she searched, the door clicked and swung open. She whirled to face the door and found herself staring into the radiant blue eyes of one of her kindred.

"What... Lady Cass?" she said, surprise evident in her voice and on her face. It was Kit. "Lady Cass, what are you doing here?"

Kit came forward and embraced her in strong arms, and then stepped back quickly, as if remembering her place. "Oh, I'm sorry, Lady," she said. "I was just so surprised..."

Cass smiled in spite of herself and hugged Kit in return.

"Kit, it's so good to see you. I feared you were dead."

"No, ma'am, not yet," she answered. "Though not for lack of trying. But really, what are you doing out here? How did you *get* out here?"

"I climbed. I need to see Aron."

"OK," Kit said. "OK, sure. He's inside."

Kit led her inside, through a large open room with wooden floors and a number of chairs. It was warm and comfortable, dusky with its lights turned low. There were several Awakened throughout the room, and others besides. The conversation all but stopped as Kit escorted Cass through.

They found Aron sitting in a small upstairs room in what looked like a workshop. He was sitting on a stool and had something on a workbench in front of him. He was hunched over it intently when Kit tapped on the door. There was a long wide bandage across the back of his head.

"Yep?" Aron said, without turning.

"Sorry to bother you, Aron, but someone's here to see you."

"Oh yeah? Who's that?" he said, swiveling on his stool.

He blinked a couple of times as his old eyes adjusted, and then his eyes opened wide and he shot to his feet.

"Easy, Aron," Cass said. "I'm not here to fight. I just want to talk."

His shoulders relaxed, and his eyes went a little sad.

"I'll leave you two alone," Kit said. She squeezed Cass's arm as she passed by, and disappeared down the hall.

After she left, Cass and Aron just stood staring at one another for a time, neither sure of what to say or where to start. Finally, Aron just shook his head.

"I'm sorry, Lady. I know it don't make any difference now, but I *am* sorry." He held out his hand, offering her a seat in the chair tucked in the corner of the room. Cass nodded and moved towards it, but she stopped when she saw what was lying on the workbench. It was a rifle. Long-barreled, old but well-cared for; well-worn, well-used. A deadly thing.

Aron followed her gaze, and then looked back up at her.

"It's OK, she's safe," he said, and picked up a piece that looked like the trigger mechanism from his workbench. "Puttin' her back together. After a long time away."

Cass went to the chair and sat, and Aron returned to his perch on the stool.

"If it hadn't been for Mister Sun," Cass said, "you would have been first on my list to find and string up."

Aron nodded.

"But he seems to think there's been a change of heart. And from what I see here, I have to admit I could be persuaded to believe it."

"I wish you would," he said. "But I won't blame you if you don't."

"How did we get here, Aron?"

He shook his head and looked down at his hands with a sigh.

"It's what happens when people lose their way," Aron said. "Me, I lost sight of what I came to do. Forgot I was there for the people, not for the Council. Let others convince me that what was good for the Council was good for the city." He looked up at her then. "We see where that got us. I ain't tryin' to make excuses. I'm my own man, I made my own decisions. And I'd undo a bunch if I could. But I think maybe that knock on the head put some things right."

Hearing him confirm what she'd suspected didn't immediately upset Cass as much as she'd thought it would. There was anger, of course, but there was a strange sort of relief, too, in knowing that her instincts had been right, that she hadn't just imagined it all. Still, she hadn't asked the big question yet.

"Did you try to have my son killed?"

Aron clenched his jaw and squinted, grimacing at the question. But after a moment he answered, "She was never supposed to get that close."

Cass felt a knot of rage tighten in her chest, but she swallowed her wrath. For now.

"You gotta believe that," Aron said, holding his hands up. "I would never have gone along with it if I thought for a second he was gonna be in any danger. It was never supposed to go that far. But that girl... that girl was better than any of us ever expected."

Cass wondered. Aron seemed sincere, genuinely pained by the close call. He'd always loved Wren, in his own gruff way. But Connor. Connor had been in charge of the guard.

She thought back to that night, how long it'd taken the guard to show up, after she and Able had already cornered the girl.

"Was it Connor who assured you that Wren would be safe?"

"Of course," Aron said. "He was gonna put some of his men in the right spot, make a couple of heroes in the process..." He trailed off, and his eyes widened, only now making the connection. He shook his head again and cursed quietly. "I don't like to speak ill of the dead, but I shoulda seen that. Even then we were at odds. I was just too blind. It was only supposed to scare you. Get you over on our side."

"Your side? Your side of what?"

"Forcin' 'em out. There was just too many people for the city. That's why Underdown had such strict laws, so little tolerance. Always an excuse to push someone out if ever there was threat of trouble."

"So all this time," Cass said, "you've been working to undermine Wren as governor, so you could enact your own policies. Why the game then, Aron? Why proclaim him governor, if you were all against him from the start?"

"It's all games, Cass. Always has been. Once Underdown was gone, somethin' had to be done quick. The people out there, most part they don't care who's in charge, as long as someone is. There was a good story there, made it easy for them to believe that nothin' was really gonna change, and that's what they wanted. Underdown's son. Looks just like him. Sure he's young, but he's got the Council.

"I think it started right, or close to it. When we started, we all just wanted to keep it all together. But after the big attack, and Wren makin' that announcement that we were bringin' everybody in... it didn't take long for us to start wantin' other things. Different things."

"And you were going to murder my little boy for it."

He shook his head again forcefully. "No, Cass. I don't blame you for not believin' me, I know I wouldn't. But no, I just

thought it'd rattle him. Make him see why it was dangerous
to have those people around. But then your son, that boy, he
went and surprised us all. Said to let it go. Forget about it, move
on like it never happened. Well, not a one of us had thought
of that. After that, everyone started spinnin' their own plans.

"And then when we found out it was Painter's sister. Well,
good God, I wanted to hang myself. And I thought maybe
when he found us in that room with Wren, I thought maybe
he'd found out. And Connor..." He looked over at his rifle.
"Well, I guess maybe there's something to that... reapin'
what you sow."

His eyes went glassy for a moment, and Cass left him to his
own thoughts while she wrestled through her own. Pieces
were starting to come together for her, in a broken kind of
way that made it seem all the more true. Factions within
factions. Plans gone awry, either from sabotage or because
the plans themselves were poorly made. Overreactions,
overcorrections.

People usually talked about conspiracies like they were
so clean-cut, always perfectly executed. The schemes
revealed in her mind were a tangled mess. And that made
them believable, because they were so utterly human.

"Hondo and Vye, I understand," she said. "I never felt
right around those two. But what about North? Rae?"

Aron came back to himself and looked at her.

"Rae, no, Rae's too much a straight-shooter, too strong-
minded. I don't think she ever knew much about what the
rest of us were up to. And North... well, I never could read
North. He's a power player to be sure, and he looks out for
himself. But truth be told, I got the feelin' he's careful about
stayin' in the inner circle because he don't like what might
happen if he wasn't."

"And what about you, Aron? What now?" Cass asked.

"Now… now I'm trying to do what I should've been doin' all along. Just takin' care of people with my own hands, the best I know how."

"Kicked off the Council?"

He made a dismissive sound. "Naw, I quit. Told 'em what I thought they could do with their High Council." He shook his head. "No, I'm goin' with 'em. Been talkin' with the Awakened here, and some others. Once we all move outside, we're gonna run the patrols, keep these people safe. It's what I shoulda been doin' all along. What about you?"

Cass got to her feet. "I think I'll pay a visit to our High Council in the morning."

Aron stood and nodded. "You're welcome to stay here tonight, if you don't mind sharin' some space. Might be safer than tryin' to go somewhere else."

"I may take you up on that," Cass said. She wanted to catch up with Kit, and as much as she wanted to stay angry at Aron, she felt his change of heart had been genuine and thorough. There wasn't much point in harboring hatred for a repentant man when she already felt so short of allies. She wasn't ready to trust him yet, but she could see maybe doing it again one day. She nodded and started towards the door. Just before she left, Aron cleared his throat. Cass stopped and turned in the doorway.

"I know it don't change nothin'," he said. "But I am sorry for hurtin' you, Cass. For all of it."

She nodded. And for some reason, an old dusty box on the workbench caught her eye. It looked like rifle ammunition. Cass nodded towards the rifle.

"Didn't know you were much of a shooter."

"Was, back in the day," Aron said. "Been a long time." He

smiled and gazed down at the weapon, and rested his hand lovingly on it. "She looks like a sweetheart, but she hits like an angry drunk."

"What's she shoot?"

Aron flipped up the lid on the old box, and pulled out a large shell. He held it up for Cass to see.

"Thirty kilojoules," he said. "You ever seen anything that mean before?"

"I have," Cass said. "Got any extra?"

Aron looked puzzled and a little taken aback. "I don't know about extra," he said, "but how many you need?"

"How about three?"

There were still plenty in the box. He took out two more shells and handed her the three hefty rounds.

"Don't lose 'em," he said. "They don't make 'em much anymore."

Cass slipped them into a pocket.

"I'll be sure to keep my eye on where I put them."

She gave him a parting nod and left him to his work.

Wren's room was small, but nicely furnished, with a bed, a couple of chairs, a table, a desk, and a small lamp that glowed with a warm orange, almost like firelight. They had brought him dinner, and Joris had stayed with him while he ate. But that had been a couple of hours ago, and no one had come by since.

Outside, night had fallen completely, and Wren had been growing increasingly anxious as darkness closed in, wondering if perhaps tonight would be the night that Asher would make himself known. But now as Wren sat quietly on his bed, he could hear no calls or cries from the Weir. At first he'd wondered if he'd been placed in a room where the windows were too thick to hear any noises of the night. Then he'd heard the low murmur of occasional voices in the courtyard and known that the silence of the Weir was genuine.

But, strangely, the air seemed heavy. Wren didn't really know how else to describe it. It was like the night itself had weight, and was pressing down on all the city. Even when he tried to stretch out through the digital, it took more effort. He had made several more attempts to connect to the machine, and had each time had the same result. The signal was just too complex for him to hold on to.

Wren's body was overwhelmingly tired from the day, but his mind was too active. He was just thinking about trying to see if he could fall asleep anyway, when there was a gentle knock at the door. It seemed strange for someone to knock on his door, given the fact that he couldn't open it himself. Or rather, he could if he wanted to risk it, but he knew that would very likely invite the wrath of the three guards they had posted outside. The Council was too well aware of his talent for locks.

"You can come in," Wren said.

The door clicked, and the handle turned; when the door opened there was a hulking frame behind it. North.

"Hello, Wren," he said, stepping into the room. "May I join you?"

"Sure."

North bowed his head slightly, and then closed the door behind him.

"I can't stay long," he said. "But I wanted you to know that I am sorry for how things have gone."

"OK. Are you going to let me go then?"

North gave a small smile and shook his head. "Not at this time. But you should know that not all is at it appears." He stepped closer, as if someone might be listening in. "Is what you said about your brother true?"

"Yes."

North paused in thought. Then he nodded to himself. "I will see what I can do about getting you access to the machine. If not tomorrow, the next day."

"There may not be a next day," Wren said.

"The walls are strong, little one," North said. "We need not fear the Weir."

Wren shook his head. "You're wrong, North. You don't understand."

"I know these are hard times. But you are young and have seen fewer of them than I have. We'll find our way through, you'll see."

Wren thought for a moment about trying to explain, trying to describe to North what he had seen, and felt, and what it meant. But he knew it would be useless. North was right, he had seen many more difficulties than Wren had. And he had been blinded by them, thinking that this was no different than anything he had faced before. And Wren didn't know how to convince him otherwise.

"Can I ask you something?" Wren said.

"Of course."

"Why did you order us exiled? I thought you were our friend."

"I was, and I am," North said. He seemed hurt by the implication that he would be otherwise. "I know it is hard to understand. But at the time, issuing that order was the only way I could warn you. I didn't know whether it would keep you away, or if it would cause you to return. But either way I knew it would tell you something was wrong. And I hoped your isolation would make you harder to find for those who may have been looking."

Wren didn't know whether to believe him or not. It made some sense. If Wren believed him.

"I must go," North said. "But I will make every effort to help you gain access to the machine."

"Tomorrow," Wren said.

North nodded. "Or the next day." The big man bowed his head again, and then knocked twice on the door. "Rest now," he said. "You still have friends in this city."

The guards opened the door from the outside, and with a final nod, North was gone. The guards closed the door, and Wren heard the lock click into place. Prisoner in a place he had once called home.

He didn't know what to make of all North had said. Little of it mattered at this point. They didn't seem to understand how the affairs of the Council were meaningless in the face of what Wren feared was to come.

But there was nothing more he could do for now. He got up and switched off the lamp, and then lay down on his bed. Wren closed his eyes and listened for the cries of the Weir that should have been there, and weren't.

TWENTY-SIX

It was midmorning when Cass gained entrance to the compound. She had walked up to the gates and caused quite a stir amongst the guards posted there. Some wanted to arrest her and take her before the Council immediately, while others were convinced that to do so would be to fall into her trap. None of those could actually explain what exactly her trap might be, but they were convinced it was both devious and deadly.

At length, a captain had been called out, and after he assured the others that he would assume all responsibility, he bound her hands behind her and, with a contingent of six others to back him up, led her to the new seat of power.

Cass kept calm and let them guide her where they would. She had expected to go to the Council Room, and so was surprised when they led her down to the old throne room. They kept her waiting in the hall. The guards were careful to keep their distance.

When they finally let her in, Vye, Hondo, and North were seated on their thrones – and Wren was with them.

"Mama!" he said, and he ran to her and hugged her waist. She bent forward and pressed her cheek to the top of his head before one of the guards separated them.

"Are you OK, baby?"

"I'm fine, Mama, are you?" Wren asked.

She nodded, relieved to see her son looking so well. It was almost too much for her at that moment. She hadn't expected to see him, at least not yet, and she was thrown off momentarily. Wren was dressed in fresh clothes, and he looked cleaner than she'd seen him in days. His hands were free, though two guards were clearly assigned to stay near him.

"We thought you'd want to see your son," Vye said. "He's being treated very well."

"And so here we are, gathered again," Hondo said. There was an edge in his voice, and an arrogance. "And I suppose you've come here to challenge our claim to authority."

"Not at all," Cass said.

"Oh?" Hondo said. "Then to what do we owe the honor of your presence?"

"I've come to ask for your mercy."

Hondo's eyes narrowed, and Vye glanced over at him, and then back at Cass.

"What did you have in mind, Lady Cass?" Vye asked.

"That you show mercy to the people you've sworn to protect," Cass answered. "I understand that you have a plan underway to move a number of people outside the wall. I've come to beg you not to do so. You would be sending them all to certain death."

"Despite what you may think," Hondo said, "we aren't monsters. We also have a plan for the guard to provide protection. They'll take care of any Weir that may stray too close."

"It won't be enough."

"The Weir haven't come in any number for a long time."

"They attacked the gate less than a week ago," Cass said.

"And it was repelled. They haven't returned since."

"Please, North," she said, looking at him. "There is an attack coming. On a scale that you cannot imagine. If you prepare now, the city may weather it. But if you waste your time forcing people out in the open, I believe we will all be destroyed."

"Your son already tried this tactic," Hondo said. "It sounds very noble, returning not for power, but for the greater good. But you should be careful setting yourself up as a savior for a people who may not receive you as such."

"Hondo, don't be a fool. I know what you've done. I know how this Council conspired against my son. But this isn't a game for power."

"It's always a game for power," he said. "And I know you're upset with how things have turned out. But trying to cause a panic now doesn't help anyone."

"That's funny, coming from a man who went out of his way to stir up trouble for the rightful governor."

"There was already trouble. We may have accelerated the process on occasion, but it was underway before we ever got involved."

"It's not like you think, Cass," Vye said. "We just wanted to get ahead of it. To make sure we could control it. Otherwise the city would've eventually torn itself apart."

"The sentiment was always there," Hondo said. "It just needed a little push."

Cass thought she'd prepared herself for this confrontation, but she was aghast at the absolute lack of remorse they showed.

"People died so you could have your way," Cass said. "And more will die now."

"And are they not acceptable losses, Cass, if the end result is peace and security for everyone?" He lowered his voice and leaned forward. "People are sheep. They need a shepherd to tell them where to go, what to do, what to think. They *want* a shepherd. Everything we have done has been for them."

It was no use. There was nothing more Cass could do here.

"You fools. You've made enemies of friends and allowed the wolves to claim your doorstep. What good will it be to rule a kingdom of dust and ash?"

"It'll work out," Vye said. "You'll see, Cass. You'll understand when it all settles."

Cass was still trying to work out a response when a guardsman came in. He bowed when he entered, and Hondo waved him forward. It turned Cass's stomach to see that. Wren had never asked anyone to bow to him.

"An Awakened has come with a message," the guard said. "He said he must deliver it himself, in person."

"Another plea?" Hondo asked.

"I don't believe so, sir. It seems urgent. He's very serious."

"Alright, send him in."

Hondo motioned dismissively towards Cass, and two of the guards took her by the arms and moved her off to one side.

She heard the door open behind her, but before she could glance over her shoulder to see who it was, Wren called out, "Painter!"

Cass turned and saw Painter stride into the room and immediately knew something had changed about him. He was standing taller, with his shoulders back and his chest out. His face was grave. He didn't acknowledge Wren or Cass, or anyone else, other than those seated on the three thrones.

He stopped before them, but did not bow.

"You look familiar," Hondo said. "A friend of Wren's, aren't you?"

"I am a herald, and I have come with a message for the rulers of the city."

Cass was shocked to hear the voice coming from Painter. It was full and powerful, confident. And he hadn't stuttered once.

"Oh, well, by all means, please deliver it."

"One is coming with a host at his command. He does not wish to take you by surprise, for he longs to test his strength against yours. When the sun sets, his army will appear and make your city desolate."

Vye sat upright, but Hondo only laughed. He leaned forward in mock seriousness. "And what tribute does this mighty warlord desire to spare us this fate?"

"It is no threat. There is nothing you can give to see it pass over. There is nothing you can do to prevent it. It is a prophecy. Your city has seen its last sunrise."

Hondo sat back with a bemused look, and then he looked over to Wren and Cass.

"I can appreciate the theatrics," he said. "But really, next time you should find someone with a more..." he waved his hand up and down in Painter's direction, "imposing figure."

Cass was too stunned to pay any attention to what Hondo had said. Painter seemed wholly in control of himself, but the change was too sudden – too severe – and she knew the ominous words were not truly his. The thought was too terrible to admit, yet too certain to dismiss. Asher had found a way into Painter's mind. And Painter had given himself over.

"Get him out of here."

Two of the guards approached Painter, but he held up his hands with such authority that they halted. He turned on his own and walked to the door, without so much a glance at Wren or Cass. Before he left, Painter paused and stretched out his hand towards Hondo, as if pronouncing a blessing.

"Come tomorrow you shall no longer be called Morningside, for by then I shall have given you a new name."

And with that, he exited. The throne room was silent for a few moments after. Cass and Wren made eye contact, and Cass wondered if the fear and horror was as apparent in her eyes as it was in his. Vye had gone pale, and even North looked unsettled. Only Hondo remained unmoved.

"Will you now do as I've asked?" said Cass. "Shut the gates, and prepare."

"And please, Hondo, let me use the machine," Wren added, pleading.

"So you can help bring this army? It was an impressive performance, but I'm not so easily taken as that. Because you have such compassion for the people, how about this? You both may go and live among them." He motioned for the guards to take Cass and Wren from the throne room.

"Hondo, wait," North said. "Let's talk about this…"

"There's no need to discuss it, unless Vye is in disagreement?" Hondo answered, looking at Vye, who was watching Wren. Vye glanced at Cass and for a moment they locked eyes. But then she lowered her gaze and shook her head.

He said, "As I thought. The ruling stands. Escort them from the grounds, and see that they leave with the first relocation."

The guards forced Cass and Wren from the room, though neither she nor her son offered any resistance.

They were corralled and placed near one of the western gates, with what Cass estimated to be roughly two hundred of the most unfortunate citizens that Morningside had to offer. There were a few rough-looking characters who looked like they might start trouble once the move began, but for the most part, everyone seemed resigned to their fate.

After spending some time among them, Cass realized this too was part of the plan. The first group to leave wasn't made up of the worst offenders, or the most vocal critics. It was comprised almost entirely of those who would go along quietly, those who trusted the promise of the Council, or who were too afraid of reprisal to make any fuss. These were people who just wanted to live their lives in whatever peace they could find. They would make an example for the others. They would prove it wasn't so bad if you just went along.

There was a large contingent of guardsmen stationed around the area, an impressive show of force, though it was largely unnecessary. No one seemed to have any plans to do anything other than move out when they were told to do so. Cass overheard some conversations of people discussing which buildings beyond the wall they were planning to occupy. Some even went so far as to claim that their options would be better outside the wall than they had been inside.

The people they were with didn't seem to know quite what to make of them, and though there were occasional nods of recognition, or puzzled looks, for the most part there was a concerted effort not to notice them: *Don't make trouble. Just go along.*

Cass wanted to be angered by the attitude, but she couldn't find it in herself. Walking amongst them, she realized that she'd spent much of her own life doing that very thing. Going along, doing whatever it took to get through one more day. It was how she'd hooked up with RushRuin. It was why she'd let a city crown her son. She wondered if she was doing it even now.

She kept Wren close and together they tried to figure out what to do. Try as he might, Wren just couldn't keep a connection established to Underdown's machine, and it didn't seem likely that they'd be getting a chance to ever return to the compound. There was no doubt in either of their minds that Painter's pronouncement had been no idle threat. Though neither of them understood exactly what had happened to Painter, it was just like Asher to call attention to himself ahead of time. To give them a warning, and dare them to defy him. And to leave them in terrible anticipation of what was to come.

Even escape was out of the question. There was simply nowhere for them to go. It was too late in the day to try to make the run to Lil's refuge, and neither of them knew the location of any wayhouses within range. The doom seemed inevitable, but neither of them had yet accepted it.

They'd been stuck with the others for about an hour when Cass heard someone call her name. Glancing around, she didn't immediately recognize where it had come from, but after a moment she spied a hooded person waving her way. She and Wren approached, and when they got close she recognized who it was.

"Kit," Cass said, "what are you doing here?"

"Aron asked me to keep an eye on you. Glad he did. What's going on?"

Cass glanced over at the squad of guards that had been specifically assigned to watch her and Wren closely. There were six at least. She moved past Kit and drew Wren along with her.

"We're being watched," she said over her shoulder. "Probably best if they don't see us talking."

"Just pretend you're talking to me, Mama," Wren said. Cass looked down at Wren and smiled. Clever boy. She knelt in front of him, and put a hand on his shoulder. Kit remained close by, facing slightly away from them.

He "listened" intently, nodding now and then, as Cass quickly explained to Kit what she could; her confrontation with the Council, Painter's message, and the attack they believed would be coming that night. Kit didn't quite grasp all of it, and Cass couldn't blame her. It was too much to absorb. But Kit understood enough.

"We have to get you out of here," she said.

"We can't let them put all these people outside," Cass said.

"I don't know how we can stop that right now," Kit answered.

"And I'm not sure how we can get out of here," Cass replied. She surreptitiously nodded towards the guards that were watching them. Kit waited several seconds and then casually scanned them.

"We can take 'em," Kit said.

Cass shook her head. "I don't want to start a riot, Kit. And we're going to need as many guards alive and well as we can get. Did they just let you walk in here?"

Kit nodded. The guards were still watching them, and Cass was concerned that if they spent any longer talking, Kit might get marked.

"Are they going to just let you walk back out?" Cass asked.

"I hope so," Kit said. "They better."

"Do me a favor and get back to Aron and try to talk to Mister Sun, let them know the situation. Maybe they'll be able to put something together."

"You got it," Kit said. She risked turning towards them, and spoke in a low voice as she passed by. "Stay safe, Lady. You too, Governor. We're not going to leave you out there."

It was around noon when the order came down to start moving the people out. One of the captains of the guard started giving commands in a loud voice and reminding everyone that it would be an orderly process, and he had the means to ensure it. There were a few scuffles around the edges, but with the overwhelming response from the guard, they neither lasted long nor spread. By and large, the mass of people seemed content to gather their belongings and set off to start a new life in the open.

The lack of protest or struggle was easier to understand when Cass realized that most if not all of these citizens had spent most of their lives outside the wall anyway, under Underdown's reign and protection. For them, perhaps living inside the city had been the anomaly, not being forced back out. Many of the dwellings that had been established outside still remained, and there seemed to be some kind of unspoken agreement that these people would simply return to where they once had lived. Maybe for some, it felt like going home.

Cass and Wren were near the middle of the crowd, and before they started moving, a guardsman weaved his way over to them. Cass recognized him from the compound. It was Joris. He was carrying Wren's pack and coat.

He nodded in greeting as he approached, and smiled apologetically.

"Lady, Governor," he said. "I'm not supposed to be doing this, but I couldn't stand to see you go out there empty-handed." He handed Wren his belongings.

"Thanks, Joris," Wren said.

Joris glanced around quickly, and then produced something else from within his uniform. He handed it to Wren. "And there's this."

Wren accepted it and looked at the item laid across his palm. His knife. "Oh, Joris, thank you so much."

"Might want to hide it for now. I know it's special."

Wren nodded and tucked the knife away in his belt.

"Thank you, Joris," Cass said.

"I'm sorry I couldn't do more," he said.

"It means a lot that you did anything at all," she answered.

He gave her a sad smile. "Good luck to you," Joris said to Cass, then he gave Wren a nod. "Governor."

"Bye, Joris," Wren said.

Joris turned to go, but as he did so a murmur arose from behind Cass, and there was a commotion. When she looked at the source, she saw a number of guardsmen were forming up in a line, shoulder-to-shoulder, but facing away from the crowd. It was hard to see through the crowd and the guards, but Cass was able to make out what looked like a large group of people approaching.

"Here, Wren," she said, "come here." She grabbed him around the waist and boosted him. "Can you see what's happening?"

"It's Aron," he said. "And a whole lot of people. He's got a gun."

Cass's heart fell. She thought she'd made it clear to Kit that a fight wasn't what she wanted. There was no point in starting a battle inside the city when a war was coming from without. She let Wren down, grabbed his hand, and started pushing her way through the crowd towards the guards. She had to stop it.

But when before she reached the edge, she was surprised to see the line of guards parting. Aron was there, with Mister Sun, followed by many others. They started filtering into the crowd, and she saw now that many of them were wearing packs, or carrying large bags.

When they got close enough, Cass called out to them, and they made their way towards each other.

"What are you doing?" she asked.

"Comin' with you," Aron said. His rifle gleamed in the noonday sun. A bandolier full of rounds hung across his chest.

"What? What do you mean?"

"I told you I was gonna do what I could to protect these people," he answered. "So we're movin' out to stand guard. All of us."

Cass looked past him and saw Mister Sun and Kit, leading a crowd. If all the Awakened weren't gathered there, Cass couldn't immediately identify who was missing, and there were many others besides. People she'd seen guarding Mister Sun's and staying at Aron's. She was completely overwhelmed with emotion.

"Aron," she said, shaking her head. "This isn't what I meant. I can't ask you to go out there to die."

"Don't plan on it," he said. "We're goin' out there to fight. And we're countin' on you to lead us." Aron handed her the pack he was carrying in his hand. Her go-bag.

As they stood there, the others started filing by, many with nods in Cass's direction as they passed. They were a grim people and armed with whatever they'd had on hand. A ragged army to be sure, but one with purpose and determination.

They streamed by, and she knew these, too, were men and women who'd spent most of their years out beyond the wall. But they weren't the docile ones, going to their fate at the direction of another. These were a hard people, who knew what they would face and chose willingly to do so on the behalf of others. She recognized another haggard face that seemed to be trying to slip by unnoticed. Swoop.

"Swoop, no," she said. He stopped and looked at her with a raised eyebrow. "You're in no shape for this."

"Don't reckon that's for you to decide, ma'am."

"Please, Swoop. I can't have you on my conscience."

He stepped in close, leaned forward. "They got me, Cass. I can feel it in my blood. So I figure I'd rather die out here on my feet than in some bed on my back."

The news hit Cass hard. She'd known Swoop was in trouble, but after Mister Sun had stitched him up, she'd thought he was going to make it. Now knowing his death was inevitable was almost too much to bear.

But then she remembered what Mouse had told her back at the refuge. About how he'd rather follow his brothers and sisters to war than sit back in safety while they went off to die. And it wasn't just Swoop. All of these people passing by Cass were on the same errand, by choice. Maybe here were his kindred. Courage stirred within her. And slender hope.

She wiped tears from her eyes and squeezed Wren's hand.

"Alright," she said. "If this is to be our end, let's at least make it worthy of legend."

Cass and the others spent the afternoon organizing, planning, and fortifying what little they could. The citizens that had been displaced were left to mostly go about their business. Cass had decided it would do no good to frighten them at this stage, not knowing what kind of panic might break out. If anyone actually believed her.

In the end, she and the others with her spread the word of an emergency plan, just in case. Everyone was to gather at the eastern gate, through which they had come. Cass and her warriors would form a barrier of protection against the Weir, and the hope was that by sheltering as close to the gate as possible, the guards on the wall of Morningside would be able to lend support. Cass knew they would be able, and hoped they would be willing.

Cass would lead her Awakened kin. They would form the point of the spear, with the hope that they might be able to sow some confusion among the Weir. Swoop led a group of the most seasoned fighters in place directly behind the

Awakened. Mister Sun and Aron, each, were captain of their own contingent, protecting the flanks. There were few guns among them, so it would largely be hand-to-hand combat. But Mister Sun had his vicious three-barreled weapon, and Aron his rifle, and Cass hoped that they'd be able to at least thin the numbers.

Mister Sun's demeanor had changed drastically. No longer the eager-to-please, friendly curator of teas, he now had a no-nonsense air, a hard edge, with no patience for inefficiency or poor tactical thinking. And as he moved throughout the assembled warriors, exhorting them, he seemed to know far more about killing than Cass would ever have guessed.

And she could tell that Swoop wasn't at full strength, as he checked his lines and ran them through some communication drills, and gave them final pointers on hand-to-hand combat. He was wielding his tomahawk, a weapon she'd seen him carry but never use. But as he went through the motions, his stride wasn't as certain, and his voice wasn't as full. Even so, she was willing to bet that none of the men and women under his command could tell anything was off. He still had a powerful presence.

At some point while she and Kit were discussing how best to organize their force, Kit stopped midsentence as someone appeared from out of a nearby alley and approached.

"Uh oh," Kit said. "You know this guy?"

Cass looked over her shoulder to see who she was talking about and saw the old man headed for them. Chapel.

"Yeah," Cass said.

"Good guy or bad guy?"

"I'm not sure he's either."

Chapel stopped a few feet from them and bowed. "I have considered," he said.

"And?"

"I will stand with you."

"We welcome the help."

He dipped his head, and something about his expression dispelled the notion that he was doing it out of concern for the people. Perhaps it was a fortunate aligning of purpose. Or maybe he was just going where he felt led. Whatever the case, he moved off again with no further exchange.

"How much help can a blind old man be?" Kit asked, after he'd walked away.

"You'd be surprised."

The final hour of sunset was the worst, when all the plans that could be made had been made, and all that could be prepared had been prepared. The citizens who had seemed so unconcerned were beginning to grow restless as the reality of their new circumstances closed in with the night. The lower the sun got, the more friendly they became towards the Awakened and the warriors gathered.

Wren had taken some stairs up to the roof of a one-story building, and he sat there now with Chapel, watching as the westering sun slipped slowly towards the horizon. Chapel had found him in the midafternoon and had remained with him since. They hadn't spoken much, but Wren found it comforting to have the old man around.

"Do you remember your village, Chapel?" he asked.

Chapel nodded. "In part. It is as a faded dream to me now."

"And Lil? And Mister Carter?"

"The same. But the memories have become clearer with time. Perhaps one day I will remember again. Perhaps not."

They sat quietly again, both looking out over the city, towards the setting sun. Wren glanced up at Chapel with his blindfold. He'd wanted to ask since he first recognized the man, but he hadn't had the courage. Now, he wasn't sure he'd ever get another chance, so he thought it was worth it.

"What happened to your eyes?"

Chapel didn't turn towards him.

"They were no longer mine," he said. "I removed them." He spread his fingers on his lap, showing the dark and cracked nails. "These too I reclaimed."

"But you can still see?"

"In a way. I have other senses, some which I did not have before. But as I could not expel them, I learned to harness them, and so again became master of myself."

"I wish you could've gone back to the village," Wren said. "I think it might still be there today if you had."

"My sins are many," Chapel said. "I doubt hell has room enough to hold them all. But I could not return there."

"Why not?"

"It was a mistake. Selfish. I withdrew there. Hid myself away. And darkness grew." He turned his face towards Wren then. "There is much evil in our world. No longer will I let it rest."

He turned back towards the sunset, and for a time Wren pondered his words. As the sky deepened from blue to purple above, and the orange disc disappeared at last behind the horizon, Cass called to Wren from below and waved him down.

"I guess it's time."

Chapel dipped his head.

"Do you have a new name for today?" Wren asked.

"Today?" Chapel said as he stood. He thought for a moment. "Today, I am War."

He motioned for Wren to lead the way, and together they descended the steps.

Cass and her small army took their positions. Some of the citizens had chosen to gather at the gate already, knowing from all the plans and preparations that something was about to happen. Others were still setting up in their reclaimed shelters around the area. But all of them seemed to be keeping their heads up, ever watchful for any hint of danger. Cass expected them to panic when the time came. She just hoped they would remember to run towards the city and not away from it.

In the very picture of irony, Wren was now under the care of Aron. Aron was stationed in the rear-most portion of the fighters, on a slight rise in the terrain, which afforded him a view from which to command as well as a perch from which to shoot. Chapel, too, was with Wren, and Cass felt certain that those two would do everything in their power to protect her son.

Her natural instinct had been to keep him near her, of course, but she realized that she could protect him best by leading these people. And she understood something of his heart, now, in his earlier desire to separate himself from her for her own safety.

Cass drew the massive pistol from the holster on her thigh and checked its cylinder. Three rounds, ready to go. She'd only fired the weapon once, long ago, in a moment of utter despair. Well, she'd fired it three times, wasting ammunition far more precious than she had realized at the time. She wondered what Three would have thought of their predicament now, and she smiled in spite of herself. Probably wouldn't have surprised him much. She snapped the cylinder shut with a flick of her wrist and replaced the pistol. Shooting had never been her greatest strength. But it was nice to have the option, just in case.

The attack didn't begin the way she had expected. Rather than the sudden eruption of electric howls, it started with a pronouncement.

"People of Morningside," a loud voice called, impossibly loud, as if it was coming from all around her, or from the heavens themselves. "Your time has ended!"

There was a figure standing atop a building not far from the gate, silhouetted black against the night-blue sky. His glowing eyes radiated their starlight-blue as he looked down upon them. Painter.

"The one you once knew as Master has returned that you should now know his wrath and ruin."

His booming voice echoed through the streets and alleys, off the surrounding buildings and the wall.

"He is Asher, Mind of the Weir, and I am his Voice. Thus he says to you: I will slake the thirst of Death with your blood, the mouth of hell I will glut with your flesh, until all that remains is the echoing horror of what once you were!

"No more shall you be called Morningside. Instead, I name you the Grief of Dawn!"

As soon as those words were spoken, shadows sprang forth from the ruined city beyond, shadows with electric eyes, sweeping like a black tide towards them. A cascade of Weir poured forth, and their shrieks rent the air. Cass felt those nearby shrink back in the face of the onslaught, but she leapt forward with a shout.

Thunder exploded behind her, and the Weir at the front of the charge disintegrated in a shower of gore, and several behind it fell to the ground. Aron was already at work with his mighty weapon.

But those deaths did nothing to slow the surge, and seconds later, the lines crashed together. Cass met them head-on and was forced backwards by the impact. But Swoop was there. And then Kit, and then another of her Awakened brethren, and another. And together they fought, side by side, shoulder-to-shoulder.

And then others joined in with a cry, and all became chaos. Citizens who hadn't made it to the gate fell before the storm, but Cass had no time to mourn them, or even process their deaths. All around her, the Weir writhed and strove against her, and she beat them back with fist and claw.

Aron's rifle continued to thunder, though Cass couldn't see its effects. And while always fear threatened to overwhelm her, she fought to focus on destroying the enemy closest at hand, and again and again succeeded in doing so. Swoop was never far from her side, his tomahawk smoking black in the melee.

But no matter how many they slew, it never seemed to stem or even to slow the assault. She grabbed one Weir by the side of the head and spun, slamming it to the ground, and as she rose, she realized how much closer they'd already been pushed towards the wall. They were practically at the gate, maybe twenty yards away.

She risked a glance up, and saw a number of guards were firing down from the wall, and that gave her hope, until she turned back and saw how many still remained. Claws stung her. But Cass refused to let them take her. She smashed her palm into the face of a Weir and drove it backwards into its advancing kin, fighting to gain space for the people trapped between the Weir and the gate.

Someone fell to her left, claimed by the Weir, but she didn't have time to see who it was. Already her arms and legs grew heavy, her strikes inaccurate, and still so many remained.

But then on her right, the Weir peeled back and wheeled, and there a radiance fell among them. And above the roar of combat and the shrieks of the Weir, a voice arose. Singing. And Cass knew that somehow, beyond all hope or imagining, Lil had come, and her warriors with her.

Where those avenging angels went, the Weir fell before them, or scattered, and Cass heard now as well the sounds of gunfire. Gamble was there too, with her team. And together Lil and Gamble and all those with them drove back the Weir from the flank.

Still the bulk of the Weir fought on, pressing their way towards the gate, and Cass was helpless to prevent them. She strained against the Weir, but their numbers were still too great. She could only hope to survive long enough for Gamble to cut a path to her, but with each second that passed, it seemed a more and more distant hope.

And then.

The crush stopped. And the Weir before her turned their eyes from her to something behind her, and they halted their advance. Cass dared not turn, and she crushed her fist into the throat of the Weir before her. But as it fell, she became aware of a pressure growing, and a light, and there were screams of dismay from some of her own.

And when she turned she saw now, there, walking among them, a being of lightning and flame. And terror entered her heart.

But also hope. For she had seen this being before. It was Wren, revealing himself in power, and he was coming to save her.

The Weir fell back before him, and some collapsed to the ground. The warriors that had stood with Cass surged forward, many unable to perceive what had caused the change, but determined to press their temporary advantage. Cass fought with strength renewed, and the Weir melted away and fled back into the night.

The survivors all stood in shocked silence after the assault ended. No one could really believe it was over. The ground was strewn with corpses, many Weir, and many of Cass's own people. The loss was too great to seem like a victory. But the number of slain Weir scattered around them was astonishing.

She glanced up at the wall and saw the guards arrayed along it. They had lent their aid after all.

A voice was crying out from the top, "Open the gates! Open the gates!" She recognized the deep baritone. It was North.

The gates clanked and groaned open, and as soon as they did the citizens pressed against it began flooding back inside the city wall. Cass looked down to find Wren standing before her, once again himself, knife in hand.

"We did it, Mama," he said.

She picked him up and hugged him. "We did, baby. We did."

"Maybe now they'll listen."

"I hope so."

"Hey," came a voice behind her. "Sorry we're late." Gamble. She looked grim and exhausted, but Cass thought she'd never been more beautiful. She set Wren down and embraced Gamble. The whole team was there, even Wick, pale and eyes heavily shadowed. Cass greeted them all, as did Wren.

Lil joined them, with nine of her warriors.

"I can't believe you came," Cass said.

Lil smiled. "Gamble can be very persuasive."

"We should get inside," Gamble said. "They might've run off, but there are still a lot of 'em left."

Cass nodded and picked Wren up again. Together they all started towards the gate, but Finn, Mouse, Able, and Sky broke off from the group and started checking bodies. Whenever they found one that wasn't a Weir, two would work together to lift the body and carry it back inside the city. Once others realized what they were doing, they too came to help reclaim the fallen, before the Weir could do so. Aron, and Kit, and even Mister Sun joined in.

There was one man just sitting on the ground, staring off in the direction that the Weir had gone. A ridiculous number of Weir lay sprawled around him, and he sat amongst them, paying no heed. Cass approached to see if he was all right, and realized it was Swoop. He was so covered in ichor, she hadn't recognized him at first, and she went to his side.

"Swoop, you OK?"

He didn't answer, but just stared ahead. Cass put her hand on his shoulder, and when she did, he slumped slightly towards her. "Oh, Swoop..." she said, and she cradled him and wept softly.

After a time, she called the rest of the team over, and they paid their respects, and took care of the body. Able let his tears fall freely, though he did it almost without other expression. Mouse, too, was clearly upset. But the others seemed to swallow their emotion for now. Finn said there'd be time to hurt later, but now wasn't it.

There was still work to do, and it was heavy. Most of the people Cass helped carry, she didn't know. She didn't know which was worse. To carry the body of a fallen friend, or to have fought alongside someone and lost them without ever having known their name. But these were heroes, all. People who had willingly laid down their lives for their own. She would see to it that they were honored as such, no matter what their station in life had been.

North was there at the gate, assisting, giving directions, keeping order. He had a natural command that provided some comfort in times of crisis. Cass had just laid a body inside the wall. An Awakened whose name she just couldn't place at that moment, and she felt terrible for the fact. She was just turning to go talk to North when a terrible sound came from the outskirts beyond the wall.

It was a cold, mocking laughter, echoing from the darkness. It was Painter's voice, but Cass knew in her heart it was Asher who laughed. He was toying with them.

"Get them back inside," she called. "Get everyone back inside!"

Most of the people were already gathered back within the city, but three or four remained outside, still searching the bodies. Aron among them. When the laughter started, they stood, stunned at the sound. But then from out of the night, a horrible sound rose and swallowed the laughing. At first it sounded like rushing water, or some swarm of insects, but as the noise grew, it sharpened and became electric. And out there beyond the gate, the streets filled with Weir. Hundreds. Thousands. A number beyond comprehension.

"Close the gates!" North roared. "Seal the gates!"

The massive gates began to roll closed, and two of the people broke and ran towards them.

"Aron!" Cass called. "Aron, run!"

But he was the farthest out. He turned back when he

heard his name called, but when they made eye contact, they both knew it was too far. Aron gave a nod and hoisted his rifle. It thundered as the gates closed. And then it was silent.

Moments later the gates rang with the impact, and people scattered. North dashed up the stairs to the top of the wall, and the guards at the top fired wildly down into the throngs below.

Wren caught Cass's hand. "Mama, I've got to get to the machine!"

It was hard to process with everything happening around her, but she nodded and called for Gamble.

"We've got to get to the compound!" she said. "We've got to get Wren inside!"

Gamble nodded and called to her team. Cass picked Wren up, and together they all raced to the governor's compound. People in the streets were panicking, even those who hadn't been in any danger of relocation. The sounds of the battle spilled over the walls and carried through the streets, and the echoing cry of the Weir drove people to madness.

But Gamble's team spread out in a protective ring around Cass and Wren, and cleared a way through. When they reached the compound, Cass was aghast. Not surprised, but aghast. The gates were sealed, and the number of guards tripled. All of them were needed on the wall, and yet here they remained, guarding the compound against nothing.

"You've got to let us in," Cass called as they approached. "We've got to get inside!"

The captain at the gate waved her off. "Gate's sealed by the Council's orders," he said. "No one's getting in or out tonight."

"The city's under attack!" Gamble yelled. "Your men should be on the wall!"

"We have our orders, ma'am."

Gamble actually reached through the bars and caught the man's uniform. She jerked him forward and smashed his face against the bars.

"Open this gate, or we'll blow it open."

Powerful floodlights switched on and bore down upon Cass and her crew. No one could see beyond them, but the sound of coilguns and other weapons spinning up was unmistakable.

Gamble released the captain.

"I recommend you folks move off," the captain said. "If I see you approach the compound again, I'll have no choice but to open fire."

"The whole city's in trouble," Cass said. "There's a very real chance we're going to lose the gate. Let the people come here."

"I'll give you ten seconds."

"Please," Wren said. But the captain wouldn't be moved.

"Seven."

Gamble seemed like she was considering taking the shot anyway, but Cass called her off, and they all withdrew across the street.

"So, what's with the machine?" Gamble asked.

"Wren thinks he might be able to stop Asher through it," Cass said.

"But you have to be near it, or what?"

Wren nodded. "I've tried to connect to it, but I just can't. It's too... slippery. I can't keep it."

"But you can connect?" Finn asked.

"Yeah, kind of."

Finn waved him over. "Can you help me find it?"

"I think so."

"If you can help me find the connection, I'll feed you the signal," Finn said. "I don't know what you'll be able to do with it, but I'll keep the connection stable, if that helps."

Wren nodded. "We can try."

Wren did something internal, found the connection, shared it with Finn just before he lost it. It took a few attempts, but after a couple of minutes, Finn seemed to understand what they were looking for.

"OK, got it," he said. "I'm going to try and boost it. You just ride along, do what you have to."

Wren nodded and sat down on the ground, next to the wall of a building. Finn knelt next to him, and together they went into a realm none of the others could see.

The first thing Wren noticed was how dense it all was. Like a mass of wires crushed together. Connections to connections to connections, and none with any meaning to him. Processes flashed like lightning, gone in a blink, with only an after-image remaining. It wasn't long before Wren was completely overwhelmed.

But as hopeless as it felt, at least he knew the machine's purpose. And he knew Asher was in it. And he knew Asher. So that was where he started, looking for the things that reminded him of his brother.

Wren realized he didn't even have words for what he was doing. He couldn't reduce the thoughts or the impressions to anything he could describe. But it was something like how a scent could trigger a vivid memory, or a particular color could summon a flavor on the tongue. A fleeting impression was enough to trigger a stream of interactions, and Wren found himself falling deeper into the void of the machine.

He floated, lost for a time, flailing, grasping. And then Wren realized how hard he was searching, and he took a breath, and he stopped trying. Moments later, or maybe minutes, it was impossible to tell, as he let his mind rove where it would, something caught his attention. Something that seemed out of place. And he stretched out and touched it through the ether.

And he was answered.

Asher. There was something of him still within the machine. And he sensed Wren. And he laughed. A cold, mocking laugh.

And a voice came into Wren's mind.

"You're too late, Spinner. So, so very late," Asher said.

"You don't have to do this, Asher," Wren said. "You can stop. Call off the Weir."

"Why would I? I'm enjoying it."

"Stop it, or I will."

"Oh, Spinner. I wanted to love you, you know. I really did. But you're impossible to love. You think you're special, but you're not."

"I've fought you before, Asher. I've defeated you before."

"Not this time."

Wren knew better than to waste much time talking to Asher. And now that he knew Asher was here, Wren bent his whole will towards forcing his brother out of the machine. Out of the Weir's minds. Back to wherever he'd come from. Anger grew, and Wren invited it. Fed it. All that Asher had done, and all that he'd caused, Wren remembered it, focused on it, and used it to drive him.

And then he unleashed himself within the machine.

And Asher laughed again.

"Even now you don't understand, do you? Underdown's toy was a beginning. The first baby step, ten thousand miles ago. I know it seems impressive to you, but it's nothing to me now. And *you* shouldn't be here."

A sudden pressure came into Wren's head then, and a searing pain that felt like it was right in the middle of his brain. But he grappled with his brother and pushed him back. Asher was too big – too strong now. He'd changed since Wren had last dealt with him. Wren didn't know how he was controlling the Weir now, but Wren knew the machine still connected to them somehow. He changed tactics.

He tried to Awaken the Weir through the machine. It was a terrible strain, but he visualized how he had helped Mama, and Painter, and Kit. Wren focused on Kit. She'd been the easiest, because she'd been fighting it on her own. Like Chapel. Wren searched the machine for that same sensation, that feeling of struggle. And when he found one, he touched it, and it sprang free. Quickly he searched for another, and then another.

"Oh, clever. But see how slowly you think, little brother. Already I perceive your mind."

Wren had no way of knowing what effect it was having, but it had disrupted Asher, and so he kept trying it. And he noticed that once those connections were severed, Asher didn't seem to have any way to repair them.

"Fine," Asher said. "I was done with it anyway."

A blinding white light entered Wren's mind. Not one seen with his eyes, but no less powerful and painful to his senses. Something was happening. The machine was collapsing. And Wren felt himself thrown violently backwards. He cried out, and all was dark.

"What happened?" Cass screamed. "What happened to him?"

She was cradling Wren in her arms. Finn was holding his head like he was in severe pain.

"I don't know," he answered. "It was like… I don't know, like feedback or something. The connection broke itself. And it hurt."

Cass put her ear to Wren's chest. He was still breathing; his heartbeat was still strong. Whatever had happened to him, it wasn't something she could fix right now. It might be something she could never fix, and that thought terrified her. She held him close.

The sounds of the battle were intensifying, and it was clear that many others had thought to retreat to the governor's compound. A crowd was gathering, and it wasn't just frightened citizens. Some guards were there as well. One of the guards on the wall fired a warning shot, but that only made the crowd more frightened and angry, and some started pulling on the gates.

"We've got to get out of here," Sky said.

"Where else is there to go?" Finn asked.

"They can't have surrounded the whole city," Wick said.

"The train," Cass said.

"What?" Gamble said.

"There's a train. To Greenstone. It runs under the Strand."

"Do you know where it is?"

Cass shook her head. "They wouldn't let us use it."

"It's underground?" Wick said. "Where? Where does it come out?"

"I don't know."

"In the city? Close to it? Far away?" he asked.

"Close, I think. I'm not really sure."

Wick's eyes went unfocused, but his face was intense. Searching. "How big a train?"

"I'm not sure."

"Big, small?"

"Small. Just a few passengers. Like an old shuttle."

He was silent for a few more moments.

"People of Morningside," the Voice boomed. Cass couldn't

comprehend how it was possible that she could hear him from so far away. And then she realized that his voice was coming from every system in the city. The compound's public address system, the exterior alarm of the building next to them, everything with an output was broadcasting his voice. "The very heart of your city is corrupt. And so shall you fall from within."

The echoing voice had stunned the heaving crowd across the street into silence. And then they started screaming, and fleeing away from the gate. The guards reacted, and some turned to face inwards, and Cass felt a shock of realization.

Painter. Painter had used the tunnel that ran from the compound out under the wall. And he had revealed it to the Weir.

She didn't have to see what was going on inside the compound to know the truth. The Weir were inside its walls. The city had fallen.

"Got it," Wick said. "It's a run, but we can make it."

"Lil? Gamble," Gamble said. "City's compromised, we've got Weir inside the governor's compound. We gotta evac... Yeah, we'll ping you a route now."

The team got to their feet and started moving out, with Wick in the lead. They kept a steady, aggressive pace, and Cass had to struggle to keep up, with her unconscious son in her arms. Mouse offered to carry him for her, but she refused. Wick led them to a smaller gate, more of a reinforced door, really, on the north-western side.

As they approached it, Lil and her warriors were coming from the opposite direction, along with several Awakened, and a few of the people who had fought with them at the gate. Kit was with them, and when they met, she and Wick embraced without hesitation.

Chapel too appeared, sword in hand, shoulders and face spattered with the red-black dew of war.

"What's the plan?" Lil said.

"There's a tunnel," Cass said. "We're going to try to make it."

"Abandon the city?" Kit asked.

Cass nodded. "It's already lost. There's nothing more we can do here."

"Lead on," Lil said.

Mouse popped the door, and Wick, Able, and Finn swung out to make sure it was clear. Once they were certain, they motioned everyone else to follow. Able hung back as a rear guard until everyone was through, and then closed the door behind him. Wick set a hard pace, and the terrible sounds of the Weir and their attack pursued them as they went. They'd made it about a third of a mile before the first of the Weir spotted them.

It was quickly dispatched, but after that, it became clear that their plan was blown. Two Weir showed up soon after, followed by a group of three. And though they never faced a major attack, it was only a matter of time.

Gamble told Wick to find them a place to button up, and he did so in a low one-story building, about a half mile from the tunnel. It was solid, mostly concrete, with only two entrances and a window. Gamble's team shared ammo out as much as they could, but they were all low. Everyone packed in. This would be their last stand.

"Gamble," Cass said. "Whatever happens, I don't want Asher to get my son. I can't let him take my son."

"I understand," Gamble said. "Wick can take you to the tunnel. We'll do our best to hold them here as long as we can."

"No," Cass said, "I'm not leaving these people behind. I want you to take Wren to Greenstone."

"Nope. Out of the question, Cass," she said. "These people won't last long without us. Take your son. None of us will blame you."

"I can lead them," Cass said, looking at the other Awakened gathered with them. "And we may be able to cross the Strand without you."

"If you survive the night." She looked over Cass's shoulder. "Wick, take Able, get Miss Cass and Wren to the tunnel. Make sure they get to Greenstone."

"Wait, what now?" Wick said.

"No, Gamble," Cass said.

"It's an order, Wick."

"Alright, check."

"Gamble—" Cass said.

"Cass, Wren needs his mother. Only you can be that. Go."

"If we're gonna do it, we gotta go now," Wick said.

"I will aid you," Chapel said from behind Cass. "Come." He took her arm and pulled her towards the back entrance.

And somehow again, Cass found herself following Wick. There was sporadic gunfire behind them, but they didn't come into contact with any Weir themselves. In about six minutes, they reached the station. The train, of course, wasn't there. It belonged to the Bonefolder, back in Greenstone, and she controlled it jealously. But she couldn't do much to control the tunnel.

"You can take it from here," Wick said. "Straight on down the tunnel," Wick said.

"What about you?" Cass said.

"I can't leave my brother back there. Able can take you."

You're my brother, too, Able signed.

Wick reached behind Able's neck and pulled the man's forehead to his own in a show of affection. Able patted his face before they separated.

"Go on. Godspeed."

Wick turned and started back towards where the others were holed up. Cass felt like her heart was about to break. She was Wren's mother, and she loved him more than she loved herself. But deep in her heart, she knew that she would rather die fighting alongside those people back there than live with herself knowing she'd left them behind.

"I will take the child," Chapel said.

Somehow he had perceived her thoughts.

"Wick, wait," she called.

It was the most terrible decision Cass had ever made, and her heart seemed to tear within her chest as she handed Wren's unconscious form over to the blindfolded old man. But he had cared for her son before, when she had been unable. And though Cass did not know Chapel well, she knew she could trust his word. Chapel laid him on his shoulder. Cass kissed Wren on the forehead as he lay there, as if he'd been asleep, and she was kissing him goodnight. He had once been forced to say goodbye to her. Now it was her turn to bear that pain.

"Bye, baby," she said.

She took Three's pistol from its holster on her thigh, and handed it to Chapel.

He shook his head. "I have no need."

"It's for Wren. I want him to have it."

He nodded, then, and took it and tucked it away inside his coat.

"Careful, it's loaded," she said.

"Go," Chapel said.

Cass brushed Wren's hair with her fingers, and kissed him one last time. And then she turned back, and she and Able together caught up with Wick.

When he first woke, Wren couldn't tell he had opened his eyes. But he could tell he was lying on a hard surface, with something squishy under his head, and he blinked his eyes several times. His next thought was that he had gone blind. He called out. "Mama!"

A hand pressed into his shoulder, firm, with strong fingers. Not his mother.

"Shhh, child," Chapel said. "She is not here, but you are safe."

"Where is she?" he asked.

"Away."

"What happened, Chapel? Where are we?"

Chapel explained in his patient way, gentle in truth, but hiding nothing. Wren wept then, deeply and bitterly, and Chapel comforted him, not with words, but with his presence.

After a time they resumed their journey. He rode on Chapel's back through the long darkness, sometimes sleeping, sometimes wakeful, and often unable to distinguish the two. His sorrow was heavier than any he had known. And now he understood something of Painter's agony. The uncertainty of the loss. Unable to grieve fully because weak hope continued to cling whether bidden or no.

But it was indeed a weak hope, too frail to support the belief that Wren would see his mother again. And so he felt trapped between the two thoughts: that his mother was dead, or that she was alive but never to be seen again. He had grieved for her once in his lifetime. It was even harder the second time.

And all those others. Gamble, and Sky, and Able; Wick, Finn, Mouse, and Swoop. Swoop alone among them could be mourned.

And Painter. Wren had no words to describe the pain that thoughts of Painter caused. He too was dead, in a way. Wren didn't understand it exactly, but he knew that somehow Asher had reached Painter, had changed him. Or that Painter had allowed himself to be changed, which was even more tragic.

And then there was Asher. He'd had his vengeance on Morningside. It was probably too much to hope that Asher believed Wren to be dead. How long would it be before he came to claim his little brother? Or would he be content to have destroyed everything that Wren had loved?

Wren lost all sense of time during that journey. He still had his pack with him, which had a little food and some water. Enough to get them through, though Chapel never ate. When they finally reached the end, dawn was breaking over the city.

And together they walked towards Greenstone, the last known survivors of the once great city in the east.

EPILOGUE

"A blind old man and a kid, huh?" the Greenman said. "Might be kinder of me just to put you both down myself. I'm not sure I'd feel right letting you walk around alone in there."

"I have friends inside," Wren said.

"Oh yeah? Who's that, little man?"

"jCharles. He runs the Samurai McGann. He gave me a book once."

The Greenman let out a low whistle. "Well, alright then. It might not stop anyone from messing with you, but I guess they'd be sorry enough after the fact. You know your way?"

Wren nodded.

"Alright. I suggest you go straight there, quick as you can. And watch your step."

Nimble, the bartender, recognized Wren as soon as he came in the door. Nimble called up to jCharles, who practically sprinted down the stairs to see them. Of course jCharles knew immediately something was wrong, and he took them both up to the apartment where Mol was.

Wren was amazed to see her holding a sweet baby girl, maybe six months old. When Mol saw him, she handed the baby off to jCharles, and she held Wren for a long, long time.

They did everything they could to care for Wren, and though Chapel declined their hospitality, he remained nearby, and spent a great deal of his time sitting in the bar downstairs.

One night, jCharles took them both up onto the roof of the Samurai McGann, and they sat there staring out over the wildness of the city. Wren opened up then, about all that had happened. He told jCharles all about Morningside, and what had become of Three, and Swoop, and Gamble, and her team. And about his mama.

"They sound like they were great people," jCharles said.

"I wish I could be that kind of person," Wren said.

"You cannot be *that* kind of person," Chapel said. The words stung Wren, and jCharles looked over at the old man with an ugly expression. But Chapel was nothing if not honest.

But then he turned his face towards Wren and lifted the boy's chin. "You cannot be *that* kind of person, Wren, because *you* are the kind of person for whom such men and women willingly lay down their lives."

Wren's chest tightened, and a lump caught in his throat.

"But why?" he said, voice thick with tears.

Chapel turned his face back towards the city.

"That is the question your life must answer."

ACKNOWLEDGMENTS

A lot of people deserve thanks for the many kindnesses they showed me while I was working on this novel. Hopefully I already delivered those in person, though, so here's just a quick list of folks I'd like to appreciate in print. Many doubly extra-special thanks to:

…Jesus, for your constant faithfulness and ever-present help.

…my wife and children, for your continual support and love, for being so generous, and for being the very best thing ever.

…Marc Gascoigne, Lee Harris, Mike Underwood, Caroline Lambe, and everyone else at Angry Robot for all their patience, hard work, and tireless devotion to global domination.

…all the friends and family who picked up my first novel and said things like "Wow, I can't believe *you* wrote this!" or "This is, like, actually a real book!". These comments were all far better than "Yeah, it seems like something you'd write."

…all of the readers out there who took the time to send me kind words of encouragement, which I often re-read in the wee hours of the morning to keep me going. Feel free to send more. Frequently.

PEACEMAKER

MARIANNE DE PIERRES

"TWO LINE AUTHOR SHOUT ABOUT THE
FANTASTIC PEACEMAKER WILL GO HERE."
AUTHOR NAME